Whispering Women

A Delafield & Malloy Investigation

A novel by

Trish MacEnulty

PRISM LIGHT
PRESS

978-1-7375751-7-7

Published by
Prism Light Press

Manufactured in the United States of America.

For the Fourth Estate
with gratitude

And for Celina Bartlett,
always and forever my inspiration

"Miss Jennie Creagh, a dashing brunette, has splendidly furnished her palace at 17 Amity street, from top to bottom, sparing neither expence nor labor to render it a palace of beauty forever, with its French mirrors, English and Brussels carpets, rosewood furniture, superb bedding and everything in character. This emporium of love and beauty is one of the finest in the city."

A Gentleman's Directory, 1870

Contents

TRAGIC END FOR PROMINENT NEW YORKER

Financially Bankrupt Pillar of Society

Found Murdered in Tenderloin Hotel

New York, Nov. 27, 1901 – Richard Milton Delafield of Manhattan was found dead in a rented room at the Hotel Empire late yesterday evening. After receiving complaints about screams on the second floor, a hotel clerk found Delafield alone in his room stabbed to death.

The murdered man was 46 years old. He and his family lived in a first-class neighborhood and, until recently, owned a cottage in Newport. He was married to Anna Neubecker Delafield, whose family is one of the original Knickerbocker families of Old New York. Avid socialites, the couple were frequently seen at exclusive parties, charity balls, and yachting competitions. In addition to his wife, Delafield leaves behind a 12-year-old daughter.

Delafield is a direct descendent of John Delafield, who brought the provisional peace treaty from England to the United States in 1783. The family made their fortune in the insurance business. He attended private schools in New York and later enrolled in Yale University, where he was heralded for his skill in poetry and his performances in several plays.

While Delafield did not work in the family business, which his older brother moved to Philadelphia, he did dabble in various investments, using the large inheritance he had received upon his father's death.

The police have no suspects or motive for his death at this time. However, it is known that Delafield was in financial straits. In March 1899, he fell victim to the "Franklin Syndicate" scheme, perpetrated by Brooklyn bookkeeper William Miller, who claimed to offer a 520 percent return on investments and is now serving a sentence in Sing Sing, as he never invested a dime of the $1 million he collected. Earlier this year, only two years after losing the sum of more than $300,000 to Miller, Delafield invested his remaining fortune with a member of a gang of New York swindlers selling phony deeds to land on Staten Island.

Police do not know if the murder is connected to the swindles. His remaining assets will be sold to pay his creditors, according to the family attorney, Mr. Herbert Markham.

Chapter 1

Louisa

Louisa perched on the edge of a wooden chair in the outer office of Herbert Markham, Attorney at Law. His secretary, who also happened to be his mother, pecked at a typewriter on her desk and ignored Louisa. The feathers on her black hat bobbed as she typed. She had the wide, tight-lipped face of a New England-bred Yankee, the sort of face prevalent in meetings of the Daughters of the American Revolution.

Louisa had never been to the attorney's office before today. Usually, they received a notice at the end of every year that a deposit of approximately six hundred and fifty dollars had been made to their bank account. This year, instead, she received a letter asking her to come see him.

The door to the inner office opened, and Herbert Markham smiled warmly when he saw her. He had a clean-shaven face with a crease in the middle of his forehead. His graying hair, which had fled the top of his head, curled incongruously above his ears. He'd been overseeing her and her mother's financial affairs for the dozen years since her father had died and hadn't charged them a dime. A good thing, since they didn't have any dimes to spare.

"Come in, Louisa. Aren't you a vision of young womanhood?" he said, beckoning her inside. "How is your dear mother? Well, I hope."

His office was tastefully decorated with a claw-footed Chippendale desk, heavy mahogany bookshelves with glass doors, a bust of Marcus Aurelius on top, and a framed colonial American flag between two tall windows looking out onto Wall Street. Outside the window, snow fell in silver drops as round and shiny as coins from the sky.

She sat down in a leather chair and folded her hands to exude an air of calm, but her knee vibrated under her long wool skirt. She felt Aurelius' stone eyes glaring down at her.

"Mother is fine," she said, which was not exactly true but she was in no mood for small talk. "Mr. Markham, why did you ask me to come here? Has something happened to our yearly allotment?"

He sighed. He was in his late fifties, about the same age her father would have been if he were still alive.

"I'm afraid it's all gone, my dear," he said in a gentle tone that might as well have been a slap across her face.

"But... I don't understand," she said, silently cursing herself for not having paid more attention to the accounts. Too busy with work, she had told herself, but the real reason was that she didn't want to face the truth. She much preferred the illusion that their small well of money would magically refill itself the way it seemed to do in all the wealthy families. She should have been spared from any financial concerns, but there was no getting around the hard kernel of truth — the Delafields were poor now, and their family name meant nothing to the rest of the world.

"We've been quite frugal," she said, clutching her purse.

"Yes, you have been. I wouldn't have thought that Anna would be a good money manager, but..."

Louisa interrupted him.

"The annuity covers our basic expenses. Now that I'm working, most of my salary goes to clothing and transportation to various events. Writing a society column seems to be the only work for which I'm suited, but unfortunately it doesn't pay well. We've been relying on that yearly allotment," she said. "How could it be gone already?"

"There wasn't much to start with," he said, looking down at his desk and then up at her. "I couldn't invest it or you wouldn't have had anything to live on. Besides, your mother absolutely forbade it, and I can't say I blame her after your father made such regrettable mistakes." Then he leaned forward with a perplexed expression on his face and said, "Frankly, Louisa, I assumed you'd be married by now."

"I'm afraid the scandal of my father's death has tarnished my glow," she said.

"Certainly, you might have found someone," he said. "My nephew is coming to visit us in a few weeks. He lives in Cincinnati and isn't married. Why don't you come over for dinner and meet him?"

A tremor ran over Louisa's shoulders but she stilled herself. The very last thing she wanted to do was marry, especially some relation from *Cincinnati*. She'd seen what could happen when a woman's livelihood was dependent on marriage. Her once vibrant mother now lived like a hermit, sitting in her invalid chair all day, reminiscing about days long gone.

Louisa cleared her throat and said, "I do not believe marriage is the answer for me." She paused and then asked, "So, there's nothing left at all?"

"I stretched it as far and as long as I could. I'm afraid you'll need to tighten the purse strings. Perhaps you could let go of your servant?"

He might as well ask her to cut off her right arm, she thought. Suzie had stopped even taking a salary, and Suzie was the reason they had survived as well as they had.

"At least the townhouse is paid for," Louisa said.

"The townhouse is yours free and clear," Mr. Markham said, "as long as you've kept up with the property taxes."

Louisa froze. Property taxes? They had to pay property taxes?

"I thought you were in charge of doing that..." she said.

"Oh no, my dear. The bill for 1912 should have come to your mother by now," he said, rising. The meeting was over. "Merry Christmas, Louisa, and please give your dear mother my regards."

"Merry Christmas," she said, though her tone of voice was about as merry as a case of typhus. She forced her head high as she strode out the door.

As Louisa got on the elevator, a single tear trickled down her cheek. She brushed it away with an angry swipe of her hand. Property taxes. She didn't remember a bill for taxes, and Suzie hadn't mentioned it.

"Are you all right, Miss?" the elevator operator asked.

"I'm fine, thank you," she answered. "I must have gotten something in my eye. It's gone now."

The elevator creaked down to the ground floor, and the operator opened the doors. Louisa stopped short in surprise. An elegant middle-aged woman in a dark-purple velvet dress and a felt hat with a large purple plume looked just as surprised to see her.

"Louisa!" Natasha Bloodgood said. "What a surprise."

Louisa stepped out of the elevator, and Natasha held her hands and kissed her cheeks.

"I'm on my way up to see Herbert about some property I'm buying," Natasha said with a smile. "What are you doing here, *cherie*?"

"Checking on our annual annuity," Louisa said, unable to keep the squeak out of her voice. The precariousness of her situation gripped her, and she imagined she stood teetering on the edge of a cliff.

"I see," Natasha said as she stepped onto the elevator. The operator was about to close the doors, but Natasha stopped him. "Louisa, please come by the house soon. I have some lovely day dresses that no longer fit me. I wonder if you'd do me the favor of taking them off my hands."

"Thank you, Natasha," Louisa said. If it had been anyone else, she would have been humiliated, but Natasha had looked out for her in so many ways since her father's death.

The doors began to close, but once again Natasha stopped him.

"I hope you're covering the Christmas ball this weekend, *cherie*," she said with a wink. "There will be so many eligible bachelors."

The elevator doors closed.

Not you, too, Natasha, Louisa thought. At twenty-four years old, Louisa was past the age of interest to anyone but the desperate old widowers.

She headed out of the building and into the blustery winter day. Snow drifted down and dampened her cheeks. She pulled her coat tight, worried about the property tax and thinking she must find a way to make sure they could keep the house. It wasn't impossible. Nixola Greeley-Smith wrote for *The Evening World* and she was doing well. She interviewed the most esteemed people in the world. Then there was Djuna Barnes who was making a name for herself as a writer and illustrator at *The Daily Eagle*. Unfortunately, *The Ledger* where Louisa worked was stodgy and set in its ways. Louisa didn't know about anything other than society, and society writers earned next to nothing.

She turned the corner onto Broadway and nearly bumped into a beggar woman with a large, protruding belly. The beggar was young and dirty in a threadbare coat with a small boy clinging to her. She held out a cup and pleaded to the passersby, "Please, help. Please."

Louisa was in no position to give money away, but she dug into her coin purse, pulled out a nickel, and dropped it in the cup. She'd intended to buy lunch with that nickel but she no longer had any appetite.

"Thank ye, Miss," the young woman said, and Louisa made the mistake of glancing into her desperate eyes and seeing her own reflected fear.

She quickly turned away, but the panic which had been a burning ember bloomed into a flame. If they lost the house, would that woman be her, standing on a sidewalk, holding out a tin cup? She grimaced and shook her head. She must extinguish her fear, smother it, and figure out how to keep a roof over her head. She was a Delafield, after all. Her father may have besmirched the name with his ill-conceived investments and his ignoble death, but she would reclaim her place in society. She would restore their respectability. She simply had no idea how.

The snowfall thickened as she hurried along the sidewalk. In the middle of crossing the street to get to the subway station, she slipped on a patch of ice and fell forward, landing hard on her hands and ripping her dress at the knee. A motorcar swerved around her, and a man in a top hat stopped to help her up, but she waved him off, pushed herself up onto her feet, and continued numbly toward the subway.

Chapter 2
Ellen

Ellen slipped off her shoes and curled up in the big overstuffed armchair by the fire in Miss Hattie's bedroom. The servants had been allowed to welcome the New Year at midnight with a single glass of champagne while outside, New Yorkers of every stripe thronged the streets, making an awful din as they celebrated the arrival of 1913. Since coming to New York six months earlier, Ellen had discovered that the city's denizens lived in an endless blitz of revelry and noise. Not the servants like her and the others, of course. They rose at dawn to do a thousand little chores and could be beckoned at a second's notice. As a lady's maid, she often stayed up until the wee hours when the family returned home because her poor unfortunate mistress couldn't undress herself. She wondered how the ruling class had ever garnered so much wealth when they seemed unable to perform the most mundane tasks.

Ellen relished the few hours of peace when Miss Hattie, her mother, and brother were off celebrating with their own kind. She flipped through the pages of the latest *McClure's Magazine* and landed on a poem by someone named Willa Cather. The poem was about the prairies of America, but it reminded her of home, of Ireland:

"The toiling horses, the tired men;
The long, empty roads,
The sullen fires of sunset fading,
The eternal unresponsive sky."

She rested her head against the soft back of the chintz-covered chair. She'd been a maid at the Salt Hill Resort back home for the past few years and thought she understood what it meant to be in service, but if she were honest with herself she'd had no idea what she was getting herself into. She'd only known she had to get out of Ireland and the stranglehold of the priests and the nuns who claimed she was on the sure path to Hell. Confessing her sins had been a mistake. She thought there'd be opportunity in America, opportunity to be herself. Now, she was not so sure.

She gazed around the room. The surroundings were certainly pleasant. Hattie Garrett had recently turned 18, and Ellen got on with the girl well enough. The only problem was the sheer dullness — the sewing, laundering, tending to the girl's wardrobe, brushing her shoes, fixing her hair, and most importantly praising and admiring her. If Ellen wanted a life, she had to live it through Hattie, and the life of a debutante wasn't all that stimulating, at least not from the outside. Silly parties and tea dances and such.

She sighed and opened the magazine again. Reading provided an escape from the monotony of service — that and the weekly trip she took to the Nickelodeon with Silvia. Aside from the occasional poem, there were illustrated stories of all sorts. Her favorites were the detective stories. Such adventures. Women in those stories were not always the most upstanding creatures, but their lives were never dull.

The Seth Thomas clock on the mantel chimed twice. Ellen's head lolled and her eyelids slid down.

"Happy New Year, Ellen!" Miss Hattie hooted as she burst into the room.

Ellen jerked awake and stood, the magazine falling from her lap and spilling onto the floor.

"Happy New Year, Miss," Ellen said. She picked up the magazine and placed it on the table. "Did you have a nice time?"

"I did, and you can read all about it in Louisa Delafield's column tomorrow," Hattie said and plopped down on the chair in front of her vanity. "I believe that 1913 is off to a most auspicious start. Mother says we can go to London in the spring. You might even come with us. Mother takes Smith everywhere."

Ellen helped the girl un-jewel, un-coif, and un-dress herself. London might be interesting, but how much of the city would she actually get to see? She knew little enough of New York and she'd been here for months. As she tucked Hattie into the big, soft, canopy bed, she noticed a whiff of champagne on the girl's breath.

Ellen was expected to do this for the rest of her life, she realized, as she put the clothes away. She saw no way out. A portion of her salary was still being kept back to pay for her passage from Galway, and it was near impossible for an Irish girl to get work other than as a domestic. She was lucky enough to be a lady's maid. It wasn't like she had any other skills. Best to keep her sights low.

She turned out the light and went upstairs to the servants' floor. She entered the room quietly so as not to wake Silvia. A bright winter moon slid westward, spilling a beam like an afterthought on the floor. Ellen had gotten into her flannel nightgown and crawled into bed when she looked across the room. Immediately, she sat up and stared. Silvia was not there.

Ellen wondered for a moment where the girl could possibly be, but then she knew. That older brother of Hattie's had a dangerous cock in his eye. It was the same everywhere. The rich took what they wanted, and the poor lived in the abyss. She slowly lowered herself down onto the bed, a fist clamped 'round her heart, squeezing it tight.

Chapter 3

Louisa

Two burly men wearing tweed flat caps, workmen's clothes, and thick-soled muddy boots hefted the large crate between themselves and carried it out of the parlor, through the hallway, out the open door, down the stoop and onto the street where a truck waited. Louisa stood in the doorway of her West Harlem townhouse and watched as they carefully lifted it into the back of the truck and trundled off.

"What have you done, you wicked girl?" Anna Delafield cried after Louisa went back into the parlor to stare at the empty space above the mantel. "That painting was the last vestige of our former life. And now you've sold it!"

"Mother, we were out of money and if we didn't pay our property tax we would lose the roof over our heads," Louisa explained once again. She put a log on the fire to try to heat up the room. "The Metropolitan

Museum will take good care of it. It's an Emil Fuchs, after all."

The fact that Fuchs also painted Queen Victoria had made her offer to the Metropolitan Museum especially enticing, and the money they had given her would mean they could pay the taxes on the townhouse and put some coal in the coal bin. Suzie had explained she usually paid the tax out of the annuity each year, but this year there was no annuity.

"They will put our misfortune on display for the whole world to see," Anna said, her voice choked with humiliation.

"Not right away," Louisa said. She refused to feel the loss of the painting even though every morning she'd looked into her father's eyes and felt him encouraging her to go forth and restore the family name. He was a good man and had never intended to put them through such shame.

The portrait of the three of them had been painted in London by John Singer Sargent's protégée, an acclaimed society portrait artist, when she was eight years old. She remembered that trip with fondness — seeing Big Ben and the Tower of London, walking along the Thames, even standing for hours while the painter stared at them had been rather fun.

Suzie came in with a rag to wipe up the muddy bootprints.

"I'm sure they'll let Louisa buy the painting back when she's got some money," Suzie said.

"What makes you think Louisa's ever going to have money?" Anna asked, bitterly. "She's too old for someone to marry."

Louisa glanced at Suzie with a raised eyebrow.

"We didn't scrimp and save all those years for Louisa to go to college so she could depend on a man for her bread and butter," Suzie said, hands on her wide hips. "Louisa will make money all on her own. You mark my words."

Suzie almost never spoke harshly to Anna, but the drama over the painting must have worn her nerves. Louisa looked up at the blank space again. Was Suzie right, she wondered. Could she ever make the money to buy it back? Suzie's belief in her defied reason, but it was all she had to go on.

***

A week later, Louisa bent over her cherry wood writing desk — the same desk her grandmother had used to write letters in support of abolition — and composed her column for the evening edition.

She put down her fountain pen and flexed her stiff fingers. She reached a hand toward the heat of the radiator, grateful for the warmth that emanated. Before she sold the painting, they'd had no coal and the meager fire in the fireplace had little effect.

"Look what I found in the back of your mother's wardrobe."

Louisa turned and saw Suzie holding up a red velvet dress with puffy sleeves, a lace bodice, full skirt, and a high collar. Louisa had been complaining for a week that she had nothing to wear tonight to the opening of Grand Central Terminal. Suzie's bronze eyes gleamed. Her hair was gray, and over the years, worry wrinkles had formed between her eyebrows like a set of train tracks.

"It was lovely thirty years ago when Mother wore it to Alva Vanderbilt's first ball," Louisa said. "But I can't wear that to the opening. I wasn't even born when that dress was made. Look at that ridiculous bustle."

"I can alter it. If I open the sleeves here, cut the neckline down like this, add some lace around the collar," — Suzie used her finger to indicate a V-shape — "and take out the bustle so it makes a nice straight line, nobody'll be the wiser. High quality fabric like this lasts forever."

"Can you finish it by tonight?" Louisa was skeptical.

"It might not be perfect, but it'll pass for one night."

Suzie shooed the little ginger cat off the sofa and laid down the dress. Louisa came over to inspect it. She imagined her mother purchasing it from some Parisian *vendeuse* when she was young and had everything she wanted at her fingertips. Louisa wondered what it would be like to be so carefree. Then she noticed a faint mothball smell.

"*The Ledger* should at least provide me with a clothing allowance if they expect me to do my job properly," Louisa muttered.

"Are you destroying another of my dresses?" Louisa's mother had woken up and wheeled herself over to the sofa in her invalid chair. Louisa and Suzie exchanged a look. The trick to mollifying Anna was to send her on a trip down memory lane.

"Mother, do you know who will be at the Grand Central Opening tonight? William Vanderbilt," Louisa said. "He's come all the way from Paris to witness this triumph." She may not be able to afford a new dress, she thought, but she would be rubbing elbows with the men who ran the world.

"That old scoundrel? He cheated on Alva. Everybody except her knew about it. They all thought it was such a scandal when she divorced him. Not I. I told her to go right ahead," Anna said.

"That gossip is a million years old. Alva is doing quite well these days. She's a suffragist, you know," Louisa said.

"Then she's come down in the world," Anna grumbled and rolled the chair to the window to stare outside at the snow-dusted sidewalk. Anna was able to walk, but she preferred not to, claiming that her heart was too weak for the exertion.

Louisa gazed at her, sitting in the stream of light from the window, bundled up in a wool shawl. The cat leaped onto her lap, and her mother stroked it absently.

She turned to look at the blank wall over the mantel, which Suzie was dusting.

"How much is left?" she asked Suzie in a low voice.

Suzie shook her head. "Very little," she said.

"I have an idea about how I might make more money," Louisa said. "We have a new editor at the newspaper. I haven't met him yet, but I've heard he intends to make some changes. I'm going to suggest that we expand the women's page. I'd like to add a home decor section and maybe an advice column for all those parvenues who need to learn the rules of old society. Of course, I wouldn't word it like that. But, honestly, some of them walk about in the middle of the day, dripping with diamonds."

"Abominable!" Anna piped up from her spot by the window. "Diamonds during the day are the height of poor taste."

"Exactly," Louisa said and then continued, "We could have the best women's page in the whole city, and I'd be in charge of it. They'd *have* to give me a raise."

"Then what are you waiting for?" Suzie asked.

***

On the way to *The Ledger*, Louisa hung onto a leather strap in a crowded train car on the 6th Avenue elevated train as it barreled through the air, ignoring the press of humanity around her. She felt a nervous fluttering in her stomach. Asking for money went against everything she'd been raised to believe. Women of the upper class didn't even acknowledge money. It was beneath them. The fact she was no longer in the exalted upper class and hadn't been since she was twelve didn't seem to matter. Standards of ladylike behavior had been ingrained into every fiber of her being, and generations of breeding didn't evaporate overnight. Fortunately, the one skill she possessed, writing about society, kept her among respectable people. If one had to work, there was no better path as far as she could tell. She was able to enjoy the glittering entertainments and yet still have a sense of purpose. Society writing kept her foot in the door of the world to which she'd been born.

The train jerked to a stop, and she wormed her way out of the car and onto the platform. She'd worn her wool maroon skirt and jacket with a silk blouse, and a large hat with a black ostrich plume in an effort to impress the new editor, but she looked incongruous in this crowd of working men and women, and the unwieldy hat was not made for public transportation. A few of her fellow travelers looked up at it as if she were wearing a camel on her head. She held onto the brim with one hand as she hustled down the stairs and headed past Macy's toward 34th Street, clutching her coat against the wind with the other, striding past clumps of dirty snow and the occasional pile of horse manure.

She pushed through the revolving door, took the elevator to the third floor, and with great determination wound through the maze of desks as phones rang, typewriters clattered, and the copy boy dashed past her carrying fresh stories for the typesetter. The odor of tobacco and newsprint perfumed the air.

The Ledger was not a large paper like *The Times* or *The Herald*, but it was prestigious, catering to wealthy men who wanted to keep up-to-date on stocks and bonds and other business matters and their wives who cared about one thing and one thing only: society. Louisa told herself that an expanded women's page was vital for the health of the newspaper. Readership had declined in recent years — hence, a new editor.

***

After she typed up her column and dropped it into the basket for the copy boy, she sat at her desk and combed through the stack of letters and invitations. She glanced over some publicity material from B. Altman's and sharpened her pencils. She made a note of upcoming weddings. When she'd finally run out of things to fiddle with, she looked over at the editor's office. A workman had just finished stenciling the letters "Virgil Thorn, Editor-in-Chief" on the door. He stood back to admire his handiwork. As soon as the workman left, she pulled her shoulders back, marched across the room, and knocked.

"Enter!" a voice called.

The office was filled with heavy oak furniture and cluttered with papers, books, and boxes not yet emptied. The new editor stood over his desk, blue pencil in hand, marking up the layout of the front page of tomorrow's paper. She waited for him to acknowledge her. He finally straightened to his full height and gazed at her with gray eyes behind wire-rimmed spectacles. A crisp mustache adorned his upper lip like two slender wings.

"You're rather fancy for a secretary," he said, giving her the once over. His British accent was not a surprise. She'd heard that he came from Fleet Street, and his origins were reinforced by his attire — the high stiff collar, narrow silk tie, and worsted vest with a gold chain across the front — much more formal than what American newspaper men wore these days.

"I'm not a secretary. I'm the society writer," she informed him. "Louisa Delafield."

"I see," he said, lifting a newspaper from his desk. "I've been reading your columns, Miss Delafield. Apparently, Miss Dorothy Bloodgood wore a yellow chiffon 'Poiret' to a dance party. And the esteemed sculptress Gertrude Whitney attended in a clingy sheath dress by 'the fashionable Fortuny.'" He stopped and looked at her. "Does anybody actually care what these toffs wear?"

Louisa's mouth dropped open. The previous editor had exhorted her to write about "babies and bonnets," but had never questioned her judgment as to how she covered society doings.

"Of course, my readers want to know what society women are wearing," she said, trying to quell her indignation. "The designers want their names in the paper, the ladies want the public to know they have the very best, and women all over the world are curious as to the wardrobes of Manhattan's socialites."

"We're not publishing a paper to aggrandize a bunch of French designers..." Thorn began.

"Fortuny is Italian," Louisa corrected.

"Forgive me. European designers. You do know you have American readers, don't you? How many ordinary

Americans do you think can actually afford to dress like these socialites?" he asked.

"People want to know about the upper crust, what they do, what they eat, and most of all, what they wear," she said. "And many of our readers are these socialites."

This conversation was not going at all the way she had planned. She decided to change tactics and try to mollify the man. Her imperious façade might work well when she was covering society, but this man didn't give a fig about her family name or her high society airs.

"You may be right," she said in a conciliatory tone. "I was thinking that we could expand the women's page to add more relevant stories. Perhaps include a feature or two..."

He waved a hand at her.

"Miss Delafield, I must inform you that we shall not expand the women's section. I'm thinking of getting rid of it altogether," he said. He noticed the stricken look on her face and added, "I'm sorry, but you must understand. I've been hired to increase circulation. To do that, I've had to make certain changes. The men who read our paper are interested in business, sports, motorcars, and that sort of thing."

Louisa stood perfectly still. It didn't seem to matter what the women readers wanted.

"You'll keep your column, of course, but not on a daily basis," he continued, then formed his lips into a grim, tight-lipped approximation of a smile. "We'll still run it three times a week."

"I see," Louisa said. Louisa no longer had wealth, but she was still a Delafield. Her lips would not tremble, and tears would not stain her face. Without a word, she turned to leave, and the editor turned back to his work, but then he called after her.

"Miss Delafield, I'll consider running your column more often if you spice it up a bit."

She turned to face him again. "Spice it up?"

"Dig up some dirt on these socialites. Throw in a scandal or two. Trust me, readers are much more interested in seeing the high and mighty brought down a notch than they are in their clothing styles. Give them what they really want," he said as he hovered over a dummy sheet with his pencil in hand. "Dirt."

Louisa walked slowly back to her desk, afraid the floor might collapse under her feet. Dirt? He wanted her to destroy the reputations of people she'd known all her life? Not only would they would hate her, but she would hate herself. After the first scandal appeared in her column, she'd be lucky to get invited to a Bowery clambake. He expected gossip and innuendo from her, but she was not that person. Gossip and innuendo had nearly destroyed her mother after her father's murder, and she couldn't be the instrument of those twin prongs of evil.

She sat down and stared at her Remington. Her fingers felt leaden, but she rolled a sheet of paper into the carriage and stared at it. The blank page mocked her. She hadn't the slightest idea what to write. The whole building rumbled slightly as the presses in the basement began their daily churn. She had always loved that sensation. It made her feel as if she were part of a living organism, but now she only felt heartsick.

She had pecked out a sentence about the Grand Central Terminal opening when Billy Stephens, the police reporter, came bouncing in. He fell back into his chair and tossed his hat over her head to the hat rack where it twirled around one of the pegs and softly landed.

"Have I got a story," he crowed.

"I hope it's better than the exploding cats story," she said without looking up from her typing. The previous week a man in charge of animal control had lost a toe when a cat he placed in the gas box exploded. Dogs apparently didn't explode, but cats did. Knowing her own cantankerous cat, she had no trouble believing the story.

"Much better than exploding cats. This one is about an exploding police matron," he said, rather too gleefully. Billy was notorious for his gallows humor.

"Excuse me?" she said.

"Happened early this morning in Hell's Kitchen. The bomb squad said she was investigating an abortionist and got a little too close to some 'explosive' information," he said, rolling a sheet of paper into his typewriter.

"What do you mean?" Louisa asked.

"Someone set a trap for her. They lured her into a building and then *kaboom!*" he said, spreading his hands apart to mimic the explosion.

"My God," Louisa said. "But why would a police matron be on an investigation? I thought they were hired to take care of women prisoners, to protect them."

"That was the original purpose, but some are ambitious. According to the scuttlebutt, they are actually good at police work. No one suspects women of being cops. They still call them matrons though. That way they don't have to give them a pension," Billy said and began pecking out his story.

Of course, the women would be cheated out of their rightfully earned pensions, Louisa thought.

"What was her name?" she asked.

"Adele Cummings. She was a widow, leaves behind one kid," he said, reading over his notes. He lit a cigarette. "And what earth-shattering events are you covering today? Luncheon at Delmonico's? Or tea at The Vanderbilt?"

He didn't wait for her to answer, but instead plunged into his story.

Louisa looked at the page she'd been typing. What was wrong with writing about luncheon and teas and soirées, she wondered. With an index finger, she rubbed the metal carriage arm. She looked over at Billy, a cigarette wedged between his lips, his eyes peering through the smoke at the words materializing on the page in his typewriter, totally absorbed in his work. He must have felt her staring at him, for he looked up and winked at her. She quickly turned her eyes back to her typewriter and chased the wayward questions from her mind. She had an event to cover tonight and a lovely red velvet dress to wear. With some *eau de toilette*, she could easily cover up the mothball smell. Unlike all those teas and luncheons which only women attended, men would be at the event tonight. That meant she might have a chance to write about something more weighty than who wore what dress by which designer.

Billy pulled the sheet of paper from his typewriter and dropped it into a basket for the copy boy before heading over to the coffee pot. Louisa reached over and pulled out his story. She read it quickly. All the who, what, and when was there, but nothing about the police matron herself. Louisa dropped the sheet back into the basket and wondered what she was like. A thought wiggled its way into her brain. This police matron's life was certainly as important as some society event. Someone should write a story about this woman's life, not just her death. Louisa shook the thought out of her head. She was lucky to be a society writer, she told herself, the next best thing to being in society itself.

Society Notes

GRAND CENTRAL TERMINAL OPENS TONIGHT;

Vanderbilt Returns to New York to Celebrate with Friends

---

by Louisa Delafield

NEW YORK, Feb. 2 — Tonight at midnight a great monument to the 20th Century opens its door to the public at precisely midnight. The auspicious opening of the Grand Central Terminal is the result of a decade of blood and toil. This Beaux Arts marvel, designed by the charismatic and prolific architects Whitney Warren and Charles Wetmore, represents the largest construction project in the city's history and the first all-electric train terminal in the world.

Tucked away in an exclusive new restaurant, specializing in oysters and cocktails, the men behind the magnificent railroad terminal will celebrate their achievement. Many of high society's most sophisticated ladies and loveliest debutantes will also be in attendance. Yours truly will be there, as well, to capture the glitz and glamour of this momentous event.

Chapter 4

Ellen

Rage pulsed through every vein in Ellen's body as she held back Silvia's long dark hair while the girl, barely seventeen, heaved into a ceramic basin. Snow drifted past the narrow window of their fourth-floor quarters.

"I'm sorry, Ellen," Silvia said, wiping her mouth with a rag.

"It's not you who's at fault," Ellen said. The anger burned like acid on her tongue. "It's him should have known better than to take advantage of you." The heat that high up in the house was stifling, so Ellen cracked open the small dormer window. Across Fifth Avenue, children with sleds and skates ran through Central Park to enjoy the snow. It was her first New York winter, and it was colder here than back home in Ireland, but she was hardly ever outside to tell the difference.

"I couldn't say no to him," Silvia whimpered.

"No, I s'pose you couldn't," Ellen agreed, turning away from the view outside. "Not if you wanted to keep your job. And now you're....." She looked at Silvia's belly.

"At least he's taking care of the problem. And with a real doctor," Silvia said. She held up a note on Mr. Garrett's stationary. Ellen perused the note.

My dear girl,

Please don't worry. You will be in good hands.

Marat will be with you when it happens. When this is over, all will be well, and we'll see about getting you a position as a lady's maid somewhere.

Your Friend

He hadn't signed it, but the stationery was enough to give him away. Silvia took the note from her and placed it in a drawer among her clothes.

"I'd like to give Hugh Garrett a piece of my mind," Ellen said, but she could not afford to do anything that might cost her the job. Hattie's older brother was the man of the house since their father had been dead and gone for years now.

"Will you go with me tonight? Marat will come get me as soon as he drops the family off at the Grand Central opening," Silvia said. "Please, Ellen, I need another woman with me. Not Marat."

"I should have known that chauffeur would be involved. He's as shady as a sycamore. Miss Hattie told me they wouldn't be leaving for the opening till near midnight," Ellen said. Going on this devil's errand with Silvia would mean she wouldn't get any sleep at all. She was tired all the time as it was. She ought to say no.

Silvia gripped Ellen's arms and looked up at her with deep dark eyes. Ellen gazed at the Italian girl — as pretty and fresh as a summer strawberry.

A loud knock on the door startled her.

"Girls! Get up. Mrs. Garrett doesn't pay you to sleep all day."

"We'll be right down," Ellen answered. The family wasn't awake yet, but there were shoes to be brushed or shined, washing and mending to do, and the preparing of breakfast trays with fresh flowers and polished silverware.

She glanced at Silvia, who stared at her with imploring eyes. Ellen could never live with herself if something happened to her.

"All right, girleen," she said in a softer voice. "I'll come with you. But you'll owe me some darning." Silvia smiled weakly, unable to hide the fear in her eyes.

Chapter 5

Louisa

Louisa's breath turned into clouds in the frigid air as she hastened toward the 125th Street station to the El. Crossing the street she barely evaded a speeding roadster. More and more touring cars and racing cars and all sorts of motorcars crowded the streets of New York these days, making crossing the road a dangerous enterprise.

She handed a paper ticket to the attendant who dropped it into a cutting machine and let her pass on to the platform where people were already filing onto a waiting train. Once she transferred trains, it was a quick trip, filled with other people heading to the event. It seemed all New York was dressed up and ready to celebrate. Louisa felt elegant in the velvet dress that Suzie had refurbished beautifully, and even Virgil Thorn's threats couldn't dim her excitement at seeing the massive monument that William Vanderbilt's money had made possible.

She approached the new terminal among throngs of people, surging toward the building to witness the first train leave. Just a decade ago, this was a dirty, chaotic train yard filled with smoke and steam and crisscrossing tracks that divided the city. And now this engineering marvel stood before her: a magnificent edifice covering a subterranean network of tracks, all made possible by the advent of electric trains.

She heard the chugging of a motorcar and turned to see a red Rolls Royce with big yellow-spoked wheels roll past her. A moment later the car stopped and out stepped Dorothy Bloodgood, whose perfect face could surely launch as many ships as the fabled Helen's. She looked resplendent in an Eastern-inspired gown of green velvet with a hand-beaded overtop. An emerald coronet in her dark hair glowed, and a white fox stole hung over her shoulders.

In the next moment, out poured the debutante Hattie Garrett in a full-length ermine coat. Hugh Garrett, Hattie's older brother, emerged last in tails and white tie, a cowlick sprouting from his otherwise neatly combed hair.

Louisa hurried to catch up to them. Both Hugh and Dorothy were her childhood friends. The three of them had all lived within a block of Central Park on the same street, and they'd spent their summers playing in the backyards of Newport. Even Hattie remembered when Louisa was one of them. Hugh leaned into the front window of the car, deep in conversation with the chauffeur. He straightened up as Louisa approached them.

"Louisa, you ravishing creature! Come join us," he said, holding out his arm. His jolly eyes and ready smile were a welcome sight. Of all her past acquaintances, he managed to pull off the pretense that her status had never changed with the most sincerity.

"You're too kind," Louisa said, afraid that she did not look ravishing at all compared to Dorothy or Hattie. "Isn't your mother with you?" she asked. Amelia Garrett was one of Louisa's least favorite people.

"She's already here," Hugh said. "She and Natasha are guarding the doors of the party against interlopers." Then he perfectly mimicked his mother's nasal voice: "You can never be too careful."

Louisa giggled even as she felt a little wistful. If her own family had not suffered disgrace, her mother would probably be there with them, rifle at the ready to shoot any commoners who dared set foot in Social Register territory.

Dorothy turned and bestowed a smile on her.

"Worth and Cartier," she said, referring to her dress and coronet.

"Duly noted," Louisa said. Louisa didn't have her notebook out yet, but she'd have no trouble remembering those sartorial details.

"Louisa," Hattie gushed, eager to see her name in Louisa's column. "What do you think of my dress? It's a Lucile! I'm so glad she didn't drown when the Titanic went down."

The tragedy was still fresh in all their memories, and Louisa thought of the many heart-breaking obituaries she'd written almost a year ago. All those helpless people. She shook off the thought.

"I'm sure nothing could kill Lady Duff Gordon," Louisa said. "Not even an iceberg."

"No talk of that dreadful shipwreck," Dorothy insisted. She tucked her arm in Louisa's and whispered, with a touch of sarcasm, "I'm sure *all* of New York is dying to know that Hattie's wearing a Lucile."

"All of New York" wasn't the least interested in Hattie Garrett or her dress. As the most beautiful heiress in town, Dorothy had seized the imagination of the city, and she would occupy the center of Louisa's story as she nearly always did.

"Lovely design on your coronet, Dorothy," Louisa said.

"It's called a lover's knot," Dorothy confided, then added, "I've always wondered how lovers get into a knot."

"Cheeky girl. I'm sure I don't know," Louisa said. "At twenty-four, I'm an old maid."

"Just because you're not married doesn't mean you have to be an old maid," Dorothy said with a slight rise of her eyebrows. Louisa wondered what she meant by that. Dorothy was two years younger than she and in possession of a fortune. She had beauty, wit, and charm. She could marry whenever she felt like it — or not. At the moment, she didn't seem interested in settling down.

"Look," Hattie said and pointed to the clock. It struck twelve, and there was a collective roar as the doors opened and the crowds entered. The fashionable quartet hung back as the hoi polloi pushed their way inside. As soon as it was possible to enter with a modicum of dignity, they did so.

Grand Central Terminal was as stunning a marvel as had ever been built in New York City. Marble floors gleamed as the crowds pushed through the long sloping hallway. The loud, excited chatter around her dimmed as soon as they entered the Grand Concourse, thousands of milling people awed and humbled by the enormity of the place.

Louisa's head swiveled: the Botticino marble, the opal faces on the clock — heaven only knew how much that was worth! — the enormous arching ceiling, encompassing the entire zodiac with 2,500 stars. And the electric lights! It was a secular cathedral to progress and capitalism.

"You mustn't gawk, Louisa," Dorothy said, her expensive perfume wafting across Louisa's cheeks in a sweet and smoky composition of frankincense, almond, and vanilla.

"But it's spectacular," Louisa said. "Look at all the lights!"

"I'm told there are four thousand electric light bulbs," Hugh said, gazing up at the twinkling ceiling. His arm brushed against Louisa's as he turned in a circle. For a moment, they stayed there in each other's orbit, and Louisa admitted to herself, she didn't mind. Then the spell was broken.

"The train!" someone shouted. They followed the crowd out of the concourse to the platforms and heard, rather than saw, the Boston Express pulling out of the station.

"Let's find the party," Dorothy said, unimpressed by the departing train. "I'm desperate for champagne."

Louisa glanced once more at the arched doorways down into the bowels of the building where trains waited like subterranean beasts, then followed her friends back to the main concourse, knowing that her readers would be eager to learn how the elite celebrated the momentous event.

Dorothy's mother, Natasha, stood guard at the entrance of the Oyster Room, wearing a towering hat of feathers shaped like a mohawk. A filthy young woman in rags slouched near the doorway. Natasha appeared to be saying something to the ragged woman, but as they got closer, Louisa saw she was handing her a sandwich before shooing her away.

That was so like Natasha, Louisa thought, to take the time to alleviate someone else's hunger. She was the epitome of class.

"If it isn't my winsome daughter and her beautiful friends," Natasha said with a bright smile. Dorothy breezed past her mother, but Louisa stopped and accepted a peck on the cheek before following the others into the restaurant.

Once inside, Hugh wandered off in search of something stronger than the ubiquitous champagne. Louisa gazed around the room. Diamonds, emeralds, and sapphires dangled from women's necks, earlobes, and wrists. Glasses clinked on silver trays. The grand dames, Mrs. Fish and Mrs. Cornelius Vanderbilt, claimed one corner of the room. The younger set claimed another corner. Louisa would need to include all their names in her column, a rather tedious part of the job.

"Notice the Guastavino tiles," William Vanderbilt declaimed in his sonorous voice as he pointed to the terra-cotta tiles covering the great arched ceiling. A tall, slightly stooped man, he was surrounded by his cronies along with the building's architects and engineers.

"Those men. So boring and old," Dorothy said with distaste. "You'd think architects would be dashing. They're like a bunch of toads in the bog."

Hattie turned to Louisa and asked, "Do you know I have a lady's maid now that I'm a debutante?" Hattie had just turned eighteen. She was round and soft with a slight double chin like a baby's, a distinct contrast to the elegant, angular Dorothy.

"Of course you do," Louisa said, thinking how much simpler life would be if she had a lady's maid to help with her thick hair, which roamed over her head like an animal with a mind of its own.

"She's Irish," Hattie prattled on. "Mother says that foreigners make the best servants. American girls are too impertinent. And, of course, no one has colored servants."

"Really? Suzie has been indispensable," Louisa said.

Louisa turned to see Hugh's mother, Amelia, bearing down on them. Amelia saw Louisa and displayed a brittle smile that went no further than the lips.

"Louisa, how nice to see you, and what a lovely dress," Amelia said with a slight sneer as if she remembered the same dress three decades ago on Louisa's mother.

Hattie looked eagerly at Louisa. "We will see you at Mama's party for the Portuguese princess, won't we?"

"Hattie!" Amelia said sharply. "The soirée is a private affair."

Hattie looked chagrined, and Louisa felt the color rise to her face. Hattie had been a little girl when Louisa's family fell from grace, but as a girl she'd idolized Louisa who'd always included the younger kids in the summer games. Hattie hadn't yet absorbed her mother's worldview that money meant everything.

"I don't mean to offend, Louisa, I know your family is quite distinguished, but you are a member of the press," Amelia said, as if she were noting that Louisa had leprosy.

"That I am, Mrs. Garrett," Louisa said. "And I should get to work."

She turned away abruptly, determined to put Amelia's Garrett snobbery out of her mind. A few of the old guard, it was true, only tolerated Louisa's presence at their affairs because of her family name, but the younger women and the ones who were newer to society — the climbing roses — fawned on her in the hopes of seeing their names in her column and their dresses described in glittering detail. Still, Mrs. Garrett's snide comment had fanned the flame of fear in her chest, and she remembered that her livelihood was in peril.

Tonight presented Louisa with the opportunity to write about something other than whether hats would be smaller this year, or whether Miss Rothschild carried orange blossoms or tea roses at her debutante party, or what kind of china cups were used for coffee at the charity luncheon for orphans. She would prove to the obnoxious new editor that her column could be substantial — even if she didn't come up with any "dirt." She wound through the drinking, flirting, and gossiping crowd to make her way to William Vanderbilt, who had emerged from his chateau in France and come to New York to see to the continuation of his grandfather's railroad legacy. He stood in a circle of admirers.

"I don't care how much money the income tax will supposedly raise. It's unconstitutional and you know it," Vanderbilt said, waving a cigar at his listeners. His hair had gone white since she'd last seen him when she was a child, but it was still wavy and parted in the middle. He noticed Louisa. "And you can put that on the record, Miss Delafield."

Louisa smiled, pleased that he knew who she was. While women often courted Louisa's attention, the old captains of industry like William Vanderbilt could not care less whether their names were in the society section.

"Thank you, Mr. Vanderbilt. I may just do that," she said, smiling at him, not averse to using feminine wiles. "Our readers, of course, want to know how you feel about this mammoth achievement." She indicated the building.

"Twice the size of Penn Station," Vanderbilt boasted. "My grandfather Cornelius built the first depot on this spot more than forty years ago. If he could see it now! We have systemized every activity with which it will henceforth be astir."

"And tell me about the 'kissing galleries,'" Louisa said, pen poised.

The men who had been listening to this exchange burst into laughter.

"Leave it to a woman," one of them said.

"Whitney thought it only right that passengers and their loved ones should have a space outside of the mainstream of the concourse to say their good-byes," Vanderbilt said, pounding the architect on the shoulder.

"And is William Wilgus getting credit for having conceived of 'taking wealth from the air'? It was his idea to put the terminal on top of the tracks, wasn't it?" she asked.

Suddenly, the men went quiet. Louisa held her breath. They expected questions about kissing galleries from her, not questions about scuttled engineers. Wilgus had been thrown off the project after one of his electric locomotives had an accident, killing twenty people. The railroad had tried to lay the blame on him, but he'd outwitted them. He'd saved his designs showing that the railroad had not adhered to his instructions and the accident was their fault, not his.

"I believe he recently got some sort of award from the Civil Engineers," one of the architects said.

"Yes, yes," Vanderbilt said. "We wish him the best."

Then he turned his back on her, and she realized she'd foolishly stepped out on a limb. She didn't know what had gotten into her. She was a respectable society writer, not a muckraker.

Louisa left the men to their self-congratulations, stopping by a table piled with trays of shucked Blue Points, Rockaways, Cape Cods, and Shrewsburys — oysters from everywhere except the polluted New York harbor — to relish a few of the salty morsels.

She slipped away from the party. The corridors of the building resembled a Gothic cathedral with vaults and stone arches. She stepped under an archway about twenty feet wide and noticed a young woman in a crocheted hat and a black wool coat with her face in the stone corner. Across the expanse of the corridor, another young woman faced the diagonal corner.

"What are you doing?" she asked the one nearest to her. A crowd of people passed by them, chattering loudly. The other girl was some distance away.

The young woman giggled and said, "It's a whispering wall! Listen."

Louisa edged closer and leaned her ear into the corner of the wall. At first she heard nothing but the noise of people passing by, fragments of conversations.

Then she distinctly heard a woman's voice say, "I'm in love with Harry."

The young woman standing with Louisa gasped, then giggled.

She whispered into her corner, "I think he's in love with you, too."

The two of them turned to face each other, burst into laughter as they rushed to meet in the middle and then hurried down the corridor, arm in arm.

Louisa looked curiously at the stone corner and put her ear into the cool space. Bits of conversations floated around her: "I don't want to go home," "These shoes are killing me," "What do you think?" and so on. Then a strange sensation came over her and she felt a lifting, as if her spirit were skimming along the tiled ceiling and she heard a soft murmuring, as if thousands of women were all whispering their secrets to her. What on Earth were they saying, she wondered. She stood unmoving, listening to the whispering, straining to hear what the voices were saying. The edges of her vision grew dark and it seemed she was in a long tunnel. She felt a terrible sense of dread and sorrow.

"Miss? Miss?"

She seemed to wake from a dream, turned and saw a policeman. He wore a black armband over the sleeve of his uniform. She stared at the armband and then asked, "Is that for the police matron who was killed in an explosion?"

He nodded.

"It is, Miss," he said. "Are you all right?"

"I'm fine," she said, trying to steady the trembling in her voice. Then she stepped into the stream of people, who were enjoying the night like cackling birds. She looked back to see the officer watching her, the black mourning band clasped around his upper arm. Once again she wondered about the woman who had been so dangerous that someone had decided to blow her to bits.

Chapter 6
Ellen

Ellen's chest tightened as she watched Silvia on the gurney in the windowless little room. A chain with a small silver cross dangled from Silvia's neck. She had told Ellen that her grandmother back in Italy had given it to her when she was little. Ellen had grown up in the church, too, and she said a prayer now for Silvia. She hoped it wouldn't matter that the prayer came from a sinner such as herself.

The doctor arrived. He wore no jacket but his high-collar and white bow tie made it look as if he'd just come in from a party. He slipped on an apron that hung from a hook and suddenly noticed Ellen.

"What in the Hell is she doing here?" the doctor asked Marat.

"The girl was scared. She wanted her friend with her," Marat said.

"The girl will be fine. Get her out of here," the doctor said, pointing at Ellen.

"I'm not going anywhere," Ellen said. "I promised Silvia I'd make sure she was all right, and I won't leave till it's over."

The doctor looked grimly at her.

"You better be gone before the orderlies get here."

"Orderlies?" she asked.

"Yes. They'll take her to the hospital where she'll convalesce after her unfortunate miscarriage. I take good care of all my patients," he said.

Miscarriage? Ellen thought.

The doctor placed a mask on Silvia's face and rotated the knob of a gauge. Ellen turned her eyes away as the doctor, sleeves rolled up, bent in between Silvia's raised legs. By the door of the poorly lit room, Marat stood, feet apart, hands folded together in front as if he had seen a hundred such operations. He probably has, Ellen thought.

Marat sidled over to her. He was a large man, but he moved quietly.

"She's lucky," Marat said. One of his eyes wandered so she was never sure where he was looking.

"Lucky?" Ellen couldn't keep the disdain from her voice.

"Most poor girls drink henna or throw themselves down stairs to kill it. But little Silvia was made pregnant by a rich man, and so she gets the same treatment as a rich woman," Marat said.

Ellen kept her eyes on Silvia's face as the doctor conducted his vile business. Her breath stuttered with worry for the girl. Time passed slowly, and Ellen looked around the cold little room. The doctor had mentioned to Marat that his usual place of business was unavailable when they first came in. This is just temporary, he'd said. In the corner were boxes of castor oil, Vapo Cresolene for coughs, and Mrs. Winslow's Soothing Syrup, so she assumed they were in the back of an apothecary. To get there, they'd driven through the worst areas of town: women standing in doorways and by streetlamps with low-cut dresses, hiking up a skirt to reveal a leg, men openly drinking from bottles, other men still as statues glaring at the passing motorcar with their hands dug into their pocket, and even children out in the middle of the night — filthy, ragged, wild children running from whatever crimes they'd just committed. Barred storefronts, rundown hotels, taverns, and, tumbling out of an alleyway, two men brawling. They drove past a Chinese laundry and a Chinese restaurant, and then turned into a dark, quiet alley. If this doctor was so reputable, then why, she wondered, did he do his business in such a treacherous place?

Finally, the doctor pulled Silvia's dress back over her knees and plucked the mask from her face. He turned toward them. He was a handsome sort with dark hair brushed back from his face and a thick mustache suspended over his mouth like a half-moon. Like the moon, though, there was something distant and cold about him.

"She's done. Keep her feet elevated to stop the bleeding," he said.

Marat handed him an envelope. The doctor opened it with blood-stained hands and quickly scanned the contents. Ellen gazed at the sedated girl. A fine spittle of drool leaked from the corner of her mouth. Then to Ellen's horror, Silvia's body began convulsing, heaving up and down.

"What's wrong with her?" Ellen called out. The doctor cursed, dropped the envelope on the ground, money spilling onto the floor, and rushed over to the girl.

"She's had a reaction to the ether," he said, slapping Silvia's face. "Jesus Christ!"

Ellen felt a prickling sensation across her scalp. The doctor pushed with both hands against Silvia's chest. After an eternity, she stopped convulsing but showed no sign of life. Ellen stepped in to look closer. The girl's eyes had rolled back in her head, and her face had turned livid. A gurgling sound came from her throat. A moment later her head dropped to the side. Everything was still. A cold, black feeling swam through Ellen's body, and her hands trembled. Death hung in the air like icy smoke.

"What have you done?" Ellen asked in a choked voice.

"It happens sometimes," the doctor said, wiping his brow with his sleeve.

"She was just a girl," Ellen said, balling her fists in rage.

The doctor glared at Marat.

"Get her out of..." He stopped speaking and stared behind her.

Ellen felt a cold gust of wind. She turned and saw two Chinese men standing in the doorway. The closest one had a pointed goatee and wore a shiny black jacket. He was wiry, and his eyes glowed like a cat's. The other man was shorter but burlier with a round scowling face. These were no orderlies.

"Where is the girl?" the taller one asked.

"She died on the table," the doctor said, rolling down his sleeves.

"The boss won't be happy."

"It's not my problem," the doctor said.

Ellen couldn't understand why these men were here. What had they intended to do with Silvia?

One of the "orderlies" suddenly noticed Ellen.

"We'll take this girl then," he said. Ellen turned toward Marat, who watched the two men warily. Marat stepped toward her, but one of them suddenly pulled out a knife and waved it in his face. Marat froze and then slowly backed away.

"Marat! You can't let them..." she said, panic flooding through her. "I don't understand."

She looked from the men to Marat and back. Marat stood by, doing nothing.

"Sorry," he said, and looked away.

"You come with us," the man said. He reached out and gripped her arm tightly. The other man replaced his knife and also came toward her.

Ellen did exactly what her older brother, Michael, had taught her to do when they brawled with other kids back home in the Claddagh. With her free hand, she punched the first man in his throat with her knuckles, lunged forward and kicked the second one in the groin.

"Stop her!" yelled the doctor, but before they could catch her she was out the door, running through the night, her footsteps ringing on the cobblestones.

Chapter 7

Louisa

Louisa stopped in the ladies' lounge to gather her thoughts. The room was large and luxurious with wood paneled walls and plush seats strategically placed around the room. She sat in one of the chairs and wondered what had come over her. She was not the sort of woman to have fancies and visions. She was pragmatic, practical. Most of all, she was respectable. She couldn't afford to be anything else. Her poor father's ignominious death had ruined the family name, left it to wallow in the gutter like a piece of refuse. She had sworn to herself that she would pull that name out of the gutter, she would clean it and polish it and never allow it to be sullied again. She must have just had a drop in blood pressure. Or perhaps the champagne had gotten to her. It must mean it was time to go, though she didn't have anything salacious for her editor.

Louisa gathered her cape from the coat-check in the Oyster Room. She was embarrassed she had no tip for the clerk so she quickly ducked away while he was attending to another guest and headed toward the Lexington Avenue exit. She had enough material for her column, and she could include the quote about the kissing galleries. Her readers would like that.

When she got to the door, she looked out at the bitter night. There were plans to have a subway station right in Grand Central but no subway tunnels had been built here yet. In the meanwhile, she'd have to walk several blocks in the cold to the El.

The Garretts' chauffeur pulled up in the red Rolls Royce and a moment later she heard a voice call her name.

"Louisa!" Hugh exclaimed. "Let us give you a ride home."

His mother glared at him.

"Hugh, that would be completely out of our way," Amelia complained. "And Hattie's exhausted."

"No, I'm not, Mother," Hattie said. "I'd love for us to take Louisa home. I can tell her all about our plans for a London tour."

"It's settled," Hugh said, ignoring his mother's pique. "Louisa, hop in the tonneau with Mother and Hattie. I'll sit up front with Marat." He opened the motorcar's door.

Louisa was only too happy to comply. She didn't care if Amelia was miffed. Unlike many of the motorcars, the Rolls Royce was closed in. No one seemed to have figured out how to put a furnace inside a car yet, but a couple of mohair coach blankets would make the ride comfortable enough.

"Here, Louisa," Hattie said, inviting her to share the coach blanket with her while Amelia sat frostily next to the door under her own blanket.

A glass partition separated the back seat from the front where the chauffeur and Hugh sat. Louisa wondered what Hugh and the driver could be discussing. It seemed quite intense. Hugh even glanced back once with a scowl on his face.

Meanwhile Hattie chatted about the particulars of her day. Since she'd turned eighteen everything was different, she explained.

"First, Ellen brings me breakfast in bed, just like Mama's lady's maid. Ellen's ever so smart. She reads your column to me while I'm eating my breakfast or sometimes when I'm taking a bath," Hattie giggled. "She gets very excited when you mention one of my dresses."

Louisa doubted it was the maid who got excited by seeing Hattie's name in her column.

"You must learn to treat that girl like a servant," Amelia interjected. "Whoever heard of calling your maid by her first name. I always call mine Smith. She's British, and that's how they do it."

"I'm not calling Ellen by her last name. That would be silly," Hattie said. "Anyway, then we go calling on other ladies or go to a luncheon. No more boring lessons from the governess. It's so much fun. And we usually get the most delicious little cakes when we visit other people."

Hattie's day sounded not much different from her own mother's society days, Louisa thought. She had her notebook out and dutifully scribbled down notes. Perhaps there was a story here: "A Day in the Life of a New York Debutante." Thorn would probably say it was too dull unless her day involved dalliances with various lotharios.

"I especially enjoy the tea dances," Hattie said. "And I know lots of new dances."

"The Turkey Trot is indecent and disgusting," Amelia interjected.

As Hattie prattled on about the details of her daily life, Louisa noticed something shiny on the floor of the automobile beside her boot. When Hattie stopped babbling long enough to ask her mother for a handkerchief, Louisa leaned over and scooped it up. A silver cross no bigger than a quarter dangled from a thin silver chain. She gazed at it. And then. It happened again. Everything in her peripheral vision disappeared. All she could see was the silver cross twirling in her hand. She felt paralyzed. Hattie's voice sounded as if she were far away.

"Louisa!" Hattie said. "Why did you stop taking notes?"

In an instant, Louisa was back in the moment.

"What's that in your hand?" Hattie asked.

"A necklace," Louisa said.

Hattie peered into Louisa's hand and said, "Cheap." Then she glanced at Louisa. "I'm sorry. Is it yours?"

"No, I found it," Louisa said. She was about to tell her that she'd found it there in the car, but something stopped her. That eerie feeling settled in her shoulders. The necklace obviously didn't belong to Hattie or her mother. She looked up front and wondered, had Marat given someone a ride in the car? She wasn't sure what to do so she slipped it into her bag and took up her pen again. "I'm listening."

Hattie smiled and continued the detailed account of her thoroughly uninteresting life. Louisa licked her pencil and continued scrawling words across the page of her notebook without really seeing them.

Chapter 8

Ellen

The cold air burned Ellen's lungs, and her cramped muscles ached as she huddled in a doorway behind a mound of trash in an alley. She was in the seedy, desperate area of the city where the poor eked out bitter lives of destitution. It was the life she'd thought she'd avoided by going into service for a wealthy family with comfortable quarters for the servants and good food on the kitchen table to give them the strength to do their chores. The smell of human waste and rotted food wrapped her in a sickening embrace. A rat stood on its hind legs to sniff curiously at her. She'd always been horrified by the whiskered, twitching creatures, but still she didn't make a move — even as the cold seeped through her thin wool coat, stinging her skin.

She'd been in this same spot for nearly an hour, she reckoned, and it had been a good while since she'd heard the footsteps pounding down the cobblestones.

She told herself they had probably given up the search for now. Marat would have to do something with poor Silvia's body and then he'd have to go fetch the Garrett family from their entertainments. She wasn't sure what his role was, but she knew the doctor hadn't wanted her to escape. He was probably afraid of what she could tell people. Hugh Garrett might also be concerned. She had put herself in a precarious position by coming with Silvia.

She thought of standing, of finding her way out of this network of alleys and dark streets and felt waves of fear flow down into her knees. Where could she go? She had no money, and this area was no place for a woman alone.

Finally, she knew she must rise. She must stretch out her legs or they would collapse underneath her and she'd fall into the disgusting heaps of garbage that surrounded her and find herself at the mercy of the scuttling rats. She used her hands to pull herself up the brick wall of the doorway and forced her feet to move through the refuse to the clear part of the alley. She shook out the skirt of her dress and brushed off her shoes. Then she wiped her hands on her coat. There was no getting away from the smell. It was part of her now.

She figured it was some time past three in the morning. Should she try to get back to the Garretts' house or should she wander the streets until daybreak or find a bench to sit on, maybe fall asleep sitting up? She had no idea how far Fifth Avenue was but it seemed like it might as well be on a distant planet. Worse, the doctor surely knew who paid for the operation. He might send his orderlies to the Garretts' to search for her. And what would Hugh Garrett do when he knew she'd been a witness to his crime? No, she was better off not going back there for now.

She shivered and made her way to the street. She'd been to the tenements once with Silvia when they came to bring some goodies to Silvia's Italian family for Christmas. The family had welcomed her into their tiny apartment and they'd had a feast of sorts in the little living area. Ellen had enjoyed herself but was under no illusion that the food and the laughter was an everyday occurrence in that tenement apartment. Her own family back in the Claddagh was also quite poor, but they had their own little cottage kept warm by a turf fire, and they ate nourishing food from the sea which their father plowed with his hooker boat like a farmer plows the fields.

The streets were fairly empty. Men slept in doorways, hands clutching bottles of liquor like lovers. One of them snored so loudly she thought he'd surely wake the families in the tenements above the stores. Many of the stores had Irish names. They would be owned, she supposed, by the sons and daughters of those who'd fled the Hunger. And they would cater to the poor immigrants who continued to leave the homeland in droves. Though she'd been in America for a half a year, she hadn't gone out looking for her countrymen. She hadn't even known where they congregated.

Instinct took her down the long blocks to the waterfront. She could smell the brackish water of whatever river it was crept toward the sea. She desperately missed her little room on the top floor of the Garretts' Fifth Avenue mansion where furnaces and fireplaces heated every room in the house and even the servants had their own water closet. It was not lost on her that just a few weeks earlier she'd thought her life too dull. She thought of Silvia, who had been in America since she was ten. She'd been helpful to Ellen, explaining as much as she could about the ways of America and they'd built a comfortable friendship. Then Hugh Garrett took advantage of Silvia's sweetness and innocence. Murderer, Ellen thought, and in her mind's eye he swung from a gallows. But she knew better. Men like him never faced the consequences for what they did.

She came to an empty lot at the foot of a large bridge and saw a fire in a canister. A few figures stood around it, huddling close for warmth. The fire drew her in. It wasn't safe, but she could not help herself. She had to get warm.

One of the men looked at her warily as she approached.

"What have we here?" he asked as she stepped into the circle of light. He was slight of build with a long face, no front teeth, and a single black brow across his forehead.

"Nothing for you," she snarled. She was already looking around for a stick or a brick to wield as a weapon if necessary, but the men were too cold and tired to present much of a problem. A lone tenement stood a forlorn watch over them.

Another man piped up, "An Irish girl. Where are you from, lass?"

"County Galway," she answered.

"Well, then," he said, "You might have some friends among the peelers, I'm guessing. Maybe that's why no one locked you up tonight."

Ellen didn't say anything, but his comment got her to thinking. Galwegians had flocked to New York City over the past few decades, and not a few of them had joined the police force. Might one of them help her?

She edged closer to the fire and held out her hands. The warmth was meager. She realized that even if it was safe to go back to the Garretts', she could not do it. Silvia had died in front of her. She couldn't pretend that hadn't happened, and she couldn't pretend that Hugh Garrett wasn't responsible.

She stood there, fighting to stay upright and to keep her eyes open, until the fire burned down to embers. The men eventually wandered away. It would be dawn soon. She figured she'd be safe as long as she could stay awake, but it wasn't easy. She was knackered and needed to pass water.

The fire died, and she headed back toward the city. She remembered passing some sort of park, but she was turned around and had no idea where it might be. She wandered the streets, block after block, passing shops and tenements until she came to an iron fence surrounding a patch of land. She found an opening and went inside. She followed a path through bushes and trees. Finally, she wedged herself behind a bush, pulled up her skirt, tugged down her bloomers and relieved herself, trying to steer clear of her boots, which she realized was pointless as she'd already walked through all sorts of muck. Then she crawled further behind the bushes and sat with her back against a sturdy tree. Her eyes fell closed, and her head bowed. Sleep took her.

***

Ellen awoke to the sounds of the city rising. She was dirty and smelled bad, but she found a fountain in the park where she could dab herself with some ice-cold water. The horror of what had happened the night before hung over her, but at least the sun had begun to crawl up the sky. Bells from a nearby church pealed. She followed the sound, and upon exiting the park she saw the church across the street. She crossed quickly, dodging a milk cart pulled by a shaggy horse, and went to read the sign outside. St. Brigid Roman Catholic Church. She could have fallen to her knees and wept in gratitude. St. Brigid, our Lady of the Irish. An old prayer to the saint came to her mind: "May the mantle of your peace cover those who are troubled and anxious, and may peace be firmly rooted in our hearts and in our world."

The church doors were unlocked for morning mass. She went inside and found a spot on a wooden pew. There she'd wait for as long as she could, kneeling on a cushion so anyone who bothered to look would think she was deep in prayer. She wanted to light a candle for Silvia but didn't have a penny for the collection box. The faint smell of incense hung in the air. It smelled like the church back home, and for a moment she felt deeply homesick. It seemed such a long time since she'd gone by her parents' cottage to bid them farewell though it was only last summer. Her mother had squeezed out a tear or two, and her father had railed that she was "na daughter o' mine." Her younger brother Martin was the only one to hug her and wish her Godspeed. When she walked away, she hadn't looked back.

Now she was hungry and tired, afraid she might fall asleep again. The church was comforting, but she wouldn't turn to it for help, for she didn't trust the priests. She knew what they thought of the likes of her. She rested her head on her hands, shut her eyes, and thought of a field of bluebells. She was running through the field as butterflies pranced across the flowers. She shook herself awake. No bluebells. No butterflies. Just a few old women praying and the stern faces of saints looking down on her from the stained-glass windows. She rose and went outside.

The sun was climbing towards its zenith when she headed back to where she'd seen the Irish shops and saloons. Her stomach growled with hunger as she walked.

She remembered passing a saloon with an Irish name — Murphy's — and imagined it wasn't much different from the ones where she'd fetched her father when she was a girl. The men would not be drunk yet, and no matter how rough the bartender or how slatternly the barmaids, she would not be cowed. She was an Irish woman in need of help, and when she told her story she'd not leave a dry eye in the place. Of course, the story might need some embellishment.

She entered the saloon and let her eyes adjust to the dark. The place had a dank, sour smell. A bartender stared at her with a puzzled look on his face. A few old men gazed up at her, blinking like moles.

"What do you want?" the bartender asked.

"I'm a girl from Galway, and I need help," she said.

The men and the bartender all exchanged glances.

She continued, "I've been working for a well-known family that lives in a big house off Fifth Avenue. The man of the house had his way with one of the housemaids and got her with child."

The men guffawed.

"T'weren't funny. Not a bit," Ellen said vehemently. "The girl killed herself in despair. I'm the one found her body hanging in the attic."

This silenced the crowd. The lie seemed an easier explanation than the truth and was sure to draw more sympathy.

"I foolishly blurted out what I knew and the man of the house — whose name I cannot say for fear of recrimination — swore he'd have me killed. He dragged me outside and took me into the carriage house, yelling that I was responsible for the girl's suicide. Then he picked up a wrench and hit me in the head. Next thing I know I'm in the back of his motorcar down by the waterfront. It was the dead of night, but in the headlights I could see the chauffeur outside with chains that he was surely going to drown me with. So I slipped out and ran for my life. I barely managed to escape. I've been wandering these streets all night. I'm tired and cold and scared. And I could sure use something hot to drink."

Silence cloaked the dingy little room.

Then one of them said, "Give the girl some tea, Mick. She's a mighty fine storyteller, she is."

"Aye," another one chimed in. "I don't believe a word of it but there's a future for her on the stage, eh, boys?"

The bartender motioned for her to sit at the bar while he fetched her some tea and a slice of brown bread.

"'Tis true?" he asked as he slid the mug of tea and plate of bread toward her. She scarfed the bread and scalded her tongue on the tea.

"Some of it," she said after a good gulp of the tea.

"And what do you have in mind to do about it, sweetheart?" he asked, leaning on his beefy arms. He had scars on his cheeks, and his beard was in sore need of a trim, but he looked like an angel to her.

She wiped her mouth with the back of her hand and said, "You know any peelers from Galway? Maybe I can trust someone from home."

The bartender scratched his head.

"Paddy O'Neil hails from Galway City. He's a detective now. Fifth precinct." As soon as she heard the name, her ears pricked. There was a family she knew of by that name back home. Could he be one of them?

"I don't suppose you can tell me where that is," she said.

"Sure I can. Haven't I been hauled down there more times than I can count?" he said, wiping the bar with a dirty towel as she finished her tea and bread.

Chapter 9

Louisa

Louisa walked toward the narrow five-story stone building that housed *The Ledger*. She took the elevator to the third floor and made her way through the maze of desks, removed her hat, and settled herself at a desk in the corner of the large newsroom. The steady clack-clack of typewriters and the low hum of conversations made a soothing backdrop to her work. She felt a bit lighter since it was payday. She refused to think about what might happen if Thorn made good on his threat to cut her column to three days a week.

"Why do you suppose Mr. Calloway hired a butcher instead of an editor for the paper?" she asked Billy Stephens, who was blowing the steam off a hot cup of coffee.

"I don't mind old Thorny," Billy said with a shrug. "He gave me a raise. Says he wants more local flavor in the paper."

A raise? Her paycheck was in an envelope on her desk. She opened it up. The payment was exactly the same as it had always been. She hadn't had a raise in the entire three years she'd worked for the paper.

After she finished her story, she took it into the lion's den. She clasped her hands and awaited Thorn's judgement as he scanned her story on the opening of Grand Central Terminal.

"Nothing scintillating at all?" he asked.

"I did mention the kissing galleries," Louisa said.

He continued to peruse the story. Then he yawned and handed it back to her.

"I do have something," she ventured. "An American princess is coming to town. There's a soirée..."

"You don't say?" he asked, peering up at her through his spectacles. He blinked his slate gray eyes.

"Actually, she's an American woman who married the Prince of Portugal," Louisa explained.

"Get an interview with her," he demanded. "Everyone loves royalty."

"It's not that simple," she said, remembering how Amelia had specifically not invited her.

"Are you a journalist or a copyist?" he sneered.

"I'll get the story," she snapped. She strode back to her desk, placed her hat on her head and jabbed the hatpin into her mass of hair. She accidentally pricked her scalp, readjusted the pin, and headed toward the elevator.

She must have been looking the other way as she opened the heavy glass door of the building and stepped out because her face was suddenly inches away from a wall of fine wool. As she stepped back, her eyes traveled up from the lapels of a man's charcoal frock coat to his striped vest, up to the ascot around his collared neck and then to a strong clean-shaven chin, full lips, ruddy cheeks and into the amused mahogany eyes of the paper's publisher, Mr. Forrest Calloway.

"Mr. Calloway," she said, utterly mortified she'd been so careless and at once blaming old Prickly Thorn for causing her to be distracted. "How clumsy of me."

"Not at all, Miss Delafield. It's my fault entirely," he said.

"Of course it isn't," she disagreed. "I wasn't paying attention."

"It's quite all right. Your mind is on higher things, I'm sure," he said. His accent carried the hint of desert and sunlight — a reminder that he was not a New Yorker.

"How kind of you to think so," she said. What a fool she must look, and yet this was more conversation than she'd had with the man in her entire tenure at the paper. He rarely made visits to the office.

"I won't detain you any longer, Miss Delafield. I'm just in to meet with my new man," he said. "And I've no doubt you're off to cover some important social event. Luncheon with Mrs. Vanderbilt?"

"Not today, I'm afraid. They're all sleeping off last night's opening of Grand Central Terminal," Louisa said. She had no idea what else to tell the man — that she was a failure at dishing dirt and probably about to be fired? She decided that dishonesty was the best policy. "I do have an interview with a princess, however."

"A princess?"

"An American girl who married a Portuguese prince."

Calloway smiled and said, "Everyone loves a Cinderella story."

Then he stepped into his newspaper building. She wished she'd told him that his "new man" was a butcher and he should find a replacement immediately.

***

She cashed her paycheck and went to the Knickerbocker Café for a cup of coffee and a Sally Lunn breakfast bun — a small luxury. The room was warm and cozy. Not yet crowded. She grabbed a copy of *The Times* from the counter. On the local page, she saw a story about the murdered police matron. Apparently, the police had no leads. She thought of that strange sensation she'd had the night before. Twice! She'd never experienced anything like that. A memory rose in her mind of the day her father was murdered. She had been lying on the Oriental rug in his study, looking at maps of the world, imagining where she might go when she was a grown woman. Her father had come in the room. He was distracted. "Where are you going?" she had asked, hoping he would take with her as he sometimes did. "Just some business. I'll be back soon." Then she'd heard a voice in her head — not a pleasant voice and certainly not her own — say, "No, you won't." That was all. The next day when the police came to tell her mother that his corpse had been found in a hotel room in Greenwich Village, she had not been surprised. Devastated, but not surprised. What if she'd warned him? Instead she'd been silent.

She stuffed that memory back into the mental box where she kept such things and pondered her current situation. She needed an invitation to Amelia's soirée.

She absently looked down at her notebook as she wondered how she might change Amelia's mind. Amelia was stubborn and snobbish, but then again so was her own mother, even without money. The words in her notebook caught her attention. She had the key right there in her hands. For one year in her life a young society woman was allowed to be a tyrant. It was time to make a deal with the debutante. She might also take the opportunity to remind people who her own mother once was.

Society Notes

A Day in the Life of a New York Debutante

---

by Louisa Delafield

NEW YORK, Feb. 4, 1913 — When my mother was launched into society in 1883, the event was heralded as the etiquette writer Mrs. Sherwood has described, "by the order of dresses from Paris, a ball at Delmonico's or home, and the most extensive leaving of cards on all desirable acquaintances." At the ball my mother stood to the right of her mother and then danced the German with a gentleman her mother chose. She had a little book to keep her promised dances straight, but on the fourth dance, she was smitten by a rather clumsy, but amusing green-eyed young man named Richard Delafield and she somehow managed to lose her little book.

For the rest of the season she performed the rites and traditions of the day, attending the balls of her peers, daily visits with other members of society, some small tasks for charity, and accepting visitors. Her mother was her guide in all things and her chaperone at all times. She obeyed the dictates of Mrs. Sherwood in that she never wore jewelry, never painted her cheeks, and never laughed too loudly. As soon as her first season reached its finale, Mother accepted a diamond ring from Mr. Delafield and their future was settled.

Thirty years later, some things have changed but others are just the same. Last December, Miss Hattie Garrett stood at the side of her mother and greeted a ballroom full of guests at the Waldorf Hotel. She wore a white, lacy confection and her hair was coiffed on top of her head for the first time in public. She was no longer a little girl. As Hattie related to me, her daily activities are similar to my mother's thirty years ago. Her governess has been let go, and an Irish lady's maid hired to help her in matters of hair and dress. She breakfasts in bed each morning, then rises, dresses, and it's off to call upon friends or attend to the visits of potential suitors. Afternoons are sometimes spent dancing at the tea dances so prevalent this year.

Unlike my mother, Miss Garrett is permitted to wear one or two pieces of jewelry — a simple gold necklace, perhaps, or a pearl bracelet, and all the young ladies are allowed to slightly rouge their cheeks if they choose. She is also not expected to select her mate for life in her first season. Women today often wish to take their time in making such a momentous decision.

When asked about her thoughts on the subject, Miss Garrett replied, "I'm not in a hurry for matrimony. We're going to London for the season next year, and who knows whom I might meet?" Who knows, indeed? Perhaps, there's a title in Miss Garrett's future.

Chapter 10
Ellen

Ellen sat on a wooden bench and waited. Police in their long blue jackets and boxy hats came and went, billy clubs at their side. Men and women who looked like they had little to live for sat on benches waiting to be processed or waiting for arrested loved ones to be released, she assumed. A couple of gangsters in flashy suits with hats dipped over one eye stood in the corner on some sort of dubious business.

Worries crowded her mind. Could they put her in gaol just for having witnessed what happened last night? Maybe they could even charge her with accessory to murder. The Garretts wouldn't defend her, of that she was sure. She clenched her fists, sniffled, and wished desperately for a handkerchief. She was actually trembling. She should flee, she thought, but her body would not do it.

Then a stocky man with black hair, eyes as blue as the midday sky, a big square-jawed face, and full frowning lips stood in front of her with his arms crossed. He wore a brown suit and a bowler hat, and she could have sworn she'd seen a hundred versions of him on the narrow streets of Galway City or on the farms in the surrounding countryside or even in the seaside villages where they lived by the hook and the net. Paddy O'Neil was Irish through and through.

"Y'asked for me, Miss?" he said. She gazed up at him. No turning back now.

"I did indeed. I'm in a terrible fix and I'm absolutely moidered about what to do," she said. "I thought maybe you could help me."

"Moidered, are ya? And what might your name be?"

"Ellen Malloy," she said. "Just came here from Galway City less than a year ago. I think you might have known my brother, Michael Malloy. You're about his age."

"Galway City, you say?" he asked.

"Actually, I grew up in the Claddagh, but moved into the city to live with my aunt when I was sixteen," she said. "I remember a family named O'Neil."

The man looked at her blankly, and she felt a surge of panic. She'd hoped some feeling of kinship would save her, but this man might as well have been from another planet. She rose to leave.

"I'm sorry to have bothered you," she said.

"You wait just a minute," he said. The detective walked off and left her standing. She wasn't sure what to do. After a few minutes, he returned with a uniformed police officer at his side. Was he going to have her arrested? Maybe the Garretts had accused her of something?

"This officer is going to take you to my house, Miss Malloy," the detective said. "My wife Paula will look after you till I get home. Then you can tell me about your troubles and we'll see what we can do. Paula will know if there are any jobs out there for you."

"Jobs?" Ellen asked. "But..."

He'd already walked away. She followed the policeman out of the building and down the crowded street. Lord, if her feet had to walk any more they'd turn into stumps, but she put one in front of the other and eventually found herself in front of a narrow brownstone. The policeman pointed at the door, and said, "There you go."

He left her standing on the stoop.

She knocked on the door, and a pretty, harried-looking young woman with a pudgy little baby on her hip opened it. A black-haired toddler peeked around her knees. Ellen and the woman stared at each other for a moment. Then Ellen's legs buckled and she sank to the ground.

She had no idea how long she'd been asleep, but she woke to the sound of a child laughing and the smell of cabbage cooking in a pot. She rubbed her eyes and sat up. The baby was squirming on a blanket in the middle of the floor like a fish trying to swim on land. The toddler, a small replica of his da, shouted and pointed to her. "Look, Ma!"

"Hullo, sleeping beauty, welcome back to the world," Paula said. "I had to get the neighbor fella to help me get you inside."

"I'm sorry. I did some rough sleeping last night, and it didn't agree with me," Ellen said.

"Paddy sent word you were a Galway girl looking for help. I don't know what I can offer but we'll give you a hot meal and a sofa to sleep on for a night or two. You might get work in a factory. Seamus, give your brother the bottle."

Seamus looked to be about three. He dropped the bottle in front of the baby, and then stared at Ellen with two fingers in his mouth and snot running from one of his nostrils while Paula busied herself in the kitchen.

"I'm not so much looking for work as looking not to get killed," Ellen said.

Paula stopped her pot-stirring and stared at Ellen. Then she turned back to her cooking and said over her shoulder, "Then I guess you'll be needing to talk to my husband."

They chatted about Ireland while they waited for Paddy to come home. Ellen learned that he had been sent over by his family when he was fifteen to live with his uncle, a sergeant in the 23rd Precinct. When he was sixteen, Paddy started working at the Fifth, "just helping out around the station." A couple of years later he had a beat on the streets, and now he was the youngest detective on the force. Paula relished talking about her husband. She was obviously proud of him, and Ellen could understand why.

"What made you leave home?" Paula asked.

"Oh, I wanted a change of scenery. Not much opportunity for a woman back there," Ellen said.

"You might have married," Paula said.

"I suppose," Ellen said. The truth was that her hand had been requested in marriage by the nicest fella she could have hoped for, Colm Feeny, a greengrocer's son. But that summer she had shared a long, deep kiss with a woman on the beach at Salt Hill. And that kiss had ruined her for any man.

Paddy arrived home a short while later, causing the Devil himself to break loose as the toddler lost his mind with glee and the baby decided to scream loud enough to shatter windows. The ruckus sounded like a cat on a melodeon.

"Made it, I see," he said, holding the laughing wean over his shoulder like a sack of flour.

"I did, and I thank you," she said.

Over a dinner of meat loaf and boiled potatoes, he admitted he did remember her brother.

"My da was in the Garda back home and used to bring Michael to the house sometimes after he'd been out on the streets causing trouble," he said with a grin.

"Your da was a policeman like yourself then?" she said.

"Aye. Michael would eat dinner with us and promise to do better next time. I remember you even showed up one evening to fetch him home. You were a wild looking thing with your red hair and your lower lip stuck out like you dared anyone to touch you. Rumor had it you were as tough as your brothers."

"Not so much any more. I've had to grow up," she said. "I've been working as a lady's maid for the past half year, sewing and washing and doing up hair and such. I'm afraid I've gone soft."

They kept to small talk during dinner. Afterwards, Paula took Seamus and the baby into another room of the apartment while Paddy and Ellen sat with mugs of hot tea.

"I've been party to a criminal activity," Ellen blurted out, gripping a teaspoon in her hand as if she might strangle it.

"Why don't you start from the beginning?" he said. So she did. She told him the whole sordid story as he listened impassively. When she was done, he shook his head.

"An Italian girl, you say. About seventeen?"

She nodded.

"Let's go," he said.

"Where?"

"To the morgue."

She put her boots back on her swollen feet, donned her coat and followed him out the door. They walked to the subway station, and he paid their fare. The train car smelled of the unwashed masses, but after having hidden amongst the garbage the night before she was sure she didn't smell much better.

"You know," he said as the train took them north to Bellevue. "We have a few women joining our ranks in the police force. If they have ambition, they can work their ways up to a good job. Mostly it's widows, often times widows of policemen. They need to support their kids somehow."

"What sort of work do they do?"

"They deal with women's crimes. They're the best ones for it. A man can't exactly pretend he's pregnant and in need of a little 'fix up' from one of these so-called midwives, can he?"

"Midwives? Why are they the ones getting arrested? Would you rather have those unwanted children be born and then starve to death? Or should we follow Mr. Swift's proposal and feed them to the rich?" Ellen asked. It wasn't a topic she had thought much about before now since she was sure it would never be a problem for her. And never would she dream she'd be on the side of an abortionist, but somehow when she thought of all those women back home with all those hungry mouths to feed, she wasn't sure anyone should be forced to have a child they didn't want.

"Look, I won't be debating the moral aspects of the issue. The law is the law. We may not be able to catch the men who get the girls, you know, in the family way, but we can get the midwives who break the law when they 'fix' the problem. Police don't make the laws, but we must enforce them," he said, spreading his big hands.

"A law that only applies to the poor," Ellen said. She was conscious of the hypocrisy of her stance. She wanted the doctor arrested, but she didn't think it fair that these police women targeted midwives, who were surely all immigrants, new to this country, trying to survive like anyone else.

"Adele Cummings would have agreed with you on that point," Paddy said.

"Who's she?" she asked, watching the city lights flicker past in the black windows.

"She's one of our police matrons. *Was* one of our police matrons, I should say. She was getting to close to nabbing an actual doctor, American, not immigrant. Might be the same fella as you're talking about. But somebody sent her into a townhouse and blew up the building."

"I wouldn't be surprised if it was him. Paddy, will I have to testify against this doctor if we find him?"

"You will," he said.

"I'm not too keen on that idea," she said and looked out at the blur of the city outside the window.

The man had already proved he was ruthless what with his "orderlies" trying to snatch her. If he was the cause of that police matron's death, then he could be capable of anything. Fear fluttered in her rib cage like a trapped bird.

"I'll be taking you to see Captain Tunney in the morning," Paddy said as they got off the train at their stop. "We're going to need to hide you somewhere. You aren't safe in the Lower East Side. There may be a price on your head already."

She shuddered and followed him down the long staircase from the platform into the crowds below as the train clattered away.

Bellevue was already close to a couple of centuries old and looked it. The cold gray stones matched the winter air. Paddy led her through corridor after corridor until they came to a chilly, tiled room. Four long tables were spaced a few feet apart, and a sharp chemical smell hung in the air like a layer of fog. A nozzle dangled from the ceiling above each of the tables. On the table closest to the door was the naked corpse of a headless man. Ellen's hand flew to her mouth as she stifled a scream.

A stout man in a white coat, looked up from a microscope on a counter on the other side of the room. "What can I do for you, Detective?"

"Need to identify the girl," he said. "Do you know what killed her?"

"Well, now, the operation didn't kill her," he said as he led them to the end of the room. "That was expertly done in my opinion. And she didn't drown in the river. She was already dead before someone tossed her in. I think she had a reaction to the ether. Who knows? Maybe they gave her too much or maybe she had an allergy. I've seen it happen before."

There stretched out on a metal table was a form under a sheet. The coroner pulled the sheet down and Ellen saw Silvia's puffy, livid face partially covered by thick strands of hair. Her body was bloated, her skin wrinkled and splotched. Ellen pushed back the long black hair. There was no mistaking that face even with every grain of life gone.

"Oh, sweet girl," she said, sadly. "Aye, this is Silvia Marie Ricci, a housemaid for the Garrett family."

Silvia's black eyes were open as she gazed into eternity.

Chapter 11
Louisa

Louisa twirled a spoon in her cup of coffee, watching the cream blend into the dark liquid. A copy of that morning's *Ledger* lay on the table in front of her.

"Billy doesn't mention anything about who this poor woman was as a person. She could have been a stray animal for all anyone knows," Louisa said to Suzie, who sat across from her at the kitchen table, buttering a piece of bread. Suzie never sat with them in the dining room. She still held by tradition, but in the kitchen, which was always her domain, Louisa sat with her each morning while Anna slept in. They sometimes talked about how to stretch their finances or had their coffee and breakfast in a comfortable silence, but Louisa had woken up agitated this morning with whispering voices in her ear.

"Maybe you should write a story about her," Suzie said.

"Me? I'm not a police reporter," Louisa said. "I don't even know how I'd get any information on her."

"Same way as you get information on those society ladies," Suzie said. "Ask somebody who knows 'em."

Louisa contemplated the idea but then dismissed it.

"Thorn would never publish it," she said, shaking her head. "Not in *The Ledger*."

"How do you know unless you try?" Suzie asked.

Louisa took a sip of coffee. She was so grateful they could afford cream again, and yet always nagging at her was the thought that there were no more paintings to sell.

"It would mean writing about something I'm not familiar with, a world I don't know," Louisa said. "I mean, what would people think?"

"Louisa, you have to stop worrying about what people think because their opinions won't matter if you're in the poorhouse. And you've said yourself that writing about society doesn't pay," Suzie said. "Now, if you want I could take in laundry..."

"No!" Louisa said. She rubbed her hand across her forehead.

Suzie buttered a piece of toast.

"I suppose that if I simply wrote a profile of her, who she was, her family, that sort of thing, maybe some quotes from the people she worked with..." Louisa said.

"People might like that," Suzie said. "I've seen stories like that in McClure's."

Louisa knew that McClure's paid much better than the newspapers, but Thorn would throttle her if she wrote for another publication.

"I'll write it first," Louisa said. "Maybe I can persuade Thorn that it should be a companion piece to one of Billy Stephens' pieces about the bombing."

The two women locked eyes as the morning light cut its way through the clouds and pierced the window to spill a shard across the table. A slow smile spread across Suzie's face.

"That sounds perfectly respectable to me," she said.

***

"Miss Cochran, I don't suppose you know where Mr. Stephens is?" Louisa asked the young woman who happened to be the secretary this month. The last one had married the business editor.

"Probably at Tuck's Tavern. That's his 'other office,'" she said.

Louisa pondered this information. She knew where the tavern was located, and she knew that the male reporters liked to congregate there. However, she'd never been inside, and if it was like many of the taverns she might not be allowed to set foot in the doorway. There was only one way to find out.

Ten minutes later, Louisa tugged open the door and walked into the gloom of Tuck's Tavern. She'd entered another world. The ceiling was blackened from decades of smoke, glimmering gas jets emitted weak light, and on the walls, framed front pages from various newspapers hung, including just to her right, a front page featuring the funeral of Edward VII, which she found odd in what she assumed was an Irish tavern.

"Top of the morning, Miss," said a burly, aproned man with a head as bald as an egg. "Can I help you?"

"I'm... looking for someone," Louisa stammered.

"Who might be that be?" the man asked.

She peered around and saw Billy Stephens at a table by himself in the corner with a racing sheet in his hand.

"There he is," she said and smiled graciously at the bartender as she edged toward the corner table. She'd never felt so out of place in her entire life. She sat down hesitantly.

"Delafield?" he said in surprise.

"Good morning, Mr. Stephens," she said.

"Not many ladies grace us with their presence," the bartender, who had followed her, said, "but we'll make a happy exception in this case. Ale, Miss?"

"Oh, no thank you," Louisa said. "Do you have tea?"

The bald man guffawed and walked away, but within moments a china cup full of steaming Irish tea sat on a chipped saucer in front of her. The room smelled of pipe smoke and ale and fried foods. The table was of a dark wood, and the armchairs quite comfortable.

"Welcome to the Old House, Miss Delafield," Billy said as he hoisted a pewter mug.

She raised her cup of tea and sipped nervously. The imperious manner she usually hid behind with the men at the newspaper failed her utterly.

"What are you doing here?" he asked.

"I wanted to talk to you...to ask you...I want to write about that police matron. A feature piece on her," Louisa said. "As a supplement, you might say, to the grittier crime angle."

"Why?" he asked.

"I think it will be an interesting story," she hedged.

"You're trying to branch out, aren't you?" he said. "I take it Thorn won't give you a raise."

"No. He's under the impression that only men need to eat to survive. We women can live on air," she said.

"Probably figures you're as well off as your readers," he said with a shrug.

"I'm not," she said. "One of the advantages of my job is the free food."

Billy stared at her as if seeing her for the first time, his customary smirk replaced by a quizzical frown.

"It's true," she said. "My father died deeply in debt. We lost our house, our furnishings, almost everything. There was a pittance left over once everything was sold and the debts cleared, but even that has run out. The only thing I know how to do is write about people."

Billy sipped his beer thoughtfully. She hoped he didn't pity her.

"You're not a bad writer. No reason you shouldn't have a decent wage," Billy said. "How about I introduce you to Captain Tunney. He's in charge of the investigation."

Louisa had almost hoped he wouldn't help her. What would she say to a police captain?

"Thank you, Mr. Stephens."

"Billy."

"Thank you, Billy."

"This afternoon then?"

"I have a charity tour at the new maternity hospital," she said, not to mention she needed to prepare herself to talk to this Captain Tunney.

"Tomorrow morning then," he said. "Ten o'clock."

He picked up the racing sheet and studied it while Louisa drank her tea and wondered what she had gotten herself into.

Chapter 12
Ellen

"And this is what you consider protection?" Ellen asked Captain Tunney after he parked his police car in front of an innocuous looking building. "Locking me up like a common criminal?"

"Safest place for you. These women aren't dangerous. Most of them are here for drunk and disorderly behavior. Usually they aren't in but a week or so. They get out and then come right back."

"It doesn't sound like a very efficient system," Ellen said.

"It's not, but it keeps us in business," he said. "And gives them a chance to sober up."

The police captain led her to the front door of the gray granite building. The building had an institutional feel to it with a long dark hallway leading to some stairs, and an antiseptic smell. Ellen noticed a tired looking woman sitting in a corner, knitting what looked like a baby's blanket.

A tall, angular woman in a matron's uniform came out of an office and greeted Captain Tunney. A sorrowful frown was etched amongst the crevices of her narrow face.

"Do you have any leads on what happened to Adele, Captain?" the matron asked, peering at the big man.

"I'm sorry, Mrs. Wallace, not yet," Captain Tunney said. He put a hand on Ellen's shoulder. "But we think that a crime this young lady witnessed may be connected, so I'm asking you to take special care of her."

"Of course, we will. You know, all us women on the force are just heartbroken," she said, shaking her head. She thumped her chest once, and seemed to be holding the reins on her pain. Ellen thought of her own pain over Silvia's loss and felt a kinship with the matron.

"As are we all," Tunney said. He turned to Ellen, "All right, Miss Malloy, I'll leave you here for now. I'll come back as soon as I find a better situation."

"What if you don't get him? The doctor, I mean. How long will I need to stay here?" Ellen asked. "What if he isn't who you're looking for? And how do I know those so-called orderlies aren't still after me?"

"I don't have answers to those questions right now, but if the case dead-ends then you're free to go and do what you like. Perhaps your employer will take you back," he said.

Ellen felt a wave of despondence as he walked out of the door. It could take weeks for them to track down this doctor, and then they might not be able to prove anything. He would have powerful friends like Hugh Garrett. She didn't think the police would even be pursuing this if not for the dead matron.

The matron took her by the arm and led her away from the door.

"Come on then. No one's going to eat you," she said.

They walked to the end of the hallway and up a flight of stairs.

"Hello, Myrtle," the matron said to a thin, white-haired woman in a plain dress with her arms crossed over her chest, who seemed to be standing guard at the top of the stairs. The woman looked as stern as a country school marm.

"Hello, Matron," Myrtle responded.

Ellen looked at her curiously.

"Myrtle's an inmate," the matron said, and led her down a hallway past rows of cell-like rooms. "She takes care of all the women here. Comforts the ones who need comforting and scolds the ones who need scolding. Less work for me."

They reached a room at the end of the hallway and the matron opened the door. Two bunks occupied one side, two hard benches the other, and a small barred window let in a feeble light at the end of the room.

"The bottom bunk is occupied. There's a blanket on the top one, but you better shake it off good. Lunch is at one," she said. "You don't have lice, do you?"

"No," Ellen said.

"I'll take your word for it," she said and left Ellen alone.

Ellen shook out the blanket; a few mouse pellets sprinkled onto the floor. She noticed a foul smell in one corner of the blanket. She left the blanket on the floor and climbed up onto the thin mattress and wondered what the Garrett family had made of her disappearance. Had anyone spoken to Silvia's family yet? Maybe Paddy O'Neil had gone to tell them. She hoped he wouldn't tell them about the abortion. It would break her poor mother's heart.

Eventually, Myrtle stuck her school marm face in the doorway and said, "Let's eat, girl. No sense going hungry."

Ellen followed her to a dining room on the first floor. It was a large unadorned room with yellow walls and four oblong tables where inmates and a few staff sat. The windows looked out onto a brick wall.

"How long you in for?" Myrtle asked her.

"Don't know," Ellen said.

"Could be a while then, I guess," Myrtle said. Ellen suppressed a feeling of despair.

Myrtle pointed out an elegant woman in her forties.

"That's your bunkie," she said. "You better sleep with one eye open."

Ellen couldn't imagine what the woman had done to wind up in this place. All the others looked like the drunks, street walkers, drug addicts, or vagrants they probably were. But this woman wore an expensive gray silk dress and her thick auburn hair was tied back with a ribbon. She didn't have the sallow pallor of the rest of the women. And yet, Myrtle had implied she was dangerous.

Ellen figured she'd better find out the worst, so she sat down across from the woman.

"Hello. I'm Ellen Malloy," she said.

"How nice to meet you. My name is Lillian. What are you in for, dear?" the woman asked as if she were asking if she liked one lump or two with her tea.

Ellen thought of telling the truth and then thought better of it.

"Vagrancy," she said. "And you?"

"Prostitution," Lillian said. "But they'll never make it stick."

"Oh?" Ellen didn't know much about "ladies of the evening" but this woman certainly didn't fit the image. She seemed more like some rich man's mother.

One of the other inmates placed plates of watery beans, white rice, and rye bread in front of them.

"Thank you," Ellen said.

"Nothing has any flavor," her lunch companion said, "but it won't give you the runs."

Ellen took a bite. The food was indeed as bland as butter, but it was edible.

"D'you think you'll be out soon?" Ellen asked.

"Look, they can't make the charge stick because I never asked for money. In fact, I paid for *her* — her meal at the Astor, her ticket to the show, a night in a nice hotel room," she said in between bites.

"Her?" Ellen asked.

"A lady cop. She had me fooled. I thought she was one of us." She leaned over and tapped Ellen's arm with a long elegant finger. Ellen stiffened. Us?

"I see," Ellen said. "Why did they call it prostitution?"

"Nothing else on the books! Look, honey, take it from me. I run a place called the Will o' the Wisp Teahouse in the Village. It used to be a girl could meet a friend there, have a little fun, but these days you're just as likely to be cuddling up to a cop," she said and shook her head in disgust.

"I'll remember that," Ellen said, wondering why the woman had assumed that Ellen was one of "us." What had given her away? She also felt a strange hope at the thought that there was a place where women could meet other women, women like her.

As they walked back to their room, Myrtle pulled Ellen aside.

"She's a degenerate," she whispered, nodding at Lillian who proceeded down the hallway. "And a bad influence on young girls, that one is."

Of course, Ellen thought, Myrtle would believe in her sour, little heart that a woman wanting love from another woman is a degenerate. Once they were back in their cell, they talked for a while about ordinary things. Lillian asked Ellen about her home in Ireland and what it was like to come to America.

"I'm right about you, aren't I?" she asked from the bunk below.

"I guess you are, but how did ya know?" Ellen said.

"I just had a sense. I'm going downstairs to play cards. Join me?" Lillian said.

"Maybe in a bit," Ellen said.

After Lillian left, Ellen sat on the bench by the window. Her thoughts wandered back alleys and narrow streets past teahouses and mansions and found their way back to that cold room in the morgue. All of a sudden, she wondered what had happened to Silvia's crucifix? It hadn't been on her body. She ran a finger over her own neck and shivered.

Chapter 13
Louisa

Louisa entered the thick, overheated air inside the hospital. The charity tour had already started. She removed her coat and hat, left them in the cloak room, and then found a hospital assistant to take her to the tour. She caught up with the ladies as they followed the doctor through the maternity ward. Lining the walls were beds with tired new mothers, holding babies. Some of them, ignoring the parade of strangers walking by, nursed their babies, their large veiny breasts fully exposed.

Dorothy lingered at the back of the tour with her mother, Natasha. Natasha had the austere look of Russian nobility with her ivory skin and long slender nose. When she saw Louisa approaching, a bright smile lit up her face. Unlike Amelia Garrett, Natasha Bloodgood always made Louisa feel welcome at any social gathering. Of course, Natasha had been like a second mother to her after her family's downfall. She'd brought Louisa into her home every day so she could continue her education with Dorothy's tutors and encouraged Louisa to apply for a scholarship at Barnard.

"Good afternoon, Natasha," Louisa said, warmly.

"Louisa," Natasha said. "Dorothy tells me you're going to the soirée for the princess tomorrow night, after all."

"Yes, dear Hattie invited me," Louisa said.

Natasha winked at her. "Your article was quite flattering."

"I suppose I'm temporarily in Amelia's good graces."

"Oh, look at that darling baby. I cannot wait to be a grandmother," Natasha said as a nurse walked by, holding one of the swaddled infants. Dorothy, in green velvet, stared up at the ceiling. It was obvious the sight of these women and their squalling babes repulsed her.

Just then Hattie in a dress with a bit too many ruffles sidled up next to Louisa. Her hair was pulled back in a plain bun.

"Your hair..." Dorothy said with raised eyebrows.

"Don't say a word. My lady's maid went missing," Hattie complained.

"Did she?" Louisa said. "What do you think happened?"

"I don't know, but she and one of the house maids just disappeared. Didn't even take their belongings. Mrs. Strauss is fit to be tied. And Mother says that immigrants are as useless as American girls. She promises we'll find someone else in London, but I liked Ellen," Hattie huffed.

Ahead of them, Natasha and Amelia were deep in conversation. Natasha was probably sympathizing with Amelia over her servant problems. There were few things that women of society liked to do more than complain about how unreliable or incompetent their servants were.

Louisa turned her attention to the doctor at the front of the group. He was a well-dressed man in his forties with an urbane air about him. The women hung on his every word, Amelia smiled obsequiously at him, and Louisa realized he was as popular as his cause.

"Poor women still have their babies at home. They use untrained midwives and the results are often disastrous," the doctor informed the ladies. "But we are encouraging them to come to the hospital if there are any complications."

"Everyone knows those midwives are criminals," Amelia announced. The women around her murmured their agreement, and the tour continued.

After the tour, Louisa went back to the office to file her column. She sat at her desk and began to type up the details, but she kept making mistakes and had to rip out one sheet of paper after another. Finally, she stopped what she was doing and looked into her bag. The silver cross with its broken chain nestled at the bottom. She pulled it out and let the chain dangle from her finger. She wondered if this necklace belonged to one of the missing maids.

***

The next morning Louisa accompanied Billy to the Fifth Precinct.

Billy knocked on a door just below a brass nameplate which read "Captain T. Tunney." The door opened and there stood a bear of a man with a Wild Bill Hickok mustache and pale blue eyes that glared at them with an electric sort of energy.

"The press," he said with a shake of his head. "Come in and take a seat."

Billy stepped aside for Louisa and they sat in hard back chairs. Captain Tunney sat across from them. He clasped his hands together and looked from one to the other. On his desk lay scattered pieces of what looked like a broken watch and a ham sandwich.

"Captain Tunney, this is Miss Delafield," Billy said. "I told you about her. She's a reporter for *The Ledger*."

"So you did. A society reporter?" Tunney looked with suspicion at Louisa.

"Pleased to meet you, Captain Tunney. Is that what killed Adele Cummings?" Louisa asked, pointing to the metal pieces, ignoring his skepticism. "It looks like pieces of a watch."

"It is. What we have here is the inner workings of a precision Swiss timepiece, perfect for setting off a bomb just powerful enough to bring down a small townhouse," he said. "Not generally what my wife reads about on the society page."

"I know that, sir," Louisa said. "This isn't for the society page. I'd like to write about Adele Cummings, to tell her story."

"There's been plenty of articles about the murder of Mrs. Cummings," he said, leaning back in his chair.

"Not from a woman's point of view," she said. "She is a heroine, and other women should know about her." If Nixola Greeley Smith could corner the market on celebrity interviews, then Louisa would stake out the territory of unsung women who were changing the world and sometimes sacrificing their lives to do so.

Captain Tunney shook his head.

"This is an ongoing investigation," he said. "We suspect a doctor, possibly even a respected doctor, may be responsible for the explosion that killed our officer. If he is willing to kill a police matron, think what he might do to you." He huffed and waited for her reaction, but Louisa would give him no satisfaction.

"I merely want to write about Mrs. Cummings," she said. "Perhaps speak to some of the officers who knew her. I have seen the armbands and I know how the force feels about their fallen comrade."

"I cannot have you meddling in police business, Miss Delafield. Stick with the women's page. Gossip and that sort of thing."

He pulled the ham sandwich toward him, and took a bite.

"Captain Tunney, your department hires women to do investigations that would be difficult, if not impossible, for men. I believe that same rule applies in my case. Though I'm not asking you to hire me," she said.

"I will not stop you from doing your job," he said, chewing his food. "But I will not help you either. If you were to be injured or, God forbid, worse, it would look bad for us, very bad indeed. There has already been public outcry that a woman officer was killed and in such a vicious manner." He wiped some mustard from his lips. "I'm afraid you are on your own."

"Could you at least give me her home address? I looked in the public directory but can't find her name," Louisa said. "I'd like to speak to her family and get a sense of what she was like as a person."

Captain Tunney stood up and walked to the window.

"I'll tell you what I will do," he said, his back turned to her. "I've got a key witness and I need to keep her somewhere safe. She's a servant of some sort. You take her into your household, and I'll give you free reign to write your story. You do have servants, don't you?"

Louisa felt her heart drop. Suzie hardly counted as a servant and she couldn't afford another mouth to feed. She stammered.

"A key witness?"

"She has seen this doctor's face, and now she's in a wee bit of danger," he said.

"I don't know," Louisa hesitated. This was certainly not in her plan. "My mother is not well and..."

"That's my offer," he said, turning to face her. "Take it or leave it."

She looked up into the icy blue eyes. What would she do with a servant on her hands? She should tell him no. She should walk out before she got in too deep. It wasn't too late. She stood up, and as she did so, a picture sprang to her mind — Suzie up to her elbows in someone else's laundry.

"I'll take your offer," she said.

He opened a box on his desk, pulled out a file card, and handed it to Louisa.

She looked at it and saw an address for Matron Adele Cummings.

"She lived with her widowed mother and young son," he said. "Do right by our girl, Miss Delafield."

***

That evening the lion head knocker banged on the door. Suzie got up from the couch with a groan and went to answer it. Louisa stayed on the chintz-covered armchair with her hands in her lap. She heard voices, and in a moment Suzie showed Captain Tunney into the parlor. He was followed by a rangy, red-haired woman who created the impression of a large bird about to take wing.

"Miss Delafield, may I introduce Ellen Malloy," Captain Tunney said. The woman's head snapped toward her, and she stared at Louisa.

"How do you do?" Louisa asked, rising and holding out her hand.

The woman didn't answer her or take her hand. Instead she turned to Tunney with hands on her hips.

"I know very well who Miss Delafield is," she said. The red-haired woman turned to Louisa and looked her up and down. "You're a friend of the Garretts. Miss Hattie lived and breathed just to be in your column. What's to stop you from telling your friends where I am?"

Louisa stared at her dumbfounded. So this was Hattie's missing lady's maid, but why would she be afraid of the Garretts? And where was the other maid?

"Stay inside and be careful, you should be fine," Tunney said. "Miss Delafield has given me her word that you'll be safe here."

The woman's green eyes continued to assess Louisa, her lips sealed in a tight line.

"I write about society, but I'm not one of them," Louisa said. She gestured to the modest surroundings, the faded fabrics, the small dimensions of the room, the lack of a telephone or a gramophone. All they had for entertainment was a rickety, out-of-tune upright piano that no one had played in years. "Once upon a time, this was referred to as genteel poverty. I suppose the description is just as apt today."

From the corner of the room, Louisa's mother piped up.

"I'm still one of The Four Hundred!" she said.

"Of course, you are, Mother," Louisa said.

The red-haired woman scrutinized the place.

"Better than the workhouse, I s'pose," she said and turned to Louisa. "My life is in your hands."

***

There'd been no time to get Ellen Malloy settled or discuss anything with her, but Louisa trusted that Suzie would make sure she was comfortable. Louisa hurried out of the house as soon as her hair was coiffed and she was dressed for the soirée.

When Louisa stepped out of the cab, she spotted *The Ledger* photographer waiting at the entrance with his big boxy camera and flash at the ready.

"Be sure to get a picture of the princess when she arrives," Louisa told him. "And also one of Dorothy Bloodgood."

On her way up the steps she noticed a female vagrant huddled in a doorway nearby. Amelia wouldn't like that, Louisa thought. The wealthy preferred to pretend the poor only existed to give them an excuse for charity balls and luncheons. They didn't want to have to actually see them.

She walked into the grand foyer as a servant came to take her overcoat. An elegant staircase spiraled around curved walls, a tiger skin sprawled on the floor, and a French Empire crystal chandelier spilled light across the Carrara marble floor. The butler led them into the drawing room where he announced her to the rest of the party. She made her way through the crowd, making mental notes of which luminaries were in attendance and which weren't. In every corner a Louis Quatorze table was topped with an Oriental vase or a Roman urn.

Louisa wandered into the ballroom where a small Hungarian orchestra played Strauss and dancers waltzed elegantly around the room.

"Shall we do the turkey trot?" a voice said in her ear.

She turned to see Hugh standing behind her with a grin.

"We're not in a public dance house, or hadn't you noticed? A turkey trot would cause a bit of a fuss," she said.

"A waltz then," Hugh said with a grin. "Wait till they see our Boston dip."

He took her hand and led her into the middle of the dancers. With one hand around her waist and the other holding her hand tightly in his, Hugh led her in a lively waltz. They weren't dancing the notorious turkey trot, but he did dip her once, and she felt a little dizzy as he brought her back up.

She laughed and said, "My boss wants more scandal in my column. I'll write that we were doing the tango."

Hugh twirled her around past huge vases of lilies, filling the air with their scent.

"Speaking of your column, how did you ever get past my mother?" he asked. "She despises the press and she's not terribly fond of you."

"Hattie persuaded her. I absolutely have to interview the princess if I want to keep my job," she said. "I'm sorry your mother isn't fond of me. I don't know how I could possibly be more obsequious."

"By the way, you look lovely," Hugh said. Louisa had a quick glance at herself in one of the ubiquitous mirrors. She was wearing an inexpensive dress, and tendrils of hair snaked out of her Grecian hair design, but her skin glowed in the light of the chandeliers, and for a moment, she agreed with his assessment.

She whispered, "I got the dress from Wannamaker's at a discount. Suzie gussied it up with some sequins and lace."

"Louisa, it's not the flamboyance of a woman's apparel that matters," he said, pulling her close. "It's her bearing. Every woman of distinction and breeding has it. You could come in wearing rags, and you'd still be among your peers."

Hugh's flattery was reassuring. For a moment, she'd forgotten she was working. She had slipped into a different reality — one in which she still had her father and he still had his fortune, and a rich and handsome man might consider her a worthy prospect for marriage. Then she saw Hattie across the room and remembered that strange Irish woman who had been Hattie's maid and who was now hiding in Louisa's house like a fugitive.

"Hugh, Hattie says that two of your servants have disappeared," she said after the dance ended.

Hugh didn't respond for a moment. Instead he reached for a glass of champagne from a passing waiter and picked up one for her as well.

"Yes, one of our young house maids is dead," he said, shaking his head. "A detective came by to inform us. The other maid was with her when it happened."

Dead? Louisa stifled a gasp. Was this the danger to which Captain Tunney had referred?

"How did the girl die? Do you know?" Louisa asked.

"I've no idea," he said. His expression was inscrutable. "Why do you want to know, Louisa?"

"I'm just curious," she said. She had to keep her promise not to tell him about the Irish woman. Ellen Malloy and Captain Tunney had been adamant, but why? What did Hugh have to do with any of this?

"If you'll excuse me," he said. "I'm afraid I'm obligated for the next dance. Best of luck with your interview."

He took her hand, kissed it like an old-fashioned gallant and walked away. Louisa wandered through the crowd, nibbled on some canapés, took note of the women guests and their attire, and drank another glass of champagne.

At the other end of the room, Amelia raised a bell and rang it.

"Attention, everyone. Attention. The princess is here, and I must ask one favor of you. She insists on no applause. Too much noise might disturb the cat."

The cat? All around the room people traded glances.

The door swung open, and a black-haired woman in a black dress trimmed in gold entered the room — with a leopard on a leash. The gasps were audible. Eyes widened. Women clutched their pearls. The princess smiled regally and moved around the room to greet people, but most of the guests backed away in terror. The princess seemed to find this amusing. When she came to Louisa, Louisa smiled and curtsied, eyeing the cat. His gold eyes gleamed as he looked around the room. His pink tongue lolled out of his mouth. The poor thing was probably as terrified as everyone else.

"What a gorgeous companion you have, Princess," Louisa said. "Does he have a name?"

"I call him Chaka, after the great Zulu warrior. And who are you?" For all her glamour, her accent was decidedly Upper Midwestern. An American Cinderella.

"Louisa Delafield. I'm the society columnist for *The Ledger*," Louisa said.

"A member of the press. Wonderful. Let's chat," the princess said. "I want to tell you all about my latest cause."

The princess took Louisa's arm with her free hand and led her through the crowd as if she were another pet. A path appeared before them, and the princess located an armchair as big as a throne where she sat down and smoothed her skirt. Louisa found herself sitting on a foot stool like a supplicant. The big cat settled on his haunches on the other side of the princess. He yawned, showing large scythe-like teeth.

Within a few minutes of the interview, Louisa learned that the Portuguese princess was not actually a ruling princess of Portugal, though she was nominally a princess.

"I am the princess of nowhere," she said with a laugh. That would make a good headline, Louisa thought.

"Tell me about this cause you are championing, Princess," Louisa asked, notebook in hand.

The princess's expression grew serious.

"It's called contraception. Have you heard of it?"

"You mean birth control?" Louisa asked and quickly glanced around to see if anyone else was listening. All wealthy women had causes — usually orphans or clean milk or something like that; they didn't often choose something so intimate.

"Did you know that it's illegal for a doctor to even discuss the prevention of pregnancy with married women?" she asked, leaning forward. The diamonds on her neck were positively blinding. "The world doesn't need more mouths to feed. It's the old Malthusian trap — as life gets better, the population grows and then we have too many people again and we're back where we started. Those tenements, for example, filthy and crowded, but women keep having babies."

"You're absolutely right, your Highness," a man's voice interrupted.

Louisa turned around and recognized him — well-built with even features in an oval face and a bushy mustache over full lips.

"Dr. Alan Swanson," he said, bowing to the princess. "I own a hospital solely for women."

The princess smiled.

"What do you think of these laws, Doctor?" she asked as she gazed up at him.

"Absurd. And yet I dare not break them," he said as he swirled a snifter of brandy. "However, those who are well off can always find a way around the law."

"That's the problem," the princess said. "It's the ones who can't afford to feed all those children who need access to contraception. Have neither of you heard of Margaret Sanger? She's a lone voice in the wilderness."

"I've heard of her. She doesn't seem to be making much headway, and she's likely to wind up in jail. What do you propose to do about the problem?" Louisa asked.

"Information!" she declared. "That's why your job is important. Women must be told there are ways to prevent pregnancy after pregnancy after pregnancy. They must demand this information from their doctors. And if the police arrest the doctors" — she pointed to the doctor, who clasped a hand to his breast — "then we must work to change the laws."

"How can women change laws when they can't even vote?" Louisa asked.

"There's the rub, isn't it?" the princess said as she reached over and stroked the cat's head.

Amelia suddenly appeared at the doctor's side.

"Dr. Swanson, I see you've met the princess," she simpered. "Princess, won't you join us in the parlor? So many of my guests wish to meet you." She threw a hard glare at Louisa, who realized the interview was over.

Louisa found the butler, who retrieved her coat for her.

"Mr. Strauss," she said as he helped her into her coat. "May I ask you something?"

"Of course, Miss Delafield," he said with a thick German accent.

"I understand two of your staff disappeared," she said. "What happened?"

"I'm not at liberty to say, Miss," he said.

"Were they good servants?" she asked.

"They were. Little Silvia will be missed," he said. His eyes watered and he bowed slightly. "Have a good evening, Miss Delafield."

Silvia must be the maid who was dead. What could have happened to her? Strauss would say no more. Louisa walked outside and found Dorothy Bloodgood on the sidewalk, talking to the Garretts' chauffeur.

"Dorothy?" she asked. "Are you leaving so soon?"

Dorothy turned to her, eyebrows arched, a smile playing across her face.

"Marat's taking me somewhere more fun. Would you like to come?"

A cloud of confusion descended over Louisa. Society women simply didn't leave a party for a princess to go have "fun." She stood dumbstruck as Marat opened the door to the back of the red Rolls Royce. Dorothy got inside and ran her fingers down her long, elegant neck. The chauffeur shut the door, and started toward the front of the car. Louisa thought of Thorn and his directive to spice up her stories, and her paralysis unlocked. She opened the car door and settled in next to Dorothy. Dorothy smiled in triumph.

"Where are we going?" Louisa asked.

"Take us to the Winona Club, Marat," Dorothy said as she leaned forward to drop a ten-dollar bill through the window between the driver's seat and the back.

"Winona Club? What is that? I've never heard of it," Louisa said.

"Of course, you haven't. It's a gambling house in the Tenderloin," Dorothy said. Louisa thought she couldn't possibly be more shocked than she already was, but she was wrong.

The big motorcar pulled into the street.

"Does your mother know about this?" Louisa asked.

"Mother thinks I have a headache."

"Are... are you slumming?" Louisa asked. She'd heard the term but never knew of any ladies who actually did it.

Dorothy turned to her, no longer smug. Instead her expression reminded Louisa of a time when they were children and Dorothy had discovered some baby rabbits in a field near their Newport cottage.

"Louisa, it's so much fun. Last time I was there, I met someone so interesting," she said.

Louisa felt a moment of confusion.

"Who is this someone?"

"Owney Madden. He's the head of the Gophers, and he's only twenty-three," Dorothy whispered and then settled back in the seat like a house cat with a canary in its mouth.

Louisa was vaguely aware that the Gophers were some sort of gang, so named because of their tendency to hide in the basements of the slums. In spite of her poverty, Louisa's world was a rarefied one: balls, soirées, the opera, and luncheons in winter; polo, tennis matches, elaborate dinner parties, and horse races in the spring and summer.

"Your mother will never forgive me if she finds out about this," Louisa said.

The car prowled down the cobblestone streets. As they passed pool rooms, saloons and clubs, women walked the streets, opening their velvet wraps to reveal pale flesh bulging from the tops of their dresses.

The world was changing, she thought. And yet for all its changes, her life was still a galaxy away from this other dark and dangerous world, which she'd read about in the newspapers, where gangsters warred with each other, women sold their wares on the streets, and politicians and company presidents bought the services of killers and hoodlums to keep their enemies at bay.

"You'll like Owney, Louisa," Dorothy said. "He's so different from the men of our set."

"I'm sure he is," Louisa said.

Marat laughed from his place in the front of the car. The partition was wide open so he'd heard every word. "So different they call him Owney the Killer," he said.

Louisa stared at Dorothy. She was consorting with a killer?

"He's not in jail, is he?" Dorothy asked.

"Not yet," Marat said.

"How do you know so much about these gangs, Mr. Marat?" Louisa asked.

"You can just call me Marat, Miss. I know about them because I came up in Monk Eastman's gang. The toughest gangster in Manhattan. When he went to jail, I figured I oughta change my ways if I didn't want to wind up there myself," he said.

They drove into The Tenderloin, an area that got its name — or so the story went — from a police captain who claimed his men would be eating "tenderloin steaks" from the abundance of bribes. Cabarets and theaters lined the streets. They pulled in front of a club, located on the ground floor of a sandstone building with an awning that jutted out to the street. A burly doorman with a face that looked like it had withstood a thousand punches stood sentinel.

"Marat, come back in a couple hours. There's another ten spot in it for you," Dorothy said. Then they got out of the car.

"Does Hugh know you've hijacked his chauffeur?" Louisa asked.

"Hugh doesn't mind. He's got his own secrets," Dorothy said.

Louisa had no idea what Dorothy was talking about. Hugh was a perfectly respectable man, a philanthropist, a pillar of society. Then she thought of the dead maid and the Irish woman who was probably sleeping under her roof at that very moment. What had happened at the Garrett house to these two women?

"Hello, Rolf," Dorothy said and flashed a dazzling smile at the dour doorman, who gave them a quick nod.

"Rolf works for Owney," Dorothy said under her breath.

"Is this Owney's club?" Louisa asked.

"I think it's owned by some city alderman, who lets Owney run it for him. The politicians and the gangsters aren't so very different."

Inside, flashy men, playing dice, baccarat, and other card games surrounded felt-covered oval tables. Smaller round tables were set here and there with silver bud vases, each one sporting a red rose, where women of dubious character drank cocktails, cigarette smoke snaking overhead. An elegant Negro woman in a black velvet dress sang a torch song in a husky voice on a platform while a piano player in a tuxedo accompanied her. Waiters rushed to and fro, carrying colorful concoctions. Dorothy plucked some champagne glasses from a tray and handed one to Louisa.

"Ladies drink free," she said and grinned over her glass, showing her perfect white teeth, which reminded Louisa of the princess's leopard. Under the smell of smoke, the place reeked of warring perfumes and colognes.

A man about Dorothy's height walked toward them. As he swaggered through the room, older men deferred to him with a polite nod and women eyed him slyly. Smiling confidently, he exuded a brazen air as if he owned the world. How men of society must pale in comparison to someone with so much bravado, Louisa thought.

"Who is this lovely lady?" he asked, smiling at Louisa. He was young and tough, his eyes like pieces of onyx, but his face was smooth as ivory and just as pale.

"This is my friend, Louisa," Dorothy said. "Louisa, this is Owney." So informal. She would never have been introduced to a man by her first name in their world. But she was rather glad he didn't know her last name.

"Nice to meet you," he said and took her hand in both of his. She remembered the sobriquet that Marat had used for him: Owney the Killer. She thought, *a killer is holding my hand.* And while his voice was warm and welcoming, his soft, perfectly manicured hands were frigid as the night air.

Chapter 14
Ellen

Ellen woke up on the sofa and heard a scratching noise. Rats? Sitting up quickly she glanced around the room. No rats. Louisa Delafield was bent over a writing table near the front window. The scratching was the sound of her pen.

"Writing your column, are you?" Ellen asked in a voice thick with sleep.

Without turning around, Louisa said, "I often write my first draft by hand at home and then take it into the office to type it. This one is about a Portuguese princess who has a pet leopard."

"So you were at the Garretts' soirée then? Did you say anything about me?" Ellen asked.

"I did not," Louisa said. "I told you and Captain Tunney I would not discuss you with anyone. Even your former employer."

"I appreciate it," Ellen said.

Louisa put down her pen and turned to face her.

"I don't understand why you're afraid of the Garretts. I'll admit Amelia can be unpleasant enough, but Hattie is a dear girl, and Hugh is a pillar of society, a philanthropist," Louisa said. She sounded exasperated, but Ellen wasn't inclined to talk about the Garretts with her.

"Do you enjoy writing about all those doings and the dresses and what not?" she asked.

Louisa pondered the question and then said, "I do. Each column I write is a capsule, a moment preserved. Oh, I know a newspaper isn't exactly a historical record. People read it in the morning and by evening it's being used to light the fire. And yet, some young woman will clip my column and save it because it mentioned her in a particularly pleasant light. Years later she'll remember who she was in that moment just by re-reading what I wrote about her. My mother has a scrap book full of society columns from when she was younger."

"What happened to yer fortune?" Ellen asked.

Louisa looked above the fireplace for some reason and then shrugged.

"Who knows?" she said. "Somehow my father lost it."

She seemed sad, and Ellen felt a little sorry for her.

"This doesn't seem too bad," she said, indicating the room. "Nicer than those tenements."

"I only hope I can keep it," Louisa said and turned back to her writing.

Ellen stretched and blinked. She was stiff from having slept on the sofa, but at least it had been more comfortable than the hard little mattress back at the workhouse. She stood up and put on the dress that she'd laid on one end of the couch. She'd been wearing it for several days now.

Louisa looked up at her. "Do you not have any other clothes with you?"

"I left everything at the Garretts' house, Miss," she answered. "I didn't know when I left that night I wasn't going back."

"Well, when you freshen up, we'll see what we can find for you."

Later, Ellen stood in Louisa's room while Louisa pored through the wardrobe and pulled out dresses to hold up in front of Ellen.

"You have a lot of clothes," Ellen said. Louisa's wardrobe wasn't nearly as full as Hattie's and the dresses weren't nearly as fine, but they were nicer than Ellen had ever owned.

"With my job I need a lot of clothes. And it's one reason we struggle. Last month we ran out of coal," Louisa said. "Here, try this. It might hit above your ankles, but that's the style these days anyway." She tossed Ellen a brown cotton day dress with a white collar. Then to Ellen's complete surprise, Louisa helped her put it on.

"Tell me what happened to Silvia, Ellen," Louisa said as she buttoned the back of the dress.

"Captain Tunney didn't tell you?" Ellen asked.

"No," Louisa responded. "He just said you witnessed something. Something to do with a doctor?"

Ellen wasn't sure what to say. She had no idea whether or not to trust this woman.

Louisa seemed to sense her hesitancy.

"I have something to show you," Louisa said. She went to the vanity where her bag was draped over a chair. She dug into the bag and then held out her open palm. Silvia's crucifix.

Tears sprang to Ellen's eyes.

"Is this yours?" Louisa asked.

"It was Silvia's," Ellen said.

"I found it in Hugh's car," Louisa said. "What happened to her?"

"She was murdered," Ellen said, the words ripped from her heart.

"Murdered? My God!" Louisa exclaimed. "How?"

Ellen closed her eyes. She didn't want to relive that night, but there it was right behind her eyelids — Silvia's face gone white and her eyes gone black.

"That doctor said it happens. Said there was nothing he could do," Ellen said.

"Doctor? I don't understand. I thought it was a murder," Louisa said.

Ellen looked at her. This woman for all her sophistication didn't have a clue.

Suzie stuck her head in the door.

"Girls, come get breakfast," she said as if they were a couple of teenagers.

Ellen happily complied. She didn't want to continue this conversation.

They went downstairs and sat at the dining table. Mrs. Delafield was already there, dabbing at her lips with a linen napkin. At the Garretts' house, Ellen would never be allowed to sit at the dining table. She noticed that Suzie didn't sit at this one. She was glad not to be a servant any more.

"How was Amelia's soirée?" the old woman asked Louisa.

"Fascinating. All the princess wanted to talk about was the prevention of unwanted pregnancies. You would have been scandalized, Mother," Louisa said.

"Hardly conversation for polite society," she agreed.

"It's about time someone talked about it," Ellen piped up. The sadness she felt earlier was replaced by her anger about Silvia's death. "If Silvia had known, she might still be alive."

"What do you mean?" Louisa asked.

"She died having an operation to end her pregnancy," Ellen said. "That doctor was going to send her to a house of wanton women afterwards. And the police think he's involved with the matron's murder. She was investigating him for being an abortionist."

Louisa's mother looked positively horrified.

"This is no topic for the table," she said with disgust.

Ellen knew she shouldn't have blurted it all out. They'd probably want to get her out of the house as fast as possible now. She'd wind up back in the workhouse. But Louisa put a hand on hers.

"This is perfectly dreadful. You must have been so frightened," she said.

This sympathetic response surprised her.

"So how do the police expect to catch this doctor?" Suzie asked, pouring Ellen a cup of coffee.

"I don't know. Marat said the doctor usually provides his services to the society ladies — or dames as he called them," she said.

Louisa remembered riding in the back of the Garretts' motorcar while Marat boasted of his underworld connections.

"That's what Captain Tunney said," Louisa said.

"Why did Tunney bring me here? To your house?" Ellen asked.

"Well, I plan to write a profile of Adele Cummings, the matron who was killed," Louisa said.

"Why would you write about her? She's not a member of society," the old woman exclaimed.

"It's what they call a feature, Mother," Louisa said. "The paper pays more for features, and I need to start bringing in more money. We're out of paintings."

It was all starting to make sense to Ellen now. Louisa Delafield needed money. She wanted to write about all this, maybe even to exploit poor Silvia. Then again, maybe it was time people paid attention to what happened to the Silvias of the world.

"That doctor is one of yours," Ellen said, remembering the fancy clothing he wore that fateful night.

"One of ours?" Louisa said. "Do you mean he's a member of society? Why would they have anything to do with an abortionist?"

Ellen gave her a look.

"Haven't you ever wondered why poor women have seven, eight, or even more children while your set usually has only two or three?" Ellen asked.

"I assumed that had to do with different degrees of appetite," Louisa said.

"Appetite? No one has an appetite like the rich. I used to wonder why the dining table at the Garretts' didn't collapse under the weight of all that food. You...you can't even imagine who got Silvia pregnant, can you?"

"Marat?" Louisa ventured.

"It was Hugh Garrett himself," Ellen said.

"Oh my," Mrs. Delafield said.

"It was not," Louisa exclaimed and threw her napkin on the table. In an instant she rose and fled the room. Ellen and Suzie exchanged glances. Louisa's mother ate her cereal as if nothing had happened.

Louisa came back in and glared at Ellen. "How do you know it was Hugh?"

"Because Silvia told me, and I saw him calling her to his room at all hours. Also, he paid for the doctor," Ellen said.

Louisa sat back down and stirred her coffee glumly.

"First Dorothy consorts with gangsters and now Hugh...with a servant," Louisa said.

"She wasn't just a servant," Ellen said. "She was my friend."

"I am sorry," Louisa said. "I didn't mean to be insensitive."

"It would not be the first time," the old woman in the wheelchair said.

"What do you mean, Mother?" Louisa asked.

"That business between men and their lessers has been going on forever," she said. "That's why smart women never hire servants who are too comely. Instead they hire girls like this." She waved at Ellen.

"Mother, how rude," Louisa said. "Miss Malloy is a fine looking young woman."

"Your ma's right. I'm as plain as dirt. Beauty causes nothing but trouble," Ellen said.

"My daughter is naïve," Louisa's mother said, leaning toward Ellen. "I had hoped she could stay that way forever. An absurd notion."

"I need to clear my head," Louisa said.

Ellen was sorry she'd upset her benefactor but also felt relieved that she had spilled the truth. It was a burden to carry dark secrets.

Louisa stalked out, and Ellen wondered if she'd be rethinking this arrangement. Would the society writer send her back to the workhouse now?

Chapter 15
Louisa

Louisa loosened her coat. The rapid pace of her walking had warmed her — not to mention the heat of her emotions and the onslaught of memories. Fireflies. The ocean crashing against the cliffs as the children scrambled dangerously over the rock face. The breath hard in the chest from furiously running in a game of tag. A waltz floating in the air from the grown-ups' party. Night falling. Nannies calling, "Children! Come in now. Time for bed." Muffled laughter as they hid from their caretakers. These memories assaulted Louisa as she strode along the sidewalk. Memories of Newport summers with Hugh and Dorothy and a dozen other children. Winter memories were equally idyllic. Bundled up under blankets as they traversed Central Park in a sleigh pulled by snorting horses, steam billowing from their nostrils. An only child, she had loved it when the children all piled together like puppies and the parents pretended they didn't exist.

She climbed some granite steps up to Morningside Park and walked along the wide path through the neglected park. The trees were bare and the light weak. Harlem was a far cry from her Fifth Avenue childhood. They had moved here in 1902 when Harlem was a Jewish settlement. It was the only area where they could afford a house after her father's murder. When she was younger, she'd been ashamed of their shabby surroundings and frightened of her neighbors. Now it was her home. Here is where she had learned how to survive.

Survival was not something Dorothy or Hugh had to think about. They had never been hungry, never been cold. They didn't have to dress themselves or fix their own food or sell their family portraits to pay a tax. Dorothy was pretending to be a gangster's moll, but eventually she would no doubt marry a prince or a duke. Hugh ran his family's shipping business, which had been dropped into his lap. He hadn't had to learn the ropes, kowtow to superiors, or scrape his knees scrambling up the ladder. He simply walked into an office and assumed his father's seat with a room full of older, more experienced businessmen to tell him what to do. And worst of all — taking advantage of a servant girl, a girl now dead because of his carelessness.

Louisa wandered into Morningside Park and sank onto a bench, dejected. For all these years, she'd dreamed of making her way back into "respectable" society, but just how respectable were they? She had willingly stayed in a self-imposed prison, fawning over society in her column, so she might win their approval. She'd been a fool.

Pigeons swirled around her feet, clucking and cooing, occasionally pecking at each other or ruffling their feathers. The night before at the Winona club, Dorothy's gangster had talked about his love of pigeons.

"They can survive anything," he'd said. "They're the toughest mob out there. Smart, too. They've been carrying messages for people since the times of the Egyptians."

As the pigeons continued to circle her feet with their incessant mutterings, she remembered that strange feeling she'd had in the "whisper room" at Grand Central — as if countless women were whispering in her ear. She thought of all the women whose stories were left untold, whose voices were silenced forever. Perhaps the Irish woman with her anger and her sorrow had been brought into Louisa's orbit for a reason. Louisa smoothed out her gray wool skirt. She was like these pigeons. She would survive in spite of Virgil Thorn and his edicts and in spite of her sense of betrayal.

When she returned to the house, she went directly to her writing desk. Ever since she'd gone to the Winona Club, she'd had the itch to write about it. If she were going to start writing the truth, this was as good as any time to begin. She picked up her pen and began. The words flowed like water.

When she was done, she stood in the doorway of the kitchen and found Suzie and the Irish woman at the stove. They didn't see her and seemed to be fascinated by whatever it was Suzie had brought out of the oven.

"My granny always said to make sure your cast iron pan was good and hot before you pour in the batter," Suzie said. Suzie cut a piece of the bread and handed it to Ellen, who held it gingerly and then popped some into her mouth.

"This is good," Ellen said, licking her lips. "You learned how to make this when you were on the plantation?" The plantation? Louisa wondered how this woman knew about Suzie's childhood.

"It was. They had sold my mama when I was six, but Granny was the cook and they wouldn't have sold her for any price, so she took care of me," Suzie said.

The Irish woman muttered something that sounded like "gears-music."

"What was that?" Suzie asked.

"Irish for 'disgusting.' That business of buying and selling other people's labor. The English didn't sell us but they did let us starve a time or two without shedding a tear, and if his lordship decided he wanted a man's wife, wasn't a thing to be done about it," she said.

Suzie shook her head.

"Granny knew all about that," she said. "You can take one look at me and see that."

Louisa gasped. She'd never even questioned Suzie's light brown skin tone. The other two women turned and stared at her.

"I'm sorry. I didn't mean to eavesdrop," Louisa said.

"We're making cornbread to go with dinner tonight. I picked up some pork chops on sale," Suzie said.

"Last night I met a gangster," Louisa said.

Ellen's eyes widened.

"You did what?" Suzie asked, aghast.

Ellen grabbed an oven mitt and placed the pan of cornbread on the table.

"It was perfectly fine," Louisa said and sat down at the kitchen table. She took a bite of the cornbread. "Delicious."

Ellen and Suzie sat down on either side of her. Ellen reached over and pulled a piece of the crusty part of the cornbread free from the pan.

"My mother was right," Louisa said. "I have been a naïve fool, but no more." She turned to Ellen. "I want to discover the identity of this doctor who killed your friend. And I want to find out what happened to that matron, Adele Cummings. I will expose the perpetrators of these crimes so that they won't do it again."

Ellen's jaw dropped, and she stared at Louisa.

"Are you sure?" Ellen asked.

"I am," Louisa said.

"I don't like this one bit," Suzie said, crossing her arms over her chest. "It's one thing to write a story about the matron but this sounds dangerous."

"It probably is," Louisa said. "However, these are stories that need to be told. And I am the one to do it."

Suzie gave her a quizzical look. Ellen stared thoughtfully at her hands resting on the table.

"What do you think, Ellen?" Louisa said.

"You've been writing about trifles forever," Ellen said. "It could be time for a change, and I know someone who might be able to tell us more about the dead police matron."

"You can't go out," Suzie said to Ellen. "It's not safe."

"Suzie's right," Louisa said. "You should stay here."

"I'll do no such thing," Ellen objected. "I'll wear a disguise."

Louisa and Suzie glanced at each other. Ellen was not an inconspicuous woman.

"I could cut your hair," Suzie suggested.

"Short hair on a woman will make her stand out even more," Louisa said.

They were silent for a moment, lost in their own thoughts. Then Suzie's eyes brightened.

"I know what to do," Suzie said and took Ellen by the wrist and led her out of the room. A full half hour later, Suzie came down the stairs, followed by a lanky young man in well-made if not very stylish trousers, vest, jacket and homburg hat.

"Where- where on earth did you...?" Louisa stammered. She sucked in her breath. "Suzie."

"Your father's clothes have been in a trunk upstairs all these years," Suzie said. "Not doing anybody any good."

Louisa stared at Ellen in the striped pants, the gray vest, the high collared shirt with a cravat tied around the neck, and the tailored jacket that was a bit too large. Underneath the homburg was a head of short red hair.

"My God," Louisa said. "You've lost your beautiful hair."

"The hair will grow back," Ellen said. "I'd rather keep my life."

"Men's fashions don't differ that much from your father's day," Suzie said.

"I suppose not," Louisa said.

Ellen crossed an ankle and leaned on the newell post like a young rake. Utter madness, Louisa thought, but it just might work.

Chapter 16

Ellen

The trousers fit well, but the shoes were a bit large. As Ellen walked down the street next to Louisa, she began to feel more comfortable in her costume. Having grown up with brothers, she easily embodied their gait, the way they tilted their heads up to look at the sky, and the way they swung their arms, always consuming space. She felt a sense of invulnerability. This must be how it feels to be a man, she thought.

As they walked Ellen explained about the workhouse. The overcast sky hung low above them.

"It's a jail for women," she said. "But not so stringent."

"I can't believe you had to stay in such a place," Louisa said. "If I'd known..." The sentence trailed off and she looked away. As they walked the next block in silence, Ellen wondered what would have happened if she'd had to stay at the workhouse. She'd probably still be there.

"Why did you agree to shelter me?" Ellen asked.

"Captain Tunney asked me to," Louisa said.

"That's it?" Ellen said. She'd soon realized that the Delafield household was a far cry from the Garretts' and wondered if her presence created a burden.

"Well, once I realized you had worked for the Garretts, then I felt it was only right," Louisa said. "As you know, I've known the family forever."

Ellen did know that, only too well, and worried that Louisa's loyalty to her own class would make it impossible for them to actually learn anything that might help her situation. If this doctor serviced the upper classes, which she was sure he did, he would not be easily caught. Her da always said there were some wily fish in the sea that wouldn't go near a net.

When they came to the workhouse, the matron opened the door and looked at them with a perplexed expression.

"Mrs. Wallace, it's me, Ellen Malloy."

"Oh my!" the matron exclaimed. "Captain Tunney's witness, aren't you? You look like a man."

Ellen took that as a good sign that her disguise was working.

"It's necessary. I'm still in danger. This is Miss Delafield, a reporter for *The Ledger*. We'd like to talk to you. It's about the murder of Adele Cummings," Ellen said.

The police matron looked suspiciously from one to the other and finally waved them in. Ellen noticed Myrtle standing a few feet away and ducked her head.

"Come into my office," the matron said. "Myrtle, make sure I'm not disturbed."

They sat down in an office, walls adorned with pictures made by a child. For a moment, Ellen thought of the Garrett house, every wall covered with masterpieces, and yet not a one as fresh and sweet as these.

"My little granddaughter," Mrs. Wallace said, indicating the pictures. "She's a regular Rembrandt."

"With a dash of Titian," Louisa noted. "Mrs. Cummings was also a matron, and it seems your job is to guard and protect prisoners, but she was on some sort of assignment, wasn't she?"

"A few of the gals want to do more. They volunteer for other duties and their help is most welcome... Not me. I'm perfectly happy here with the ladies. But all of us matrons look out for each other. We have to. We haven't been on the force all that long."

"Captain Tunney said Adele was investigating an abortionist. How would a police matron actually do that?" Ellen interjected.

The matron hesitated and looked pointedly at Louisa who had taken out her notebook. Ellen motioned for her to put it away. Louisa glanced from one to the other and put the notebook away.

"I can only speak in generalities, you see. Part of a police matron's advantage when she is investigating a case is her anonymity. We have our secrets," the woman said.

Didn't everyone, Ellen thought.

"Mrs. Wallace, I'm not interested in giving away the secrets of the police matrons. What we want to do is to find out why Adele Cummings was killed," Louisa said. "And the only information we have is that she was investigating a certain doctor who takes care of unwanted pregnancies. If we can find information leading to this doctor and have him arrested, then Ellen will be safe again."

"I see," the matron said. "Catching an abortionist is extremely difficult and it's humiliating, to be honest. You must fool them into thinking you're pregnant and then allow them to look at your private parts. And then somehow jump up from the table and signal the detectives. And then that's only an attempted abortion, which rarely gets a conviction. That's why so few of the gals pursue it. Most matrons who do police work go after shoplifters, swindlers, and fortune tellers."

Ellen felt a chill, remembering Silvia lying on that little gurney, so vulnerable and exposed.

"Why would a woman choose this profession?" Louisa asked. "It sounds quite dangerous."

"Women on the force are often widows with a family to support. We're hired to deal with crimes involving women," she said.

"The policemen use you to trap other women, you mean," Ellen said. So many poor women had to survive by hook or by crook. They didn't have a choice.

"That's one way of looking at it," the matron said. "Another way is that we're here to protect women. Do you have any idea how many young, innocent girls come to this city every day? They're prey, thrust into the jungle. I remember one case that Adele worked. A girl ran away from her family's farm in Virginia. Her parents were terrified for her and notified us. She came to New York and wound up in the clutches of a man who seduced her and then intended to sell her. Adele infiltrated the saloon where this type of activity took place, and at great risk to her own life, saved the girl and shut down the operation. Just a week ago we got a letter from the girl, who's safe and happy back home with her family."

"I do know how easy it is for that to happen," Ellen said. "After Silvia died, two men showed up. When she was no longer available, they planned to take me. I imagine it was just those sorts of plans they had."

"Take you?" Louisa exclaimed and stared at her.

Ellen nodded. She realized she hadn't told that part of the story to Louisa, and yet those men were still out there, still looking for her.

Louisa recovered and turned her attention back to the matron.

"What was Officer Cummings like as a person?" Louisa asked.

"A real pistol. Maybe a little foolhardy, but she was ready and willing to take on anyone. She wanted to be the first woman detective. Can you imagine? A woman detective." By the wistful tone in her voice, Ellen was sure the woman could imagine it. She couldn't help but feel some admiration for the women who had chosen this work even though at times it also seemed wrongheaded.

"What about women like Lillian?" Ellen said. "What harm is she doing, running a tea shop for other women like herself?"

"Those women corrupt the morals of young college girls," the matron answered and slapped her desk. She really believed what she was saying, Ellen thought.

"I see, and you're sure those college girls aren't looking to be corrupted?" Ellen asked.

"If they are, I can't help it. The law is the law."

"How do you think Adele Cummings found out about the doctor?" Louisa interrupted.

Ellen realized she shouldn't have gone off track, and she certainly shouldn't sympathize too openly with Lillian and her ilk, especially not sitting here dressed like a man.

The matron leaned forward, elbows on her desk and looked at each of them in turn. Then she glanced at the door as if to make sure it was closed tightly. She lowered her voice.

"There's an old lady gangster. Well, 'lady' probably isn't the right word. Her name is Battle Betty. Back in her day she was as ferocious as any man. She was the leader of the Lady Gophers. They were a terrifying army of women. When I was a little girl, I saw them in action once. A union hired them to go after scabs. There must have been a hundred of these Amazons all wielding clubs, banging heads, and hurling bricks," she said, wide-eyed as if witnessing the spectacle all over again.

"She sounds quite formidable," Louisa said.

"She was. Now, she's old and not so important. She's reformed, so she says. Adele coaxed her into being an informant. Adele had heard of a doctor conducting abortions but she didn't know where he was doing his work. He may be a respected doctor, but he had to have somewhere to ply his side trade. So she found out. From Battle Betty," the matron said. "The place to start, if you ask me — and you're the first ones to do so — is with Battle Betty, Queen of Hell's Kitchen in her day."

"Where can we find her?" Louisa asked.

"That I can't tell you," the matron said and shrugged.

Ellen's mouth went dry. How did you begin to find a woman like that? Ellen wondered.

"I'd better talk to Captain Tunney," Louisa said, and Ellen thought it was the first sensible thing she'd said all day.

***

Louisa's mother was asleep in her chair when they came in. She woke with a start at the sound of the door shutting and stared at Ellen.

"Richard?" she asked.

"No, Mother, it's Ellen. She's dressed in men's clothing as a disguise," Louisa explained.

"I thought Richard had come for me," Mrs. Delafield said, blinking her eyes.

"I'll go upstairs and change," Ellen said.

"I'll come with you," Louisa said.

When they got upstairs, Louisa shut the bedroom door.

"Why didn't you tell me about the men who tried to abduct you?" Louisa asked.

"I didn't realize you were going to become a Pinkerton detective," Ellen said.

"This makes the story so much more important," Louisa said. "This is white slavery."

Ellen had heard Mrs. Garrett use those very words a few times in a tone of absolute horror.

"Suzie might wonder why white slavery is so much worse than black slavery," Ellen said.

"Whatever you call it, it means women who are enslaved for... immoral purposes," Louisa said. "The Comstock Act of 1873 was very clear on that. And it sounds like you were almost a victim of it."

"That's true," Ellen said. "Two men came for Silvia, but she was dead. So they grabbed me."

Louisa gasped.

"How did you get away?"

"I fought back," Ellen said. "I punched one of them in the throat and kicked the other in the crotch, and then I ran."

Louisa sat on the bed and looked at her, mouth agape.

She must think I'm a perfect hoodlum, Ellen thought.

"You're terribly brave, aren't you?"

"I was scared," Ellen said, remembering the sick feeling of fear churning in her gut. "And I did whatever I had to do to save myself."

Louisa rose and went to look out the window.

"I'm sure Hugh couldn't have known that was going to happen to her," she said.

"I have no proof that he did," Ellen said. "But Marat didn't seem surprised."

"Marat is a former gangster. He's probably up to his eyeballs in this," Louisa said.

Ellen thought she detected a sadness in Louisa's voice when she talked about Hugh Garrett, and then something occurred to her.

"Are you in love with him?" she asked.

"With Marat?" Louisa asked in astonishment.

"With Hugh Garrett," Ellen said.

Louisa contemplated the question.

"With my income, love is not an option. I always thought of him as a brother, I suppose," Louisa said.

"I have three brothers," Ellen said. "One I hardly know since he's so much younger, and I left home at fifteen. One I love with all my heart, and one that terrifies me. Brothers come in all forms."

Louisa nodded as if she understood, but Ellen didn't think she did. She wondered why Louisa had written off the idea of love. Ellen did not want marriage or the love of any man, but she still wanted love. She would always want love.

"I'll go talk to Adele's family tomorrow," Louisa said. "I have been avoiding it because I've been afraid of facing a grieving mother, but I can put it off no longer."

"Say, Miss Delafield," Ellen said.

“Please, call me Louisa,” Louisa said.

“Louisa, may I have Silvia’s cross? I’d like to give it to her ma,” Ellen said.

“To be honest, I’m glad to get rid of it,” Louisa said. She went to her vanity, retrieved the small silver crucifix, and dropped it into Ellen’s palm.

Ellen held it and thought of Silvia’s dark, imploring eyes. Would her spirit ever be able to rest?

Chapter 17
Louisa

Black crepe hung on the door, but inside it was a cheerful, pleasant house with knick-knacks in every corner and a poorly done painting of an old sea captain on the wall. A table underneath the painting was laden with flowers, and the smell of lilies filled the room. On a cot in the corner a small child slept.

Adele Cummings' mother-in-law was a round, middle-aged woman in a black dress who smiled at the same time as tears dribbled down her face.

"I don't know where they get these flowers at this time of year," she said, waving at the bouquets. "The police officers come by every day with flowers or envelopes of money. They swear they'll find whoever did this to my daughter-in-law and send him to the electric chair. I hope so," she said and sat down wearily in an armchair. "She didn't have a pension but the money will help me keep a roof over her son's head for a bit.

Then I suppose I'll have to find some kind of work or go to the poorhouse."

"I'm so sorry for your loss, Mrs. Cummings," Louisa said.

Louisa stopped by the mantel over the fireplace and looked at a wedding picture. The bride and groom stared solemnly at the camera. The bride, who Louisa assumed was Adele, had a wide open face with a prominent nose and a firm chin. She looked like a woman of conviction. She lifted the picture for a better look at the woman. Her hand tingled and she set the picture back down quickly.

"Tell me about Adele," Louisa said, turning to look at the older woman who had sunk into the sofa.

"Well, she was married to my son, Jack, in '09. He died two years ago. He was working on the Woolworth building when a new guy fell and took Jack with him. They call all the new fellas 'snakes' because they're deadly — they don't know what they're doing. It was a long way to the ground and he was nothing but blood and bones when he landed." She wiped a tear away.

"That is a lot to bear," Louisa said and sat next to her. She could not imagine how hard it must have been for this woman to lose first her son and then her daughter-in-law.

"Thank you," the woman said, and took the handkerchief Louisa offered. Her face was ruddy, wrinkled, and round.

"How did Adele get into police work?" Louisa asked.

"She never had no intention of being in the police but she needed to earn a living. So she took a job in a department store, selling ladies' underthings. She had such an eye for shoplifters and such that the store detectives recruited her to work for them. Turns out she was well suited for it. She went on to make more arrests of shoplifters in one month than anyone else did all year. Then she started doing other kinds of investigations. She had a closet full of disguises," Mrs. Cummings said.

"Do you remember how she was dressed the night someone killed her?" Louisa asked.

"I do indeed," the woman said. "The department store where she used to work sold her a very fancy dress for next to nothing since some rich woman had ordered it and then changed her mind. Fit Adele like a glove, it did. Then she went to one of those thrift stores where the wealthy ladies get rid of their old clothes and found a hat that looked very sharp. Once she was all dressed up, she could have been an actress. You should have heard her talking like a grand dame." Mrs. Cummings smiled at the memory. "That night she was pretending to be a wealthy lady from down south. She practiced her accent on me, and I found it very convincing."

This was interesting, Louisa thought. Adele's costume and accent lent credence to the theory that the police matron was dealing with a high-end abortionist. If she was pretending to be from elsewhere, did that mean that women came from all over the country for the doctor's services?

"Did Adele ever mention a woman named Battle Betty to you?" Louisa asked.

The older woman shook her head.

"She never talked about her cases," she said. She glanced over at the table full of flowers and then seemed to recall something. "I did get a big wreath — that one right there — from someone named Betty, but I have no idea who that is."

Louisa looked in the direction the woman had pointed. A wreath made of red and white carnations bore a banner: R.I.P. It seemed quite expensive. Could it possibly be the same Betty?

At that moment, she heard a cry and turned to see the child — a boy — sitting up on the cot. He was looking toward her.

"Mama?" he asked.

The old woman hurried over and caressed the boy.

"No, son. Your mama's gone. She's not coming back. This lady is just a visitor," she said.

Louisa felt a blade of pain slice into her heart. For the first time she understood what the loss of Adele Cummings really meant.

"Thank you so much for your help," she said to the woman, clutching her bag as she escaped the small house.

***

They were still in the throes of late winter, but the afternoon sun had beaten back the clouds, the snow had melted, and the day was relatively warm. Louisa strode down Park Avenue, past a crop of shiny new buildings and formidable older ones to the Colony Club, where she found Dorothy at a table in the marble-floored alcove, handing out sashes to a line of women.

"Are you finally going to write about our cause, Louisa?" Dorothy asked.

"I'm afraid not," Louisa said. "Our editorial policy is still that women have no business in politics. The new editor actually told me that women have enough power running their households. More than that would corrupt us, apparently."

Dorothy scoffed and said, "I suppose all those women without households to run don't count." She indicated the line of working women who were waiting to get their sashes.

"Thank you, Miss," said a lean woman, taking the sash from Dorothy in her rough hands. She rolled up the sash and put in her purse, probably to hide it from her husband, and she left.

"I thought the club wasn't open to non-members," Louisa said. The Colony Club had been established by the wealthy women of Manhattan in response to the men's social clubs that excluded them.

"True, but we're trying to recruit as many women as we can to go to a march next month in Washington, D.C.," Dorothy said. "So they made an exception."

Louisa looked at the women in line, their worn dresses, their tired eyes, and the hard set of their mouths. In the view of the men who decided what was important, these women didn't even exist, much less deserve a vote. She turned back to Dorothy, beautiful in her understated burgundy suit, a double strand of exquisite South Sea pearls draped around her neck.

"I'm actually here to see if you would like to lunch with me," Louisa said.

Dorothy was happy to take a lunch break. She put aside her pamphlets and donned her wool coat.

As they strode out onto the sidewalk, Dorothy said, "Lunch is my treat."

"No, I invited you," Louisa objected.

Dorothy waved a dismissive hand.

"Louisa, you're practically a pauper. Look at your gloves," Dorothy said. "We'll go to Delmonico's and charge lunch to the Colonel."

"If you insist," Louisa said. The Colonel was Dorothy's father, known to one and all including his wife and daughter by the dubious military title he had earned sometime in the Spanish-American War.

The maitre'd took them upstairs to the Palm Garden and showed them to a linen-covered table next to an enormous potted palm tree in the middle of the room. A waiter arrived within minutes to take their order. Louisa asked for the chicken croquette, Dorothy the halibut.

"You're right about my financial status," Louisa said, once the food had arrived. "We can't quite make it on my salary alone and the funds from the sale of our house have run out. I need to do something more with my skills."

"Such as...?" Dorothy asked, fork aloft, a flaky piece of fish balancing on the tines.

"Something other than society news," Louisa said.

"Like a sob sister?" Dorothy asked, excited. "You could be like Nellie Bly. Go undercover in a madhouse."

"I was thinking of something less drastic. For instance, a police matron was murdered last week," Louisa said. "If I could find out why, think of the story that would make."

"Why are you interested in that story?" A valid question, but Louisa couldn't let on that the Garretts may be involved or that their former maid was staying at her house. Dorothy may be her friend, but she was no different from all the other society women who ate up gossip like sweet cakes.

"Well, I didn't even know women were working for the police in investigative roles. She, apparently, was looking into illegal...I don't know how to put this delicately," Louisa said.

"Abortions?" Dorothy asked.

"Yes. An issue that affects all women, don't you agree?" She hoped that Dorothy's interest in suffrage would extend to other problems women faced. One could never tell with society women. Some, such as Alva Belmont, were quite progressive. Others, like Mamie Fish, liked things exactly the way they were.

Dorothy coughed and looked around the room to see if anyone was listening.

"It's rather salacious," Dorothy said, leaning forward. "You're not just doing this for the money, are you?"

Louisa swallowed a sip of water and admitted Dorothy was correct.

"Society is such a confined world. Even you're breaking away from it with your gangster and your trips to the Tenderloin," Louisa said. Then she leaned in close and whispered, "I think there was a Lady Gopher involved."

"A what?"

"A Lady Gopher," Louisa said.

Dorothy clapped a hand over her mouth, suppressing her delight. Then she said, "I didn't know the Gophers had lords and ladies. Of course, they are all so aristocratic."

"I'm glad I'm amusing you, Dorothy," Louisa said. "I need help finding her."

Dorothy wiped a tear of laughter from her eye, and they finished their lunch. When Dorothy suggested dessert, Louisa couldn't resist a chocolate eclair.

"Come to the Winona Club tomorrow night. Owney's taking me out for Valentine's Day," Dorothy said when the desserts arrived. "See what information you can pry from him. Just don't tell him that you're searching for the killer of a cop. The Gophers hate the police from what I understand and they can be quite vicious."

Louisa thought of Owney Madden's cold eyes, as hard as black pearls, and suppressed a shudder.

"Where are you headed?" Dorothy asked as they left the restaurant.

"Oh, I'm interviewing Hugh about his foundation's upcoming gala," Louisa said, breezily. She didn't mention the real reason she wanted to talk to Hugh.

***

The Garrett Family Foundation kept an office in The Singer Building. The Mission Statement of the organization read, "Promoting the well-being of humanity, especially widows and waifs." Louisa had already covered the annual winter fundraising event, and now Hugh was promoting a spring event so the organization could do bigger and better things. Hugh might even know the name of the dastardly doctor. After all, he'd sent Silvia to him, according to Ellen.

"Hello, Hugh," Louisa said when she entered the office. "I'm here to get some information about your upcoming initiative. I understand you are planning a gala to kick it off."

"Indeed," Hugh said, kissing her cheeks in the French fashion. "Sit down, and I'll tell you all about it."

While Hugh went into detail about the gala, which would be at the Plaza Hotel and was to be a costumed affair, Louisa took notes and pondered how to broach the subject of the servant girl.

"Have you got any more questions?" Hugh asked after they had exhausted the topic of the gala.

"Just one," she said and hesitated. "I spoke to Hattie's former lady's maid, Ellen Malloy. She said that the girl who died, the maid, Silvia, was with child."

"You spoke to the Irish girl?" Hugh asked. His brow wrinkled in consternation. "How did that happen?"

"Well," Louisa said, feeling a sense of panic fluttering at the base of her throat. "I'm not at liberty to say."

"Not at liberty?" he said, leaning away from her as if she smelled bad. "What are you doing, consorting with such a person?"

He had managed to put her on the defensive almost immediately.

"She also said you were the one who..." Louisa began, and then stopped and stared at Hugh.

He looked perplexed and then seemed to understand her meaning. He barked a sharp laugh and stared at her with incredulity.

"Me? And a housemaid? You know me better than that. Louisa, we've been friends since we were children. And how long have you known this Malloy woman?" He rose from behind his desk and walked around toward her. Louisa didn't answer him. He leaned over, took her face in his hands, and looked into her eyes. His hands were soft and smelled like soap.

"Louisa, I swear to you it isn't true. Yes, she got pregnant. And yes, I gave her money to help her out. Perhaps your new friend thinks I'm responsible, but she's mistaken," he said. "You shouldn't listen to the gossip of servants, especially those who may bear a grudge."

A tiny crack of doubt appeared along the surface of the story. She was no longer sure what to believe.

"You don't know who the doctor is, do you? The one who performed the ... operation?" she asked.

"Of course not. Marat is the one who took her, but even he doesn't know the man's real name. After the police came, I asked him, but a doctor like that doesn't hand out calling cards," Hugh said.

Louisa looked at him. He had such startlingly blue eyes and he looked at her with such a forthright expression she found it impossible not to believe him.

"I'm sorry, Hugh," Louisa said. "I should not have brought it up."

She rose to leave.

"Wait, Louisa," he said. She looked down at his clean, soft hand, wrapped around her arm. "Why don't you ride with me and Hattie to Tuxedo? We're opening up the cottages next week. And Gertrude Whitney is hosting a luncheon. Have you ever ridden in a roadster? You won't believe how fast it goes."

He spoke with such enthusiasm that Louisa couldn't help but smile. She remembered the two of them racing ponies on the beach when they were only ten years old. He always won.

"Of course. I should cover it in my column anyway," she said.

"Good. See you then," he said and kissed her again on the cheek.

She let herself out. As she rode down the elevator, she felt a sense of reassurance, even peace. She could still try to find the identity of the doctor and solve the police matron's murder, but it needn't involve her friends.

Chapter 18
Ellen

Ellen had helped Suzie clean. It wasn't a large house, and Suzie seemed perfectly capable of handling the work, but it felt good to do something other than sit and wait for Louisa to return, so she swept and mopped the kitchen, washed some dishes, and dusted the furniture in the living room. All the while the little ginger cat made figure eights around her feet and meowed for attention. As Hattie Garrett's lady's maid, she'd had different sorts of duties, but she never got airs about it and had always been willing to help out the house maids when she had the time, especially Silvia.

Ellen still wasn't sure how much she trusted Louisa to find out the identity of the doctor who had killed her friend, and if she did, what then? They wouldn't have the proof that Tunney needed to arrest the man. It was her word against his. She doubted Marat would corroborate her statement. She also held out little hope that some reformed lady gangster would have any answers for them.

After the house was clean, Suzie left for the market.

"Some coffee, girl, and something to eat," Louisa's mother commanded, so Ellen fetched her a cup of coffee and a sugar cookie.

"At one time, I had twelve servants," Louisa's mother said, holding the china cup up to her lips to blow on the hot liquid. "Our house was much bigger then. In fact, we had two houses and a sailboat."

"I don't see why anyone needs more than one house," Ellen said. "And they ought to be able to clean it themselves."

Mrs. Delafield stared up at Ellen. Then she turned to look out the window.

"I liked you better when you were Richard," she said. "You may go."

Ellen went upstairs to the room she was sharing with Suzie. They'd dragged a small bed down from the attic and squeezed it into the room.

Ellen picked up Silvia's silver cross from the dresser and held it up to the thin light coming through the window. Outside the branches of a bare tree looked like cracked china against the sky. She sank onto the bed. A nap was a luxury she'd never had while working at the Garretts', but now sleep called to her like a siren in the sea. Gray light curtained the windows, and she allowed her eyes to shut. Just for a minute, she told herself. Then she was gone and dreaming. Silvia appeared, holding a torch and beckoning her into a cave. Ellen hesitated. She wasn't sure where they were. Italy? Silvia called her to come, and Ellen obeyed. She walked into the blackness with only Silvia's lamp for a guide. They walked further and further down into the cold ground.

Silvia held the torch low and they saw red liquid flowing over the floor of the cave. Ellen was horrified, realizing it was blood. Silvia set the torch down and the blood caught fire.

When Ellen woke up, the dream came back to her vividly. What had it meant, she wondered. Blood? Fire?

There was a knock on the door.

"Come in," Ellen said, sitting up and rubbing her eyes.

Louisa entered and sat down on Suzie's bed across from Ellen.

"I spoke to Hugh today," Louisa said. She clasped her hands in her lap. She seemed conflicted.

"And? Did he tell you who the doctor was?"

"No, he didn't," Louisa said. "He said even Marat didn't know his name."

"He's lying," Ellen said.

"I'm not sure he is," Louisa said. "I've known him my whole life, Ellen, and he's just not like that. You must be mistaken." Louisa picked at a thread in her skirt.

A sour nausea gripped Ellen.

"Your mother was right," Ellen said. "You are naïve." She stood up and went to look in the mirror above the dresser. Her face had sheet wrinkles and her newly shorn hair stood up like clumps of heather.

"Perhaps you're just angry," Louisa said. "And you want to find someone to blame. It's perfectly understandable."

Ellen bristled. Perfectly understandable? It was bad enough to have her word called into question, but this condescension was unbearable. Louisa might not have wealth, but she was one of *them*. It was in her blood. Ellen turned toward her.

"Of course, I'm angry. My friend is dead, and your friend is at fault. Who wouldn't be angry?" Ellen said.

Louisa rose and said, "Look, it doesn't really matter who got Silvia pregnant. What matters is that we learn the identity of the doctor. Don't you agree? It was his fault. Do you remember what he looked like?"

Ellen swallowed her anger.

"He was a good looking fella. Dressed expensive," she said. "Mustache, thin face. And his manner was cold as a well digger's arse, as my da would say."

"That's not much to go on," Louisa said. "Perhaps we'll have some luck with Battle Betty. I'm going to the Winona Club tomorrow night with Dorothy. If Battle Betty is a former Gopher, then the head of the Gophers ought to know where to find her."

"Be careful," Ellen said.

"Dorothy has Owney Madden wrapped around her finger, so I should be safe as long as I'm with her," Louisa said. "I will admit it's a little disconcerting to be sitting at a table with a man whose nickname is the killer."

"Really? I should think you'd be used to killers by now," Ellen said, immediately regretting the harshness of her words.

"That's not fair," Louisa said and left the room. Ellen turned back to the mirror. She held Silvia's crucifix and remembered her dream — the flowing blood and Silvia's dark eyes. With slow deliberation, she took the necklace and clasped it around her own neck. She looked in the mirror and patted the silver cross where it lay on her pale skin. Silvia would be avenged.

Chapter 19

Louisa

Virgil Thorn took off his spectacles to stare at Louisa with wide, incredulous eyes.

"Contraception?" he asked in a low voice, though there was no one else in the office. "What were you thinking?"

"This is a topic of great importance to women," she said. "The princess is the one who brought it up, after all. And you did want an interview with her."

"Miss Delafield, what I want, occasionally, in your column is a little titillation, perhaps. Maybe some innuendo. But controversy? In the women's section? Next you'll want to write about the damnable suffrage issue," he said with utter disgust.

"As a matter of fact..." she said.

He held up a hand and stopped her.

"Do you know who doesn't like controversial topics? Mrs. Fish. One of your so-called American royalty. At least that's how they like to think of themselves. She called and threatened to boycott the paper if we continued to publish such trash."

Louisa was flummoxed.

"I didn't intend..." Louisa said, but Thorn cut her off.

"From now on, you will bring your columns to me before they go to the typesetters," he said. "And don't worry. There's no need to write anything for tomorrow's paper. There's no space for it."

Louisa left his office without another word. She wasn't sure if she would cry, scream, or throw a typewriter at the man if she didn't maintain absolute control over herself. His admonition should have made her hesitant to continue on her present course, but it had the opposite effect. She would find Battle Betty, and somehow she would find out who killed Adele Cummings. Then she would write a feature article about the murder. Maybe *McClure's* would take it. If she didn't at least try, she might as well get used to a life of utter poverty.

***

Louisa stood in the hallway and examined herself in the mirror. The black velvet dress — another one of her mother's refurbished gowns — clung to her like a second skin. She placed a velvet cloche atop her head and her mother's old mink cape over her shoulders. Ellen had helped her fashion her hair in the Grecian style which was all the rage these days. Earlier Louisa had noticed the silver crucifix dangling between Ellen's collarbones. She hoped Ellen had forgiven her for believing in Hugh, but it was difficult to tell with the tight-lipped Irish woman.

She turned to the three women silently watching her.

"I promise I will return home safely," Louisa said to them.

"Do not let that Dorothy Bloodgood lead you into a life of indecency and shame," Anna said, clutching the ginger cat to her bosom.

"I will try not to let that happen," Louisa said as she bent over and kissed her mother on the top of her head. She turned to Ellen and Suzie. "Au revoir."

***

Louisa hurried outside and hailed a cab to the Winona Club, her throat constricted to the size of a pin-hole from nerves. It was one thing to go slumming with Dorothy, but quite another to go into one of these dens of sin by herself. Once inside, she grabbed a glass of champagne from a passing waiter.

"Thirty cents please," he said.

"I thought ladies drank for free," she said.

"Only on Saturday night. However, I'm sure one of these fine fellas would buy you a drink." He leered at her. Louisa dug into her bag and brought out thirty cents, her money for a cab ride home.

She drank quickly in the hopes the alcohol would steady her nerves as she wandered around the outskirts of the gambling tables. The gamblers shouted their bets, the women laughed, and the glasses clinked. The same Negro woman as before sang from the platform in the corner. Her voice was lovely and lilting, but every so often something plaintive sounded in the notes and managed to touch Louisa at her core.

"Louisa," Dorothy called to her from a table in the corner.

Relief flooded through her as she saw Dorothy in a sheath dress with gold beading, sitting next to Owney Madden.

"Happy Valentine's Day," Louisa said, sitting down in a chair next to the gangster. He grinned and looked at her from the corner of his eyes.

"Planning on gambling, Miss?" he asked.

"I'm already gambling. On your generosity, Mr. Madden," she said.

"Call me Owney. I'm always generous with beautiful dames," he said and poured her some champagne from a bottle in an ice bucket next to the table.

"Thank you, but this is about more than champagne," Louisa said. "You see, my paper has asked me to write about ... other aspects of New York life."

"What sort of aspects?" he asked. His voice had gone ice cold, and Louisa felt perspiration pooling in the backs of her knees.

"Nothing that might incriminate anyone," she said hastily. "I'm more interested in matters of the past, and as a woman you know I must focus on women. Such as the Lady Gophers." Light from the chandeliers glinted in the champagne bubbles.

Owney relaxed and smiled.

"They were hellions back in their day," Owney said, "but then they got old."

"What about Battle Betty?" she asked.

"That old relic? She's gone soft, and she's not a Gopher no more," he said and shrugged. "Betty feeds bums on Mott Street. She'll talk yer ear off about her Mission."

"That seems an interesting turnabout for a lady gangster," Louisa said.

"Yeah, well, what else is she gonna do? She's probably conning people out of money in the name of her charity," he said.

Louisa was about to ask another question but Owney stopped her.

"Let's go to the tables," he said with a wide grin.

"I don't know how to play," Louisa said.

"Well, that's craps over there where the fellas are throwing dice. You got a roulette table over there. I never saw the fun in that one. It's all luck. But over there, that's Baccarat. Now that's a good game for a beginner. You have to be able to add and subtract. Then you rely on instinct. Want to give it a try?" he asked with a mischievous gleam in his eyes.

"I'm afraid I don't have the means to gamble," she said. For once, she was grateful not to have any money.

"You can watch me," he said. "Watch and learn."

"Come on, Louisa," Dorothy said. "Loosen up a little."

"But I don't know the rules," she said.

"The only rule you need to know is that you want your cards to add up to nine points," he said.

"What happens if they add up to more than nine points?" Louisa asked.

"Then you drop back to zero. Let's say you get ten points, that's zero. Eleven points is one and so on," he said.

Owney stood up and beckoned her over to the table. He seemed determined to show her how to play, so she followed him and Dorothy over to the table. With a wave of his hand, he let one of the players know his turn was up, and he sat down in the chair at the far end of the table. Louisa and Dorothy sat on either side of him.

"Hey, Mick," he called to the dealer. "Give me a round. I wanna show these society dames how to play the game."

"Sure thing," the dealer said. He pushed a lever on a card dealing machine and slid two cards on a paddle over to Owney. Then he took two more cards and placed them on the table. Owney looked at the cards, a two and a three, and tapped the table. The dealer drew another card. Owney showed her the new card. It was a king.

"Oh, that's a good card, isn't it?" she asked.

"It's worth nothing," he said. The fourth card was another three. "And so we'll stop here. See, the dealer's got seven, and we've got eight. We win."

Louisa watched another few rounds of play. It was starting to make sense, and when Owney turned to her and asked if he should get another card or stop, she nodded that he should take another.

Louisa was on her third glass of champagne when she looked across the room and felt her heart drop. Standing at one of the tables, shaking a pair of dice in his hand was Forrest Calloway, esteemed publisher of *The Ledger*. He wore an impeccable black jacket and white tie. His hair was brushed back from his face, and for a moment he looked exultant. The dice must have landed in his favor. But nothing about this was in her favor. If her publisher saw her in this place, her job would be a distant dream. It wouldn't matter that he was here, too. He was a man, after all. And wealthy. She was the *society* writer, for crying out loud. She couldn't afford to be seen "slumming." She would become the scandal that Virgil Thorn craved.

"Dorothy, I'm afraid I should go now," Louisa said in an apologetic tone. Owney looked askance.

"What gives?" he asked.

"I have to be up early tomorrow morning for work," she lied and rose from the table, slipping the mink cape over her shoulders. She had to get out that instant. She'd gotten what she came for.

Louisa kept her face averted as she maneuvered through the crowd. Finally, she reached the door and stepped out into the freezing cold. Sleet fell in silver needles, and she wished she would have thought to borrow some money from Dorothy. She looked out into the dismal night.

"Miss Delafield?"

She recognized his voice. She should probably start running, she thought. She might get murdered or catch pneumonia and die, but anything would be better than turning around. Yet turn around she did and peered into the dark eyes of her publisher.

Chapter 20
Ellen

Louisa didn't believe her. That was the crux of the matter. *You must be mistaken.* But Ellen wasn't mistaken. Silvia had slept with no one else. Suzie softly snored in the other bed. Louisa was gone out to the gangster's club to try to get information on the whereabouts of Battle Betty, and Ellen lay there in the dark alone with her anger and her helplessness. The rage she felt toward Hugh Garrett throbbed inside her veins. He had seduced the girl. With his money and his charm. Just like he was seducing Louisa. It hadn't ended well for Silvia. How would it end for Louisa? She seemed to think she was invulnerable.

Ellen tossed in the small bed. She thought of her da. He was a hard man, prone to the back hand more than the loving touch. He would call this mess a "fine kettle of cod." A stalwart Irish Republican, he had no love for the rich and he'd passed that disdain onto his children.

"I did na raise ye to cater to 'em fancy britches," he'd said before she left.

But Louisa had been raised to admire people like the Garretts. She would need convincing. Ellen sat bolt upright in the bed. It was as if a curtain had been lifted in her mind. The note! The note would prove that Hugh Garrett knew Silvia was pregnant and knew the doctor. As she fingered the chain around her neck, she felt Silvia's presence.

Her gran had always said that those who died before their time lingered, unable to rest, and Ellen knew this was true for Silvia. Her spirit was troubled, and it was up to Ellen to help her find peace.

She put on her old dress. She didn't think there was any need to disguise herself at this hour. She stepped quietly out the back door and made her way through an alley to the street.

The train to downtown was nearly deserted when she got on. At one point a drunk man got on, sat down, and sang in a loud, terrible voice about the Peg of his heart. *You're not even Irish*, Ellen thought, looking at the slovenly old fool.

She got off the train and walked to Fifth Avenue and found the street where the Garretts lived. She stopped. She couldn't go waltzing up to the front door and demand to be heard. She walked past the house. It was dark. Her eyes traveled up to Hattie's bedroom window and then higher up to the room she had shared with Silvia. Once again she felt the sorrowful presence of the girl and her body trembled slightly with the chill of the night. She walked around the block to the driveway that led to the carriage house behind the mansion.

The key was where she knew it would be — under a planter beside the kitchen door. It was left there for servants who might be returning after the housekeeper had locked up and gone to bed. The key slid easily into the lock, and the door creaked open. She froze and waited but all was quiet so she slipped inside and gently shut the door behind her. She crossed the kitchen quickly, glad for the warmth of the house. The whole house was dark, and she hadn't thought to bring a candle. Like a blind person, she groped through the drawers of the kitchen and finally found a candle and matches.

In the flickering light, she made her way to the servants' stairwell and climbed the four flights to the servants' hall, then removed her shoes and padded as softly as she could down the hallway to the room she had shared with Silvia. She slipped in, shut the door behind her and stood in the silence. The candle flame cast shadows on the walls, and a shiver crept down her spine. Silvia's bed had been stripped, and the top of her dresser was bare. Ellen rushed over to the dresser and opened the top drawer where she'd seen Silvia put the note. Empty. She opened the other two drawers. Both empty.

She looked around the room and wondered what they had done with Silvia's things.

"What are you doing here?"

Ellen wheeled around and saw Mrs. Strauss standing in the doorway in her flannel nightgown.

"I've come to get my things," Ellen said.

"In the dead of night?" Mrs. Strauss asked.

"I didn't want to see anyone," Ellen answered.

"You are no longer employed here. You must return at a decent hour," Mrs. Strauss said, her German accent thicker than usual, perhaps from being half-asleep.

Ellen turned to her side of the room. It looked the same.

"You haven't hired anyone to take my place yet," she observed.

"Mrs. Garrett plans to hire someone in London," Mrs. Strauss. "Now, I insist that you leave, Ellen. Come this way."

"Where are Silvia's things?" Ellen asked.

"With her family, I assume," Mrs. Strauss said. "Please don't make me tell you again. Or I shall have to call a footman to escort you out."

Ellen followed the older woman out of the room, down the hall and back down the stairs. They entered the kitchen, and Mrs. Strauss stopped short. Hugh Garrett stood in the center of the kitchen, holding a revolver. He wore an elegant paisley dressing gown over pajamas.

"Mr. Garrett, what are you doing up?" Mrs. Strauss asked.

"I heard noises," he said.

"There's no problem, Sir," she said. Her heavy accent had nearly disappeared. "Ellen Malloy has come to get her things. But I have told her she must come back when the family is awake."

Hugh stepped closer.

"What was so important that you needed to sneak into my house?" Hugh asked.

"I need not be telling you what it was," Ellen said and glared at him.

"Ellen!" Mrs. Strauss admonished her.

"Leave her to me, Mrs. Strauss," Hugh said. "Go on back to bed."

"Are you certain?"

"Go," he ordered.

Mrs. Strauss responded with a quick nod of her head and then turned abruptly like one of the Kaiser's good soldiers and headed out of the room.

When she was gone, Hugh put the gun down on the kitchen table and leaned back with his arms crossed.

"Where have you been, Ellen?" he asked.

"As if I'd tell you," Ellen said. "You lied to Miss Delafield. I know it, and I can prove it."

Hugh pulled a piece of paper from the pocket of his gown.

"Is this what you were looking for?" he asked and waved it in the air.

He walked over to the stove and lit one of the burners. Then he held the note to the flame. Ellen stared as it crumpled into black ash and smoke. Ellen thought of Silvia, her eyes as dark and round as a deer's, her laughter, even her scent like a garden after the rain. Ellen's heart felt as black as the ashes falling to the ground.

"She was so young," Ellen said.

Hugh wheeled around, his eyebrows raised in indignation.

"You act like I wanted her dead," he hissed.

"Didn't you? You were going to let those men take her. And I know it wasn't to convalesce in some hospital," she said.

"I don't know what you mean. You should leave now," he said and walked to the kitchen door. He opened it and turned to face her. His mouth formed an "o" of surprise when he saw she held his gun.

"Tell me the doctor's name," she said.

"If you shoot me," he said, "you'll go to the electric chair, you know. A nasty way to die."

He was right, of course. Even without that threat, Ellen knew that as angry as she was, she couldn't kill him.

"I could injure you and say it was an accident," she said.

"Do you really think that would convince Louisa? She knows I never touched that girl," Hugh said.

With her left hand, Ellen held up the cross around her neck.

"Who do you think found this in the back seat of your Rolls Royce on the night Silvia died?" she said.

Hugh didn't say anything for a long moment, and then he lunged for her. Startled, she fell back against the counter and fired the gun. The loud explosion nearly caused her heart to burst. They stared at each other for a moment as the sound of the gunshot reverberated. Dust floated from the ceiling where the bullet had hit. Then Ellen's instincts took over. She dropped the gun and scrambled out the door.

Outside she continued to run as she was pelted by sleet. When she finally found herself hiding in a tunnel in Central Park, trying to catch her breath, she was cold and wet, but she felt a strange sort of exhilaration. Maybe Louisa Delafield did believe Hugh Garrett, but now he wouldn't be so sure.

When she got back to Louisa's house, she stopped short. The rain had slowed down to a drizzle. A large motorcar rumbled in front of the house. A driver opened the back door and Louisa got out. She looked quite stunning in her velvet dress and mink cape as she rushed up the steps to the door. As she went inside, the motorcar slowly pulled away. Ellen hurried inside after her.

"Ellen!" Louisa said. "Where have you been?"

"To the Garretts'," Ellen said.

Louisa tossed a log on the fire, and they stood close to the warmth of the flames.

"You should not have done that," Louisa said.

"Maybe not. Your friend, Hugh Garrett, pulled a gun on me," Ellen said.

Louisa's eyebrows furrowed and she gazed down into the flames crawling over the logs.

"Oh, Ellen," she said finally. "I don't know what to think."

"Did you find out anything about Battle Betty?" Ellen asked.

"I did. I'll tell you about it later," Louisa said. "You should get out of those wet clothes and go to bed."

"Who brought you home?" Ellen asked.

"No one," Louisa said. She sounded upset, and Ellen wondered what had happened.

"Well then, goodnight," Ellen said and climbed the steps to Suzie's room. When she got to the top of the steps, she startled. There stood Louisa's mother in the doorway of her bedroom, the gaslight shining behind her. Ellen hadn't even known she could stand on her own.

"You are playing with fire, girl. The Garretts are dangerous people. I should know," the old woman said. Then she turned and shut the door. In a moment the light inside her room was extinguished.

Chapter 21

Louisa

Louisa's eyes cracked open. Someone was knocking on her bedroom door. Her stomach ached and her head pounded. She hadn't gotten more than three or four hours of sleep.

"What is it?" she croaked.

The door opened and Suzie stood in the doorway.

"It's after nine o'clock. Why are you still in bed?" Suzie asked.

"I feel sick," Louisa said and turned her face into the pillow.

"Did you drink spirits last night, Louisa?" Suzie's voice was filled with recrimination.

"No," Louisa said, pushing herself up and swinging her feet off the side of the bed. "But I may have lost my job."

"What?" Suzie sat next to her and clasped her arm. "What are you saying?"

"I lost my temper with Mr. Calloway, my publisher. Oh, Suzie, what have I done?" Louisa covered her face.

"I don't know what you've done," Suzie said, rising to open the curtains and let the unforgiving light of day come in, "but whatever it is, you have to face up to it."

Louisa got out of bed and walked over to her vanity. She was a mess — eyes puffy and red, hair that had been through a tornado.

"Mr. Calloway insisted on giving me a ride home from the club last night, and he began scolding me for being in such a place. Even though he was there! Gambling!" Louisa pulled a robe over her nightgown.

"Come downstairs and eat something and tell me what happened," Suzie said, heading toward the door.

"I have no appetite," Louisa said.

"Then come down and get some coffee and tell me what happened," Suzie insisted.

Louisa turned and faced her.

"I told him everything. I don't know what got into me — maybe it was the champagne — but I couldn't stand that condescending tone he took with me. I told him that my wages weren't enough to feed squirrels. I told him that I intended to write stories about things that were more important than luncheons and yacht races. He has no idea what it's like to struggle, riding around in his chauffeur-driven Packard," Louisa said, thinking of that comfortable leather back seat and the burled wood and the brass fixtures.

"What did he say to that?" Suzie asked.

"Nothing. He looked at me as if I were a lunatic. And then he laughed," Louisa said, feeling hysterical. She could still hear his low chuckle in her head, mocking her. She turned toward the lavatory and saw Ellen in the doorway.

"Are we going to find Battle Betty today?" Ellen asked.

"First, I have to find out if I still have a job," Louisa said. "If you'll excuse me."

She pushed past Ellen, went into the small lavatory, and shut the door. She splashed cold water on her face, looked at her reflection in the mirror, and then excoriated herself for being a fool.

***

Billy Stephens sat at his desk, smoking a pipe and reading over police reports when Louisa sat down at her desk.

"Lady Sherlock," he said. "How is the sleuthing going?"

She summoned all of her reserves, smiled and said, "Swimmingly. I have a lead on Adele Cummings' source."

"Do tell," he said, leaning forward.

"Not on your life," she said.

He laughed and said, "You learn quickly. But you better keep Tunney in the loop. You do not want to get on his bad side."

"Speaking of displeasing men," she muttered as she saw Virgil Thorn crossing the room toward her.

"Miss Delafield, my office please," he said curtly. She smiled, hiding behind her mask, rose, and followed him.

"Have a seat," he said, and she demurely sat across from him. "I met with our publisher this morning."

"Oh?" she asked. She assumed a curious, unconcerned expression but inside she was churning.

"We were discussing ways we might increase readership among the ladies," he said.

"Pardon me?" she asked. This was not the turn she had expected. "Did you say increase?"

"Of course, I did," he said. "Why would we want to decrease readership?"

"We would not want to do that. No," Louisa agreed.

"I came up with the idea of having a weekly feature about some topic of import to women. Something other than bonnets and babies. Something for the modern woman," he said and looked across the desk at her with a great deal of self-satisfaction.

"The modern woman," she repeated. How had Mr. Calloway made Thorn think this was his idea? "Then I'm not being fired?"

"Heavens, no," he said. "I even suggested that *you* write these features, Miss Delafield. There's no need to hire another writer when we have you. However, Mr. Calloway insists that you use a pseudonym. He doesn't want to taint the society column."

Louisa took a deep breath. She wanted to laugh and she wanted to weep. She did neither.

"Of course, this will entail a raise," she said, making sure she did not phrase it as a question.

"Two dollars a week increase. I think that's a generous offer, don't you?"

An extra two dollars a week was no fortune but it would make a difference in their lives. She was already imagining a new pair of kid gloves on her hands.

"Yes. Thank you," she said.

"When can you get me the first feature?" he asked.

"I already have one written," she said. She rose, excited to get back to work. "What name should I use?"

"Whatever you like," he said.

She gazed at his name on the door and thought of Virgil leading Dante through the rings of Hell.

"How about Beatrice Milton?" she said. "Beatrice inspired Dante. Perhaps she'll inspire me."

"And are you also inspired by John Milton? Is this to be your version of 'Paradise Lost?'" he asked.

"Milton was my father's middle name," she said softly and turned to leave.

She floated back to her desk, found her notes from her first night out slumming with Dorothy, and began to type.

***

"Battle Betty runs a mission for destitute men in Chinatown," Louisa said over dinner. "I suggest we go there and question her."

"Chinatown? And what if those fine gentlemen see me? You know the ones who wanted to take me in place of Silvia?" Ellen asked. Ellen's fear was perfectly understandable, but Louisa didn't think anyone would come after her in broad daylight.

"Wear your disguise," Louisa said. "You can pretend to be one of the derelicts and get inside. Listen to their conversations. Maybe you'll pick up some information."

"What kind of information would they have?"

"I don't know. Who knows what they might know?"

Louisa had the newspaper's blessing now, and she'd follow this story to its end.

"Why don't you come with me to the paper tomorrow?" Louisa asked. "We can dig through the archives and see if we can find anything on Battle Betty."

"Why should I go with you when you don't believe what I tell you about Hugh Garrett?" Ellen said. Her lips were pulled in tight, and her eyes fairly blazed. "He as good as confessed to me that he got the girl pregnant. You should have seen how he reacted when I showed him the necklace."

Louisa's mind went dark. She had known Hugh Garrett all her life. Maybe he had gotten the girl pregnant, but she couldn't believe he would lie to her like that.

"It doesn't matter what I believe. We have to find Battle Betty and discover who this doctor is," Louisa said.

Ellen glared at her and then softened.

"I s'pose you're right," she said.

Whatever the outcome, Louisa thought that Battle Betty might make a great topic for one of Beatrice Milton's features.

Chapter 22
Ellen

Ellen followed Louisa through the revolving glass door into the gleaming lobby of the building. A huge bronze sign announced THE LEDGER over two elevators.

"Good day, Miss Delafield," a man in a red suit with gold braid and brass buttons said when they got on the elevator. "Third floor?"

"No, James," Louisa said. "Second. Today we're going to the morgue."

Ellen threw Louisa a horrified look but didn't say anything.

On the second floor, the elevator man pulled the door open, and they stepped off.

"Morgue?" Ellen asked.

"It's where we keep old papers," Louisa said and led her to a room filled with cabinets and rows upon rows of papers hanging on wooden dowels.

"Mother Mary, where do we begin?" Ellen asked.

"The mid-1880s, I believe," Louisa said. "Look for anything involving strikes. I believe both the companies and the unions hired gangs to aid them."

They spent several hours combing through thirty-year-old newspapers. At one point a great rumbling came from below and Ellen wondered if the gates of Hell had opened.

"What is that?" she asked an unperturbed Louisa.

"The presses," Louisa said. "They're in the basement, but they shake the whole building."

"Do you like working here?" Ellen asked.

"I do," Louisa said.

Ellen inhaled deeply. She would have liked to work in a place such as this. But she didn't have the background or the education like Louisa did. They said America was the land of opportunity. Not exactly true, was it? Her opportunities were to work as a servant or in a factory. She perused the papers, one after the other. So much news and yet even though they were looking at events from twenty to thirty years ago, most of the headlines didn't seem any different from today — police corruption, unions striking, people being murdered. She'd been searching for nearly a half an hour when a headline caught her eye: "Longshoremen Strike Broken. Gangs Involved."

"Here's something," she said. She skimmed the article and there it was — a single mention of a woman named Betty Walsh. She read the passage aloud. "Upwards of one hundred women, hurling bricks and insults, attacked the strikers with such ferocity that the startled men backed down and ran. These war-like women were led by Betty Walsh, also known as 'Battle Betty.' A coalition of shipping companies hired the women to break the strike. Money well spent, according to Henry Garrett, president of Garrett Shipping."

"Henry Garrett?" Louisa said. "That was Hugh's father. He died a few years ago. The perfect caricature of a greedy capitalist. At least Hugh is a philanthropist."

"Sure, unless you're a pretty servant girl," Ellen said. She thought of the fancy Garrett house by Central Park, just one of their possessions. That one family should have so much while a longshoreman's family went hungry filled her with disgust.

Louisa took the article and read it.

"Good work," Louisa said. "But this doesn't mean that the Garrett family is still involved with these people."

"Put two and two together," Ellen said. "This doctor gives abortions to the wealthy. When a police matron investigates him, she's killed. The link is an old lady gangster who was once hired by the Garretts to disrupt a strike? I suggest you take care when you talk to her. What if they try to bomb your brownstone?"

Louisa looked aghast, but had no answer.

***

Ellen looked at herself in the mirror. Suzie had altered the jacket so the sleeves were the right length, but otherwise left it loose to better hide her torso. Ellen had wrapped strips of cloth around her chest to minimize her bosom, which was small to begin with.

She had a strong-featured face, not delicate. Her nose was long and her eyebrows thick. She thought of the fake mustaches and beards that actors sometimes wore and thought if she could get one, that would help complete the transformation. She had to be careful not to let Louisa Delafield find out the real reason she'd never married. Louisa would probably be horrified to learn she was harboring a criminal. That's what women like her were, according to the law. Criminals. Deviants. She thought of her first and only kiss with a woman. That didn't make her feel like a criminal or a deviant. It was as natural as singing.

"Ready?" Louisa asked.

"I am," Ellen said.

They got on the subway at 110th Street, sat next to each other on the rattan seats, and barreled underground. Ellen didn't speak for the whole trip, worried that her voice would give her away, and Louisa seemed lost in thought. Even if she did feel safe speaking to Louisa, Ellen wasn't sure what to say. Louisa may not have wealth, but she had something else. She had a place in the world, which Ellen no longer had. She hadn't liked being a lady's maid to Hattie Garrett, but hadn't hated it either. At least she had a purpose. Now she felt aimless.

"Are you nervous?" Louisa asked in a low voice.

"I am. The men who tried to take me were Chinese men, and I'm not sure this costume adequately hides the fact I'm a woman," Ellen whispered.

"Your look is quite convincing," Louisa said.

They got off at Canal Street and walked several blocks past tenements and stores.

"Why am I doing this again?" Ellen asked.

"Because you might learn something useful. Who knows if this woman is really reformed? Those men will. So listen to what they have to say. You might hear something that no one would ever tell a reporter."

Ellen tried to imagine herself as her older brother, Michael, who feared no one and nothing. She slowed her breathing and thereby slowed her heartbeat. She could do this, she told herself.

They reached Mott Street and turned a corner. Across the street stood a three-story brick house with a fancy sign over the front door, saying THE PINK PALACE. Curtains covered most of the windows, but one of the curtains on second floor window was parted. A young woman in a camisole leaned against the window with a cigarette in her hand. She caught Ellen staring up at her, smiled, and lowered the strap of her camisole to expose her white breast.

"Early bird gets the worm," she called out. Ellen's mouth dropped open. The woman laughed and turned away from the window.

"That's a house of ill repute," Ellen said, realizing she had been mistaken for a young man.

Louisa glanced at the house, but didn't seem very interested.

"We should separate here," Louisa said. "Will you be all right?"

Ellen nodded.

"Don't speak to anyone unless you absolutely have to," Louisa advised.

Ellen walked on. She wondered how she might manage to stay mute. If she did speak, could she lower her range to convince anyone listening that she was a man?

The Mission House was in a narrow building between a laundry and Chinese restaurant. A few derelicts stood outside, huddled in their flimsy coats, waiting for lunch. Ellen shoved her hands in the pockets of her trousers and shuffled to the end of the line. She kept the hat low and her shoulders hunched. Her clothes weren't as dirty as the man in front of her, but she'd purposely torn the pockets of her jacket and put a stain on the shirt. Another few men formed in line behind her.

"Got a match?" one of them asked her. She shook her head and looked the other way.

She heard Louisa's footsteps, but didn't look up as she passed by the line of men and knocked on the front door. In a moment the door opened, and Louisa went inside.

"What the Hell is that dame doing here?" one of the men asked.

"Maybe one of the donors," another one offered. "Betty's in with all sorts of rich types."

"She can donate a little something to me," another grumbled and rubbed his crotch in a filthy manner. A few of the others chuckled. Ellen kept her head low.

As they waited, one man groused about the weather but most of them stood next to the wall like dumb cattle. Then a scruffy man who looked older than the rest turned to the other man and said, "I ain't lying. The bounty's twenty-five dollars. Just for information. Keep your eyes peeled. Some bigshot wants her…" He made a slicing motion across his throat.

"Lemme take another gander at that picture," the second man said. The scruffy old man took a piece of paper from his pocket and unfolded it. "I can't read what it says."

Ellen peeked over his shoulder and saw a fairly accurate likeness of herself. This couldn't have been made by the Chinese men. They barely saw her. Could Marat or the doctor have provided the description? Or worse, Hugh Garrett himself?

"Says here she's a redhead, goes by the name of Ellen," the second man said, studying the sheet of paper. "And tall for a dame. Last seen at the waterfront."

They knew her name!

"That was me," one of the men piped up. "I seen her. Irish girl."

Ellen glanced up, saw the man with no front teeth grinning at the others, and realized he was the same one she'd spoken to as she stood by the fire at the waterfront. She quickly lowered her head. She needed to get away from here. Now.

"Come on, boys. Come and get it," a stout woman called from the steps in front of the Mission. As the men pushed forward, Ellen bent down to tie her shoe. She waited until they were inside and then turned and walked away as fast as she could. She was almost to the corner when suddenly two men stood in front of her. She raised her eyes and saw them. The Chinese men. The wiry one with a pointed goatee and the other burly with a clean-shaven face. They stood without moving. Fear reared up inside her like a horse that's been spooked by a snake. She stepped back.

The taller one sneered and pointed to the street. They didn't recognize her, she realized. They just wanted her to move. She shrank inside the coat, hunching her shoulders, and shuffled out of their way. Her breath had disappeared but she didn't notice until she was around the corner when she began to run and it came back hard and filled with terror.

Chapter 23
Louisa

In the front room stood a long table with stacks of sandwiches, bowls of fruit, and a large metal pot filled with steaming soup.

"Hello, Miss. I'll be right with you," said a cheerful, stout woman with red cheeks and black, pearly eyes. Her face reminded Louisa of a friendly French bulldog she'd had as a child. Two other women, past their prime and coarsened by a hard life, busied themselves bringing bowls and cutlery from the kitchen.

"I'm looking for Betty," Louisa said.

"I'm Betty," the stout woman said. "The one and only. Have a seat in the kitchen while I call in the gentlemen." She opened the door and called out, "Come on, boys. Come and get it."

This was the notorious Battle Betty? She hardly looked like the famous "brick hurler" or the leader of the Lady Gophers. Louisa stood at the kitchen door and watched as the older woman beckoned the men inside. One old gray beard reached for a sandwich but Betty stopped him.

"You gotta thank the Lord before digging in," she said. A quick prayer was mumbled, and soon the men were devouring the repast with trembling hands. Louisa didn't see Ellen among the group of men.

The woman who said she was Betty left the other two in charge and ushered Louisa to a table in the kitchen.

"How can I help you, dear?" Betty asked. "Are you looking to help with our cause?"

"Actually, no, I'm a reporter for *The Ledger*. My name's Louisa Delafield," she said.

"*The Ledger?* That's an impressive paper. Lots of fine ladies and gentlemen read that paper," Betty said with a knowing look. "Are you wanting to write an article about the work we do here at the Mission?"

Louisa hesitated and then said, "In a manner of speaking, yes. I want to tell your story. I understand that when you were younger, you had a very different sort of life..."

"Oh, youse want me to talk about the bad old days," the woman said and sank onto a wooden bench on the other side of the kitchen table.

Louisa took a moment to study her. She was probably close to sixty years old, but her hair was still a thick brown with one shock of silver.

"Truth is I don't like to reflect on it much. I'm doing the Lord's work now."

"That's quite admirable, Mrs....?" Louisa said, pretending she hadn't already learned about her.

"Name is Betty Walsh. I never married. Many of 'em wanted to marry me, mind you, but I like being my own boss," she said. "A man always wants something. Seems like they can't do nothing of themselves."

"I understand, but I think it's a powerful story — your transformation into a charitable woman looking to do good. It might inspire people to help you in your mission," Louisa said.

Betty perked up and flashed a smile. Her canine teeth pointed inward and made her appear slightly wolf-like.

"Tell me about your youth, Betty. Why did you turn to a life of crime?" Louisa asked. Louisa was genuinely curious.

"You really want to hear about all that?" the older woman asked.

"I do. I think my readers will be enthralled," Louisa said. "I understand they called you the Queen of Hell's Kitchen."

"Enthralled? Well, I don't look like much now, but in my day there weren't a Gopher in the whole of Hell's Kitchen didn't want to get ahold of me," she said. She warmed up to her subject and seemed to lose herself in memories. "I was a fighter. Loved it all. The blood tingling my skin." She rubbed her arms, then thumped her chest and said, "The pounding drum inside, the grunts, the moans. The smell of blood made me drunk. Better than sex. Better than money even. That sound, the crunch of bone." Battle Betty grinned. "I once made a bully club with a lump o' lead in the corner of my kerchief and put down a Captain He-man with one swing. I'd rather have blood on my hands than flour. If I'd had a home, I would not've stayed."

Louisa scribbled furiously in her note pad and then looked up at the sweet-faced woman before her and tried to imagine her beating a man with a club.

"Did you ever know Henry Garrett?" she asked.

"Who?"

"He was the president of Garrett Shipping. You helped break the longshoreman strike, didn't you?" Louisa asked. She studied Betty's reaction, but the woman's face was blank.

"I never dealt directly with them people," she said, glancing away. Louisa wondered if the woman was lying, but chose not to pursue the matter. She preferred to think that the Garretts had nothing to do with this sordid affair.

"I see. So, you left that life behind?" Louisa asked.

"I'm too old for it, now, and I spent some time in prison. So now I do this," she said and waved toward a big black stove.

Louisa scribbled more notes and then changed tack.

"Betty, I understand you knew Adele Cummings, the police officer who was killed not far from here. Was helping her out part of your effort to reform?" she asked.

A sour expression flickered across the woman's face.

"Terrible business that. Just terrible," she said, shaking her head.

"She was investigating a shady doctor, was she not? An abortionist?"

Betty tilted her head. Louisa's pen was poised above the note pad.

"Say, I thought you was writing a story about me," she said.

"I am," Louisa said. "But I am also interested in what happened to Mrs. Cummings. Was she a friend of yours?"

Betty ran her fingers over her lips and appeared to be deciding whether or not to continue the interview. Then she smiled broadly.

"I suppose you'll be wanting to mention to your readers how much it costs to support a mission. Right now we can only afford to feed the men lunch. If we had some support from some of them millionaire readers of yours, we could feed them two meals a day and maybe feed women and children, too," Betty said.

Louisa paused as if she were considering this information. Battle Betty may be reformed, but she was shrewd, and she didn't give something for nothing.

"That's an important aspect of the story. You're doing good work and the citizens of the city should support you," Louisa said. That seemed to satisfy her.

"An abortionist, you say? I don't know anything about that. Adele were asking about a doctor doing business around here. You know, offering cures that don't do anything but fatten his wallet. I told her I'd heard about such a man and gave her an address for him," she said and then squeezed her hands into fists. "How can I ever forgive myself?"

"Betty, what was the doctor's name? Do you know what he looks like?"

"Never saw him myself. And his name? Hmm. I don't recall. My memory isn't what it used to be," she said. "He's long gone now, I bet. Probably up to his tricks in some other city."

"Who do you think set that bomb off?" Louisa persisted.

Betty looked around the kitchen before speaking. There was no one in there but the two of them.

"You want to know what I think? I think someone in the police force didn't want her going after that doctor," she said, leaning forward. Louisa got a heavy whiff of floral perfume.

"You think she was set up?" Louisa asked.

Betty leaned back in her chair, arms folded across her ample bosom, and raised an eyebrow. "I have no idea," she said. "I only know that Adele was a straight arrow, and she might have been talking to that commission. You know the one I mean, right?"

"Yes," Louisa said. "I've read about it. The Curran Committee, but what makes you think she was talking to them?"

"She said she was. And nobody likes a stool pigeon. Especially not the cops," Betty said.

"I see," Louisa said. This was a new wrinkle, she thought.

"I hope I've helped you, Miss," Betty said. "I'll be looking for your article. What newspaper did you say?"

"*The Ledger*," Louisa said, and for some reason, she wished she had lied. As she left the Mission, she noticed a flyer lying on the floor and saw Ellen's likeness looking up at her.

Chapter 24
Ellen

Ellen walked quickly away from the Mission. She kept her head low with the brim of the man's hat shading her face. She crossed the street, slipped down an alley, came out on another street and kept walking. In a few blocks, the signs were no longer written in Chinese characters and she might as well have crossed onto another continent. She slowed down and sauntered along the street. The houses on the street were modest but it was in no wise a slum. Children played on the sidewalk in front of the houses. She turned onto a busy thoroughfare and suddenly came across a massive stone arch. She'd never seen such a stunning work. This must be Greenwich Village, she thought. One of the Garretts' footmen talked about it often. He'd grown up here, he said, and anytime he had a day off, he went home to his family for a hearty Italian meal.

As she strolled along the streets, she passed bookstores, small gift shops, cafés, and art galleries. Strange figures were painted on the walls, and the people did not rush the way they seemed to in other parts of the city. The women were even dressed differently. They wore sensible hats and dresses, but they still somehow managed to be stylish. They displayed a confidence completely unlike the haughtiness of the women on Fifth Avenue or the beaten down aspect of the women in the tenements. She stopped in front of a little brick shop with a big window and read the words HER SHOP painted above the doorway.

Ellen stepped inside. She was acutely aware that she was still dressed as a vagrant, but no one paid her any heed. The shelves of the shop were filled with Persian scarves, Mandarin rugs, odd rings and all sorts of things that were unlike anything one would find in the houses of the rich, and yet she decided they were treasures nevertheless. She left the shop and continued to comb the streets until she found what she'd been looking for: a sign that said THE WILL O' THE WISP TEAHOUSE. This was the place that her friend in the workhouse mentioned, a place just for women. She knew she shouldn't go in there. Not dressed like a man. Still she stopped and looked in the window.

The tables were occupied by women of various ages and classes who seemed engrossed in conversations. One woman in particular caught her eye. She looked to be in her late twenties, big boned with a narrow face, an affable smile, and big brown eyes under thick eyebrows. Ellen could tell by her tailored gray jacket she had money, but she wasn't showy. A strand of pearls hung carelessly around her neck. A feeling swept over Ellen like a dull ache — the kind of ache you don't want to stop. The woman laughed at something her companion said. Ellen swiveled her head to look at the companion. Small, blond, and delicately holding her tea cup. When the woman with the pearls got up to get some more tea, Ellen saw the blond woman glance out the window and wave a handkerchief. Curiously, Ellen looked around. Two men stood across the street, smoking cigarettes with their eyes fixed on the window of the tea shop. Peelers, Ellen knew immediately.

Ellen stepped in the shop and walked up to the proprietress, whose silver hair was elegantly coiffed.

"What do you want?" the woman asked, glancing down at the scuffed shoes and shabby pants.

Ellen pulled off her hat, looked the woman in the eye, and said, "Lillian, it's me. Ellen."

Lillian's eyes lit up in recognition and she smiled. "Look at you!"

"There're two policemen outside, and I happened to notice the blond lady over there, waving at them with her handkerchief. Thought you might want to know. You might warn your customer, that pretty woman with the pearls."

Lillian glanced quickly at the blond woman and then called to the other woman as she headed back to the table, her tea cup in hand.

"Hester, come here. I need to talk to you a minute," she said.

Ellen turned to leave, but as she did, she caught the eye of the brown-eyed woman with the pearl necklace. They stared at each other for a moment before Ellen hurried out, her heart leaping in her chest.

***

When Ellen got back to Louisa's house, Louisa was waiting for her in the parlor.

"There you are," Louisa said, sounding relieved. "I was worried when I didn't see you inside the Mission with the men. I saw that flyer with your picture."

Ellen sat down.

"Very accurate likeness, don't ya think? I even saw my two Chinese friends while I was down there, but fortunately they didn't recognize me," she said.

Louisa turned pale.

"Oh no," she said.

"I don't suppose your friend, Hugh Garrett, had anything to do with it," Ellen said.

"It could just as easily have been Marat," Louisa said.

"Maybe," Ellen said. "What did Battle Betty tell you?"

"She's got a theory that Adele Cummings was set up by someone on the force. She said that Adele was talking to the Curran Committee," Louisa said.

"If 'tis the police, they already know where I am," Ellen said.

"And if it is the police, they are probably perfectly happy to lay the blame on the doctor," Louisa countered.

"All right then. I'll ask Paddy. He has offered to accompany me to the Garretts' so I might get my things," Ellen said.

"Why would he tell you?"

"Paddy is an honest cop," Ellen said. "I can at least plant the idea in his head and see what he thinks."

As she went upstairs to get out of the men's clothing, she thought of the woman with the pearl necklace back at the tea shop. Had the woman — Lillian had called her Hester — thought she was a man? No, Ellen told herself, a woman like that wouldn't have even seen her.

The look that passed between them was only something Ellen had imagined.

A Woman's View

By Beatrice Milton

NEW YORK, Feb. 17, 1913 – Readers of this paper may be surprised to discover that not all society entertainment happens in the mansions on Fifth Avenue, the luxurious new hotels in Midtown, or the summer playgrounds of Newport or Saratoga. On occasion, members of the younger social set have been known to stray outside the boundaries of their class to see how the other half lives. The derogatory term for this activity is "slumming," but the establishments they patronize are hardly slumlike. They are often appointed with leather and gilt, waiters patrol the rooms with trays laden with the finest champagne and delicious hors d'oeuvres, and the fashions on display would rival the Easter Parade.

Such adventurings have always been common among a few wealthy and powerful men. The murdered Stanford White is a perfect example of what can go awry when crossing class boundaries. However, even members of the fairer sex sometimes seek out entertainments far from their own green pastures.

Just the other night I had the opportunity to travel into this wicked world with one of society's darlings —

a young woman of both wealth and pedigree, who shall remain unnamed for the sake of discretion.

We went to a gambling establishment in an area known as the New Tenderloin, between 42nd and 62nd Streets. The door was guarded by a burly fellow whom one would not want to meet in a dark alley. Inside, felt-covered gambling tables occupied the floor while a raised platform over to the side was open for dancing. The tango is especially popular.

An elegant Negro songstress in a black velvet sheath serenaded the revelers as they drank daiquiris, Delmonico cocktails, and dry martinis. Dice flew across the tables, stacks of chips shrank or grew, depending on the vagaries of luck. And a rushing river of money flowed from one pocket to the other. Your frugal correspondent, however, took no chances with the contents of her purse.

I spoke to one of the esteemed denizens of this world, a Mr. Owney Madden, who cut quite a dashing and debonair figure, and learned that when he is not keeping an eye on the activities of the club, he may be found caring for his prize-winning pigeons — just as a Whitney or Vanderbilt may be found caring for his thoroughbreds or sailing vessels.

Fortunately, my companion and I witnessed no murders and made it safely home.

Chapter 25
Ellen

Ellen and Paddy O'Neil walked along Fifth Avenue, the mansions on one side of them and the park with its bare trees etched against the pale sky like shattered china plates on the other. Since she was with the police detective, she felt safe not wearing her disguise. She'd told him about the bounty on her, and he promised to look into it, but she didn't hold out much hope that he could find the culprits.

"We'll get your belongings, I'll question the chauffeur, and you can get your final wages," Paddy said.

"I doubt that last part," she said. "Mrs. Garrett will pinch a penny till it screams. Sometimes she simply 'forgot' to pay us, and then poor Mrs. Strauss would have to hector the woman until she coughed up our salary."

"Typical," Paddy said. "About this chauffeur, is Marat his first or last name?"

"I don't know. I'm not sure it's his name at all," Ellen said.

They turned onto a side street and within spitting distance of the park, they came to the Garrett house. It was five windows wide and five windows high with a wrought iron fence across the front, and two pillars with carved lions' heads on either side of the gate.

"Christ on the cross," Paddy said. "This is a far cry from yer dingy old cottage in the Claddagh."

Ellen looked up at the hooded dormer windows on the fifth floor where she and Silvia and the other servants had lived. She would need to go up there to retrieve her things and she dreaded it. She remembered that fiasco when she tried to get the note from Silvia's dresser. Well, they'd have to let her in to at least get what few possessions she owned.

Paddy rang the doorbell, and Mr. Strauss, the stiff German butler, opened the gate for them. He didn't acknowledge Ellen at all, merely bowed briefly to Paddy and said that he was expected.

She could tell that Paddy was intimidated by the huge marble-floored foyer, but that he was trying his best not to show it. He was used to the everyday mayhem of Hell's Kitchen, but this sort of absurd opulence was beyond his realm of experience. Beyond the foyer Ellen saw the ballroom where Hattie had been presented to society just a few short months ago.

Mr. Strauss led them to one of the smaller drawing rooms but pointedly did not invite them to sit. Statues occupied the corners and an imposing portrait of the family's late patriarch adorned a wall above one of the home's fourteen fireplaces.

After they'd stewed a bit, Hugh Garrett strode in, followed by his mother, the formidable Amelia Garrett.

She wore a velvet dressing gown and a pinched expression which turned into a scowl as soon as she saw Ellen. Ellen wondered if she knew about the late night visit. Hugh Garrett's expression was inscrutable. He kept a half-smile permanently affixed to his face.

"My apologies for disturbing you and your mother, Mr. Garrett," Paddy said, his Irish brogue submerged underneath a tortured English that many an Irishman and woman assumed when speaking to the overlords at home. No matter where you were in the world, if you were Irish, you were never any better than you should be.

"Quite all right," Hugh said. "Such unfortunate circumstances. The whole family is distraught by poor Silvia's death."

Mrs. Garrett took the opportunity to sneer and say, "Disgusting and immoral is more like it. She's brought a scandal down on the house with her loose ways."

"She didn't do it by herself," Ellen snapped. "I assure you she had help." She glared at Hugh, who shook his head as if he were dismayed by the whole affair.

"I've brought Miss Malloy along with me so she can collect her belongings and her final payment whilst I have a conversation with your chauffeur," Paddy said, having recovered a sense of his legal authority.

"Final payment? Detective, do you know what our housekeeper found among her things?" Mrs. Garrett asked, glaring at Ellen.

"Now, Mother," Hugh said.

"My emerald earrings," Mrs. Garrett spat. "She's not only involved in the sordid business of abortion, she's a thief, and I want to press charges."

Ellen was dumbstruck. She looked from Mrs. Garrett to Paddy, who seemed at a loss for words. In a moment, he recovered.

"Send for the housekeeper, please," Paddy said.

Hugh Garrett went to the wall and pulled a cord. If Mrs. Strauss told them about Ellen coming in to the house in the middle of the night, it would only add to their suspicions. She should have told Paddy about it on the way.

"Paddy, I did no such thing," Ellen said. "I've never stolen a thing in my life. What would I be doing with emeralds?"

"You'd sell them," Mrs. Garrett hissed.

"I did not do this," Ellen said.

Mrs. Strauss came to the doorway. She did not look happy to be standing there.

"You rang for me?" she asked. Mrs. Strauss averted her eyes from Ellen's. I am lost, Ellen thought.

"Mrs. Strauss, did you or did you not find a pair of my valuable earrings, tucked under the mattress in this woman's room?" Mrs. Garrett asked.

"I'll ask the questions if you don't mind," Paddy said, but it was too late. Mrs. Strauss was nodding her head.

"I did find them there," the housekeeper said.

"Anyone could have put them there," Ellen said. "It wasn't me."

Amelia lifted her chin and looked at Ellen as if she were atop a mountain and Ellen groveling in the valley below her.

"Let's take it to a judge and see whom he believes," she said in a triumphant tone.

Hugh stepped in between them and said, "Now, Mother. No harm has been done. You've got your earrings. There's no need to press charges. We can handle this a better way." He turned toward Ellen. "Miss Malloy, I'd like to offer you passage back home to Ireland on one of our ocean liners. Not steerage, mind you. Second class. Very nice accommodations. If you go back home, we'll consider the matter dropped."

"Home? But I don't want to go back to Ireland," she said, backing away. She thought of the smokey old cottage in the Claddagh, the smell of fish and mud. It was a dead end for her.

"Well, it's got to be better than the Tombs, right, Detective O'Neil?"

Paddy looked at Ellen.

"You're in a bit of a spot here," he said. She didn't think he believed that she'd stolen those earrings, but that didn't mean a judge wouldn't believe it.

"We have a ship departing in early March," Hugh said. "Where shall I send the ticket?"

Ellen looked at Paddy, helplessly.

"Send it to me, care of the Fifth Precinct," he said. He handed Hugh a card from his pocket. "Now if someone could take Miss Malloy to gather her things while I question your chauffeur. And by the way, she'll still be needing her final payment."

"But she's a thief," Mrs. Garrett said.

"That's for a judge to decide. If you don't pay her wages, then who's the thief?" He stared hard at Mrs. Garrett, and Ellen felt a swell of pride for her compatriot.

"Mrs. Strauss, please take this woman to the servants' quarters but don't take your eyes off her for a minute," Mrs. Garrett said. "I'll go get her payment."

Mrs. Strauss ushered Ellen out of the parlor and to the servants' stairs at the back of the house.

Once they were in the stairwell, Ellen spoke up.

"You don't believe I took those earrings, do you?" Ellen asked.

"It doesn't matter what I believe. I did find them and Mrs. Garrett's maid, Smith, was with me. Mrs. Garrett insisted I search your room when you and Silvia disappeared," she said.

"I bet Smith planted them there. She's always hated me," Ellen said.

Ellen's feet dragged as they climbed the four flights to the servants' quarters. Her da wouldn't have been surprised by this turn of events. He always said, there's some folks just aren't happy unless they know someone else is hungry. He was thinking of the British, but Ellen believed it applied to these rich Americans, too. Not all of them, sure. Hattie had always been kind to her, but Mrs. Garrett had an empty pit where her heart should have been. And her son was even worse.

She collected her battered old valise, stuffed it with her few clothes and the picture of her ma and da she'd brought from home, and went back downstairs. Mr. Strauss led her out the back to the carriage house where Paddy was still questioning Marat, who was leaning against Hugh Garrett's yellow roadster and smoking a cigarette.

"There she is," Marat said. "I'm glad to see you're safe, Ellen. You had a shock that night, didn't you? I looked everywhere for you."

"And fortunately for me, you never found me," Ellen said.

"I never planned to harm you," Marat said.

"Didn't you?" she asked. "And what about those Chinese men? Did you know about them, about what they planned to do with Silvia?"

Marat had a puzzled look on his face.

"Chinese men? I saw a couple of orderlies come to take the girl to the hospital, that's all," he said. Then he winked at her before tossing his cigarette to the ground and turning to wipe the glossy wax coat of the roadster.

***

Ellen and Paddy walked quickly from the house to Fifth Avenue and dashed across the street to Central Park.

"You're right. Marat's a dangerous one. One of the Eastmans. Claims he's reformed," Paddy said as they walked through the snow-covered park.

"Is it always this cold in the winter?" Ellen asked. She wished she had worn a scarf.

"This year's been a bit worse," he said. "Do you think he's reformed? This Marat fella?"

"Maybe he is," Ellen said. "But it was him that took us to that murderous doctor."

"He says he wasn't in the room when Silvia died. He swears he didn't know nothin'," Paddy said. "Says he was outside and never saw the doctor."

"Then it's the doctor's word against mine," Ellen said, "and he's got a powerful protector in Hugh Garrett."

"He does indeed. Tunney's been getting pressure from Commissioner Waldo to drop the whole thing," Paddy said.

They came to a man selling chestnuts. The delicious charred smell was too much to resist, so they each purchased a penny's worth.

"I've been reading in the papers about that commission on police corruption. According to Louisa Delafield, Battle Betty thinks Adele Cummings was set up by another cop," Ellen said, crunching into the warm meat of the nut. "Maybe Adele was talking to the Curran Committee."

Paddy shook his head.

"I know of no one who had a grudge against her," he said.

"Maybe you ought to do some investigating in your own back yard," Ellen said.

"I'm telling you, the men are plenty mad about what happened to Adele. She was one of ours, Ellen. If a cop set her up, they'll find out," he said. "And they'll kill him. It'll look like an accident."

He made this proclamation in such a matter-of-fact manner that it sent a chill down her back.

They reached the other side of the park and said their good-byes. Ellen caught a streetcar north. She believed Paddy, but what did any of it matter now? They'd be sending her off to Ireland with her tail between her legs. She looked out the window at the teeming city and felt an odd pang in her chest.

Chapter 26

Louisa

"She accused you of theft?" Louisa asked.

"She did, indeed," Ellen said, running her strong fingers through Louisa's thick hair and pulling it back into a French twist.

"I don't know what to say," Louisa said.

"Nothing to say. I'll be back home soon, begging for my supper," Ellen said.

"When I see Hugh tonight, I'll convince him that he's wrong," Louisa said.

"You may try, but I don't expect you'll have any success," Ellen said, sticking the last of the pins in Louisa's hair.

Anna wheeled into the room, the ginger cat draped over shoulders like a dingy stole.

"Whoever heard of an art show in an armory?" Anna asked, querulously.

"Technically, it's not an armory anymore, Mother," Louisa replied.

"Why would anyone go to this thing? It's not like you'll get to see a Raphael." In Anna's mind, there was no other artist.

"The winter season is over, Mother, and I'm excited about this show. I don't get to see what the European artists are doing very often," Louisa said.

"You should go to Europe again, dear. Every young woman should go to Europe," Anna said, rapturously. Louisa topped her coiffure with an elegant hat and gave herself one last look in the mirror.

"I'm afraid you might starve to death if I left," she said and kissed her mother on the forehead. Her mother's hair smelled like lilac powder, and for a moment Louisa was reminded of her childhood when her mother was willowy and elegant and as sure of herself as the thoroughbred Meridian, when he broke records and sailed across the finish line at the Kentucky Derby.

She turned to Ellen, "We will get this matter straightened out. I promise."

Louisa splurged on a cab as far as the Bloodgood home. Outside the house, a boxy carriage with large wheels and two robust horses waited. Natasha had declared she would never give up her pair and carriage. She didn't care that the rest of the world had turned to the automobile, a noisy and inelegant contraption, she claimed. She'd sent a note to the paper inviting Louisa to ride with her.

The ancient driver sat on his seat, bundled in a coat and fur cap, whip in hand. He got down and helped Louisa inside, though he was so old and frail that Louisa thought she should be helping him. Natasha was already inside waiting.

"Good evening," Louisa said. "It's positively freezing tonight."

Natasha didn't respond. The carriage jerked forward.

"Is everything all right?" Louisa asked after several minutes of frosty silence.

"How could you?" Natasha asked.

"How could I what?" Louisa asked.

"You wrote that slumming article, and my daughter was the so-called companion." Natasha pursed her lips angrily. "Beatrice Milton is a fiction!"

Louisa's silence gave her all the ammunition she needed.

"How dare you encourage her to consort with gangsters!" Natasha hissed.

"I don't think Dorothy can be encouraged or discouraged from doing anything," Louisa said in a meek voice. "She always has done exactly what she wants to do."

"And you," Natasha said, pulling a hand from her fur muff to point a finger at Louisa. "I thought you had more breeding than that. It's perfectly acceptable for a woman of your class to write about society, but to write about these disgusting topics."

Louisa was crushed. She bit her lower lip to keep it from quivering.

"Oh, Natasha," she said. "I'm so sorry. I promise I won't write about Dorothy in that context ever again."

Natasha stared hard at her. She looked out the window of the carriage and then back at Louisa.

"You must drop this Beatrice Milton façade. I understand you need money. You will write about society until we can find you a suitable husband. It's not too late for you to marry."

Louisa said nothing. She could not bear to have Natasha angry with her.

In front of the massive brick building waited a line of black motorcars. It still had the look of an armory with its barred lower story windows and the carved eagle perched over the door. The second floor had turrets jutting out of the wall, the better to shoot you with. A large banner hung over the doorway: "International Exhibition/Modern Art."

Louisa was careful not to slip on the ice as she stepped out of the carriage. She hooked her arm in Natasha's as they crossed the street.

In front of the Armory, an emaciated young woman stood, begging for coins from the glamorous art patrons. She stared at the two of them with hollow eyes, and Louisa had to look away from the wretched creature, but Natasha stopped and opened her beaded purse. She reached a gloved hand out and held it over the woman's tin cup. The cup was obviously empty because the sound of the coin reverberated loudly.

"That was kind of you, Natasha," Louisa said as they made their way to the entrance.

"She was such a scrawny little thing. I had to give her something," Natasha said with a shrug.

Inside, the huge open room of the armory had been divided into smaller galleries. Natasha went off to hobnob and Louisa found herself in Gallery A, confronted by the brightly colored work of a member of the Astor family. She had to admit his large wood "screens" were pleasing to the eye. She was captivated by the picture of porcupines in the woods. When she turned away, she found herself face to face with Hugh Garrett and his mother, Amelia.

"How delightful," she said, forcing a smile to her lips. She noticed that Amelia wore an exquisite pair of emerald earrings. Were those the ones she accused Ellen of stealing, she wondered.

Amelia frowned at her.

"Delightful? Your paper has turned into a sewer, Louisa," Amelia said. "Who is this new writer they've hired? I hope she isn't here tonight." She peered around the room as if looking for the Devil.

"Now, Mother," Hugh said. "Stop living in the last century. *The Ledger* has to appeal to a wide readership. It's not their fault if the public clamors for unseemly topics." He turned to Louisa with that charming boyish smile and said, "Enjoy the show, Louisa. It's a bit too modern for Mother's taste."

"Hugh, may I speak to you for a moment?" she asked.

"Of course. Mother, I'll join you in the next gallery," he said.

"What is it, Louisa?" he asked when his mother had gone.

Louisa led him to a corner of the room, and said quietly, "I understand your mother has accused Hattie's lady's maid of theft and that you have offered to pay her way back to Ireland."

"And how do you know these things, Louisa?" he asked. "Are you harboring this woman? This thief?"

Louisa stammered for a moment. She knew she should not admit to it, but she was unskilled at prevarication.

"I have spoken to her. That's all I can tell you, Hugh."

"Spoken to her? My dear, she is a servant. She should be happy to go home instead of to jail. Please, do not interfere. If my mother were to decide you had forgotten your place, then she would do everything in her power to ruin you, to keep you from any society event of any importance. I am your friend, Louisa, but even I have no control over my mother. You know that as well as anyone," he said.

"But..." she began.

"No, Louisa. Enjoy the show," he said and turned away from her abruptly.

He was right, of course. Amelia did have the power to lock her out of society. Louisa would have to figure out how to move forward with her feature without Ellen's help, she supposed.

As Louisa wound her way through the crowd, wealthy patrons scoffed and laughed at the works of art. She stopped to stare at an amazing and strange painting — all lines and distortions — by someone named Pablo Picasso. A couple of women looked at the painting, and one of them said, "Imagine being locked in here all night with these dreadful paintings. You'd surely go insane."

Louisa looked around the gallery and standing in front of one of the paintings was none other than the former president of the United States, Theodore Roosevelt, with a critic hanging on his coat tails. They stared at a strange, enthralling painting of multiple figures that seemed to move along a staircase.

"This isn't art! None of this is art. It takes no talent whatsoever to do this," the former president blustered. "I'm in favor of progress, but this is not progress. It's chaos."

"It looks like an explosion at a shingles factory!" said the critic, a tiny dapper man with round spectacles that made him look like an owl. He laughed giddily.

A crowd orbited around Roosevelt as if he were the sun, and they were all planets trapped by his gravity. She wiggled through them, determined to salvage the evening.

"Mr. Roosevelt," she called. He turned and glared at her. Then the bushy mustache curled upward, indicating a smile underneath it. "Aren't you a pretty one? What's your name?"

"Louisa Delafield. I write for *The Ledger*."

"Delafield. I know that name. Was your father Richard Delafield?"

"He was," she said.

"Oh," he paused, frowned, looked at her through his thick spectacles, and then brightened once more. "How's your lovely mother? I haven't seen her in ages."

"She's well," Louisa said. "May I ask you about something?"

"The art? I hate it," he said and waved dismissively at the paintings on the walls.

"No," she said quickly. "About police work."

Now she had his attention.

"Certainly," he said, taking off his spectacles to wipe them with a handkerchief.

"When you were commissioner and first hired women to work as matrons to guard women prisoners, did you ever imagine they would someday take on the dangerous work of investigations?"

"I'd hoped they would," he said, replacing the spectacles. "But I didn't know whether or not it would happen."

"Now that women are actually involved in real police work, what do you think of their presence on the force?"

"I believe they increase the efficiency of police work, and that their presence has a salubrious effect on the profession as a whole. They keep the men honest. And as you know in this era of public outcry over corruption, that is extremely important," he said. He raised one finger as if he were once again on the campaign trail.

"How do you feel about the murder of Adele Cummings, the police matron who was killed by a bomb while on an investigation?"

"A terrible tragedy," he answered. His thick mustache twitched. "I hope they find the person responsible."

"One final question, shouldn't they be called policewomen instead of matrons and given the same rights and privileges as the men?" she asked.

Roosevelt paused to consider her question and then said, "I do believe that. But don't expect any consideration from that rascal Wilson. He won't even consider giving women the right to vote."

Roosevelt was bitter about his loss to Woodrow Wilson, who actually had no power over the issue of city police.

He tipped his hat and walked on, surrounded by his entourage.

With a sigh, she turned and looked at the painting that had so horrified the former president. Louisa bent closely to read the sign next to the painting. It was called *Nude Descending a Staircase* by a Frenchman named Duchamp. Louisa's eyes darted from corner to corner trying to take in the colors, the shapes, the vibrant energy. She tilted her head as she studied the painting. One thing was for certain: this painting in no way resembled an explosion at a shingles factory.

She found Natasha in the American Gallery deep in conversation with the attorney Herbert Markham.

"Hello, Mr. Markham," Louisa said. "Sorry to interrupt, Natasha. I just wanted to let you know I'll take a cab home."

"Et tu, Louisa?" Natasha said with false dismay. She turned to the attorney and said, "These girls only want to ride in motorcars these days."

"Louisa," Herbert Markham said in an oily voice. "My nephew is here. Wouldn't you like to meet him?"

"Yes," Natasha said. "She would love to meet him."

Mr. Markham grabbed a tall, gangly man in a shiny top hat by the elbow and dragged him over to Louisa.

"May I present my nephew, Miss Delafield. He's also Mr. Markham. My brother's son," the attorney said.

The young Mr. Markham stared down the slope of his nose at Louisa and let his eyes rake her up and down. His lip curled but he managed a short bow and a "How do you do?"

Louisa sighed in relief. The horrid man was obviously looking for someone with more something, money or feminine assets, than she had.

"Fine, thank you," she said. "I'm afraid I must go now."

Outside, the cold had turned bitter. She looked for a cab, but there were none.

"Well, if it isn't the little stool pigeon," a voice behind her said. Louisa wheeled around to see Owney Madden leaning against the building with a cigarette in his mouth. "Maybe I should take you up to my pigeon coop."

"Mr. Madden," Louisa said trying to quell the terror in her voice. "What are you doing here?"

"I thought Dorothy said your name was Louisa, but it's Beatrice, isn't it?" he said, flicking the ash of his cigarette. "I read your article about my establishment. You know you coulda had the cops all over the joint except I pay 'em off."

"I'm sorry. I didn't mean to cause you any trouble," she said. She wondered if he'd been waiting here for her. Was he going to shoot her here in the street? What a dreadful end that would be.

“Are you kidding? We’re twice as busy tonight thanks to you. All the swells want to be seen at the Winona,” he said.

“What a relief,” she said and glanced at the road.

“Say, stick around. As soon as Dorothy comes out, we’ll go find a party. It’ll be fun,” he said.

“Some other time, perhaps,” she said. “I must go write this story right away.”

A cab turned onto the street and she waved it down.

“Sure,” he said. “Next time.”

He tossed his cigarette butt into the gutter and Louisa dashed toward the cab. Once inside she shivered, and it wasn’t from the cold.

Society Notes

New York Society Shocked by Armory Art Show

---

by Louisa Delafield

NEW YORK, Feb. 18 — Last night's opening of The International Art Exhibition at the 69th Regiment Armory on Lexington Avenue at 25th Street shocked critics and dismayed society's art lovers. The work was pronounced immoral and frightening, and many New Yorkers will agree with that assessment. The paintings and sculptures are like nothing we've ever seen before.

However, I suggest you go to the exhibit with an open mind. Follow the lead of Mrs. Gertrude Whitney and the American artists who worked so diligently to bring this art to our attention. Does art always have to be pretty? Should it strive to accurately reflect reality? Why should a painter try to do what a photographer can do better? Perhaps, instead, art can provoke us to see the world in new ways. Instead of a static view, art can embody emotion and energy.

One work in particular caused distress to those who viewed it. It is Marcel Duchamp's *Nude Descending a Staircase*, a work of astonishing originality. I've seen the parodies in the morning paper, but I predict the painting will be remembered long after the parodies are forgotten.

As for our ladies of society, they were all exquisitely clothed in Worth, Poiret, and Lucile, unlike the many nudes on the walls.

Chapter 27

Louisa

On her way in to work, Louisa thought about her conversation with Ellen that morning. She had been loath to admit that she had made no headway with the Garretts.

"Then I'll have to leave, I s'pose," Ellen said.

"At least you'll be safe," Louisa said.

Ellen smirked, and a certain gloom settled over the house. Even Suzie seemed downcast by the turn of events.

When she got to her desk, she decided she would save Roosevelt's pronouncements about women in the police force for a Beatrice Milton story — one that would go into detail about their usefulness and the dangers they encounter.

As she sorted through her invitations and letters, she came upon a plain white envelope, which she opened. Inside she found a letter in a strong masculine hand.

Dear Miss Delafield, I am eager to hear about the progress of your new venture. Would it be acceptable for me to call on you at your house this evening at around 7:30? I hope this will not be an inconvenience.
Yours truly,
Forrest Calloway

Louisa was stunned. The publisher wanted to speak to her? At her house? She glanced around the room and tucked the note in her purse.

***

"Is Mr. Calloway a suitor?" her mother asked over dinner. Ellen sat with them, and Suzie served, but stopped to listen to Louisa's answer. She'd been making cookies to serve to their expected guest.

"Heavens, no," Louisa said. "He's my employer, and he's probably twenty years my senior."

"Is he already married?" Suzie asked.

"He was married once," Louisa said, recalling the rumors she'd heard. "A floozy from California, they say. She ran off years ago."

"Then he's available," Anna said. "He's got money, doesn't he?"

Louisa tried to stifle a sudden rush of anger.

"Why does everyone want to marry me off?" she muttered. She glared at her mother. "I won't do it. I will not marry. Ever."

She dropped her napkin and went upstairs to change. Ellen followed.

"Your mother has a point," Ellen said.

"Not you, too," Louisa said. "I don't see you rushing to get married."

"I'm different," Ellen said.

Louisa wondered what she meant by that, but there was no time to ask.

At precisely 7:30 the doorbell rang, and Suzie showed Mr. Calloway into the parlor.

"Thank you for allowing me to visit you, Miss Delafield," he said.

"It is I who must thank you," Louisa said. "I was so surprised by Mr. Thorn's idea," she said. "I was quite sure you helped him come to it."

She introduced him to her mother, Ellen, and Suzie. He was the pinnacle of graciousness to all of them.

"Ellen is helping me with my investigation," Louisa said.

"And how is it going, by the way? That's the main reason for my visit. I wondered if you need anything," he said, sitting in the arm chair and taking a cookie from the tray that Suzie held out to him. He bit into the cookie and closed his eyes. "Delicious," he said.

Suzie beamed and went to get the coffee.

"I'm afraid I've hit a dead end. We know there's a doctor out there, performing abortions for a wealthy clientele. And we believe he had something to do with the death of a police matron," Louisa said.

"And we know that a servant girl died on that doctor's table," Ellen interjected. "A girl whose life seems to matter to no one, especially the man who got her pregnant."

"A doctor? I would think that it would be simple enough to learn the identity of a doctor, favored by society women," Mr. Calloway said, reaching for another cookie.

Louisa looked at him. Their eyes met, and she felt an odd tingling sensation.

"I do have one idea," she said. "However, if I'm wrong, I would be ruined."

"You know who this doctor is?" Ellen asked.

"There is a Dr. Swanson who runs a charity hospital. I wrote about it recently. He was also at Amelia Garrett's soirée for the Portuguese princess," Louisa said. She had been trying to avoid this suspicion but with Mr. Calloway sitting in her parlor and Ellen on the edge of her seat looking at her with wide green eyes, she knew she must at least consider Dr. Swanson as a suspect.

"Of course, he was at the Garretts' house. I told you they are neck deep in this," Ellen said.

"The Garretts are a powerful family," he said. "I can see why you would be careful before making an accusation."

"I'm not making any accusations about them," Louisa said and gave Ellen a look.

"Hmm, yes," Mr. Calloway said. "They would be at us in an instant with lawyers threatening to shut us down."

"I won't let that happen, Mr. Calloway," Louisa said.

He inhaled and looked around the room. How shabby it must seem to him, she thought.

"Did you know that my mother ran a boarding house?" he asked, apropos of nothing.

"I did not," Louisa said.

"It was in Colorado. I learned about mining from the men who used to stay there. If it hadn't been for their advice, I would never have figured out how to make my fortune," he said.

"Raised yourself by your boot straps?" Anna asked. "We make a lot of fuss here in New York about old money, but there's much to be said for initiative. It was something Louisa's father didn't have, and look where we are now."

Louisa wondered what could have possibly gotten into her mother.

"I think you have a lovely home, Mrs. Delafield," Mr. Calloway said. "I'm afraid I must be going. Thank you for your hospitality. There is one last thing, however." He turned to Louisa. "You must go where the truth leads you, Miss Delafield. Let me worry about the rest of it."

Louisa walked him to the front door. He took his hat and coat from the coat rack and turned to her.

"Miss Delafield," he said. He took her hand and held it for a moment, looking into her eyes.

"Yes?" A strange whirling sensation filled her.

"I..." he began and then stopped. "I look forward to speaking to you again."

He turned and walked out the door to his midnight blue Packard.

Louisa shut the door, but through the glass she saw him look back at the house. She took a deep breath. She felt dizzy, and overcome with ridiculous, absurd feelings. He was her employer, and she had sworn she would never marry. It would not do. She refused to allow herself to feel this way. Not now. Not ever.

Chapter 28

Ellen

On the day of the memorial service for fallen officers, Suzie and Louisa stood in the hallway with Ellen as she put on her hat, scarf, and a wool coat that Louisa had insisted she keep.

"I'll be in a church. Filled with police," Ellen said. "I'll be perfectly safe."

"I suppose you're right," Louisa said. "Do try to find out from your detective friend if the police have found out anything yet about the doctor."

"I'll find out what I can," Ellen said and headed out the door.

She strode down the street, a damp wind at her back.

***

Ellen entered through the massive wooden doors of the cathedral. It was nothing like the humble little church back home, and yet it felt familiar enough. The incensed air smelled of oppression, of men's musty vestments, and of old women's tears. She had been as devout as a nun herself until one day she wasn't. One day it seemed like so much hogwash, some rheumy old man always telling her what God demanded of her. The threat of Hell a constant sword of Damocles. She still believed in God and his little family, but she didn't believe the lot of them cared much about the goings on of their clay creations. Still, old habits die hard. Prayers and hymns were lodged in the marrow of her bones.

She found Paddy, Paula and the two little ones in a pew about midway in the full church. She climbed over a half dozen pairs of knees and then sat next to Paula, who reached over and squeezed her hand.

Police officers in dress uniforms, their family members and the family members of the fallen were all in attendance for this memorial service for killed men, and now a woman, in blue. Strolling down the aisle came men in the tailored suits and smug mugs of politicians.

"That's Commissioner Waldo," Paddy said, indicating a broad man walking down the aisle in his fancy blue uniform with the gleaming double row of buttons.

"Is he as corrupt as the papers say?" Ellen asked.

"Worse," Paddy whispered.

A stout woman holding the hand of a little boy waddled down the middle aisle to a seat at the front of the church. The congregation watched her with pitying eyes.

"Adele Cummings' family?" Ellen asked. Paddy nodded.

Father Sullivan stood at the podium, his white hair forming a sort of halo around his head. He had nothing but praise for the police, comparing them to Jesus on the cross.

"We, too, have our dark days of persecution and trouble, but the sun will shine again and the glory thereof will revive us."

Paddy's little boy sneezed loudly.

Father Sullivan continued, "You have passed through a stormy year. You have been criticized, plotted against, and lied about, but you have done your duty well, lived up to your oath of office and given our city its best protection against an almost unheard of wave of crime. When the clouds pass away, our citizens will realize your true worth and give the credit which is the right of heroes."

The congregation nodded and murmured their agreement with the sentiments. A few wiped tears from their eyes.

After the service, Paula took the children home and Paddy offered to buy Ellen a pint at a nearby saloon.

"Don't worry," he said. "It's a respectable place where none will molest you."

They walked the block or so to the saloon and found a table in the back. Paddy got them both a pint of Irish ale. Ellen didn't care much for drink, but she accepted it. Police crowded around the bar, slapping each other on the back. One or two looked curiously over at Paddy and Ellen, but they left them alone.

"Tell me, have you any idea who killed Adele Cummings yet? Have you found the doctor?"

"Not so far, I'm afraid," he said. "I imagine he'll turn up, but there's plenty of these quacks and charlatans around."

"I don't think this one was a quack or a charlatan," Ellen said. "Otherwise, he would not be the choice of the Park Avenue ladies."

"Then he may be untouchable," Paddy said.

"I've been hearing about this Curran Committee. Unlike Father Sullivan, they seem to think the whole police department is nothing but bribery and extortion and that your commissioner is incompetent and should be fired."

Paddy took a long drink of the amber ale, wiped his mouth with his sleeve, and then leaned on the table.

"Aye, there's some truth to it," he said. "But there's nothing to be done because, you see, the corruption starts at the top with Tammany Hall. That's not to say they don't do some good. They keep the streetcars running and help feed the poor. And we do plenty of good, too. Our boys even clean out the public privies. But there's a dark side to it. Say if a certain alderman wants us to go easy on a particular gambling saloon because the owner of that saloon contributes to his campaign, we can't touch 'em no matter what kind of hellish behavior is going on. Not only that. Some of these politicians are criminals themselves. They own gambling houses and the houses of ill repute and we canna interfere with their profits."

"But why not?" she asked.

"They hold the purse strings, Ellen, and they make the laws," he said, his voice as bitter as the ale they were drinking. "So we do what we're told and try our best to keep the filthy shite from spilling into the lives of decent people. Forgive my language."

Ellen thought about what he'd said. It seemed that the engine that ran the city was crime, and the police were there to control it but not to quell it.

"What about Captain Tunney? Is he on the take?" she asked.

Paddy shook his head.

"Tunney's under no one's thumb," he said. "Why do you think he runs the bomb squad? Even the worst politician doesn't want bombs going off in the city. I've put in a request to get on his team. Maybe go undercover myself."

Ellen sat back in her wobbly chair and looked at him with wide eyes. She hated to think of him being on such a dangerous assignment. Then again, if it meant he could be an honest cop, it might be worth it.

"Paddy, suppose this doctor's involved in more than the abortion trade. Those 'orderlies' weren't planning on taking Silvia to a hospital. They were taking her to one of those houses where men pay to have their way with women — whether she's willing or not. And if I hadn't grown up with Michael Malloy as my big brother, I'd be in their clutches right now. They didn't care who they brought back to their boss."

"Christ, Ellen. There's hundreds of those places all over the city from the Bowery to Harlem," he said.

"How many in Chinatown?" she asked.

"Plenty," he said. He took another gulp of beer and looked around the room. "Oh, I've got something for you." He pulled an envelope from his pocket.

She opened it and found a ticket for a steamer to Ireland. Her heart sank. She'd had her head stuck in the sand, pretending this day would not come.

"I don't want to go back," she said.

Paddy gave her a sympathetic look.

She finished her ale and left Paddy at the saloon. She took a street car north and then caught the Sixth Avenue line up to Harlem. She was learning how to get around the city, and decided she might enjoy living here if she weren't in fear for her life and her freedom.

She got off the train a few blocks from Louisa's townhouse, hurried down the steps to the street level and walked to the corner of Louisa's street.

"Ellen!"

She turned and saw Suzie in the corner market, beckoning to her. Ellen entered the small fruit market and looked curiously at Suzie.

"What is it?" she asked.

Suzie pulled her close and leaned toward her ear.

"Mrs. Delafield told me she saw someone outside watching the house this morning. I didn't believe her. Thought she was talking crazy. But then when I came out to go to the market I saw him. Lanky fella, standing in a doorway across the street. Couldn't see his face under his hat. So I came here and waited for you."

Ellen took a deep breath. They'd found her.

"I don't think you should come back to the house," Suzie said.

"You're right," Ellen said. "It might endanger all of you."

"I'm not worried about us," Suzie said.

"Well, I am," Ellen said. "I wish I had my disguise."

"I brought you an outfit," Suzie said, handing over a bag. "Where will you go?"

Ellen had no idea.

"Don't worry about me. I'll be somewhere safe," Ellen said. She left the market and retraced her steps to the elevated train.

Thirty minutes later she stood at the door of the workhouse.

Chapter 29

Louisa

"Where's Ellen? I could use her help with my hair," Louisa said, sitting at her vanity. She had to go to the opera that night. Toscanini was directing a production of *Tosca*. She thought it delightful that the famous conductor's name was so close to the name of an opera heroine.

Suzie sighed and shook her head.

"Suzie? Is Ellen all right?" Louisa asked, turning away from her reflection.

"There was a man standing outside the house today so I warned her away," Suzie said. "I don't know where she went."

Louisa felt her throat tighten as she thought of the flyer offering a bounty on Ellen's head. How had they found her, she wondered.

"What did the man look like?" Louisa asked.

"I couldn't see his face," Suzie said. "But I could tell he was up to no good."

"I wonder how they knew she was here?" Louisa mused. Had Hugh guessed that Ellen might be staying here? She wanted to believe he was not the man Ellen seemed to think he was, but the seeds of doubt had been planted.

"I suppose there's nothing we can do," Louisa said. Maybe this was for the best, she thought. Ellen wasn't safe at her house, obviously, and it seemed she'd be going back to Ireland, after all.

"I'm worried," Suzie said. "I'd hate to see anything happen to that girl." She left Louisa to finish getting ready for her night out.

Louisa twisted her hair and jabbed some pins in it. She accidentally knocked a pot of cold cream to the floor and stared down at the mess.

Ellen is smart, she thought. She'll be fine. But will I be?

Louisa would never have embarked on her new venture, writing features under the name Beatrice Milton, if Ellen hadn't been foisted on her. The "slumming" article was received well enough, and the piece she wrote about the reformed lady gangster had garnered quite a bit of interest, along with several complimentary letters. It seemed that her readers enjoyed hearing about the seamier side of life. She supposed she could find more topics like that, and the raise had improved their financial situation somewhat. She should be satisfied. There was no need to go chasing after doctors and abductors.

She cleaned up the cold cream with a rag and then left for the opera.

***

Louisa sat in the balcony of the Metropolitan Opera House where she could observe the more illustrious members of the audience. An opera could always provide fodder for her column, and she wanted to hear Caruso sing "Recondita Armonia." Peering through her opera glasses, Louisa made a quick pass of the boxes perched along the sides. The usual suspects were there — Vanderbilts and Fishes and Astors and Morgans in the first tier. Dorothy and Natasha were in their box with the Colonel. The Garretts were in theirs.

Natasha seemed to have forgiven Louisa for the slumming story, and Dorothy could not have cared less about it. Louisa let her opera glasses linger on Hugh. She still hadn't decided whether she believed Ellen or him. She moved her opera glasses and jerked upright. Seated behind Hugh was a handsome man wearing a jacket and white tie. It was Dr. Swanson. A guest in the Garretts' box? She put down the glasses.

It could just be a coincidence. He was a family friend, after all. But if Ellen was right, if Hugh had gotten Silvia pregnant, then it would only be natural for him to turn to Dr. Swanson to eliminate the problem. And yet, it seemed absurd to think the doctor would risk everything — his hospital, his reputation, the esteem of women like Natasha and Amelia.

She looked at him through her glasses again. He was just as Ellen had described. But how to expose him? Did she have the nerve, even under a pseudonym? She needed Ellen if she were going to do this.

On the stage below, Floria Tosca, yet another doomed heroine of the opera, betrayed her lover's friend to the police. In the spotlight, Tosca resisted the proposal of the chief of the secret police. If she would only succumb to him, he promised to save her lover. Brave, foolish Tosca. In not a single production of the opera, had it worked out in Tosca's favor. As the soprano sang about living for art, living for love, it suddenly seemed as if she looked directly at Louisa. Her black silk dress cut low, her shoulders bare, her voice rose as if it had wings.

Louisa suddenly had an idea where Ellen might be.

Maybe Tosca had the right idea. Maybe a little brave foolishness was in order. Since the dawn of time, women who stepped out of society's prescribed roles had to pay a price. But the price was even higher if they didn't.

Chapter 30

Ellen

Ellen stared down at the steamer ticket in her hand. She had two weeks before the ship would depart the New York harbor, two weeks here in the workhouse. This time Lillian wasn't around to entertain her with stories of the teahouse women. She didn't want to go back to Ireland, but if she stayed in New York, the Garretts would throw her in jail or eventually one of those men from the brothel would find her. They would kill her or force her into prostitution. If she had any money she could go to another city, Boston or Philadelphia, to look for work, but she had no money.

She put the ticket away and picked up the newspaper that Mrs. Wallace had handed over that morning after she'd finished perusing it. Ellen looked at the first page and read the headlines. There was a story about a suffragist plot to kidnap ministers in London, another about a young woman who drove a lumber truck for her father's company when the teamsters went on strike, and something about a new Panama ship line. She turned the pages until she came to Louisa's column. She'd gone to the opera the night before apparently, and Enrico Caruso's "soaring aria brought tears to the audience's eyes." Ellen shut the paper and dropped it to the floor. So Louisa Delafield was going on with her life. Ellen told herself that was as it should be, but for some reason she felt hollow.

"Ellen," Myrtle said, sticking her head into the small cell. "There's a fine lady downstairs asking for you."

Downstairs near the door, Louisa stood.

"Miss Delafield," Ellen said. "I didn't expect you. Otherwise, I'd have some tea ready."

"Don't be cheeky," Louisa said. "I'd like you to come back to my house. I've spoken to Captain Tunney and he'll have a man on, round the clock watching the house."

"I don't want to jeopardize your safety," Ellen said. She would feel terrible if anything happened to Louisa or Suzie or even that crotchety old woman.

"I insist. How am I going to get this story without your help?"

"I'm sure you'll figure it out," Ellen said.

"Not without you," Louisa said. "In fact, I've got an interview lined up with a certain society doctor, and I need your help."

Ellen's chest tightened. She flashed back to that terrible night, to Silvia convulsing on the table in that damp and awful room. Then she remembered the men standing in the doorway and the terror she felt as they pursued her.

"Why should I help you, Louisa? I'm on a ship in two weeks."

Louisa sighed and said, "I saw this doctor last night at the opera. In the Garretts' box."

"Are you thinking we might be able to implicate them?" Ellen said, the taste of revenge like a lump of sugar on her tongue.

***

"Thirty-fourth Street," Louisa said to the driver.

"Where are we going?" Ellen asked.

"To the newspaper. We've got to get a camera, and they're quite heavy," she said. "You're going to be a photographer. Don't worry. Our photographer will show you everything you need to know."

"Please explain," Ellen said. Louisa's peremptory manner was sometimes more than she could take.

"As I told you and Mr. Calloway, Dr. Swanson is widely respected in society, and before we go any further in this investigation, we must rule him out. If he's the one who performed the abortion on Silvia, then I'm afraid the ramifications will be terrible," Louisa said.

"You're worried about *him*?" Ellen asked.

"Not him. The ladies who support him and his hospital. They've gone to a lot of time and effort to support him, and it's a worthy cause. He's built a place where poor women can safely deliver their babies. I'm afraid that if he's the one and we expose him, the hospital will go under and then what will happen to them?"

"But what he did was wrong," Ellen said. "If it is him."

"Was it wrong? Silvia's death was an accident," Louisa said. "Women have gotten rid of unwanted pregnancies forever. It wasn't even against the law until recently."

"I agree. Silvia should never have had to bear a child by a man who never loved her, who only used her. But

Adele Cummings' death was no accident. I'll tell you what else wasn't an accident, those men showing up to take Silvia to Heaven-knows-where after the operation," Ellen said. She didn't have to add that she was sure the doctor and his protectors were the ones responsible for the bounty on her head.

Chapter 31

Louisa

Louisa sat in a comfortable leather chair across from Dr. Swanson, who rested his hands on an imposing mahogany desk. Behind him shelves displayed medical volumes and works of literature. A window overlooked a courtyard and on one wall hung a painting of a harbor in shades of dark blue and green. She twiddled her pencil nervously.

"Is that a Whistler?" she asked, pointing her pencil toward the painting.

"Yes, one of his *Nocturnes*," the doctor said and smiled with pleasure. "I find it soothing."

And expensive, Louisa thought. For a charity hospital, the doctor seemed to be doing quite well. He had the self-satisfied attitude of a man who led a charmed life. Her nerves were beginning to settle down.

"Shall we begin?" she asked.

"Fire away," he said.

"Tell me your plans for the money raised by Mrs. Bloodgood and Mrs. Garrett's Charity Hospital Association. It was quite a tidy sum, wasn't it?"

"Almost twelve thousand dollars. Such generous donors," he said.

"And how will you spend it?" she asked. She glanced once more at the Whistler.

"Well, we have our general operating expenses. It's expensive to maintain a building of this size. Plus, we plan to add more staff so we can provide proper care for our patients as the hospital grows," he said.

Louisa scribbled notes and pondered her next question.

"I understand you will be naming a wing after Mrs. Bloodgood," she said. She found herself hoping Ellen wouldn't recognize the man. How disappointed Natasha would be. And angry, too. Not with the doctor but with Louisa.

"Mrs. Bloodgood is one of our biggest supporters," he said.

Louisa pried a bit further into the hospital finances, but his answers tended to be vague so she changed course.

"What about your background, Doctor? Where are you from and where did you study medicine?"

"I'm from humble origins, if that's what you're asking," he said with an ingratiating smile. Humble origins, but not humble aspirations, Louisa thought, looking over his expertly tailored suit.

When he'd finished telling her about his youth in the Midwest and establishing his educational credentials, Louisa said she had a photographer in the hallway and asked if they could have a picture of him at his desk.

"Certainly," he said.

Louisa opened the door and called Ellen inside. Ellen kept her hat tipped over her face as she set up the tripod and placed the bulky Graflex camera on top of it the way the photographer had showed her. He'd already placed the slide in the back for her. She slipped her head under the cloth cover on the back of the camera and proceed to shoot the picture with a bright flash of light. When she was done, she emerged from her covering and nodded at Louisa.

"It's him," she said.

Louisa turned to the doctor.

"I have one last question, Dr. Swanson," she said. "Did you perform an abortion on Hugh Garrett's house maid, Silvia Ricci, after which she died?"

The man's face paled. His eyes traveled from Louisa to Ellen to Louisa and back to Ellen where they stopped. Recognition slowly dawned on his face.

"Get out," he said in a low growl. Ellen quickly began taking apart the camera when he rushed toward her, grabbed the camera from her hands and tossed it along with the tripod into the hall. This time he shouted, "Get out!"

Louisa and Ellen hurtled out of his office, and the door slammed behind them.

"That went well," Louisa said. Her hands were shaking, and she laughed involuntarily in relief.

"I'm not sure he's one of your fans," Ellen said as she unlatched the camera from the tripod. "Your photographer said this camera was sturdy enough to use as a weapon. Looks like he was right. It's not even damaged."

Louisa picked up the tripod and took one last look at the closed door of Dr. Swanson's office. We have you now, she thought, triumphantly.

After they returned the camera to the newspaper office, Louisa and Ellen went to Captain Tunney's office. A police sergeant informed them he was off chasing anarchists who had plotted to blow up a church, so Louisa left a short note, saying they knew the identity of the doctor who had performed Silvia's abortion.

"What now?" Ellen asked as they left the police station.

"I'm going to write my story so it will make it into tomorrow's paper," she said. "Will you be all right going home on your own?"

Ellen laughed.

"If anyone comes after me, I'll put up me dukes and bust their chops," she said, holding up her fists like a boxing champ.

Louisa watched Ellen saunter off in her men's disguise. She realized she had been telling the truth when she told Ellen she needed her to write these stories — if only for her sheer bravery. She, on the other hand, had felt quite frightened the whole time.

A Woman's View

By Beatrice Milton

NEW YORK, Feb. 20 — Today's topic is not light-hearted, I'm afraid. In fact it weighs particularly heavy in the chest as it is about a terrible danger that women face regardless to which stratum of society they belong. If you are squeamish, you may want to forego the rest of this column.

The topic to which I refer is unintended pregnancy and its sometimes lethal consequences. Often the woman is complicit in her undoing, but other times a woman is put in a position where she is unable to refuse the advances of a man, whether because of physical duress or his power over her financially. Poor women are especially vulnerable when pressed for favors from an employer.

This very situation happened recently to a 17-year-old housemaid in a respected house in this city. Her wealthy employer may have made demands of her, which she was afraid to refuse for fear of losing her job. When she became pregnant, this same employer sent her off to have an illegal operation to end the pregnancy, and unfortunately, the poor girl died on the table. According to a reliable witness, the man who performed the operation was a distinguished doctor, but until he is convicted in a court of law we cannot print his name. However, police believe this same doctor was under investigation by police matron Adele Cummings, who died in an explosion.

What can be done about this despicable situation, you may wonder. First of all, women who have domestic servants should assume responsibility for the women who work under their roofs. They must make sure they are safe from any male predators in the household or on the staff. Even a man one trusts utterly may have weaknesses, of which one may be unaware.

Secondly, is it time to reconsider these laws, making illegal an operation which many women — both rich and poor — seek out? I'm not known for advocating aggressive reforms, but when the stakes are life and death, I believe the issue merits a second look. At the very least let's have a conversation about that terrible word: "contraception."

Chapter 32
Ellen

Ellen dropped into a wooden chair at the dining table. Suzie poured her some fresh coffee and Ellen plunked a lump of sugar into it, stirring the brew with a silver spoon with a large D engraved into the handle. Louisa sat in another chair with the newspaper open. Her mother quietly munched her toast. Suzie leaned in the doorway and watched them. Ellen found it odd that Suzie couldn't sit at the dining table with them while she did. It seemed to be the one place in the house where the servant-mistress line stood firm, but Ellen held some sort of in-between status.

The newspaper rattled as Louisa closed it.

"Well, what's done is done," she said.

"You'll be lucky if the socialites don't tar and feather you," Anna said.

"They don't know it's me," Louisa said. "As Beatrice Milton, I can say things Louisa Delafield would never be permitted to say."

"May I see it?" Ellen asked. Louisa handed her the paper, and Ellen turned to the page with Louisa's column.

As Ellen read the words, the sun broke through the cloud cover outside and filled the room with light through the window that looked out on the meager backyard.

"It's about time you wrote something that was significant," Ellen said. "And it's about time that someone told the truth. What made you realize it was Hugh Garrett that got Silvia pregnant?"

"I didn't say that," Louisa said. "I said it could have been her employer. Honestly, I was writing in general terms. It could be any young, powerless woman in any household."

"But you implied it was him," Suzie said with a worried look as she came over to take the plates away.

"I'll have the chance to gauge his reaction today. I'm off to Tuxedo Park with Hattie and Hugh."

Ellen was incredulous.

"You're off with Hugh Garrett? After all this?" Ellen asked.

"If you're right, Ellen, then maybe now he'll tell me the truth," Louisa said, raising her cup to her lips.

Ellen stared at Louisa, so calmly drinking her coffee. First she'd been elated by the article, and now she felt an overwhelming sense of disappointment.

"Hugh Garrett was also in cahoots with those Chinese men," Ellen said. "He must have known they planned to take her."

"You don't know that," Louisa said. "That could have been the doctor's doing. Or Marat's, for all we know."

She might not have the proof but Ellen still knew in her heart who was the guiltiest party.

After Louisa left, Ellen stood outside on the stoop of the house. The policeman Captain Tunney had stationed to watch them stood across the street. When he saw her, he sauntered across the street.

"You doing all right, Miss?" he asked.

"Fine. Just needed a breath of air," she said.

"Didn't I see you with Paddy O'Neil and his family at the memorial service?" he asked.

"You did," she said.

The man stuck his hands in his pockets and observed the street. No one suspicious.

"Word is that you and the lady reporter are digging around into the bombing. Have you learned the name of the doctor Mrs. Cummings was investigating?" he asked as if he were just passing the time of day.

Ellen almost told him, but there was something a little too eager in his eyes. She shook her head. "'Fraid I don't know," she said.

He nodded and then said, "If you find out, let us know, will you? The boys would like to talk to him."

"I see," Ellen said. A billy club hung from his belt and she knew exactly how the "boys" intended to talk to the doctor. He deserved it, but she didn't want to be responsible for another death.

Chapter 33
Louisa

Louisa hung on while Hugh drove like some crazed charioteer with Hattie between the two of them. The sun acted as if winter had already gone. Not even a stray cumulus cloud marred the sky. They had the windows down, and the wind settled around them like an extra passenger who couldn't stop singing.

"It's a 'sport' car," Hattie told Louisa over the roar of the engine and the wind. "Hugh says it can go sixty miles an hour!"

Louisa hoped that Hugh would not test that theory.

"More than sixty!" Hugh said. "This beauty has a four-speed gearbox."

Louisa hadn't been to Tuxedo Park since she was a child, when her family took a carriage pulled by four beautiful black horses for a visit so her father could decide if they should purchase a house in the exclusive community, but her mother had not liked the feeling of enclosure provided by the surrounding eight-foot fence.

"Are they keeping others out or caging us in?" she had wanted to know, and so ultimately they had decided to keep their cottage at Newport and leave Tuxedo Park to those whose need for privacy and exclusivity was greater than theirs.

The drive in Hugh's car was quicker than the carriage by an eternity. As they drove through the stone gates and down the macadam road beside the crystalline lake, Louisa saw enormous Tudor-style palaces and ostentatious Mediterranean mansions. It had certainly changed since her last visit.

They parked at the Tuxedo Club, where not so long ago a new style of dinner jacket for men was introduced and immediately caught on with the rest of the world. On this day, however, the men would be dressed more casually as they opened up their homes and chatted at great length and in great detail about golf games, tennis matches, polo, and yacht races.

"Louisa," Hugh said after Hattie had jumped out of the car and dashed off to see her friends, "will you come with me to the cottage? I want to talk to you."

Neither he nor Hattie had mentioned the Beatrice Milton article, but that didn't mean they hadn't read it. The whole city had read it by now.

The Garretts' cottage in Tuxedo Park was a shingle-style, three-story gray house that looked as if it had emerged from the hillside of its own volition. It had a wrap-around porch and large windows that looked out onto the lake, which glittered as if its surface were made of dimes.

"It's a lovely place," she said.

"Yes. Quaint, isn't it?"

"What did you want to talk to me about, Hugh?"

"I'm sure you know," he said. "Who is this Beatrice Milton person? I thought Mother would have apoplexy when she read that article this morning. Everyone knows that one of our maids is dead. Did you give that woman this information?"

She had a sinking feeling.

"You want to tell me about her?" she asked.

He turned his gaze toward the water where a flock of ducks were floating in the reflection of the sky.

"It *was* you who got her pregnant, wasn't it?" she insisted.

He inhaled deeply and continued to stare out at the lake. Finally he turned to her with a stricken expression and said, "I'm ashamed of myself, Louisa. I have no excuse for my behavior. She was young and pretty and I..." He stopped.

"You took advantage of her," Louisa said. "And now she's dead."

"I didn't mean to hurt her. I didn't mean for anything bad to happen to her."

"Did you love her?" Louisa asked.

"No," he admitted. "I cared for her, but I didn't love her. I was driven by lust. Not love. I should have known better. I did know better. Girls like that. They make themselves available, and one thing leads to another." He saw the look of scorn on her face. "I don't mean to say she was at fault. No, I take full responsibility. She was young and poor and..."

"Then she got pregnant," Louisa said.

"When she asked me for money, I gladly gave it to her. But I had nothing to do with that doctor or her operation," he said.

"You mean, your chauffeur did that of his own initiative?" she asked incredulously.

"Marat has a past. He grew up in one of those gangs, but he's the best mechanic around, and sometimes it doesn't hurt to have someone with some muscle in your service. As a man of wealth, I'm a target for thieves and con men. You should know all about that. Look at what happened to your own father."

"Please leave my father out of this," Louisa said.

"The point is, this is a dangerous world and we must protect ourselves," he said. Then to her surprise he took her hand and continued, "and those we love."

Louisa pulled her hand away and strode to the end of the porch. He followed her and stood close. She could feel the warmth of his body but it was not a pleasant warmth.

"Mother thinks I should marry soon," he said and ran a finger along her sleeve.

What was he suggesting, Louisa wondered with alarm. She turned to face him. "That might not be a bad idea. Do you have anyone in mind?"

He didn't answer. Instead he looked at her with his enveloping blue gaze. She wondered if this was some sort of ploy to keep her quiet. Then to her horror, his face lowered as if to kiss her. She drew back.

"There you are!" Hattie came tromping up the steps just as she had when they were young and there was no getting away from the pesky little sister. "The luncheon will be in a few minutes and they've already started seating people. Come on." For once, Louisa was grateful for the intrusion.

***

Hugh and Hattie had been shuttled off to a table with a former governor and his wife and son, who surely thought that Hattie would be an advantageous match for their son. Louisa, fortunately, was seated at another table. Bustling Italian servers placed plates of squab, ducklings, and roasted quail in front of the guests. More offerings of roast beef and potatoes came by on large platters. Louisa plucked a leaf from a steamed artichoke, dipped it in a glistening sauce and scraped the meat from the bottom of the leaf with her teeth. The silky green flesh of the plant dissolved in her mouth, and she sighed. She was glad to be rid of Hugh and wondered why she'd ever thought it was good idea to ride with him. At least she'd gotten the truth out of him at last. Ellen had been right, yet Louisa couldn't help feeling just a tiny bit sorry for him. Surely, he hadn't intended for the girl to die.

Louisa turned toward a conversation across the table about the upcoming horse race. The summer was all about horse races in Saratoga, the steeplechase at the new Belmont Park, and then the horse show which ended the season in Newport with a fabulous ball. It was an expensive sport but also democratic in that anyone could bet on a horse race. At least they could until that "fool of a governor" made wagering on horses illegal. This is where the conversation had led.

"That man should be handed his walking papers," said an old gentleman seated at her side. A dribble of soup decorated his lapel.

"I don't expect the law will stand for long," Louisa commented.

"No, but now it lets the criminal element in," the man continued in his old patrician voice. "Underground wagers and what not."

"Indeed."

When luncheon was over, Louisa found a quiet spot in the club to write her notes, but Hugh kept intruding on her thoughts. Had he planned to propose to her? The idea was preposterous. They hadn't "courted." And what would she say if he did propose? Could she marry someone who had behaved so dishonorably toward one of his servants? And yet if she did marry Hugh, her financial worries would disappear. Her mother could have the finest care. Suzie could actually be paid a salary. And she'd have all the dresses and hats and gloves she could ever want. She felt a prickling sense of shame for having these thoughts. A girl was dead and a police matron murdered. That was what she needed to focus on. It was one thing to cast aspersions on an anonymous doctor, and quite another to get the goods on him.

As she finished up her notes, she saw a pale Dorothy rush into the ladies' room. She stood up quickly. Something was the matter. She followed her into the luxurious facilities and heard the sounds of retching in one of the small toilet rooms. Fortunately, no one else was around.

"Dorothy? Dorothy?" she asked.

Dorothy grunted from behind the flimsy door. In a moment, she opened the door and leaned against the frame.

"It's called morning sickness," Dorothy explained, wiping her mouth with a handkerchief. "But sometimes it lasts past the morning."

"Morning sickness? I don't understand. Dorothy, are you...?"

Dorothy nodded and said. "I'm getting it taken care of this weekend."

Louisa suppressed a gasp.

"Taken care of?" Louisa asked as it dawned on her what Dorothy meant. "It's dangerous, you know."

"So is having a baby," Dorothy said.

"The Garretts' housemaid died."

"I know. The whole world knows now, thanks to you," Dorothy said. She went over to the sink and rinsed her mouth. "I know who Beatrice Milton is, remember?"

"Will you be using Dr. Swanson?"

"Of course, I will," Dorothy said. "But it won't be in some nasty little surgery somewhere. He'll come to me. I'll have the finest care. Your little diatribe changes nothing."

Louisa looked down at her hands. She felt a compression in her chest, but Dorothy merely yawned and examined herself in the mirror.

"I understand that this doctor was planning to put the Garretts' maid in some sort of brothel when he was done with her operation," Louisa said.

"Oh, heavens, Louisa," Dorothy said. "Stop listening to gossip and innuendo. He's a well-respected man of medicine. You've met him. He's doing a good thing. It's unfortunate about the Garretts' maid. But that was an accident. He explained the whole thing to Mama."

"Your mother knows you're pregnant?"

"Why do you think I'm an only child, Louisa? Honestly, you are so naïve," Dorothy said. It was as if a shock wave passed through Louisa's body. Had Natasha also had abortions? How many?

"When is this operation happening, Dorothy? Perhaps I should be with you," Louisa said.

Dorothy stared at her and seemed to contemplate the idea.

"No, it won't do. Don't worry. I won't be alone," Dorothy said. "My maid, Justine, will be with me."

"At least tell me when and where it's happening," Louisa said. "I'm worried."

"How do I know you won't call the police?" Dorothy said. "You told me yourself you wanted to do more investigative stories."

"The police think that Adele Cummings was killed because she was investigating Dr. Swanson," Louisa said. "And if he is involved in her murder, then he should go to prison."

"If that happens because of you," Dorothy said, "you will incur the wrath of some very powerful people, Louisa."

"I'm sure your mother is upset with me," Louisa admitted.

"She's quite livid," Dorothy responded. She dried her hands on a plush towel and left the room.

Louisa stood frozen to the spot. She was terrified for Dorothy. Everything could change as the result of one wrong decision, she thought. That's all it took. Somehow the horror was so much more real when it involved someone you knew, someone you'd known all your life.

Chapter 34
Ellen

Ellen watched from the sofa as Louisa paced the parlor floor in her lady oxfords.

"What if you do find out?" Ellen asked. "You can't just show up at her abortion as if it's a dinner party. Besides, it's not something you want to see, believe me."

Louisa stopped pacing and sat next to Ellen.

"If I can just confront him after the fact, maybe I can get him to tell me who set that bomb…" Louisa said.

"Do your ears work? Can you even hear what you're saying?" Ellen threw up her hands in exasperation. "That doctor is not going to confess to knowing anything about the bomb. Murder is much worse than abortion, you know."

Louisa leaned back and sighed.

"You're right, but I can't help being worried sick. At least talk to Justine and find out what she knows,"

Louisa said. "What time did you say she usually goes out?"

"During lunch. The lady's maids usually have about thirty minutes of free time while their mistresses eat or go out," Ellen said.

"Then what are we waiting for? It's almost noon now. I'll be nearby to make sure you're safe," Louisa said, standing up and straightening out her pin-striped skirt.

"And what will you do if someone should come after me?" Ellen asked. "Belittle them to death? I'll put on my disguise."

A few minutes later Ellen came downstairs wearing a dark suit with a vest and a homburg hat that Louisa's father had once worn. She followed Louisa outside into the chilly drizzle of the day. Louisa was right — it would take more than her testimony to convict the man. And they were no closer to proving he'd been responsible for Adele's death. They needed to catch him in the act.

***

Ellen waited near the pond in the park. Just a few more days until she was to get on the boat back to Ireland. She shivered. It was cold, and she wasn't sure the French maid would even show up. She gazed over at the skaters on the pond, remembering the day Silvia and Justine had convinced her to try it. She'd felt like a cow, slipping around the ice. When Justine got on the ice, she looked like a ballerina. So graceful with an enormous smile on her foxlike face. She hoped she wasn't wrong about the maid's daily habits. Then she saw her.

"Justine," she said, coming up behind her. Justine turned and stared at her, confused.

"Is that you, Ellen?" Justine asked. She wore a mink collar around her neck — expensive cast offs being one of the benefits of being a lady's maid.

"It is indeed. I am *in cognito*," Ellen said, "hiding from Hugh Garrett."

"I'm so sorry what happened to *pauvre* Silvia," Justine said.

"Thank you," Ellen said.

"And how are you? Where do you work now?" she asked.

She had fabricated a story to tell to Justine but now found she couldn't lie to her. "I'm working with Louisa Delafield, and she needs some information."

"Miss Delafield is in the doghouse right now," Justine said. "Madame Bloodgood is horrified by the article she wrote."

"She had to write it. The doctor who killed Silvia is the same one who murdered that police matron. And now your mistress is going to see him. You know what for," Ellen said in a hushed voice.

Justine's eyes widened.

"I did not know he was the same doctor," she whispered.

"Justine, do you know where and when Miss Dorothy is going to have her operation?" Ellen asked. "Louisa Delafield wants to make sure she will be safe."

Justine looked around at the park and then leaned close.

***

Louisa joined her as she walked away from the pond. They were on a winding walkway, surrounded on either side by bare trees.

"Does she know?" Louisa asked, her hands tucked into a fluffy mink muff.

"It's not happening," Ellen responded.

"What?" Louisa stopped in her tracks. "What do you mean? Is she going to keep the baby?"

Ellen stopped and turned toward her.

"There is no baby. Not anymore."

Louisa looked perplexed.

"She had a miscarriage last night," Ellen said.

"A miscarriage?" Louisa stood still in the middle of a walkway. Louisa heard crying, and turned to see a nurse with a baby carriage passing by them. A mixture of sadness, relief, and disappointment roiled inside her.

"So now, it's over. I'll be getting on the boat to Ireland next week and that will be the end of it," Ellen said.

"No," Louisa said, shaking her head. "No, it won't. Lead me to the servants' entrance of the Bloodgood home. I don't want Natasha to see me."

Ellen stared at Louisa. The tip of her nose was red from the cold, her lips were a little chapped, but her gray eyes shined with excitement. She thought about telling Louisa to forget about it, to go back to writing about tea dances and soirées, but the fact that Louisa did not want to give up sparked a flame of hope in Ellen.

"All right. We'll have to go through the kitchen then," she said.

As they cut through the alley behind the house to get to the servants' entrance, they saw a large black motorcar behind the house.

"Where's Natasha's carriage?" Louisa asked.

"Justine says she sold it. She's got a motorcar now," Ellen said.

Ellen quickly opened the back door and looked inside. An astonished cook watched as Louisa slipped inside and hurried up the servant stairs.

"What's the meaning of this?" she asked Ellen.

"Girl trouble," Ellen said. "Spare a cup of tea?"

The woman gave her a skeptical look and then went back to shoving cloves into the side of a fat ham. Ellen sat on a stool to wait for Louisa and realized wistfully that in a few days' time, she'd be on her way back to a boring life in Galway. No intrigues with Louisa. No hot coffees with Suzie. And no possibility for that which she wanted most.

Chapter 35
Louisa

As they stood side by side on the ferry's second level, the steamer plowing over the bay waters, Louisa looked over at Ellen's profile and thought of those carved women's figureheads on Viking ships.

"I s'pose I'll be getting on a much bigger boat soon enough," Ellen said.

"I know you do not want to go back home," Louisa said.

"Neither do I want to wind up dead or in jail," Ellen said with a shake of her head.

"Tonight we'll get some information from this doctor," Louisa said. "This time we've got a real detective with us. He'll have to answer to us." She looked back at the seating area where Paddy O'Neil waited out the crossing.

"Paddy can be pretty convincing, I'm sure," Ellen said with a slight smile. "A true Galway lad."

Louisa looked out at the water. Blue slivers of light appeared and disappeared as the choppy waves jostled over each other. The wind chilled her hands. The steamer moved fast and soon the slip at Newport was visible. Louisa hoped Dorothy had been true to her word and not let the doctor know about her miscarriage. If this scheme should fail, they would not get another chance.

The detective emerged from the inside of the ferry and joined them. He was a robust man with black hair and a ruddy complexion.

"Ready, ladies?" he asked. "Do you know your parts?"

"We do, Sir Galahad," Ellen said. "Mine is to stay out of sight."

"And mine is to..." Louisa didn't finish. She couldn't bear to describe what she was willing to do.

When the ferry landed, they walked into the quaint little town, a relic of colonial days. Louisa suggested they go to the inn and rent bicycles.

"But I've never ridden before," Ellen said.

"It's not hard," Louisa told her.

The innkeeper was surprised to see them.

"Not much business this time of year," he said. He took them out to a carriage house in the back and pointed out three sturdy bicycles.

There were outfits designed for riding bikes but of course neither Louisa nor Ellen had thought to wear one. So Louisa showed Ellen how to hike her skirt just high enough to allow her to pedal. Then Paddy had to hold onto Ellen and run alongside her while she tried not to fall. It took several tries but finally Ellen was able to wobble along the road with them.

"Fun, isn't it?" Louisa said.

"It will be if I don't break my neck," Ellen answered.

Louisa laughed and for a moment, she forgot about their dreadful mission.

She guided them along the main road that cut down the narrow island. The Bloodgood mansion was one of the furthest houses out. It was March, and there were still a few patches of snow on the wide lawns. Fortunately the wind was behind them and helped rather than hindered the journey.

About halfway down the island, they came upon a granite house. Louisa looked at the great magnolia tree — even bigger than she remembered — and the expansive porch facing the roadway. As they passed she gazed across the green expanse of lawn and vividly remembered playing hide and go seek while fireflies flashed in the dark. She thought of an eight-year-old fairy princess named Dorothy, who'd fallen and scraped her knees and torn her dress. Louisa, at ten, had felt so much older than little Dorothy. She'd taken her inside to the kitchen and washed off the girl's knees. Of course, she'd had no idea that soon her childhood would be demolished forever. She elected not to tell Ellen and Paddy that this was the house her parents had owned and that she had spent every summer of her childhood there. Let the past be, she thought.

After another mile they turned down the driveway of the Bloodgoods' house. The home, a large rambling stone house with Gothic turrets, loomed at the end of the long driveway. It was not nearly as grand as Vanderbilt's Breakers, but nothing short of a palace would be.

Paddy whistled as they approached.

"This is their *cottage*?" he asked.

"And they only use it a few months of the year," Louisa said. "All these houses sit here empty all year long until summer comes."

"Let's hide these bikes and take up our positions," he said. "He'll probably be coming on the late ferry."

"Dorothy said that he'd intended to stay the night to make sure she was all right after the procedure," Louisa said. She remembered how pale Dorothy had been when she'd snuck upstairs and into her room. She hadn't the energy to be surprised to see Louisa. When Louisa asked her not to cancel the appointment, stressing the importance of finding the killer of Adele Cummings, Dorothy had shrugged and said, fine.

Ellen snorted.

"Sure, he would look after the heiress, but the servant he sends off to a brothel or would have if he hadn't killed her," she said bitterly. Louisa didn't need to tell her it was the way of the world. The lives of rich women mattered. The lives of poor women meant nothing at all — except to the people who loved them.

Louisa used the key that Dorothy had provided to let them in the front door. Inside the air was cold and stuffy. The furniture was covered with white sheets.

Paddy craned his neck to look at the high carved ceiling.

"I imagine it's pretty grand when they're all here, having their balls and such," he said.

Louisa looked around and remembered the glittering chandeliers, the handsome waiters with trays of glasses, filled with bubbly liquid, and the gowns, the beautiful flowing gowns of the women who bought all their clothes in Paris.

"It was indeed glamorous and exciting back at the turn of the century. They reveled in their wealth. It's not much different now," she said. Since she'd begun working as a society writer, she'd come to Newport the past two summers to cover Mrs. Belmont's annual picnic and Mrs. Fish's extravagant dinner parties, but it wasn't the same as being one of them. She might as well have been one of the servants. She'd been fooling herself, believing that proximity equated anything at all. She was there to do a job and nothing else.

"Let's go upstairs and find a room with a fireplace," Ellen said. "I'll get a fire going. Would you like some tea, too? I'm sure I can find some."

"No," Louisa said. She was too antsy for tea.

They chose a large guest bedroom at the front of the house with a high antique four-poster and a fireplace. Ellen brought some wood up from the kitchen and built a roaring fire.

Then they waited. Ellen and Paddy played a game of gin rummy, and Louisa doodled on her notepad. Paddy got hungry and went downstairs. He came back up with a jar of preserves and a tin of crackers.

"A little stale," he said, munching on one of the crackers, "but not too bad."

"Shh," Ellen said. "Do you hear that?"

Louisa heard the sound of tires on gravel. A car door slammed.

Ellen peeked out the window and said, "He came in a cab."

Paddy grabbed a jacket they'd nicked from the butler's pantry. "I'll go let him in. You two get in your places."

Ellen stepped into the shadows while Louisa put on the hat with the veil and lay down on the bed, her face turned away from the bedroom door. Louisa felt a fluttering inside her lower torso. Her nerves tingled, and she felt her skin flush. She clenched her fists in an effort to keep still.

"I'm nervous," she whispered.

"Shhh," Ellen said. "Paddy won't let him harm you."

Footsteps sounded in the hallway. The door opened.

"Your patient is right there, sir," Paddy said.

Louisa didn't dare turn to look at them but she heard the footsteps approach and felt something heavy land on the bed. She glanced down and saw a medicine bag.

"Good evening, Miss Bloodgood," the doctor said in an unctuous voice. "There's no need to be nervous." He turned to Paddy and asked, "Is her lady's maid here?"

"She's sitting in the corner should she be needed," Paddy said.

"Excellent," the doctor said. Then he coughed rather violently. "Sorry. I seem to have something caught in my throat. Could you ask the maid to get me some water and could you pull that table over here?"

Louisa inhaled sharply. It was all she could do not to bolt upright and run from the room. She trembled at the thought of this man touching her.

"I'll do it," Paddy volunteered. He poured a glass of water from a crystal decanter on the table and gave it to the doctor. Then he dragged the writing desk to the bedside and took the bag from the bed and placed it on the desk.

The doctor took out his instruments and laid them on a towel.

"Only one use for these, I'm supposing," Paddy said. Louisa glanced over at him through her veil. He was being too bold for a "butler."

"Yes," the doctor sounded peevish. She hoped he didn't yet suspect a ruse. "Hand me that mask and canister," the doctor said, intent on getting the job done and getting his money. "We must make sure that Miss Bloodgood feels no discomfort."

"Is that safe?" Ellen piped up from the corner.

"Perfectly," the doctor said. "But we shall administer it slowly to make sure she has no reaction to it. I thought you were a French girl."

"Oui," Ellen said. "I am."

He must suspect something isn't right, Louisa thought, but he's ignoring it. Anticipation built inside her. The doctor came around the bed.

"My dear, I'm afraid I must see your face if I'm to give you the ether," he said and pulled the veil from Louisa's face. He stared for a moment, the blood draining from his face. Then he jumped back. "You!"

Louisa sat up, and Ellen stepped out of the shadows.

"Hello, Dr. Swanson," Louisa said.

The man's face glistened with sweat as he looked back and forth at them. He grabbed his bag and began thrusting the instruments inside.

"I haven't done anything. I know the law," he said. "You can't arrest me."

"Technically, you're right," Paddy said, locking the bedroom door. "But when we get in court and Miss Malloy testifies that she saw you perform an abortion on Silvia Ricci and then when Miss Delafield and I describe your visit tonight along with your instruments, I think a jury will be inclined to believe you have broken the law."

Louisa rose from the bed and approached him. His mustache quivered in fear and indignation, and she smelled brandy on his breath.

"Ask him where his 'orderlies' are tonight," Ellen said.

"Swanson, if you were to give me information leading to the arrest of whoever murdered Adele Cummings on your behalf, you will have a more favorable outcome," Paddy said.

The doctor licked his lip. His face was livid. He coughed again and then gagged. Louisa looked at Paddy. Was he faking an illness, she wondered.

The doctor dropped his bag and sat down in an armchair by the window.

"Why couldn't you have left me alone?" he asked. "I help women. My hospital has saved countless lives of poor women."

"All the while enriching yourself," Ellen interjected. "And how many of 'em do you send off to the brothels?"

Louisa put a hand on her arm. No need to accuse him now. They needed to get him to talk.

"Dr. Swanson, do you know who planted the bomb that killed Adele Cummings?"

He looked up at her as if about to say something, but then he blew out his cheeks and coughed and gagged again. He groaned and bent over. Louisa peered at him. He looked genuinely sick.

"Stop stalling," Paddy growled. "You're lucky this lady here didn't leak your name to the boys on the force. They're not happy with whoever it was got our police matron killed."

The doctor, still bent over, looked up at them, his face twisted into a grimace.

"I...," he tried to say something. White flecks of foam had gathered on his lips.

Louisa's concern turned to panic.

"My God," she gasped. "He's dying!"

Paddy grabbed the man by the shoulders and shook him, but the gagging continued as the man's desperate wide eyes filled with tears. He groaned and crumpled to the floor.

The three of them stood helplessly as the man trembled and gurgled and then fell silent. Paddy knelt close to the body and sniffed.

"Smells like bitter almond," he said. "Cyanide."

"How...?" Louisa asked.

"They put it in rat poison," Paddy said. "You can find it anywhere."

"How long does it take to work?" she asked.

"A few hours," he said. "He must have taken it while he was still in New York."

"Then you think he took it intentionally?" she asked. "He didn't seem to know what was happening."

"Suicide? I doubt it," Paddy agreed. "Someone could have given it to him in a drink. It's easy enough to disguise."

"Who would have known he would be talking to us?" Louisa wondered. She gazed down at the dead man, curled on his side, his hands clenched in agony, the white flecks like snow on his chin. She'd never seen a dead man before. He didn't look peaceful at all.

A Woman's View: A Doctor's Demise

---

by Beatrice Milton

NEW YORK, Feb. 28, 1913, Special to *The Ledger* – Dr. Alan Swanson, founder of the Charity Hospital for Women, died yesterday of cyanide poisoning.

Detective Paddy O'Neil of the New York City Police Department said the doctor was at a home in Newport, Rhode Island, where Swanson believed he was going to perform an operation on a woman to prevent her from having an unwanted baby. In reality, the police had set a trap for the doctor in order to question him regarding the murder of one of their own, Police Matron Adele Cummings, who died in a townhouse bombing while conducting her own investigation of the doctor.

Swanson is also suspected of performing the illegal operation on the housemaid of a respected society family. She subsequently died.

A member of one of New York's families gave permission to use the Newport cottage for the ruse.

The doctor had fooled police thus far because he is a respected philanthropist. Unfortunately, before the detective could question him, Dr. Swanson succumbed to poisoning. The police suspect foul play.

This is sad news for the many society women who supported Dr. Swanson's charitable endeavors. The city has plans to take over the hospital and to continue to provide services for poor women.

Chapter 36

Louisa

Louisa sat in front of Virgil Thorn's desk and twiddled her thumbs while she waited for him to come in to his office. He'd told her to be here at 10:00 sharp and he wasn't here. A few minutes later, the door opened, and he entered, looking at the watch on his on his chain. No apology, of course.

"Now, you're not only writing about crimes, you're involved in them?" he asked, skirting his desk to sit behind it.

"I wasn't the one who killed the man," she said.

He grunted.

"I'm late because I was upstairs with our attorney," he said.

"Oh no," Louisa said. "We aren't being sued, are we? Nothing I reported was libelous."

He looked over his spectacles at her. He seemed to be enjoying her consternation.

"No, Miss Delafield. We aren't being sued — yet," he said. "I was with the attorney going over your contract."

"What contract?" She didn't remember signing a contract, but perhaps she had signed something when the paper first hired her. He was probably making sure it was all right to fire her.

"Your contract with the American Women's News Syndicate," he said and pushed a piece of paper toward her. "They liked your Princess of Nowhere story. Apparently they don't mind controversy. In fact, I think they court it."

She stared down at the piece of paper. It certainly looked like some sort of legal document.

"*The Ledger*, of course, has exclusive New York rights to all your material, but the syndicate will distribute a weekly column of general interest to women to their syndicate of papers around the country," he said, tapping the page with a pen.

Louisa heard the words he was saying, but she was having trouble processing the information. A weekly column. General interest. She wasn't sure how this had happened.

"I'll still write about New York Society for *The Ledger*, won't I?" she asked.

"Yes, yes," he said in his weary, dismissive way. "Thursday through Sunday. That should be enough to cover their dreary social lives."

Louisa read the contract.

"You sent my stories to them?" she asked.

"No, they contacted me," he said. "Is the payment satisfactory?"

Louisa caught her breath when she saw the figure but reined in her excitement.

"That's fine," she said. "I still think we should expand the women's section. At least for Saturday."

Thorn raised an eyebrow.

"Go home and celebrate, Delafield," he said. "Now, there's no need for you to write any more Beatrice Milton muckraking stories. You can leave that to the gents."

"But I don't want to stop," she said.

"Miss Delafield, you'll hardly have time to go chasing down doctors. This will keep you busy and out of trouble," he said.

She supposed he was right. The doctor was dead now. She wasn't sure what she had accomplished. But it didn't matter now, did it? She'd have a good salary with the syndicated work, and wouldn't have to worry about offending her society connections anymore. It was wonderful news. And yet she felt bereft.

***

Louisa placed an amaretto cheese cake from a bakery in Little Italy on the dining room table and beamed at Suzie and her mother, who was wearing some paste jewelry that Louisa had purchased when they'd had to sell her real jewels.

"Oh my," Anna said, peering at the cake. "Is it my birthday?" she joked. Of course, she knew it wasn't her birthday. Her mind might wander at times, but she wasn't senile.

"If you want it to be, Mother," Louisa said. "I also bought some pretty fabric. I thought Suzie might make a new dress for you." Anna gasped in delight.

Louisa turned to Suzie. "Where's Ellen? Is dinner ready?"

Suzie stared at the cake and asked, "What is this for?"

Louisa said, "To celebrate."

"Celebrate what?" Ellen asked, coming into the room.

"I am now a syndicated columnist in addition to my regular columns for *The Ledger*," Louisa said.

"What about Beatrice Milton?" Ellen asked.

"Beatrice may have to retire," Louisa said.

"Let's have some cake," Anna said.

"Dinner first," Louisa said and took some plates from the sideboard while Suzie went to the kitchen and brought back a steaming tureen of beef stew. As Louisa told them about her contract, Suzie couldn't stop beaming.

"I knew you could do it," she said, standing by the table.

"Suzie, sit down with us, please. Mother won't mind," Louisa said.

"Who says?" Anna asked.

"I do. The family money is all gone, and I'm the bread winner now," Louisa said. Anna probably wanted Suzie to sit with them as well, but someone had to give both of them the permission to go against propriety.

"I'm not sure about this," Suzie said.

"This charade has gone on long enough, Suzie. Ellen and I sit with you at the kitchen table often enough. The only reason you never eat with us in the dining room is because all these years we've been trying to pretend to Mother that she's the elegant lady of means she always was. Maybe now that the situation is not so dire, we can all stop pretending," Louisa said.

"Except when company comes," Anna said.

"Which is never," Louisa said.

Suzie sat down at the table and put a linen napkin in her lap.

"I don't mind if I do," she said.

"We can finally go back to paying you a salary," Louisa said to Suzie. She looked over at Ellen.

"I wish you would stay here in America."

"And I wish you'd keep writing real news stories," Ellen said.

"After everything we've been through...?" Louisa asked. "Besides, how could I write those stories without you around?"

"You've got a point," Ellen said. "As long as Mrs. Garrett swears I stole her earrings, I wouldn't have a moment's peace. I don't like the idea of being locked up. And I got some news today. I cabled the resort at Salt Hill to see if they had any year-round positions. There's a position for housemaid that's mine for the asking."

"Nothing wrong with being a housemaid," Suzie said.

Louisa forced a smile.

"Nothing at all," she said. Ellen didn't look the least bit thrilled to go home, job or no job. Louisa wished there was something she could do, some way to persuade the Garretts to give up this vendetta against Ellen. She still didn't believe that Hugh knew of the doctor's plans for Silvia after the operation. She couldn't believe the worst of him, but Amelia was another matter.

"Amelia and I were never friends," Anna said, spooning the last of her stew. "She's not a kind woman. Can we have some cake now?"

"You said something to me one night at the top of the stairs, Mrs. Delafield," Ellen said. "Do you remember? It was some kind of warning about the Garretts."

"Did I?" the old woman said. "I don't remember."

Suzie took up a knife and sliced through the cheesecake. Thick icing clung to the knife as she extracted it.

Louisa could smell the rich amaretto. Anna grinned in delight as Suzie handed her a plate.

Then the doorbell rang. The four of them looked at each other.

"I'll go see who it is," Suzie said and handed the knife to Ellen, who proceeded to partition the cake and put slices on delicate china dessert plates.

A moment later Suzie came back in the room.

"It's Miss Hattie Garrett," she said in a whisper.

"Hattie?" Louisa asked in surprise. "To see me?"

"No," Suzie said, "to see Ellen."

Ellen stopped with her fork in mid-air, and for a moment no one knew what to do.

"I suppose we should invite her in for some cake," Louisa said finally. She was mortified for anyone from society to see the inside of her shabby little house, but it was too late now.

Suzie fetched Hattie from the foyer.

"That looks scrumptious," Hattie said, bustling in. She sat down at the seat where Suzie had been sitting as if she came to visit every day. "Your house is precious, Louisa. It's small, but I see you've still got some of your nice furniture from when you were rich. Isn't this table a Duncan Phyfe?" she asked, running a hand over the polished mahogany. Without waiting for a response, she continued, "I wouldn't mind living in a house like this, but I don't suppose I ever will. I'll get stuck in some gargantuan palace with a bunch of servants who hate me. Ellen, what happened to your hair? It's so short. It looks nice though." She stopped chattering long enough to take a bite. "Oh my. This cake is delicious." Hattie licked some icing from her lips.

Suzie picked up the tureen of leftover stew and stepped into the kitchen.

"Suzie said you wanted to see me?" Ellen asked.

Hattie toyed with her fork and glanced around the room.

"I... Well, I've run away from home," she said.

Louisa stopped eating her cake in mid-chew, lest she choke on it.

"What?" Anna practically shrieked.

"Oh, hello, Mrs. Delafield. You're looking quite lovely," Hattie said, remembering her manners. "My mother sends her regards."

"How can your mother send her regards, Hattie, if you've run away from home?" Louisa asked, wondering if they would be tarred and feathered by the ladies of the Colony Club for harboring a fugitive from society.

"I haven't run away for long. They don't even know I'm gone yet, but you see, the women's march in Washington is tomorrow, and I'm dying to go," Hattie said and then looked at each of them in turn as if expecting applause.

Instead, a stunned silence followed this pronouncement. Then Anna cleared her throat.

"Well, she is eighteen," Anna said. "But she cannot go unchaperoned. You'll have to go with her, Louisa."

"Not I," Louisa said. "I have work to do. I have this new column..."

"Actually, I was hoping that Ellen would come with me," Hattie said. She clasped Ellen's hand and continued, "I've missed you. Say you'll come with me. There's a bus leaving tonight. We'll get there in the morning and we'll march. Then we'll be back late tomorrow night."

"Ellen can't go with you. She has to get on a boat back to Ireland, thanks to your mother," Louisa said.

"I've got a couple more days," Ellen said. "And I'd like to see as much of this fine country as I can before I have to leave. I'll be happy to go with you, Miss Hattie."

"I think you better just call me Hattie, or people will think I'm snobbish," Hattie said. "May I have another piece of cake?"

Louisa sliced a piece of cake and put it on Hattie's plate. Perhaps it was a good idea for Ellen to get out of town for her last few hours in America. After the doctor's murder, Louisa felt increasingly uneasy. His killer was still out there, and the two hoodlums were still out there looking for Ellen.

"Your mother will be out for blood if she finds out," Anna said and laughed harder than Louisa had seen her laugh in years.

After Hattie and Ellen left, Louisa sat in the parlor with her feet on the ottoman while her mother dozed in her chair and Suzie read a book. Louisa wondered what her next step should be. She'd achieved her aim, after all. She had a syndicated column now and the increased pay would make a world of difference. The fire crackled and hissed and a chunk of wood fell and disintegrated into ash. It sounded like women whispering.

No, she realized, she hadn't really achieved her aim. Ellen wasn't free to stay in America and they never did learn who set the bomb that killed Adele Cummings. She didn't believe for a minute the doctor set that bomb himself. A flame shot up and sent sparks up the chimney. She'd never even gone to see the ruined house, she realized. If she were a proper journalist, she'd at least look at the scene of the crime.

Chapter 37
Ellen

Hattie had bribed Marat to take them to Greenwich Village to catch the bus. Ellen didn't like being in the car with him and couldn't help thinking of the last and only other time she'd been in this car, when she was holding the hand of poor terrified Silvia. He, on the other hand, didn't seem bothered at all.

"Hattie," Ellen asked. "You don't believe your Ma, do you? You don't think I stole those earrings?"

"Of course not," Hattie said. "Mama's just mad at Hugh for what he did with that servant girl and she's taking it out on you. Also, I think they want to get rid of you because you know the ugly truth."

Hattie's frankness caught Ellen off guard.

"Then why don't they send Marat back wherever he came from?" Ellen asked, pointing a finger at the chauffeur.

"Because I don't go blabbing their business to a newspaper writer," he said.

"Also, he used to be a gangster," Hattie whispered. "I think Hugh's a little frightened of him."

"Well, I'm not afraid of him," Ellen muttered, though, in fact, she wouldn't want to meet the big man in a dark alley.

"Drop us off here, Marat," Hattie said. "I don't want to look too conspicuous."

Marat stopped at a corner, and let them out of the car. Hattie got out first and Ellen came after her. As she did so, Marat clasped her arm.

"Nice hat," he said.

Ellen glared at him. She had borrowed a red felt hat with a gold band around it from Louisa before she left. He grinned at her, and she wondered what mischief he had in mind. She jerked her arm away from him and said, "The sooner I'm away from you the better."

***

The women waiting for the bus were not the sort of women Hattie Garrett normally consorted with, and Ellen worried she might feel out of her element. They were working women, factory girls, mostly, a few who looked like secretaries, clerks, or telephone operators, and two who were Negro domestic workers.

Ellen and Hattie were among the last to get on the bus. The women fell silent and stared at Hattie's fine dress, her perfect hair, and her soft white hands, which had never worked at anything more difficult than embroidery. However, if there was any hostility toward her, Hattie was oblivious.

They found a seat together close to the back. Ellen was by the window and wished it were daytime so she could see the scenery as they drove south, but at least she could lean her head against it and perhaps get some sleep. An absurd notion she realized, for as soon as they were seated, Hattie piped up in her high-pitched hoity-toity voice.

"Isn't this exciting, Ellen? I wonder if Dorothy will be at the march. So many of our young society women including the debs are passionate about voting." Then she giggled. "It's quite fashionable, you know."

Ellen wanted to shrink into herself as Hattie nattered on. She could feel the women around them simmering.

Finally one of them muttered, "Why do these society dames even care? They've got everything they could ever want."

Hattie looked at Ellen with a perplexed look. Ellen shook her head. Hattie shrugged and took a small pouch from her bag. The bus hadn't moved yet, and the driver got out to check the tires.

"Anybody want a Life Saver?" she asked. "They're peppermint."

Several women glanced around and then one after the other held out their hands. Like any wealthy person, Hattie knew the way to win over others: bribery.

"Did you know that women have been allowed to vote in Australia since the 1890s?" she asked, sticking one of the small round candies in her mouth.

"We can't vote in Ireland. A woman can't even divorce in Ireland," Ellen answered.

"Well, we'll get the vote here and then we'll go kick some Irish arses," said a blond woman across the aisle in a seat by herself. Hattie laughed a bit too loudly.

They were all seated on the bus, nice and cozy. The driver had come back on board and was just about to shut the door when a voice cried out, "Wait for me. Please! Wait for me."

Ellen glanced out the window and saw a large chauffeur-driven motorcar in the street. For heaven's sake, if the latecomer could afford a car like that, she didn't need to ride the bus with commoners, Ellen thought, unless like Hattie she was defying some family edict.

"Lordy, it's another loaded dame, come to ride the bus," the woman behind Ellen muttered as the rich woman climbed the steps into the bus.

The driver shut the door behind her and didn't wait for her to find a seat before lurching onto the road. The woman — tall with a narrow face, a prominent Roman nose, and pale arched eyebrows — fell into a seat next to the blond woman and gasped for breath. Her large eyes looked about in wonder.

"Hello," Hattie said, thrilled to see one of her own kind. "I'm Hattie Garrett." She held out her hand, and the woman took it.

"Hester French," she said. Then she turned and introduced herself to every other woman around her.

Ellen felt a ripple of awe as the woman reached across Hattie and took Ellen's hand.

"Do I know you?" she said, gazing into Ellen's eyes and holding Ellen's hand for a moment longer than customary.

Ellen shook her head, but they had seen each other before. This was the woman from the teahouse.

"You look so familiar," Hester said. Her voice was warm and rich like creamy coffee, and Ellen could barely breathe. "What did you say your name was?"

Hattie watched the interaction curiously.

"I'm Ellen Malloy," she said, nodding toward Hattie. "I'm a friend of Miss Garrett, here."

Hattie sat up a little taller and seemed pleased that Ellen didn't mention she was actually her former servant. Maybe she enjoyed pretending to be a commoner for a change.

The woman was dressed plainly, but the material was high quality, Ellen knew that much. She glanced down at the woman's patent leather boots. They were handsome all right and not cheap. She recognized the Louis XVI heels from a pair that Hattie had owned.

"You're from Ireland," Hester said to Ellen and her large mouth formed the loveliest smile Ellen had ever seen.

"How perceptive of you," Ellen answered, which brought forth a few giggles from the women in the vicinity. Ellen didn't mean to be rude, but she was nervous and she hated feeling this way. She both wanted and didn't want the woman's attention.

"My brother-in-law's family is from Ulster," Hester continued, ignoring the slight.

"There's troubles up there," Ellen said.

"So I've heard," Hester said. "My brother-in-law came here as a child. He was the son of a street sweeper. Now he's the president of a company that makes train cars."

"I know who you are," Hattie suddenly said. "Your brother-in-law is the president of the French Steel Spring Company. Weren't he and your sister engaged for seven years? That's what I heard. He had to work his way up the company so that he could give her the lifestyle she was accustomed to."

"That's us," Hester said.

"And you're from Pittsburgh. That's why we don't know each other," Hattie said. She seemed relieved to have solved the mystery of this woman. "Ellen, switch seats with me. I want to lean against the window and get some sleep."

Ellen did as she was told. She was too used to taking orders from Hattie to stop now, and also she wanted to be closer to Hester French.

"You're not the only one from a fine family," Ellen said. "My father was once a guest of the Crown."

"That's impressive," Hester said.

"When an Irishman is a guest of the Crown," Ellen said, "it means the Brits've thrown him in gaol for having a bit of spine."

The women around them burst into laughter. Hester laughed as well. She was a good sport, and Ellen settled back in her seat, happier than she'd been in a long time. Then she remembered. She would be on a boat back to Ireland in two days' time, and the happiness faded.

The bus ride was dreadful, jolting and stifling even though it was early March. Women had brought all sorts of food with them, and the smells of various meats and cheeses wrapped in paper flowed through the interior of the bus, not to mention a woman in front of them who constantly passed wind.

The trip took hours, and with a bus full of women, more than a few stops were necessary for them to go into the woods by the road to do their business. She'd never imagined she'd actually get to see so much of America. It was still winter-grey with bare spindly trees and some evergreens, but it was starkly beautiful. She realized she was falling in love with this wild place where anything seemed possible. She looked over at Hester at the same moment that Hester looked at her. Their eyes locked and held for a minute before Ellen nervously looked away.

When the bus pulled into the city, the streets were clogged with thousands of women demonstrators and even more thousands of men.

"Tomorrow is the inauguration of Woodrow Wilson," Hester said, leaning toward Ellen as they staggered off the bus. "She timed it perfectly."

"Who?"

"Inez Milholland!" another woman interjected. "You don't know anything about any of this, do you?"

"No," Ellen said, gazing around at the unfamiliar street. "I'm not even a citizen. Why should I care about suffrage?"

"Well, you're a suffragist now whether you like it or not," Hattie blurted out.

As she followed the women from the bus, she felt a tingling at the back of her neck. She turned and saw a man in a flat cap staring at her. He wore a checkered jacket and had a white scar cutting from the corner of his eye to the corner of his mouth, where a cigarette was lodged. Ellen shuddered. She knew he was dangerous. Perhaps this was not such a good idea.

The women from the bus surged forward, and a loud murmur arose from the crowd. The crowds of men were mostly blotto, judging from the sour smell of alcohol and urine.

"Look," Hester said and pointed. The crowd moved backward, and someone stepped on Ellen's toe. Ellen angrily shoved back, but then stopped moving as she saw what looked like a queen riding a huge white horse.

"That's her," Hattie squealed. "That's Inez."

Ellen lost her tongue as she stared at the dark-haired woman in the cape riding past them, a golden tiara on her head. She was magnificent! Then she was gone from sight.

"All right, ladies. You're representing the New York contingent. All the states are lining up in alphabetical order. Meet by the Peace Monument," an officious woman announced.

A large contingent of women wearing caps and gowns mingled at the front of the parade with banners for Bryn Mawr, Vassar, and Wellesley.

"The college women," Hester said.

For a moment, Ellen thought of Louisa, and remembered that just before they left the house, Louisa had asked her to take notes for her.

"It's quite newsworthy. I wish I could go," she'd said.

All her notes would have to be taken in her head, but Ellen had no doubt she'd remember every moment of this day for a long time to come.

The familiar city smell of horse dung rose from the streets. The air was a touch warmer than New York had been but still chilly. The buildings were squat. Washington might be Manhattan's genteel maiden aunt. A pretty iron balcony hung above a shop door, and for a moment Ellen was struck with a sense of homesickness. The scene reminded her of Dublin, which she had visited as a child.

They came to two floats, one for Norway and one for Finland, on which pretty young women stood, dressed all in white, holding flowers. Ellen's mouth gaped. She'd not thought of her own sex as capable of pulling off such a daunting undertaking. Floats, musicians, costumes, women on horseback, banners, all of it.

As she joined the New York delegation, Ellen sensed the cautious optimism of the New York clan. They were finally assembled on New Jersey Avenue next to the Public Health Building. The parade marshals bustled around telling them where to go and passing out sashes. Each state had its own banner. A middle-aged woman and a boy, who looked to be about eight, held up both ends of the Ohio banner behind them.

"Ladies, we'll be marching down Pennsylvania Avenue to the White House. Be careful, as there will be large crowds due to the inauguration tomorrow. But we have been promised police protection," the New York marshal assured them. Hattie found a few of her society friends at the front of the New Yorkers, but Hester stayed in the back with Ellen.

"Why aren't you up there with the society girls?" Ellen asked.

"Didn't you hear what your friend Hattie said? My sister and I are from Pittsburgh. We're not old New York money even though we have as much as any of them. So we're not accepted into their society. It drives my sister crazy. I couldn't care less," she said.

"You are full of surprises," Ellen said.

Then the march began. A band at the front played a rousing march. The women stood four across and walked steadily up the broad avenue along the streetcar tracks toward a domed building. Alongside the marchers, crowds lined up behind a wire cable. Ellen marched shoulder to shoulder with her delegation behind Inez Milholland, who could have been Joan of Arc. They were too far back to see her, but just knowing she was there seemed to inspire this army of women. They hadn't gone far when the march simply stopped. An elderly woman leaned on her cane for support. They stood near a large building with a sign for the New Occidental Hotel that advertised an "electric grill room." Ellen looked around, wondering why they were stopped.

"What's going on?" a voice cried out.

"What's happening?"

"Why are we stopped?"

Bodies pressed around her. Word came back from the front lines that the spectators were no longer held back by the wire cables. They came in so thick that the procession could not pass. Ellen stared at the burgeoning numbers of watchers — mostly men, a sea of brown suits.

"Go home and make supper!" a man shouted, his mouth twisted in rage.

Foot by foot the woman moved forward, but the crowd grew thicker with every block. The women, who were walking four to a line, shrank together, shoulders touching. Men cat-called and laughed. The press of bodies was suffocating.

"Where are the police?" Hester asked.

"They're not doing anything," an angry woman yelled.

Sure enough, a policeman stood at the edge of the crowd with his arms crossed, laughing with the men who shook their fists and hollered at the marching women.

"You need a man to teach you how to be a woman? I'll teach you," a young man screamed at them with a hideous leer on his face.

Suddenly they surged forward, and someone shoved her hard from behind. She dropped her sign, wheeled around ready to fight, and saw a phalanx of men, laughing and jeering and pushing the other women back. Ellen was trapped like a hunted fox, surrounded by baying hounds.

"I'll show you what a woman's meant for," a pug-ugly man said, spewing rancid breath into her face. She threw a punch toward him but another man grabbed her hand and pulled. A man with a cap pulled low over his forehead pushed through the crowd of men and glared at her. She saw the scar and the checkered jacket and knew he had come for her. He wasn't drunk like the other men, and his pale eyes were filled with malevolent intent. A knife blade flashed in his hand. She stepped back, tripped, and fell to the ground. The man came closer, looming over her. Her legs got tangled in her skirt as she flailed on the ground, but she rolled away as he jabbed the knife toward her.

All of a sudden, the man yowled. A cane sliced through the air and landed on the back of his skull again and again. He turned, and all Ellen could see in the melée was an elegant patent leather boot with a Louis XVI heel kicking him in the arse as he ran away. Then Hester reached for her. Ellen grabbed her hand, felt the strength in the bones, the firm flesh, and something like sunlight breaking through clouds. She rose to her feet as other women shouted and beat back the men who had surrounded her. Hester returned the cane to an older woman who stood by, cheering.

"Thank you," she said, looking into Hester's glittering eyes. Someone from behind pushed her along, and they were marching again, shoulder to shoulder, Hester by her side. She glanced around. The man with the scar was gone. She kept looking behind her, but didn't see him. She remembered the look Marat had given her as he let her out of the car, the reference to her hat. He must have sent the man after her. It would be easy to get here before the bus by car, or perhaps they called a local thug. Apparently, Hugh Garrett couldn't just wait for her to leave the country.

She allowed herself to be swallowed by the crowd. Two hours passed with men jeering at them, the police standing about, either bored or mildly entertained, and a few Boy Scouts with staves trying to keep the crowds back to let the marchers through. One man stuck out his foot and tripped a red-faced elderly woman, knocking her down to the ground, but she got back up and wiped off her knees, then continued marching. A drunk man fell into the New Jersey contingent and had to be dragged out. Another man rushed up to one of the marshals and ripped the sash from her chest. A woman in the crowd screamed that her children were missing. Someone threw a bottle that burst into glass at their feet and Ellen leapt in surprise.

"Aren't you afraid?" Ellen asked Hester as the procession plowed through the crowd, thinking that someone from Hester's background would surely never willingly put herself in such a situation.

"This only means we're making a difference. It's time, don't you see? For sixty years we've been fighting. No one gives up power without a fight." Hester's hair had become disheveled; dark strands fell from beneath her hat. She looked exultant.

Then the cavalry came — men on horseback, edging back the crowd, quelling the insanity. But why was it so insane, Ellen wondered. Why was it insane to expect respect, dignity, and even equality? Then again, if you had what men had, would you ever give that up? She decided it must be all tied up with money. Everything was about money and the power to keep it.

Then the parade was over. Weariness pulled at every muscle in Ellen's body. Though the threat of violence had dissipated, Ellen would never forget that leering tunnel of men and that man with the scar that cut across his cheek. She shuddered. She would not be safe in this country, no matter where she went. She would have to leave. Then she remembered that jolt of electricity that ran up her arm and straight into her heart when she'd felt the warm, soft skin of Hester's palm. Her heart grew so heavy she could barely lift it.

Chapter 38
Louisa

It was after five when Louisa left the newspaper. She had spent the afternoon digging through her archives to find material that would be appropriate for her new syndicated column. She found an article on growing orchids, one on hat fashions, and one on the etiquette of jewelry.

She glanced out the window and realized that the afternoon would soon turn to evening and she'd better hurry.

The walk to Greenwich Village wasn't far. Soon she was knocking at the door of Mrs. Cummings, Adele's mother-in-law. She wanted to say she was sorry that she hadn't been able to find out anything about Adele's killer, and also she hoped to get the address of the bombed townhouse. Captain Tunney had declined to give her the information, and Billy didn't have it in his notes.

"You should drop the matter," Captain Tunney had said when she'd called on him that morning. "After what happened to Swanson, it's obvious you could get yourself killed."

The door opened, and Mrs. Cummings stared at Louisa a moment before remembering who she was.

"Do come in, Miss Delafield," she said. "I've gotten so many various and sundry callers since Adele's death, I can't keep up. Would you like some tea?"

Adele's tow-headed child sat at a table with a plate of beans in front of him. He ate greedily, scooping up beans that fell from the spoon with his fingers.

"No, thank you. I'm sorry. I didn't mean to interrupt your dinner," Louisa said.

"Just feeding the boy is all. A growing boy is always hungry," she said. "Have a seat. Make yourself comfortable."

Louisa sat on the couch though she was anything but comfortable.

"How are you getting on, Mrs. Cummings? You had said you might have to find some work," Louisa said.

"I thought so," Mrs. Cummings said, "but an anonymous donor has set aside a small annuity for Christopher. So we're all set till he turns sixteen."

"An anonymous donor? How fortunate for you," Louisa said with a sense of relief for the woman and the boy.

She looked around the room. All the flower arrangements were gone, and it looked less cluttered. She noticed a shelf full of curios and knick-knacks, the sort of thing that women of little means collected to make their parlors feel homey. "I want to apologize that I did not find out who set the bomb that killed Adele."

"Apologize? That's the police's job, not yours," the woman said.

"Nevertheless, I had hoped to discover who did such an awful thing," Louisa said. "I suppose you read about the doctor Adele was investigating?"

"I did. Someone put him outta his misery," the woman said with a smile.

"Do you have the address of the townhouse where Adele's body was found?"

The woman grimaced and looked down at her hands. Her jaw clenched in anger.

"Oh, I know where it is," she said. "I went there and seen it for myself."

"Will you tell me where to find it?" Louisa asked.

The woman nodded.

***

Louisa picked through the debris of stone, brick, and broken pieces of furniture where a few weeks earlier a two-story brownstone had stood. Twilight had descended and a gas lamp in front of the building shone. Much of the city had been electrified, but certain parts of Hell's Kitchen were still bathed in the amber light of gas.

She turned her head and saw the chimney clinging to the building next door. All around her chunks of wood and plaster from the two fallen ceilings formed hills and valleys. She looked around, trying to imagine the sound of the explosion, the shock of it as Adele must have realized she'd been lured into a trap. She froze in place when she saw something poking out from under a beam. Then she bent down to push away the rubble and found a woman's leather shoe.

Standing there in the gloaming, Louisa held the shoe in her hand. The darkness closed in around her, and she heard a rushing sound in her ears. They may have settled Silvia's score but this one was not settled. Someone had been protecting the doctor, and the cost of that protection had been a woman's life. She dropped the shoe, and the rushing sound slowly faded away.

As she gazed around at the destruction, she wondered who owned the property.

Chapter 39
Ellen

"Ellen, I hope you don't mind," Hattie said. "I'm going to ride back to New York with Alva Belmont. She's promised she'll make everything right with my mother." Then she leaned in and whispered, "Alva used to be a Vanderbilt. Mother will dance a jig when she sees me with her."

"Don't worry," Hester said, slipping an arm through Ellen's. "I'll keep her company."

"You're a good cookie, Miss French," Hattie said and trotted away.

The mood on the bus ride home was one of indignation, mostly at the do-nothing police. Women traded stories of insults and outrage. But others said that was exactly what was needed. The publicity of their terrible treatment could only help their cause.

Hester sat beside Ellen. Her excitement at having been a "part of history" bubbled over, and Ellen felt foolish. She'd had some momentary madness, believing they had some sort of connection. Hester was nice. That was all. It didn't mean anything. Ellen leaned her head against the window and slept.

She roused when they got close to the city and felt suddenly sad. Her circumstances had not changed. She turned to see Hester smiling at her.

"Did you sleep well?" Hester asked.

"I caught a few winks. How 'bout yourself?"

"I dozed off for an hour or so," she said.

Ellen wasn't sure what possessed her to ask the next question, but since she had nothing to lose, she blurted it out.

"What does your husband think of your activities? Is he one of the supportive ones?" she asked.

"Oh, I'm not married," Hester said. "And I don't ever plan to be. You?"

Ellen did not speak for fear her voice would tremble. She could only shake her head. No.

The bus pulled up to the old rundown hotel and shuddered to a halt.

"Well, we're here," Hester said and then sighed as she looked out the window. "And there's my sister, waiting. She's probably fit to be tied. I'm afraid I'm a bit of a black sheep."

Ellen looked out the window and saw the black and gilt Pierce-Arrow. Seeing it reminded her of the enormous, unbridgeable gulf between her and Hester. Black sheep or not, Hester was still a sheep, and Ellen was not much more than a stray goat.

As they got off the bus in the cold night air with all the other women, Ellen felt a sense of loss. She would never see Hester again. That was certain.

"Thanks for helping me out back there," she said as they made their way through the crowd.

"Oh, it was nothing. You would have done the same for me," Hester said. That's right, Ellen told herself. It was nothing, and there was no point in her trying to make it into something.

"Hester!" a voice cried out.

A short woman with curling dark hair strode toward them. She had the bearing of royalty, but her face was screwed up in a scowl.

"Hello, Katherine," Hester said. "We had a lovely time. This is my friend, Ellen Malloy. She's from Ireland like John. We got into terrible scrapes and had to beat the men off us!"

Katherine clasped Hester's wrist as if she were a child.

"What did you think you were doing? Father will have a fit if he finds out this is what I let you do in New York. Please, get in the car this instant." She dragged Hester toward the car.

But Hester broke free, ran back to Ellen and handed her a card.

"Come visit me some time," she said.

"Sure," Ellen said with a faint smile. It might be a bit of a journey from Galway, she thought.

Ellen watched the big car trundle away. She wondered, had she seen Hester turn around and look through the back window? It was impossible to tell. A lonely, hollow feeling swallowed her. She gazed around at the dispersing women — their weary, triumphant faces. It was very late and she had a long way to get home.

Ellen's feet ached but her heart ached worse. Tomorrow afternoon she'd board the ship to Ireland, and she'd never see Hester French again. She wasn't sure it would matter. Hester, after all, was one of the elite.

Surely she wasn't actually interested in Ellen. She'd just been kind.

A few minutes later she was riding the train back to Harlem. When she got to Louisa's house, she unlocked the door and crept quietly inside. A gas lamp burned in the parlor, and Ellen, exhausted and not wanting to disturb Suzie, lay down on the sofa and fell into a deep dreamless sleep.

Chapter 40
Louisa

Louisa tromped through the rain to City Hall, a majestic building at the end of the island. The beauty of working for a newspaper was that there were experts who could tell you how to find out almost anything. The man who wrote about real estate investment told her it was easy to discover real estate transactions. They kept records at City Hall.

She folded her gloved hands on the counter and asked to see any records involving Empress Holdings. The clerk, a thin man with a face like a fox, took the measure of her and then turned into a cavern of filing cabinets. He came back ten minutes later with a file.

"Empress Holdings is a land trust," he said, opening the file on the counter. He glanced over the pages before passing them to her. "There's no way to find out the name of the owner."

Louisa read over each page carefully. Captain Tunney had said as much, but she thought she'd better look for herself. In addition to the bombed brownstone, Empress Holdings owned a tenement building, and three different houses in the Lower East Side. She noticed a recent purchase of another townhouse, close to the one which had been destroyed in the explosion. The closing had been on February 14, three days before the art show at the Armory.

"Who handles the transactions if the owner is unknown?" Louisa asked.

"The attorney," the clerk said.

"Is his name in here somewhere?" she said, perusing papers filled with fine print.

"Last page," the clerk said and ran a crooked finger down the page to a line at the bottom: Herbert Markham, Esq.

Louisa exhaled. She remembered sitting in Herbert Markham's office the day he told her all her money was gone.

"Thank you," she said. She turned and walked quickly out of the building.

***

Herbert Markham's mother backed out of the inner office, carrying a stack of file folders. She was humming a Mozart horn concerto as she placed the files on her desk and began sorting through them. Louisa coughed and the woman jumped, stopped humming and dropped one of the files.

"My goodness! You startled me," she said, glaring at Louisa.

"I'm sorry. I didn't mean to. I wondered if I could have a quick word with Mr. Markham?" Louisa said.

"Do you have an appointment?" the woman asked, and stared down at a blank appointment book.

"No, I don't," Louisa said. "I..."

"Of course you don't have an appointment because Mr. Markham is out of town," his mother said, jabbing the appointment book with her finger.

"Then perhaps you can help me," Louisa said.

The woman didn't answer. Instead she looked down at the pile of files on her desk.

"You see," Louisa began, "my publisher, Mr. Calloway, is interested in buying some property owned by a company called Empress Holdings. It's a land trust company."

"Never heard of it," the attorney's mother said.

"Mr. Markham is the attorney of record. If we could just find out who owns Empress Holdings, he would like to make an offer," Louisa wheedled.

Mrs. Markham took the pince nez from the bridge of her nose and said in a steely voice, "Miss Delafield, you know good and well that all matters between an attorney and his client are confidential. I'm sure you wouldn't want the public to know your financial and legal matters, especially the fact that your family didn't even pay for his services."

"Excuse me," Louisa said, stunned at the woman's rudeness.

"I often wondered if my son's affection for your mother didn't have something to do with that," she said.

Louisa did not care for her tone or her implication, but she was out of her depth. Obviously, this woman thought she knew more about the topic than Louisa did.

"When will Mr. Markham be back in town?" she asked.

“Not until late next week,” the woman said.

“I’ll be on my way then. Good day,” Louisa said, and muttered as she left, “Thank you for nothing.”

Chapter 41
Ellen

At fifteen, Ellen had gone to work as a maid at the resort in Salt Hill in the summers. The summer she was twenty, she met a lady's maid named Sara, visiting the resort's baths with a wealthy but ailing British duchess. Sara had been the one to suggest she look for a lady's maid position herself. "I'll teach you everything you need to know," she'd said. And Sara had been the one who walked with her on a rocky little stretch of beach one September afternoon when a storm drove in from the sea, throwing the rain in billowy sheets at them as they ran to seek shelter in an old shed. There laughing and dripping wet, Sara had kissed her. Not a sisterly kiss, but a kiss full on the lips, a kiss like the storm itself, wet and powerful. Ellen had been unable to speak afterwards. She was giddy, deranged with a flood of feelings, as they walked back to the hotel in silence.

Sara's employer left the next day, taking Sara with her, and Ellen never saw her again.

Two years later, she answered an ad for a lady's maid who would be willing to move to New York. Ellen had not been able to explain to her baffled family that whilst she enjoyed the company of Colm Feeny, she could not bear his rough hand on her skin, and she did not think it fair to punish poor Colm for her inability to love a man in that way. There were girls who would delight in bearing all the babies he could muster. And he deserved that even if his heart was broken for a while.

***

The morning after the march, Ellen looked up at the tall apartment building and then at the card in her hand. Yes, it was the right address. She hesitated. Did she dare enter? It was one thing to go after a corrupt doctor, but quite another to face down the doorman of an expensive apartment building. She turned and looked back toward Broadway. An old man walked a small dog, and a nanny pushed a baby in a pram. She looked at the building again. What foolishness this was. On the other hand, she couldn't bear to leave the country without seeing Hester French one more time. She stood turning first in one direction and then the other when something took hold of her, and without thinking about what she was doing, she walked to the front door and stood there stiffly, waiting for the doorman to open it for her.

"Good day, Miss," he said.

"Good day," she squeaked back at him.

Inside another doorman asked whom she was visiting. She showed him the card and he directed her to the elevator. "Tenth floor," he said. "I'll ring to let them know you're coming."

She nodded and soon was behind the brass cage door of the elevator as it rose creakily up the building and stopped with a jolt on the tenth floor. The elevator operator opened the door, and she stepped out into a hallway and saw two doors. Which one was it? Then the door swung open and Hester stood in the doorway, smiling at her.

"I knew you'd come," Hester said.

"I didn't," Ellen replied. Ellen followed Hester inside the apartment, past the dining room. A large stone table occupied the center and Oriental prints covered the walls.

Hester led her down the hall to the parlor. They were on the other side of Central Park from the Garretts' house, and the view through the tall windows was spectacular. She'd never been so high up in her life. The park was all bare trees or evergreens, windy walkways and — oh, there was the pond! Beyond it buildings rose, their windows bright with reflected sunlight.

Ellen stood there dumbstruck.

"Tell me what kind of music you like," Hester said and walked over to a phonograph. "How about some Debussy?"

"I don't know who that is, but I'm happy to listen to anything," Ellen said, coming out of her stupor.

A maid came in with a silver coffee service on a tray and set it on the coffee table.

"Thank you, Jenny. We'll pour it ourselves," Hester said. "My sister insists on having servants, but I don't think it's very modern, really. I don't even have a lady's maid."

"So this is your sister's apartment?" Ellen asked. She didn't want to talk about servants, and certainly didn't want to mention she used to be one.

"Yes, she and her husband also have a house on Long Island," Hester said. "It's where all the parvenues like us live."

Ellen didn't know what a parvenue was. She realized she had no idea how to talk to this woman. Louisa would be perfectly comfortable, but she was not Louisa. It was just as well she was leaving the next day.

The music that came from the phonograph fell so tenderly on Ellen's ears that she wanted to weep.

"It's pretty," she said, pointing at the phonograph machine. "I mean, the music."

"I do love this song," Hester said. For a moment the two of them stood in the golden light of the sun as the music seemed to caress them. When the song ended, Hester lifted the needle and said, "Oh, let's talk instead."

"All right," Ellen said, wondering what they might have to say to each other.

"Please have a seat, and tell me about yourself," Hester said. Ellen sat and Hester handed her a cup of coffee on a dainty saucer. "How long have you been in America?"

"Since last summer," Ellen said.

"Why did you come?"

Ellen should have come up with a story beforehand, but her mind was blank. She glanced at Hester, who seemed to be merely curious. This had been a ridiculous idea. Hester was just being kind to her. She had no interest in her. Why would she?

"Well, I..." she began and then hesitated. "My parents wanted me to marry, and I didn't want to. So, I came here for the same reason anyone comes. Opportunity."

"And did you find it? Opportunity?"

Ellen suddenly felt the weight of her upcoming departure.

"No," she said. "I'm afraid not."

She glanced around the room and noticed a large painting that looked as if the paint had been smeared across the canvas. It was nothing like the art in the Garretts' house.

"What about the girl on the bus?" Hester said. "How did you meet her?"

Ellen realized it was no use lying.

"I was her lady's maid," she said.

"But no longer?" Hester asked.

Ellen shook her head. Hester watched her curiously. She must be wondering why a servant was sitting on her sofa, Ellen thought.

"I'm sorry. I've no business calling on you," Ellen said. "I'll be taking my leave."

She set down the coffee cup and rose from her seat. Hester also rose.

"Must you?" Hester said. "What if... what if we took a ride somewhere?"

Ellen looked at her in confusion.

"Where?"

"It's a surprise," Hester said.

Ellen put on her coat, Hester wrapped herself in a woolen cape, and they left the apartment. Outside Hester found an old-fashioned hansom cab, and they bundled inside.

"I do think horse-drawn carriages are more romantic," Hester said. "There are so few left. I suppose the motorcars scare them."

The driver sat on top of the cab and clucked at his horse.

"Where are we going?" Ellen asked.

"To one of my favorite spots," Hester said.

They rode in silence along the waterfront and then the carriage stopped. They got out and Hester paid the man.

"This is the southernmost point of the island," she said. "I love to come here and look at the way the two rivers meld together and become one."

Ellen saw the silvery waves churning together. Tomorrow she'd be watching from the deck of a ship.

They stood on the wharf, so close that Ellen could feel the warmth from Hester's body. Then Hester leaned close to her and whispered, "I think we're going to be very good friends, Ellen."

Ellen turned her face towards Hester's and looked into her large brown eyes. Their lips were only inches apart. Whatever there was between them was more powerful than their differences. Then a loud horn erupted. Ellen looked up and saw a large ocean liner, its funnels blowing great gusts of steam as it cruised past them on its way out of the port.

"I'm so sorry," she whispered. "It's not meant to be. I'm going back home to Ireland tomorrow."

She turned around and left Hester standing by the water.

Chapter 42

Louisa

“Where were you?” Louisa asked as she pulled her hair back and tried to twist it. She sat at her vanity, looking at Ellen’s reflection. Ellen, who had been leaning against one of the posts of Louisa’s bed, pushed herself off the post and took Louisa’s unruly hair in her hands and tamed it into a bun.

“Just saying goodbye to someone,” Ellen said. Her face was so downcast that Louisa felt her heart would break. “Shall I come with you?”

“Thank you,” Louisa said. “There’s no need for you to come along. These addresses are either in or close to Chinatown, and the last thing we need is for something to happen to you the night before you’re getting on the steamer.”

“I s’pose you’re right. My heart wouldn’t be in it anyway,” she said.

"Poor Ellen. I wish you didn't have to go," Louisa said. She rose and gathered her purse and her wrap. "Tell Suzie not to wait dinner for me. I've got a rather late night. After I look at these properties, I'm off to a reception at the mayor's mansion. I'll see you in the morning."

Louisa gave Ellen a brief hug before hurrying out of the house.

***

She'd gotten out of work later than she'd intended, and the El had been stopped half an hour around 57th Street for no discernible reason. When she finally reached the downtown area, twilight was settling in with a Gothic gloom. She stepped off the platform into the froth of the city.

Louisa walked along the street with the addresses in her hand. The day before the temperatures had been in the teens but today it had suddenly shot up to 65 degrees and now, though it was dipping again, the air felt positively balmy after the incredible cold.

The bombed townhouse had been in Hell's Kitchen, but these other addresses were further downtown. She found herself standing in front of the first address and felt a mild shock as she looked up at the building. It was the Mission where Battle Betty fed indigent men. It was closed now. She felt apprehensive as she continued to the next address.

She walked several blocks, turned onto Henry Street and saw a three-story brick building. Two well-dressed young men got out of the back of a motorcar and went inside the building. When the door opened, the sounds of laughter and music poured out. She suddenly remembered that she'd seen the building before. Ellen had pointed it out and said it was a house of ill repute. That much was quite obvious now.

Louisa backed away. So far she had learned that Empress Holdings owned the bombed brownstone in Hell's Kitchen, the building which housed Battle Betty's mission and the Chinese restaurant next to it, and now a brothel.

She looked down at the last address — several blocks away, and it was getting dark. Perhaps she should go home and wait until tomorrow. But tomorrow would be too late. Ellen would be on a ship by then, and Louisa hoped to solve the mystery before she left.

She found the street she was looking for. It was quieter than the other streets, residential with rundown but not derelict brownstones on either side of the street. Footsteps echoed on the street behind her, and her heartbeat ratcheted up a notch, fear sliding like a blade up her chest. She glanced back quickly and saw with relief it was a blond woman by herself — a woman confidently walking the streets alone, so perhaps it was safer here than Louisa knew. She had gone two more blocks before she found the address. It was an unremarkable brownstone. A light was on inside.

On an impulse she went up the steps to the front door and lifted the knocker. She could plead ignorance if someone answered. She could ask if this house were owned by the Astors. That was silly. Why would the Astors own a house down here? For a moment she felt dizzy. Something was wrong, she knew it. The voices, the whispers came out of nowhere, but this time she could make out one word: "Run!"

Louisa heard a rustle behind her and turned to see the blond woman behind her on the steps. The woman wore a bronze dress with a pink velvet wrap and looked to be in her thirties. She held her hands in a white fur muff.

"Who are you?" Louisa asked.

"A friend of a friend. I got something for you," the woman said in an incongruous little girl voice. The door creaked open behind her but before she could turn around, someone grabbed her and held onto her while the woman took her hand from her muff. Louisa's eyes widened and she screamed as the woman stepped up and shoved a handkerchief in her face. She smelled a strong acrid odor. As the woman's hand pushed the cloth against her nose and mouth, Louisa lost all strength and a fog descended over her. Her knees buckled and hit the stone beneath her. The last thing she saw was a white muff on the ground.

Chapter 43
Ellen

Ellen felt a hand shaking her, and her mind clawed its way out of sleep and into consciousness.

"What is it?" Ellen asked, looking up into Suzie's worried face.

"Louisa's been gone all night," Suzie said, wringing her hands.

"How can that be?" Ellen asked. She got up and hurried to Louisa's room. Morning light spilled across the wood floor and onto the worn yellow rug. The bedclothes were undisturbed. "Perhaps she stayed out with a friend last night."

Ellen and Suzie shared a look.

"The only man in her life I know about is that publisher who came here to call on her," Suzie said.

"That was a professional call," Ellen said.

"You didn't see the way he looked at her," Suzie said.

"She's fine, I'm sure. I need to get ready. I'm supposed to get on the steamer today," Ellen said. Her heart felt unbearably heavy at the thought, but she had told Paddy she would do it. It wasn't as if she had any work here. In Ireland, at least, there would be the position as a housemaid at Salt Hill.

"The ship doesn't leave till later today. Why don't you go to Mr. Calloway's house and see if he knows where she is?" Suzie asked, clearly worried sick.

Suzie had been so kind to her, Ellen found she couldn't say no.

"All right. But how will I find his address?" Ellen wondered.

"Go to the library and look in the city directory, you numbskull. What are you waiting for?" Louisa's mother stood in the doorway, leaning on a cane, grimacing at the two of them.

Chapter 44
Louisa

When Louisa opened her eyes, she saw a streak of light through a crack between dark curtains. Her hands were bound together and she felt the rough sensation of a rope around her neck that prevented her from raising her head more than a few inches from the bed where she lay. She felt groggy, her throat constricted as if somehow she'd swallowed a handful of pebbles.

"Don't move, or you'll cut your air off." The voice was female, young.

"Where am I?" Louisa croaked.

"Yer in a whorehouse," the voice said. A girl's face loomed over Louisa. Her hair was blond and dirty, and she was so skinny she could have slipped through that crack in the curtain.

"How did I get here?" Louisa asked.

"After you got knocked out, Madame had 'em bring you here in a motorcar. Then they gave you a shot to keep you sleeping."

"Who was that woman? With the muff?"

"Just one of the working girls."

Louisa turned her head to the side. The room was decorated in a garish pink with gold trim. Even the wallpaper was pink. Paintings of nude women in gold frames hung on the wall. Above her a large mirror hung. She saw herself bound on the bed. She was no longer wearing the gray dress she'd had on earlier. They'd left her in her slip and corset. As Louisa fully realized the horror of what had happened to her, she began to tremble.

"This is the house on Henry Street, isn't it?" she asked.

"It is," the girl said. "This house got a very favorable review in the Gentleman's Handbook, says Madame. But here in the back room is only for the high rollers."

"What are they going to do to me?" Louisa asked.

"Madame's taking bids for the first crack at you. That's where the money is. Then you'll be moved somewhere else, maybe another country, and used up like them others," the girl said.

Louisa shuddered and shut her eyes. This could not possibly be happening. The underworld did not kidnap women reporters and turn them into prostitutes. There would be too much outrage. Unless, of course, no one ever knew about it. Unless she simply disappeared. She took a slow deep breath and willed her body to relax. Struggling would be futile. She craned her head as far she could without pulling the rope against her larynx in order to look at the girl. She wore a dingy black skirt with a ripped hem, an ill-fitting sweater, and a stained scarf. She looked vaguely familiar.

"I bet you're pretty under all that dirt," Louisa said after a moment, hoping to ingratiate herself into the girl's good graces.

"Not as pretty as you," the girl said. "Madame says yer gonna bring in a boodle."

"Madame?" Louisa asked. "Madame who?" What horrible person could possibly be behind this?

"I can't tell you that," the girl said. "I can tell you she's got the fanciest bordello this side of 42nd Street. Mighty fancy men come here. You know what they do, don't you? They stick their cock in you and pound on you like yer a piece of meat."

Louisa's foot yanked on the rope involuntarily. Everything inside screamed at her to run but she couldn't, and she couldn't wake up from this horrid dream. She fell back and looked over at the girl, leaning against one of the posts, looking at her the way a child might watch an insect trying to escape from a jar.

"You'd think she'd dress you better if she makes so much money," Louisa said.

"I got to look in-con-spic-utous," the girl said. "I'm the errand girl."

Through the fog of Louisa's brain she had a memory. The Armory. A coin falling into a cup. A girl looking up with desperate eyes.

"And a beggar, too, aren't you?" Louisa asked. "I saw you outside the Armory."

"I saw you, too," the girl said.

"May I have some water, please?" Louisa asked.

"Hold on," the girl said. She left the room and came back with a mug of water. She tilted Louisa's head forward and let her drink. The water dribbled along Louisa's chin and cheek, but she got enough inside her mouth to feel a small measure of relief.

"What's your name?" Louisa asked.

"Everyone calls me Scrawny."

"That's not a name," Louisa said.

"Scrawny!" a voice outside the room called.

"I better go," the girl said.

After she heard the door close, Louisa flexed her wrists and tried to pull the ropes that bound her hands. It was no use. They were too tight. If only she could reach the rope that held her by the neck or if she could get off the bed. But when she tried to move her legs, she found that a rope bound one of her ankles. She reached up with her bound hands and found the knot around her neck but couldn't undo it. A wave of panic washed over her, and she started screaming. No one responded. Her throat grew hoarse; she stopped screaming.

She thought of what the girl had said about Louisa bringing "in a boodle." This madame was going to sell her body like the butcher sold a chicken in the market. Women had endured this sort of thing forever and survived. She realized that virginity was a blessing when one was young, but a curse the older one got. Here she was, a grown woman, and she'd never been with a man. She wished she'd been more like Dorothy or some of the bolder girls who went to college with her. It wasn't as if she didn't have longings. She woke up sometimes from dreams, yearning for a man's touch, but she'd been raised to be respectable – especially after the ignominy of her father's death. If she refused to marry, then she would simply never know the pleasures of intimacy. Now, that respectability was going to be ripped from her and no pleasure would be involved.

Scrawny returned and sat down in a chair by the window. She yawned loudly. From downstairs, piano music tinkled, mixed with raucous laughter.

"Is there a chamber pot I can use? I need to relieve myself," Louisa said.

Scrawny untied her neck and ankle and led her to a chamber pot in the corner. She knelt down and helped Louisa take off her bloomers. Louisa thought about overpowering the girl and escaping from the room, but she heard voices in the hallway and knew she wouldn't get far. Besides, the girl could be far stronger than she looked.

"You won't be needing these tonight," Scrawny said and tossed the bloomers to the corner. "And don't think about trying to escape. There's a guard outside in the hall just for you. One of those Chinese guys. Nobody messes with them."

Louisa had wondered if she was merely the victim of some random kidnapping, but now with the mention of the Chinese men she was sure she'd been targeted. But why, she wondered. The doctor was dead. Maybe someone had not liked the idea of her digging into the Empress Holdings. Maybe Mr. Markham's mother had made a phone call to someone after she'd left.

When Louisa was done, the girl led her back to the bed and tied the neck rope to a rail in the headboard. She tied the other rope to Louisa's left ankle.

"Am I the only one?" Louisa asked.

"The only what?" Scrawny looked at her with a curious expression.

"The only unwilling victim," she said.

Scrawny shrugged. "There been others. It's a special event. Madame makes a big hoo-hah of it."

Louisa's breath stuttered in her chest, and she reflexively pressed her thighs together.

The girl took the chamber pot out of the room and came back a few minutes later. She sat in a straight-back chair, looking bored with her duties.

"How much money do you make here?" Louisa asked.

"No money. Just a place to sleep and some food."

"Wouldn't you like some pretty clothes? A nice pair of shoes? I have a blue day dress that would bring out the color of your eyes," Louisa said.

"I do like some fine clothes but I never had none," the girl said. She got up and came close to the bed. A rank odor emanated from her unwashed body.

"If you let me go, I can promise you all that and more," Louisa said.

"Madame said you'd say something like that. She said you were a liar," the girl said.

"Madame is wrong," Louisa said. "And I would never call you Scrawny. What's your real name?"

The girl muttered, "Delores."

"Delores is a nice name."

"You're still a liar."

"I'm not. I can prove it," Louisa said. "I write for a newspaper. If you go out and get a copy of *The Ledger*, you'll see my picture right over the society column. It's small but you can tell it's me."

"I know who you are. Madame reads your column all the time," the girl said. "That's how we know..."

"Shut up, girl!"

The girl froze. Louisa recognized that graveled voice. A moment later the bulldog face of Battle Betty loomed into view. Her painted lips parted, and she smiled as she looked down at Louisa.

Chapter 45
Ellen

Ellen knocked on an ornate door, and a butler answered. He looked at her with a quizzical expression. She hadn't bothered to wear her disguise, but with her short hair and plain dress she was not the sort of visitor who might be expected to show up at the door of a wealthy newspaper publisher.

"How may I help you?" he asked.

"I need to speak to Mr. Calloway," she said.

She saw a large man walking through the hallway and called out, "Mr. Calloway! Is Louisa Delafield with you?"

The man turned and immediately came to the door. He wore an Oriental smoking jacket and stared at her with wide, concerned eyes.

"Come in. It's Ellen, isn't it? I met you at Miss Delafield's house?" he asked.

She nodded and entered. He led her through the foyer into an elegant parlor and invited her to sit on the gold-brocade sofa, but she couldn't. She was far too agitated. Instead she paced in front of the fireplace.

"Louisa didn't come home last night. We're worried sick," Ellen said. "We thought you might have some idea where she's been."

"I haven't seen her in several days," he said.

For a moment, Ellen felt as if she were falling down a well.

"Those men who were after me," she said slowly, "they might have decided to take her instead."

Mr. Calloway held his hand to his temple and seemed to be thinking.

"She may have been getting too close to something," he said. "Or maybe someone wanted revenge for the doctor's death. Maybe they blamed her."

"Could I use your phone to call my friend? He's a detective with the Fifth Precinct," she said.

"Of course," he said. "Then you should go back to her house and wait for her. I'll go to the paper and see what I can find out from Thorn."

***

Ellen stood outside the mansion on the sidewalk and felt paralyzed. She was supposed to get on the boat for home today, and if she didn't, she'd wind up in jail. Then she thought of Louisa, how she'd opened her house to her when she'd been stuck in that workhouse. She thought of Louisa's loyalty to those people who didn't deserve it, and she remembered how Louisa had followed her friend into a den of gangsters. Suddenly she was walking fast toward the brick and stone canyons of Lower Manhattan.

There'd been gangs in Galway City, and she knew a thing or two about their ways. She had an idea about how to find out the whereabouts of Owney the Killer. The one group of people who knew everything and might be easily bribed were children, of which there were thousands in the tenements. The trick was to find the right child — not too young or he wouldn't know anything, a boy was preferable to a girl, and she had to choose one from the breeding grounds of Owney's particular gang, The Gophers. The right one would be a boy just old enough to have ambitions.

She prowled the streets, looking at groups of urchins, mostly dirty and too young. Then as she was passing an old cemetery in the heart of Hell's Kitchen, she heard a loud thunk, a yell, and then laughter. She stopped to peer into the resting place of the dead and saw figures running and dodging among the tombstones. A tall, gangly boy stood, lifted a sling shot, aimed and let loose. A screech and a curse.

"Hey there," she shouted.

The boy turned to her. "What do you want, you old mab?"

She wasn't sure what a mab was, but she could guess.

"I'm here with some coin in my pocket to trade for information," she said. "And I'm not that old."

He sauntered over to her. Heads peeked above the tombstones and eyes watched her.

"What is it?" he asked, tilting his chin up.

"Look, I got some information for Owney. You know who I'm talking about, right? You're Slim, aren't you?" she said, as if she'd heard talk of him.

"No, I'm Lil' Jack," he said.

"Right, I remember hearing about you," she said. "You're a real pro with that sling shot."

He shrugged, but she could tell the compliment was well received.

"I have to get some information to Owney right away. I know he works with his pigeons in the afternoons but I don't know where the loft is," she said.

"If you knows him so good, why don't you know where he is?" he asked.

"Look here, kid. I heard something in the saloon where I work. The Dusters are planning to ambush the Gophers. Now, whose side are you on?" she asked. She was glad that Paddy had given her a rundown of the gangs in the area and the fact that there was always a power struggle of some sort going on. Lil' Jack seemed skeptical.

"Owney ain't scared of The Dusters," he said.

"I know that, but he don't like surprises either," she said. "If you tell me where he is, he might be promoting you into the older ranks."

Lil' Jack studied her for a moment. She stared straight into his black eyes until he glanced away nervously.

"The coin?" he asked with an outstretched palm. She thrust a nickel into it.

"That all?"

"Better than the thumping you'll get if you don't tell me where he is right now," she answered and stepped closer to him. "Or would you rather Owney cut out your little heart and feed it to the birds?"

"Forty-sixth Street. By the water. Six stories. It's white and got pictures carved on the front," he said. Not a tenement then. Of course, the area's toughest gangster wouldn't live in a tenement. He probably had plenty of money from his illegal activities. Whatever they were she could only imagine.

She turned without another word and walked rapidly up the forties to 46th Street. She headed toward the river and found a new looking building. Someone was trying to clean up the area, she guessed. She went inside and took the lift to the sixth floor and then found a stairwell to the roof.

The loft was at the far end of the roof, facing south. She approached and saw a slim, young man sitting on an overturned crate, with an upside-down bird in his hand. He was applying something to its scaly foot. She stepped into the loft.

"Who are you and what do you want?" he asked without looking at her.

"My brother back home loves pigeons. I wish he could see this," she said. The truth was that her brother Michael liked to kill pigeons and just about anything else that crawled or flew, which may be why he joined the Rangers and was off learning how to kill people.

"These aren't just common old pigeons," he said. "Some of them got a pedigree finer than the Knickerbockers."

"I don't even know what a Knickerbocker is," she said.

"They're the old money New Yorkers. The ones who never worked a day in their lives. Me, I don't work either. Never have. Never will. And while it's been nice chatting with you, Miss...."

"Malloy. Ellen Malloy," she said.

"Miss Malloy, you still haven't answered my question. So I've got another one for you, do you know who I am?"

"You're Owney Madden, also known as Owney the Killer," she said.

He gently set the bird in his hand down.

"That feels better now, doesn't it?" he said to the bird. It strutted on the ground and then flew to a perch about three feet off the floor. He turned to her and said, "You want to keep the perches low. They like it closer to the floor."

"They're fine looking birds. Especially this fellow here," she said, edging up to a large crested black pigeon. "I bet he's your favorite."

"My best breeder. He cost a pretty penny."

She took the bird in both of her hands and stroked its feathers. The other pigeons cooed and pecked in the gravel and sand in the middle of the floor.

"I used to wring the necks of my grandma's chickens whenever she was ready to throw one in the pot," Ellen said, sliding her hand around the pigeon's neck.

"Hey. What gives?" Owney said.

"I need to know who has Louisa Delafield," she said. "Then I'll be gone."

"That lady reporter?"

"You know exactly who I mean," she said and gazed at him, her hand firmly clasped around the silvery collar of the bird.

"What's to stop me from shooting you in the knee cap right now?" he asked.

"You don't have a gun on you," she answered. "Besides, if you killed me, then you'd have to figure out what to do with my body. And my question is a simple one. Where is Louisa?"

"Put down the bird and I'll tell you," he said. His gaze was so cold she got goosebumps.

"No." She edged close to the door, still firmly gripping the bird.

Owney Madden laughed and stood up. It occurred to Ellen that he could throw her from the roof and no one would be wiser. She'd be just another suicide. But he stayed where he was.

"It's none of my affair anyway," he said. "Your friend is now the main attraction at Battle Betty's brothel. Bidding has already started."

Ellen's hand tightened around the bird's neck, and it squawked.

"Hey!" he growled. "Watch it."

"Where is this brothel?" she asked.

"Not in Hell's Kitchen. We ran her out of here. She's got a stable full of goohs off Bleeker."

He could be lying, she thought, and he might kill her as soon as she released the bird.

"Detective O'Neil of the fifth precinct knows I'm up here, by the way," she said.

"I'm not scared of cops," he said. "The Gophers beat the shit out of the cops every day and strip them of their clothes. Haven't you seen us in our cop coats? We're the fashion plates of the underworld. And what can they do about it? Nothing. We got Tammany on our side."

She held the bird and studied him. His hands were so clean and soft. Not good for labor, but good enough for killing, she figured.

"My gran used to say, 'Whatever your world looks like today, it'll be different tomorrow.' I don't think you have much of a future," she said. "I'm leaving now, Mr. Madden."

"Leave the bird with me," he said, holding out his hand.

"I don't think that would be a wise course of action. I'll let him go soon as I'm safely off this roof. He's a homing pigeon. He'll find his way back to you, won't he?"

"If he don't, I know where to find you, and we'll see how good you can fly," he said.

As Ellen backed out of the coop, her heel caught on the rim of the doorway and she fell backwards, flat on her back, knocking the breath out of her. The bird flew out of her hand, up into the sky, circled once and then came back down to the roof, where it marched in circles, clucking with indignation.

Owney stood over her, his foot pressed against her chest.

"I got a rule against killing women," he said. "So I'm not going to kill you. This time. Besides, I kinda like that society writer. She's on the square. Even said I was debonair. And I got no use for Battle Betty. In fact, if she's gone, I'll just take over her stable."

Ellen felt the pressure of his foot on her chest and whimpered.

"But if I see you again around here, Irish, I might break the rules. You understand?"

She nodded. He took his foot off her chest, picked up the pigeon and held it close, cooing to it as he took it back into the coop.

Chapter 46

Louisa

"I weren't sayin' nothin'," Scrawny said, backing up.

"Go to the kitchen. Get her some food. Can't have her stomach growling when she entertains our guests tonight," Battle Betty said as she looked down at Louisa. "You are quite the little money maker."

"Why are you doing this to me?" Louisa asked.

"The two best reasons in the world — money and revenge. We lost our doctor thanks to you," Battle Betty said. "And you're just too damn nosy, Beatrice, or is it Louisa?"

"Are you going to kill me?" Louisa asked, trying to keep the tremble out of her voice.

Battle Betty pretended not to hear her and wandered across the room to peek through the velvet curtains.

"I sent out hand-embossed invitations to the very wealthiest connoisseurs. Generally, they like them a little younger than you, but the fact you smell like society adds a certain something. What's the fancy French saying? A je-ne-sez-kwa? And I told 'em you were a filly — that means virgin. I'm right about that, aren't I? I got sort of a sense about these things."

Louisa didn't answer.

Scrawny came in with a drumstick, nuts, and chocolate on an expensive gold-rimmed china plate. She untied Louisa's neck and helped her sit up.

"This is some establishment you have here," Louisa said, looking at the dinnerware and the fancy food.

"Nothing here is cheap. Customers pay ten dollars just to walk in the door," Battle Betty said. "Now eat."

When Louisa, who had no appetite, refused the food, Battle Betty struck her across the face. Her cheek stung and she tasted blood from where she'd bit her tongue.

"I said, eat."

Louisa took up the drumstick and forced the meat down her throat. When she was done, Scrawny retied the rope around her neck.

"Tie it good. Then go over to the restaurant and see if we got any last minute bids," Battle Betty told the girl.

Louisa tried to catch the girl's eye, but she was clearly terrified of Battle Betty. She gathered up the plate and scurried out of the room.

Louisa lay on the bed, her hands bound, neck tied to one end of the bed, and her ankle to the other.

"You set the bomb, didn't you, Betty?" Louisa asked, staring up at her reflection in the overhead mirror. "You set up Adele Cummings and killed her."

Battle Betty chuckled.

"I still got the old skills," she said with a grin. "But you haven't asked me who paid me."

"Paid you?" Louisa asked.

"That's right," the woman said. "I weren't in it alone. Many fine people did not want the doctor to be caught. Think of all the names he could give to the press."

She laughed as she walked out of the room.

Louisa lay on the bed, helpless, the ropes on her neck, wrists, and ankle reminding her that she had lost all control over her life and her actions. She looked up at the mirror and saw herself as no longer a woman, but a thing. It occurred to her that this is exactly what had been planned for Silvia, the young housemaid who had been seduced by Hugh. All this time she hadn't stopped to think of Silvia as a flesh-and-blood human being. She was just a servant who'd had the bad luck to get pregnant. Louisa had lost her fortune and her status in society but somehow, she hadn't lost the blindness of the upper classes, their inability to see the humanity in others. Silvia was just a girl, but she had a future. She was loved by her family and friends, loved by Ellen. She might have married and had children. Louisa screwed up her eyes in misery. Ellen had been nothing but a path to a story for Louisa, but she was honest and brave and had dreams of her own. Louisa realized now that Ellen was more than just a means to an end. She had become a friend, more so than any other friend she'd ever had, with the exception of Suzie. I've been selfish and blind, she thought. I've been pursuing this story for all the wrong reasons. I never allowed myself to see the truth about the people I admired, the people I envied. How could she have envied such superficial people? From now on she would never judge a person by some artificial standard such as birth or wealth or education. She would never again judge herself by that standard either. Amidst the clamor of fear, guilt, and rage rampaging across the pages of her mind, she did have one clear thought: somehow she must survive this.

***

The crack of light disappeared. Louisa lay on the bed. Battle Betty came in and untied her hands but left the rope around her neck and one around her ankle to the post of the bed.

"They won't mind if you fight a little," the woman said. "They like that."

With her leg tied at one end and her neck at the other, Louisa was still immobilized. The woman placed a meaty paw on Louisa's breast while holding onto the rope around her neck with the other hand. Louisa tried to slap Betty's hand away but Betty yanked on the rope and Louisa dropped her hands.

"Very nice. Your first guest is downstairs having a drink," the woman said as she stroked Louisa's neck and chest. "He paid a pretty penny for you, my dear."

"You'll go to prison for this," Louisa said. "I promise you that."

"Who's ever to know? You'll be feeding the East River fishes when we're done with you," she said and then pinched her hard. Louisa clenched her jaw so she wouldn't cry out. A knock on the door sent her heart racing. Fear clawed inside her chest like a trapped rat. Battle Betty stood up and opened the door.

"Come in," she said as if she were inviting a king to dine.

"Is she ready?" a man's voice asked.

"She's ready and waiting," Battle Betty said before she walked out of the room and shut the door. Louisa heard footsteps approaching the bed. Shame coursed through her body and she snapped her head away, closing her eyes. A stranger was looking at her. A man. She stifled a sob.

The footsteps moved away. She glanced quickly and saw the back of a large man standing at the window. She wondered what he was waiting for. She closed her eyes again. She did not want to look at him. She willed him to disappear, but the footsteps approached her again. She tried not to sob, but she couldn't help it. She didn't want him to touch her.

She also did not want to give him the satisfaction of seeing her cry.

He stopped beside the bed. Something fell over her and she jolted upward, yanking the rope around her neck. Choking, she fell back, opened her eyes, looked down and saw a man's dinner jacket covering her torso. She raised her eyes to see Forrest Calloway standing over her. His hand gently covered her mouth. With his other hand, he put a finger to his lips.

He bent down and whispered in her ear, "Don't say anything. The police are outside, waiting for my signal. Are you hurt?"

She shook her head.

"Good," he said. Then he quickly began untying her. The rope around her foot was easy, but the one around her neck required him to use a pen knife to cut through the knot. He then turned on all the lights in the room.

Clutching his jacket to her chest, she found her dress and underthings crumpled in a corner while he stood at the window, opening and closing the curtains. Once she was fully dressed, she peered at the door, dizzy with terror.

"Don't worry," Calloway said. He pulled a small derringer from his pocket. "If anyone tries to come in here, I'll shoot them."

"Do you have another one of those?" she asked.

"Come here," Calloway said gently. She went to him and he put his arms around her. His embrace soothed her, but she couldn't stop trembling. Soon she heard the clumping of men's boots in the hallway, the screams of women, the slamming of doors, and then a gunshot!

"We may as well have a drink," Calloway said. "It may take a while for the police to clear out the place."

"Mr. Calloway," she said. "How did you get an invitation to bid on me? Are you one of the connoisseurs?"

"Of course not," he said. He poured dark liquid from a silver flask into a glass he found on the dresser and gave it to her. "Your friend Ellen found me. She also found the bordello, thanks to Owney Madden, and then it seems there's an errand girl who was willing to talk for a price. When she let me know where you were, I sent Mr. Kimura to the Chinese restaurant and put in my bid. Fortunately, mine was the highest."

Then he raised his flask in salute.

"To your future, Miss Delafield," he said. "I believe you owe someone named Scrawny a blue dress."

The fiery drink burned her throat, and the fear began to uncoil.

"You're worth quite a bit of money, you know."

"I wouldn't know it from my paycheck," shc said.

"I just paid five hundred dollars for you," he said.

"Five hundred dollars?" Louisa asked. "I'll never be able to pay you back."

"Oh, I expect the police will get my money back," he said.

Louisa took a deep breath. So many things could have gone wrong. She felt for a moment as if she would collapse to the floor from the sheer terror of what might have been, but instead she flexed her fingers as she realized she certainly had a story now.

The door banged open, and Paddy O'Neil burst in. He had the exultant look of a victorious warrior.

"We're all clear, Mr. Calloway," he said. "You and Miss Delafield can leave now."

Louisa found her hat and stuck her cloisonné hat pin into it with trembling hands. Calloway put his arm around her shoulders and was leading her toward the door when she stopped in front of Paddy O'Neil.

"Detective, do you have the names of the other bidders?" she asked.

"I don't," he said.

"Well, who does?" she asked, vexed.

"Captain Tunney. He's outside, supervising."

They left the room. As they walked along a hallway, she glanced in the other rooms, doors wide open, beds disheveled, the lights left on. Each room was decorated in a different color theme. They hurried downstairs and passed a garish drawing room with Oriental rugs, damask easy chairs, bottles and glasses scattered on mahogany tables, and a gold-leafed player piano still playing a tune all by itself. Battle Betty had a high class operation.

Outside they found Tunney in the process of arresting Battle Betty, who stood glowering in her velvet and lace, her wrists in handcuffs. Louisa approached. The police milled about in their brass buttoned blue suits.

"She admitted she was the one who set the bomb that killed Adele Cummings, Captain," Louisa said. "She did it to protect Dr. Swanson because he provided abortions for her workers."

A policeman nearby stopped what he was doing and stared at her. Another slapped a blackjack in his hand.

"Filthy..."

"I didn't do no such a thing," Battle Betty yelled. "She's lying. And you can't prove nothing."

Captain Tunney glared down at the woman.

"Up to your old tricks, are you?" he asked. She spat at him, her saliva landing on his badge. He took a handkerchief and wiped it off. "Take her downtown, boys."

Louisa watched as they loaded her into the back of the paddy wagon with the other girls, in varying stages of undress.

"Where are their customers?" Louisa asked.

"Fled like rats in the night," Tunney said. "We got no authority to arrest them anyway."

"What about the Comstock Law?" Louisa asked.

"Only applies if women are being transported somewhere. Prostitution is a crime, but only for the prostitute," he said.

If it weren't for the customers, there'd be no prostitutes, Louisa thought, but the laws were written by men.

"And what about the others?" she asked, rubbing her arms. Calloway stood beside her like a knight in a tuxedo.

"What others?" Tunney asked, frowning under his thick mustache.

"The others who bid for me?" Louisa asked, her voice rippling with indignation.

"I have the names, but we cannot arrest them," Tunney said. "They can say they thought they were bidding on a horse." He took from his pocket an invitation and held it out to Louisa.

SOCIETY GIRL READY TO RUN HER FIRST RACE

You're cordially invited to an auction.
Bids accepted through 10 p.m. Friday night.
Highest bidder takes possession
of the prize filly at midnight.
~ The Pink Palace ~

"An animal. That's all I was to them," Louisa said. She thrust out her hand. "Give me the list of the men who bid on me."

"And what good would that do?" Captain Tunney asked.

"You may not be able to arrest them, Captain," Forrest said. "But this lady is a news reporter and the least we can do is expose them and destroy their reputations."

A corner of the Captain's mouth lifted in a half grin, and he handed over a list.

There were four names. The third name on the list was Hugh Garrett.

Chapter 47
Ellen

When the front door opened, both Ellen and Suzie jumped up and hurried to the doorway of the parlor. Louisa entered into the foyer like a soldier returned home from the war. She took off her coat and hung it on the coat rack, removed her hat pin and her hat, and placed them on the table. Then she turned and stood in front of them, lips held in tight. For a moment no one said anything, but then Suzie opened her arms and Louisa fell into them.

Ellen felt the worry drain from her.

Louisa stepped back and quickly wiped a tear away. She looked at Ellen, smiled, and embraced her. Ellen was not accustomed to being held but it felt so very comforting.

“Thank you so much for saving me,” Louisa said.

“You’d a done the same for me, Louisa,” Ellen said.

"I might have tried, but I don't know if I could have. Mr. Calloway says you confronted Owney Madden and then convinced Scrawny to tell the truth."

Suzie ushered them into the parlor and went to get coffee. They might all be tired, but sleep was a long way off.

"They didn't hurt you, did they?" Ellen asked.

"My neck's a little raw from the rope, but otherwise I'm unharmed," Louisa said, rubbing the red mark on her white throat. "Tell me what happened."

***

Ellen explained how she'd found Owney Madden and how she got the information from him.

"You threatened his prize pigeon? I bet he didn't like that," Louisa said.

"No, he didn't, but he does like you. He said you were 'on the square' and that's why he told me where you were," Ellen said. "Once I had the information, I went to Paddy. He said there was no way we could get in the bordello. And that by the time they broke down the door and busted in, Battle Betty could have gotten rid of you, maybe even killed you. So we waited and saw her girl come out of the place and go down to the Chinese restaurant. That's where they were collecting the bids. Paddy and I grabbed her and put her in the back of the police wagon around the corner. At first she wouldn't talk, but finally she spilled it all. So I gave that information to Mr. Calloway."

Louisa sat back and sighed. She stared down at her hands. There were red marks on her wrists from the rope.

"I'm sorry I didn't believe you about Hugh," Louisa said.

"And now you do?"

Louisa nodded.

"He was one of the bidders," she said.

Ellen felt a pang of regret. "I'm sorry. I know you were fond of him."

She studied Louisa's face. Her eyes were puffy and she looked tired.

"I was so angry to be bid on like a horse, but like a horse, I've had on blinders all this time. I couldn't look at the members of society and see that they could be just as venal and crass underneath their polished veneers as the lowliest gangster," Louisa said. She paused for a moment and then continued, "Ellen, I couldn't help but think of your friend Silvia while I was in that awful room. The doctor and Betty had the same fate, or worse, planned for her, but no one would have known until it was too late. I don't think I truly understood until..."

Ellen reached over and took Louisa's hand. For a moment they just sat there. Ellen had missed the boat to Ireland, and for that she was glad. But she'd almost lost Louisa, and as different as they were, she realized that Louisa had become a friend, and she'd be bereft without her.

"I think I'll go to bed," Louisa said. "Tomorrow we need to go to the jail to see Battle Betty and find out what else she knows." Then she paused and seemed to recollect something. "You didn't go back to Ireland. What will happen to you?"

"I s'pose that depends on the Garretts," Ellen said.

Louisa snorted and said, "Over my dead body." She rose and with a swish of her skirts left the room.

Ellen followed her upstairs, tumbled into her small bed and fell asleep.

Chapter 48
Louisa

The next day Suzie flung open the curtains, and daylight came crashing through the windows into Louisa's bedroom.

"Rise and shine," Suzie said. "You can't sleep all day."

Louisa rose from the bed. She had slept fitfully, reliving the events of the previous night. She might have been raped and murdered if not for Ellen's resourcefulness and Mr. Calloway's money. Battle Betty was nothing if not efficient. She would have gotten vengeance for the dead doctor who serviced her girls and also made "a boodle" in one night of utter debauchery. Louisa thought of Hugh and his bright blue lying eyes. She had not dreamed he was capable of such villainy.

She washed and dressed and went downstairs. She would need to write about what happened to her. She wavered for a moment, wondering what the social mavens would say. She supposed it didn't matter anymore. As Beatrice Milton, she would write what she needed to write.

She sat at the kitchen table while Suzie heated the coffee.

"Where's Ellen?" she asked.

"She's gone out to look for work. She said that if she was gainfully employed, maybe they wouldn't throw her in jail," Suzie said. "I think she's more than a little worried. I would be, too. Your mother says that Garrett woman is capable of anything. Hungry?"

"Oh, yes. It turns out that being abducted leaves one famished."

After her breakfast, Louisa went to her desk and wrote her story. She could tell with every word that readers would be glued to her account. Everyone in New York would be reading *The Ledger*.

As she wrote the story, she thought of Forrest Calloway. He had seen her in the most humiliating position a woman could be in. She wondered how she could ever face him again. She was deeply mortified. And yet. She would always remember the relief and gratitude sweeping over her — as if her heart might fly from its cage — when she opened her eyes and saw him looking down at her with such compassion — and something else. Something like admiration?

She put down her pen. For all the horror she had endured, she also felt a sense of satisfaction. The doctor who was responsible for Silvia's and Adele's deaths was dead himself. Battle Betty, the bomber, was in jail. And now she knew Hugh Garrett's true colors. Best of all, Ellen was still here in the country.

A darkness seeped over this happy outcome, however, as she felt the imprint of that awful woman's hand on her breast, her neck, her arms. *You never asked who paid me.*

She thought of Hugh and his protestations of innocence. Perhaps the apple led to the tree. Who else but Amelia was heartless enough to pay someone to end a life for her own ends? She remembered the way Amelia constantly fawned over Dr. Swanson and then there was the fundraiser for his hospital that Amelia had organized. Not only that, but the Garretts had a connection with Battle Betty from her union busting days. She put her story in her portfolio and rose from her desk.

***

On Captain Tunney's walls hung framed commendations for his service. His desk was cluttered with files and outside his second-story window was another building a few feet away.

"I didn't expect to see you so soon after your ordeal, Miss Delafield," he said when she sat down across from him.

"The ordeal isn't over," she said and rested her eyes on a silver paperweight on his desk. "Battle Betty said something interesting to me last night."

"And what was that?" he asked, leaning back in his chair, his hands behind his head.

"She admitted that she set the bomb, but she said that someone paid her to do it. And she didn't mean the doctor," Louisa said and leaned forward.

Captain Tunney sighed and placed his hands across his belly.

"Might she not tell us who that person was as some sort of deal?" Louisa asked. "A lighter sentence?"

"Battle Betty wasn't ever a rat," Captain Tunney said, shaking his head. "But we'll never know, will we?"

"What do you mean?" Louisa asked.

He looked up at the ceiling and then tilted his head sharply down and looked Louisa in the eyes. His own were fierce and dark, and his eyebrows were pinched.

"Because, Miss Delafield, she never made it to the station last night," he said.

"Well, where is she?" Louisa asked.

"Probably in Hell," Captain Tunney said. "Seems she raised a fuss, tried to escape, and my men had to shoot her. Ten times."

Louisa closed her eyes and sank inward like a deflated balloon. This was her fault. She'd blurted out in front of everyone that Battle Betty was the bomber.

"I… I was not myself last night," Louisa said. "I should have been more discreet."

Captain Tunney nodded. "You should have been."

"She should have had the chance to go to trial. To defend herself…" Louisa continued, utterly distraught. How could she have been so stupid?

"Well, you had been drugged, abducted, and threatened with defilement and possibly murdered. No one can blame you. Truth be told, it would have gotten out sooner or later. And someone woulda killed her," he said.

"That's no consolation. My behavior was unprofessional," she said.

"So it was. You're human. And you're young. There's plenty of time to learn from your mistakes," he said.

"Too late for Battle Betty," she said. "Are you going to investigate?"

"Commissioner Waldo says the shooting was justifiable. There's nothing more that I can do," he said.

***

When Louisa entered the newsroom, she was surprised that it felt no different. She expected everything to change, but the smell of cigar smoke and newsprint and the sound of the telegraphs and reporter chatter were just the same.

"Delafield!" Billy Stephens exclaimed when she reached her desk. "My God, are you all right? Tunney told me what happened."

He clasped her hands in his and searched her face. She wore a dress with a high collar to hide her raw-skinned neck.

"I'm perfectly fine, Mr. Stephens." She extracted her hands from his, and sat down at her typewriter.

"I never should have gotten you involved in this mess," he said, rubbing his forehead as if he could erase the past.

"Billy," she said, gently. "Thank you for your concern, but I'm fine. Truly."

He sighed and stuck his hands in his pockets as he wandered back to his desk. He turned and asked, "Are you sure? How did you get word to Calloway?"

She smiled and said, "I had an angel helping me."

As she typed her story, she saw him glancing at her. His concern was actually quite touching. Though he pretended to be as hard-boiled as any police reporter should be, the truth was he wasn't a particularly ambitious man — or else he would have been at *The Herald* or *The World*. If he were ambitious, she was sure he would never have helped her gain a foothold in this world to begin with. She finished the story with three hashmarks and thought, *let it fall where it will*. Then she took it into Thorn.

"Glad to see you survived, Miss Delafield," he said, peremptorily, looking at her over his spectacles. He took the story from her to peruse.

"Mr. Thorn, Billy Stephens will now know that I'm Beatrice Milton. We mustn't let the other reporters know, however. There would hardly be any point to a pen name if everyone knows who I am."

Thorn grunted and continued reading, then put down the paper, looked up at her, and uttered, "Your intrepid what?"

A Woman's View: Abducted

By Beatrice Milton

New York, March 5 – A society woman's world is filled with dances, teas, soirées, and dinners with friends and family. She is protected by the men around her and rarely encounters anything unsavory. She is never hungry or cold, and her head rests easy on down-filled pillows at night.

There is another class of woman, however, which is not so fortunate. These women are preyed upon by the worst elements, and sometimes, I am loathe to admit, those worst elements are at the very pinnacle of society.

Reader, I experienced that world myself when I was abducted and held in a house of ill repute against my will. The reason I was drugged and taken is that, as I have reported previously, I discovered that Dr. Alan Swanson had been providing illegal services to certain wealthy clients and their servants.

This same doctor also provided services for a brothel located in Chinatown, owned by the notorious female gangster, Battle Betty, who had been posing as a reformer, helping indigent men with her "Mission." This was a front and a scam. I was one of those fooled by this woman.

While investigating the bombing that killed Officer Adele Cummings, I was drugged and taken to a "bawdy house" — an ornate pleasure palace, serving the whims of wealthy men. Once I was in Betty Walsh's clutches, she sent out invitations to certain "racing enthusiasts" offering them the chance to bid on a "filly." That filly was me. Fortunately, through the efforts of my intrepid assistant, my whereabouts were discovered, and I was rescued by the publisher of this paper and Captain Tom Tunney before I could be harmed.

The names of the men who bid on my virtue cannot be printed at this time. Rest assured, however, the police know those names, and they will be conducting a thorough investigation.

Chapter 49
Ellen

"Not hiring." That's what the first man said. And the second. And the third. They were all men. And they were interchangeable in appearance, for regardless of their individual characteristics, they each had the stony expression of men who couldn't care less if you died of hunger on their doorstep. She had spent the whole morning in the factory district and found nothing.

Ellen stopped at a pushcart and bought a piece of fruit and a roll for breakfast. Her feet ached, and it was only her first day of searching for work. Too soon to be discouraged, she told herself. She rubbed her hands together. The sun passed its noon zenith, burning off some of the bitter chill of the morning.

A policeman walked by, looked her up and down, and said, "Get along. No loitering."

Walking aimlessly along the street, she came to a corner and turned. She passed people, but they seemed not to see her. She had become invisible, she thought. Maybe the Garretts would forget about her. If not, then she'd wind up in the clink. That's what they called the gaol in the flicks, "the clink."

She turned onto Mulberry Street, and there in front of her was a cathedral she hadn't seen before. She gazed up at the rose window in the center of the stone facade, and a warm feeling came over her. She might as well go inside and have a kneel down. She clasped the wrought iron railing and climbed the steps. At the top a sign welcomed her to St. Patrick's Cathedral. The tall wooden doors were unlocked, so she went inside. She found the lady chapel with an altar for the Blessed Virgin, put a penny in the box, used a long wooden taper to light a candle, and knelt down on the velvet kneeler. Clasping her hands, she said, "Holy Mary, Mother of God, pray for us sinners now and at the hour of our death. Amen."

As she gazed up at the image of the Virgin, another woman's face came to mind. Hester French. For a brief moment, she felt a blinding surge of happiness. In the next moment, her happiness evaporated, leaving her spirit depleted.

She took the El back to Harlem, and got off the train, only to find Paddy on the platform.

"Oi, Paddy O'Neil, are ye waiting for me?" she asked.

"That I am," he said and stood straight. "I'm afraid I have to put you under arrest for stealing Mrs. Garrett's emerald earrings. She came in and pressed charges this morning. Said they knew you didn't get on that boat. There's nothing I can do."

"How did you know to find me here?" she asked.

"I spoke to Miss Delafield's maid. She said you were out looking for factory work. Simple deduction. That's what a detective does," he said.

"And how does Paula feel about this? Does she know?" Ellen asked.

"Not yet, but we probably won't be making any more babies after she finds out," he said. "Do I have to put the nippers on you?"

He brought out a steel contraption with a handle and two clasps.

She shook her head.

"I'll come along peacefully," she said.

They went down the stairs of the uptown platform, across the street, and then up the stairs of the downtown platform. The train barreled toward them with a screeching of wheels and then the doors opened.

"After you," he said. He was keeping a watchful eye on her as if didn't trust her, and she wasn't sure he should.

As they swayed with the train's movement, she thought about the last time she'd been on a train with him. It had been to go see Silvia's body. Hugh Garrett caused the death of a young woman, and Ellen was the one going to jail.

Paddy took her to the Fifth Precinct where he booked her and took her to a holding cell. A white-haired woman in her nightclothes clasped the bars and screamed intermittently. Ellen balked at the door and turned to Paddy.

"Don't worry. You won't be in here long. They'll come to transport you soon. In the meantime, I'll go see Miss Delafield. She may be able to bail you out so you won't have to stay locked up until your trial," he said.

She entered and the door clanged shut behind. Ellen turned to see him walking away.

"And if she can't afford it? Will I be going back to the workhouse?" Ellen called to him.

Paddy returned to the bars.

"Ellen, my girl, you're not going to the workhouse. You'll have to stay in the Tombs until your trial," he said.

"The...the Tombs?" Ellen asked in horror. The name alone made her think she'd be buried alive.

***

She and the white-haired woman who screamed every five minutes were chained together and taken an hour later in a paddy wagon to a tall, ornate building in Lower Manhattan with what looked like steeples on the top. They were hustled onto an elevator, and then down a hallway of barred cells. Even the ceiling was barred. There were drains in the floor and the frigid air had the dank smell of a thousand lost souls.

They were put in a cell with a tall Negro woman who immediately grabbed the screamer by the throat and whispered, "Stop that." She did, and Ellen wished she'd thought of doing that. She might not have such a frayed set of nerves. She settled on a cold metal bench and waited.

Chapter 50

Louisa

Mr. Strauss opened the door and stared glumly at Louisa.

"Mrs. Garrett is not at home," he said.

"I don't believe you, Strauss," Louisa said. "Tell Amelia and Hugh I'm not leaving until they talk to me. I shall stand on this stoop until you let me in."

Strauss shut the door. Minutes later he opened it again and showed Louisa into the parlor. Amelia glared at her from her chair.

"Thank you for seeing me, Mrs. Garrett," Louisa said. She sat down and poured herself a cup of coffee since Amelia seemed to have forgotten her manners.

"Hugh isn't here, you little hussy. And if you think I'm going to let him marry you, you are quite mistaken," she said, leaning forward with her fists on her knees. "You have no money and I think you're trying to blackmail me."

"That's a bit extreme," Louisa said and stirred in a lump of sugar.

"Louisa," Hugh's voice came from behind her. Of course Amelia had lied.

"Does your mother know you are one of the names Beatrice Milton didn't mention in her story?" she asked, then sipped her coffee and watched Amelia's face as her jaw dropped and her eyes widened. Well, well, Louisa thought. She does now.

"I'm curious, Amelia," Louisa said. "What's your connection to Battle Betty? I know she knew your husband."

The surprise and shock on Amelia's face looked genuine. Then she grimaced.

"Why are you asking? Are you the one who's writing this trash?"

"I'm the editor of the women's page, Amelia. It's my business to substantiate any freelancer's work," Louisa said. "Did you know Betty Walsh?"

"We will sue your paper for every dime they have," Amelia growled. "I never met that woman, and neither has my son."

"You can't sue when we have the proof that at least Hugh knew her," Louisa said. "Hugh, are you her landlord? Do you own Empress Holdings?"

"I swear to you, Louisa, I am not her landlord," he said, looking contrite. "And I didn't know what or who I was bidding on. It was just a lark."

A lark? She held tight onto the reins of her temper.

"If your family owns Empress Holdings, I'll find out," Louisa said with a calm she did not feel. Amelia glanced at Hugh, but they both seemed confused. She was getting nowhere with this line of questioning. She suddenly wanted to get away from the two of them, far away.

"Amelia, the paper will not publicize your son's despicable nature on one condition," Louisa said.

Amelia and Hugh both stared at her. She took another sip of coffee, wiped her mouth with a napkin and then looked at the two of them: the mother sitting upright in her upholstered chair, the son, standing behind her as if they were posing for a portrait.

"You will drop this preposterous charge of theft against Ellen Malloy. Today. And neither of you will ever threaten her again," Louisa said. She set down her cup of coffee, rose and walked toward the parlor door. She stopped, turned and looked directly at Amelia.

"Detective Paddy O'Neil is outside, ready to take your revised statement," she said. Then she strode out of the room, across the marble hallway, and through the door which Strauss held open for her. She stepped outside into the bright, breezy day. Paddy O'Neil nodded and took the steps two at a time to the door.

Chapter 51
Ellen

Ellen had never been so grateful in her life to see anyone as she was when she saw Louisa waiting outside the City Prison with a cab at the ready.

"One good turn deserves another," Louisa said when Ellen tried to thank her. In the cab, they sat quietly until Louisa reached over and squeezed her hand. "Now you can stay here in America. The Garretts are no longer a problem."

That evening they convened in the parlor of Louisa's brownstone with Suzie and Louisa's mother.

"I don't remember that painting," Ellen said, staring up at a family portrait above the mantel. It showed a much younger, beautiful Anna with her hand resting on the shoulder of a handsome seated man. A child version of Louisa leaned against the chair on the other side. The man had blue-gray eyes just like Louisa's.

"The curator was kind enough to sell it back to me. He's agreed to let me pay in installments."

"I told you," Suzie said to Anna, who was too pleased to mind the jab. Suzie turned to Ellen and asked, "Did you read the article by Beatrice Milton?"

Ellen picked up the paper from the coffee table and perused the article. Finally Louisa was writing about something that mattered. Ellen couldn't help but feel partly responsible for the transformation. Then she got to the end of the story.

"Assistant?" Ellen asked.

"Now that I'm a syndicated columnist and the editor of the new and expanded women's page, I have to have help," Louisa said. "Thorn had a secretarial position open anyway. There will be plenty for you to do. I daresay the salary is higher than that of lady's maid. Does ten dollars a week sound good to you?"

"Very good, indeed," Ellen said, this time with a satisfied smile. It was not something she'd known she'd wanted. She'd only known what she didn't want. She didn't want to be a greengrocer's wife in Galway, and she didn't want to be a lady's maid. But to be an assistant. It sounded so official. She grinned at Louisa. "I accept."

"You weren't servant material anyway," Mrs. Delafield said. "Much too insolent."

Louisa laughed, and Ellen decided insolence was perhaps her best character trait.

***

Standing in the midst of a noisy, smoky newsroom, Ellen felt like a shipwreck survivor. The Garretts had withdrawn their charges against her. With Battle Betty and the doctor both dead, the Chinese men would have no more interest in finding her. And best of all, here she had a job that had nothing to do with fussing over a big grown baby who couldn't even dress herself. Who would have dreamed that a fisherman's daughter from the Claddagh would have a job as an assistant to a newspaper woman?

"I don't suppose you know how to type," Louisa said, indicating the contraption perched on her desk.

"I'm a fast learner," Ellen responded. "And I've nimble fingers."

Louisa reached into the bottom drawer of her desk and pulled out a green book with the title *Rational Typewriting*. Louisa opened the book from the top and showed Ellen the diagrams of the keyboard.

"You can practice this afternoon," she told Ellen. "But first let's go get that room for you."

They left the paper and took the streetcar uptown toward Harlem where Ellen hoped she would be able to get a room in a boardinghouse for women. She'd imposed on Louisa and Suzie long enough.

"So you had no luck finding who owns Empress Holdings?" Ellen asked.

"Mr. Markham is out of town, but that was a fool's errand anyway. He wouldn't divulge a client's name. His old bat of a mother was right about that," she said.

They arrived at a brick three-story brownstone, and Louisa said, "I met the proprietor once. She seems quite professional and upright."

"Won't she mind that I'm Irish?" Ellen asked.

"She's Jewish, so she's seen her share of bigotry," Louisa said.

They procured a pleasant room on the second floor of the rooming house for Ellen. The landlady, a woman named Mrs. Cantor, was the widow of a cloth merchant, who'd bought the brownstone thirty years ago. When he died, Mrs. Cantor told them, she had no wish to leave but didn't have the money to keep it up, and so she let out the bedrooms where her children and their governess had resided. Mrs. Cantor informed them that no gentlemen were allowed on the second floor but could visit in the parlor on Sunday afternoons. Ellen said that would not be a problem.

After the landlady left, Ellen looked at the full-sized bed with the white metal headboard in the corner and she couldn't help but imagine Hester lying in that bed, smiling up at her. She dropped the key on a silver tray on the dresser. It made a resounding clink.

Louisa came over to the dresser and picked up the key. She dropped it just like Ellen had a moment earlier. Then she looked up at Ellen with wide eyes.

"What is it?" Ellen asked.

"That sounds just like a coin, doesn't it?" Louisa said.

"I s'pose so," Ellen said.

"We need to talk to Scrawny," Louisa said. She opened the door and quickly walked out of the room. Ellen took one last glance at the bed with its pretty quilt before she followed.

Chapter 52

Louisa

Mrs. Wallace seemed unsurprised to see them when Louisa and Ellen showed up on the doorstep of the workhouse.

"You're getting to be regulars here," she said. "Do you both want to stay this time? I'll need to get permission from the captain."

"No," Louisa said. "We're not looking for a place to stay."

"We need to speak to one of your girls," Ellen said. "They call her Scrawny."

"Her real name is Delores," Louisa said. "I don't know her last name."

"I know who you mean," Mrs. Wallace said. "Sullen thing. Come on."

Mrs. Wallace led them to a large kitchen at the back of the building where several women were cleaning or cooking. They saw Scrawny sitting on a fruit crate in front of a large pot with a potato and a peeler in her hands.

"Delores," Mrs. Wallace said. "You've got guests."

Scrawny looked up at the two of them blankly. Louisa held up the bag she carried.

"I brought your dress," she said sweetly.

Scrawny's eyes searched them as if she suspected a trick was being played on her.

"Oh, go on upstairs. They want to talk to you," Mrs. Wallace said. "And be quick about it."

Scrawny got up and, eyes nailed to the floor, brushed past them, heading quickly into the hall and then up the stairs. They followed on her heels.

Inside the small room, Scrawny dropped onto the bed and said nothing. Louisa brought the dress out of the bag. It was cornflower blue.

"It's old," Louisa said. "I wore it years ago when I was thinner, but it's still pretty and I think it will fit you perfectly."

She laid the dress down on the cot next to Scrawny. Scrawny hesitated but then ran a hand over it.

"You could probably go out and apply for a maid's job in that dress," Ellen suggested. "It's not too late for you to turn your life around."

Scrawny looked up at them, still distrustful.

"Is it really mine?" she asked.

"Yes," Louisa said, nodding emphatically.

The girl picked up the dress and clutched it. Tears glistened in her eyes.

"I never had nothing so pretty in my life."

Louisa felt an odd sense of happiness. This feeling must be why the wealthy women loved their charity work. It wasn't about the people they were helping so much as the feeling of goodness one experienced, a happiness mixed with guilt, an oddly pleasurable emotion. And of course, in this case, it came with a return favor.

"Scraw...Delores, I need to ask you something about the night of the Armory Show," she said. Scrawny looked up at her, holding the dress to her breast. The color really did bring out the blue in her eyes.

***

The man at the Newport Inn happily rented Louisa another bicycle.

"You're my best customer," he said with a chuckle. "Sure you don't want a room for the night?"

"I'm sure," she said. "But do me a favor please. If I don't bring it back by 3:00, send the police to this address." She wrote an address on a sheet of paper and handed it to him.

He looked at the paper and then gaped up at her. She smiled, mounted the bike and pedaled off, wearing a recently purchased pair of dark brown cycling bloomers with a matching hip-length jacket.

The day was sunny, and a few tiny purple flowers had the audacity to poke out their heads to see if it was spring yet. The ride was a pleasant enough twenty minutes, but her heart was heavy.

A large black motorcar sat in the driveway. So it was true that Natasha had given up her carriage and her horses and joined the 20th century.

When she rang the bell, Natasha opened the door and looked at her sadly as if Louisa had broken her heart.

"I've been expecting you, *cherie,*" Natasha said and gestured for her to come inside. "I'm so sorry. There's no staff except for the chauffeur, but I did bring a picnic lunch. Let's eat out on the terrace."

"I didn't come here for lunch," Louisa said.

"No? Well, come along anyway. I know you like caviar," Natasha said, leading the way through the house to a set of French doors, which she opened. They walked out onto a brick terrace. The ocean lay like a sleeping leviathan just beyond the cliffs.

On the table sat a wicker basket and a bottle of sherry. Natasha withdrew a tin of caviar, a box of crackers, a wedge of cheese, and two wine glasses from the basket.

"I'm not hungry," Louisa said, a hard knot in her belly.

"At least have some sherry," Natasha said, and poured a glass of golden liquid.

"Is it the same vintage you gave to your friend, Dr. Swanson?" Louisa asked.

Natasha's hand froze for just a moment as she held the glass aloft. Then she sipped the drink and held the glass out to Louisa.

"I'm sorry you had to see that, Louisa. Was it terribly gruesome?" Natasha asked, still holding the glass. Louisa took it, flustered and horrified that Natasha, whom she had loved like a mother, had just admitted her guilt. Louisa wanted her to deny it, wanted her to swear this was all some sort of mistake that could be easily explained.

"And the police matron? Her, too?" Louisa asked, tilting her head.

Natasha shrugged and poured herself a glass of the sherry.

"Poor thing," she said. "I sent her mother-in-law a handsome check. To take care of the boy."

"How generous of you, Natasha," Louisa said. She felt disoriented, like Alice suddenly landing in Wonderland though there was nothing wonderful about any of this.

"Sit," Natasha said as she lowered herself into a wicker chair.

Louisa sat. It was mid-March and the wind couldn't decide if it was a lion or a lamb as it stumbled across the expanse of lawn. In spite of the sunshine, it was chilly enough for Louisa to keep her jacket on.

"This house reminds me of my uncle's dacha where we spent our summers. Those were such happy times," Natasha said.

"I've never heard you speak of your childhood," Louisa said, her heart so heavy she thought her back might break.

"Except for the summers, it was a grim childhood," Natasha said. "Did I tell you I saw my father kill my mother?"

"No," Louisa said, wondering if Natasha could possibly be telling the truth.

"Are you sure you don't want to try this caviar?" Natasha opened the tin and inhaled it. "Heavenly. The dacha was in Crimea right on the sea. Like this. But in the winter my brothers and I lived in St. Petersburg with my father. He was not a kind man."

"How..." Louisa ventured.

"How did he kill my mother? He shot her. And then claimed it was an accident," she said. "As soon as I could, I married a rich foreigner who would take me far away."

Louisa said nothing.

"Do you know how old the Colonel is? He's seventy-one. Fat and doddering around the house. When I was young, I didn't think the age difference would matter. I just wanted to get away from Russia, but now...now, things are different. Maybe I should go back. There's nothing left for me here now."

Looking at Natasha's wistful expression and the bend of her neck, Louisa suddenly saw something she hadn't seen before. She saw the raw need that Natasha kept hidden underneath her aristocratic bearing.

"Swanson was your lover," Louisa said.

"You are perceptive, aren't you? I suppose that's why you became a news girl," Natasha said.

Louisa set down her glass of sherry. "Why did you kill him, Natasha?"

Natasha's face went dark as she looked out at the thin clouds hovering over the water.

"He was weak. He would have told you and your police friends the truth eventually. And I'd had enough of him," she said. The she looked up and smiled. "Betty agreed with me."

"Betty?"

"He introduced us. He took care of her girls, you know, just like he took care of the society ladies. He thought we would be useful to each other. And he was right."

"You're her landlord," Louisa said. "And the key you dropped in Scrawny's cup?"

"A new house for the doctor."

"Were you going to get a cut of the winning bid?" Louisa asked.

Natasha grimaced. "I didn't know it was you, Louisa. I'm not evil."

Louisa shook her head.

"So Scrawny was your go-between," Louisa said.

"Yes," Natasha tried unsuccessfully to suppress a giggle. "Your column was so useful, dear. Betty always knew where to find me."

"I'm glad you find that amusing," Louisa said.

"Don't be angry with me, Louisa," Natasha said.

"Did you love the doctor?" Louisa asked.

"Ah, cherie. I stopped loving anyone the day I saw my mother shot in cold blood," Natasha said. "I was six years old. You understand me, don't you? You know what that's like. To lose a parent to murder."

"I never forgot how to love."

"Really? Then why aren't you married? I know there were men who were interested in you, but you always shut them out. Why is that?" Natasha asked.

At some level Natasha was right. Louisa had choked any sign of love from her heart as surely as pulling weeds from a garden, but she had no intention of admitting it now.

"What about Dorothy?" Louisa asked. "Don't you care about how this will affect her future?"

"Don't worry about Dorothy," Natasha said. She took a bite of caviar and raised her eyes heavenward in delight. "She's on a boat for Europe. My cousin Ludmilla is taking her on a grand tour. There's a German count quite interested in making her acquaintance."

Of course, Dorothy would eventually marry some nobleman. She'd only been toying with Owney.

"What about yourself? You won't like prison, Natasha," Louisa said.

"The police will do nothing to me, *cherie*. The Bloodgoods donated quite heavily to Commissioner Waldo's campaign. The only one who can harm me is you, Louisa, with your pathetic little ruse. I'll let everyone know you and Beatrice Milton are the same," Natasha said.

"And who will believe you once they know about your affair with the doctor? Even if I can't prove you killed him, I can prove you owned the brownstone where he did his business and where a certain police matron was killed. Scrawny will testify to your involvement. Mr. Waldo will not be commissioner forever," Louisa said. "When some reformist comes along, as they surely will, they will bring you to justice. I'll see to it."

"I have always been fond of you, my dear, but I value my own life and reputation more than yours," Natasha said.

Louisa studied Natasha's face. She had crow's feet and lines around her mouth but she was lovely regardless. Her dark hair was twisted on the back of her head and her face had the same firm jawline and exquisite neck that made Dorothy such a beauty.

"I have to leave now," Louisa said, rising from her chair.

Natasha seemed to be considering something.

"Louisa, I have information," she said. "About your father."

"My father?" Louisa's heart lurched in her chest. She sat down again.

"I know who swindled him. I know where the money went. You could probably even get some of it back," she said. "And I know who murdered him."

"I don't believe you. You'll say anything to distract me," Louisa said.

"Room 212, wasn't it?" Natasha said.

"My mother could have told you that," Louis said.

"They sent a waiter up to kill him. Then the waiter disappeared. I wonder how that happened," Natasha said. Her eyes narrowed as she studied Louisa for a reaction.

"They?" Louisa asked. "Who are they?"

"Do we have a deal?" Natasha asked.

"How do you know any of this?" Louisa asked.

Natasha shrugged her thin shoulders, her eyes were as hard as mallets. Why had Louisa never seen it before? Or maybe she had seen it. She felt as though someone had stuck a broom handle in her chest.

"Forget any of this ever happened, and I will tell you everything," Natasha said in a cajoling tone of voice. "We can go back to the way things were before."

More than anything in the world Louisa wanted things to be the way they were before. She wanted to know who steered her father into that scam and stole her family fortune. Most of all, she wanted to know who killed her father and why. But she would not, could not, bargain with Natasha. She had compromised once by not telling the truth about Hugh Garrett, but she would not do that again.

"You'll find the story on the front page tomorrow, Natasha," Louisa said and got up again to leave.

A burly man she'd seen before stood in the French doors, blocking her passage. Louisa didn't need any voices this time to tell her she was in danger.

"Louisa, have you met the chauffeur for my new motorcar?" Natasha said. "This is Rolf."

"From the Winona Club," Louisa said, remembering where she'd seen him before. "He works for Owney Madden."

"Not anymore," Natasha said.

Rolf snatched her off the ground and tossed her over his shoulder like a sack of corn meal. She hit his back with her fists but it was like hitting a boulder. She hung over him, her arms swinging uselessly as she peered around the bulk of his body to see the wide expanse of the Atlantic ocean. As they got closer and closer to the cliff, she heard his labored breath and felt the shift in his body. She reached up for her hat. A moment later, it tumbled off her head and she watched it roll over the ground. She looked around him and saw the edge of the cliff.

At that moment, she raised her arms and with both hands jammed her cloisonné hat pin into the fleshy part of his body just below his ribcage. He yelped and stumbled, dropping her body to the ground with a hard thud. She scrambled to her feet and rushed toward the cliff. She looked back and saw him turning in circles before he finally saw her. He must have supposed she would run in the opposite direction, but what he didn't know was that she and Hugh and the other kids had crawled across these cliffs for hours on those long summer days, and of all the children, she'd been the most agile, the most adept at finding hand holds and footholds and ledges.

By the time he realized what she was doing, she had kicked off her lady oxfords and was sliding down the rock face. She clasped the rocks and climbed down as fast as she could. She felt the cool stone on her cheek as she slid along, her feet clinging to the ledge. She glanced up and saw Rolf holding a large stone over his head. He thrust it down toward her and she ducked, clinging to the rock face. The stone bounced against her shoulder, and the pain made her momentarily dizzy and nauseated.

Hold on, she told herself, ignore the pain. Just hold on. She scooted along the edge of the cliff, remembering, remembering. The dip here, the bend there, the step over a jutting rock and then the slide around a smooth corner and into the crevice they had called "the cave of Doom," where as children they had pretended to hide from pirates.

The crevice was about three feet deep and four feet high. She stooped with her back against the wall of rock, gasping for air. Her breath pounded in her ears as loud as the waves below. She had no idea what to do next. Would Rolf go for reinforcements? Would he have a gun? This had been a terrible mistake, she realized.

A rock fell over the edge and careened down the face of the cliff. He was on the ledge. He was coming to get her. She looked around. There was no way past this crevice. The only way out was the way she had come in. She looked on the ground for a stick, a branch, something to defend herself with but there was nothing. She heard his loud breathing as he got closer. Louisa slid down the wall of rock behind her.

Then he was standing in front of the crevice, his eyes where her head should have been, looking down too late. She kicked at him with her bare feet. He wobbled for an instant. Then she rolled forward and shoved his legs with her shoulders. As his feet slid out from under him, he reached out and clasped her jacket. Louisa jerked away, lowering her head so the silk-lined jacket slid off her arms as Rolf fell. His body hit the rocks once, bounced, then hit the rocks again. Finally he landed at the bottom and didn't move, his arms spread out as if he were flying. Her jacket floated on a breeze gently into the water.

A Woman's View: Who killed Adele Cummings and Why?

By Beatrice Milton

NEW YORK, March 10 – Adele Cummings was a widow and a mother. She was also one of New York's finest police officers. She investigated shoplifters, confidence men, fortune tellers, and abortionists. She was adept at disguise and could change her accent for different situations. Many a worried mother is grateful to her for having rescued their wayward daughters in the nick of time.

According to former U.S. President Theodore Roosevelt, adding women to the police force has increased the efficiency of police work.

"Their presence has a salubrious effect on the profession as a whole. They keep the men honest," he said.

Unfortunately, Mrs. Cummings died tragically when a bomb in a townhouse on West 46th Street exploded in January of this year. She was investigating Dr. Alan Swanson, a respected figure in New York circles who also happened to perform illegal operations and who was recently murdered.

Before his death, Dr. Swanson had friends in high places. One of those friends was the eminent Natasha Bloodgood, wife of Colonel Bloodgood. Mrs. Bloodgood was a major supporter of the doctor and his hospital, now owned by the city. Dr. Swanson even promised to name a wing of his hospital after Mrs. Bloodgood. They may have even had an illicit romantic relationship.

Wealthy women from all over the country came to New York to have Dr. Swanson take care of their "problems." He also took care of the women who worked in the brothels owned by Betty Walsh. When it came to light that Mrs. Cummings was investigating the doctor, Betty Walsh, also known as Battle Betty, from her days as female gangster and brick hurler, gave Mrs. Cummings the address to a certain townhouse in Hell's Kitchen. Then she planted the bomb which exploded and killed the police matron.

The house where the bombing occurred was provided by a company called Empress Holdings. This company is owned by Natasha Bloodgood.

When this reporter confronted Mrs. Bloodgood about the crime, Mrs. Bloodgood admitted her part. She also admitted to poisoning Dr. Swanson. Then she tried, unsuccessfully, to have me thrown off a cliff.

Will Mrs. Bloodgood pay for these crimes? She will not. She has fled the country and gone back to her native Russia, where her transgressions will mean little. However, if she ever steps foot on American soil, she will be immediately arrested.

The loss of Adele Cummings, a brave police officer, to this city and to her friends and family, especially her young son, is enormous.

Chapter 53

Louisa

"She got away with it. Natasha left the Colonel and was back in Russia in time for the Grand Duchess' Easter ball," Louisa said as she sat in Forrest Calloway's parlor, the cabernet in their glasses glinting in the firelight. "I may have exposed her and ruined her reputation in New York, but in Russia they won't care. She's off dancing with 'honored excellencies' in some palace."

"I wouldn't worry," he said. "Russia may not be such a hospitable clime for the aristocracy much longer. That country is long overdue for its own revolution. Besides, you got your scoop. Didn't that feel good?"

His hand was gently, almost absently stroking hers.

"It did," she murmured. She looked at him and saw that he was watching her, his deep-set mahogany eyes warm and full of... love?

He suddenly seemed to realize what he was doing and pulled his hand away. Standing quickly, he walked over to the fireplace.

"My apologies, Miss Delafield," he said.

"What are you apologizing for?" she asked.

"I am quite attracted to you," he said.

A shell that had formed around her heart years earlier cracked. She could not hold herself inside it any longer.

"I'm also attracted to you," she said, and rose, stepping close to him.

They looked into each other's eyes for several long moments. Then he broke away and gazed at his hands.

"However much I would like to," he said, "I cannot ask you to marry me. I'm sorry, but the truth is that I never actually divorced my wife. She ran off before I got around to it."

Louisa had almost forgotten that he'd once been married. She felt a rush of relief and giggled.

"What is so funny?" he asked.

"I will never marry, Mr. Calloway, and I am glad you cannot marry me. I would hate to disappoint you," she said.

"Why?" he asked with a bewildered look.

She looked up at him.

"A married woman has only one place to wield her power. The home. I can't be confined to a home," she said. Louisa gazed at him. A magnetic force seemed to pull her toward him. She realized she wanted him to wash away the awful thing that had happened to her. She wanted him to make love to her. All her life she'd worried about being respectable because that was what society expected. And all her life she had strangled her feelings. Never again.

He bent down and kissed her, and she kissed him back, a deep kiss, tongues touching, hands moving of their own volition. She was helpless, but this time the helplessness was delicious.

"Would you mind very much if I called you Louisa?" he asked.

"I would like that," she said.

"And will you call me Forrest?" he asked.

"Yes, Forrest," she said and tilted her head for another kiss.

"Would you like to see my bedroom?" he asked.

She nodded.

He took her by the hand, and as he led her up the long polished staircase, she felt as if she were floating, as if they were climbing to the top of Mount Olympus. His bedroom was enormous with a writing desk and chair in one corner, two soaring windows framed by gold velvet curtains, a plush settee, a sculpture of a swan on a table between the windows, and above the bed a stunning landscape that seemed to capture the late afternoon light, streaming through the windows.

"I see you prefer American art," she said, wishing both to prolong the wait and to rush headlong into the next moment.

"I do," he said. He stood behind her, his mouth almost at her ear. "Especially these Hudson School fellows. I love all things America." How could such an innocent sentence sound so seductive.

The backs of his fingers slid along her sleeve and she felt his body against hers. She leaned into him as his fingers touched her neck, outlined her jaw and then ran across her lips. Her knees trembled. She'd had no idea.

First the dress came down in a crumpled heap of cloth at her feet. Forrest's fingers then slowly pulled at the laces along the side of her corset. As he loosened it, he ran his fingertips over her rib cage, and his eyes roamed adoringly over her thin white neck, her collarbones and the tops of her breasts. The corset fell away to reveal the chemise and her silk drawers. When she was finally naked, he simply stared at her. The first and only man to see her, to see all of her, and by the look in his eyes, she knew her body radiated a magnetic power. If women knew their power before signing it over to some husband for life, they'd never marry, she thought. Instead they'd rule the world.

The novelty of it, of lips and hands, of kisses and probing touches, drove her nearly mad with desire. Why did no one tell you, she wondered. They simply said that you grew up, you married or you didn't, you had children or not, but they never let on that there was a delicious, delirious darkness inside that was more wondrous than anything you'd ever imagined. They never told you about your fiery internal engine and the delights that were worth whatever Eve had sacrificed in order to experience it. They never told you about the male body either, the beauty of it, the perfection of his legs, the slender, soft-skinned stem perched curiously on the bone, the fine tuft of hair surrounding it — she knew "it" had a name but couldn't bring herself to think in such clinical language.

Then he abruptly stopped what he was doing, rose, and opened a drawer in his nightstand.

"What are you doing?" she asked.

"Making sure you don't get pregnant," he said. "I believe your Portuguese princess mentioned something to you about contraception?"

"Yes, she told me something about it," she said. "I just don't know how it works."

He looked at her.

"We don't have to do this," he said.

"I want to," she said. "I almost lost my virginity in a bidding war. I won't let anyone take this choice from me."

She opened her arms and he slid on top of her. She felt the weight of him, the warmth of his limbs and his torso. The sudden pressure inside her body at first alarmed her but then she was fascinated by sensations where she'd never even been touched before, and moments later she was opening and spilling like a dam bursting. He had opened her up to this heady thrill. She bit her lip and moaned. This was the final thing no one had ever told her about: the moment of blankness when time fell down a dark well and a storm thundered through every cell in the body.

"You enjoyed that?" he asked later as he pushed a tangle of hair from her face.

She laughed and stretched her arms expansively.

"I understand now what Emily Dickinson meant when she wrote, 'Wild nights — Wild nights, were I with thee, wild nights should be our luxury.'"

He kissed her cheek so gently she hardly felt it, like a feather brushed against her skin. What a maelstrom of aching pleasure. In the previous century, a woman of her class would never have been able to enjoy the pleasures of love without the bonds of marriage. She would have been ruined, but this was a new century, a new world, and she was a new woman.

Outside twilight was slipping into night. He suggested they go out for dinner, but she shook her head.

"If I don't get home soon, Suzie and my mother will be worried," Louisa said. "My abduction wasn't easy for them."

Forrest insisted that Mr. Kimura drive her. He offered to come along, but she persuaded him not to. She wanted some time alone.

"Of course," he said and planted a chaste kiss on her forehead. Their eyes twinkled as they looked at each, barely suppressing their smiles.

In the back seat of the car with a panel between her and Mr. Kimura, Louisa leaned against the soft leather seat, her body still thrumming from what had just taken place. She wondered why people called the first act of love making a "loss" when she felt she had just gained something wonderful through the experience — new knowledge of herself and of the potential depth of passion that awaited her. Already she wanted to see him again. How lovely it would be to spend a whole night in his bed, to wake up in the morning and see his face. She realized, of course, that's what marriage was, and she understood for the first time what she was sacrificing by choosing not to marry.

When she was younger, she had determined never to marry because of the anguish she saw in her mother after her father's ruin, but that night in the brothel had revealed something to her. She needed to let herself feel again whether passion, friendship, or grief. In her mind's landscape, she saw the fresh mound of dirt in the cemetery, the snow piled in drifts on either side. She remembered the dirt on her white gloves. She had thought the grief after her father's death would crush her. Her only defense had been to lock her feelings away in a box and throw away the key. It all came back in a rush. Only a few minutes ago, she'd felt deliriously happy. Now tears streamed down her cheeks. She would not let the pain crush her. Instead it would fuel her mission to find out the truth. Natasha had said she knew who murdered her father. If Natasha knew, then someone else would also know. Someday she would find that person and she would discover what had happened to Richard Delafield and why.

Louisa rolled down the window of the Packard and let the night air spill over her skin as they sped along the Great White Way.

Author's Note

Many institutions were invaluable in helping me to immerse myself in the year 1913: The Museum of the City of New York, The New York Historical Society and Museum, The Tenement Museum, The Newseum in Washington, D.C. (unfortunately now closed), The New York Public Library, and especially the archives of the *New York Times* and the Hathi Trust collection of *McClure's*. Special thanks to Kate Lanceley of the New York Transit Museum for her invaluable guidance on subways and elevated trains.

Exploring the early twentieth century has been a fascinating dive into a brave new world in which women, finally freed from the constraints of the previous century, came into their own as they fought for the vote, contraception, and the right to work outside the home in the profession of their choice.

Many books also helped open my eyes to the world of 1913. One of the most beautiful is *The Architecture of Warren & Wetmore*. The Knickerbocker Hotel has also published a gorgeous book featuring highlights of its history, fittingly called *The Knickerbocker*. I found about a dozen guides to New York history on my brother David's shelves. In addition, he always provided a place to stay and a Metro card for my frequent visits to the city.

The Ledger is a fictional paper. In the early 1900s, New Yorkers had at least 15 English language newspapers to choose from, including *The New York Times, The Post, The Herald, The Sun, The Tribune,* and *The World*. And of course, there were many others in other languages. I've always loved newspapers and in graduate school wrote a column for the *Florida Flambeau* called "Lifestyles of the Poor and Unknown." In the late 1980s, I wrote entertainment features, reviews, and society news for the Fort Lauderdale *Sun-Sentinel*.

When I first began my research on women and journalism, I came across this treasure: *Front Page Girls* by Jean Marie Lutes (Cornell Paperbacks, 2006). As Lutes writes in her introduction, "At the turn of the century, women reporters were already a visible subset of the nation's newspaper journalists." Lutes covers the great female press icons of the day, such as Nellie Bly and Ida B. Wells. Bly famously spent two weeks undercover in a madhouse on Blackwell's Island and exposed the unimaginable cruelty and horrors perpetrated there. Ida B. Wells was a Black journalist who became a publishing phenom and a crusader against lynching.

Another book that helped me understand the power of the press in general was *The Murder of the Century* by Paul Collins, (Crown, 2011), which details how the press was instrumental in helping to solve the horrific crime of a man whose corpse was beheaded by his wife and her lover. The Bowery Boys podcast offers a wonderfully instructive tour of old New York newspapers as well as tours of the Bowery. Their experts are truly that: expert.

One of my early discoveries in the research process was the story of Dorothy Arnold, a beautiful and popular socialite who disappeared in 1910 when she was twenty-five years old. There were several theories as to what happened, including that she'd had an illegal abortion, and her body was dumped somewhere, never to be found. This sent me on a search to find out more about women who died as a result of illegal abortions. I was intrigued to discover that for society women, abortion was sometimes used as a means of birth control. *Where Are My Children*, a film made in 1916 and written by reformist Lois Weber, told the story of a district attorney who finds out that a doctor he is prosecuting has been regularly sought out for his services by society women, including his own wife. Some doctors provided safe abortions for their wealthy clientele, who also had better access to birth control, but most women, especially poor women, did not have access to birth control or to doctors for their abortions. While midwives provided excellent services for birthing children, a number of those providing abortions were untrained and some were outright quacks. Unnecessary deaths did occur, but abortions were often successful and seen as necessary by many women. According to Leslie J. Reagan in *When Abortion Was a Crime*, "control over their own reproduction was as important to women as building a hospital or caring for the needy. Indeed, women's involvement in charitable and reform activities made the ability to control childbearing necessary, and that control made voluntary activities possible."

In researching the Women's March of 1913, I came across two recent books on the topic: *The Accidental Suffragist* by Galia Gichon (Wyatt-MacKenzie Publishing) and *The Women's March: A Novel Of The 1913 Women's Suffrage Procession by* Jennifer Chiaverini (HarperCollins). The first is about a woman from the tenements who gets swept up in the cause of suffrage after the Triangle Shirtwaist Factory Fire. The second book focuses on three historic figures in the fight for women's suffrage: Alice Paul, Ida Wells Barnett, and Maud Malone.

Although they are written as novels, both books provide a wealth of information about the women who conceived of and organized the 1913 march as well as plenty of historical details to give the reader a real sense of what it was like to be fighting for the right to vote, all while being beaten, groped, and mocked.

A great source for background on the suffrage movement is the Hilary Swank movie, *Iron-Jawed Angels*, which portrays the horror perpetuated on the women hunger strikers when they were thrown in jail for protesting, and it gives a vivid sense of these women and their passion for suffrage.

I also read quite a few nonfiction accounts of the March of 1913, which are available on the Internet, but what really gave me a sense for the feel of the march was participating in the Women's March in Washington in 2017. There's nothing quite like that feeling of being surrounded by a huge number of people — all so different, different ages, different ethnicities, different genders, and sexual preferences — all voicing a demand for peace, for respect, and for recognition. The Women's March of 1913 was not as diverse, and yet those marchers came from different classes, different educational and work backgrounds, and different religious belief systems. There were women of color and white women, society women and domestic workers, marching together — if not always side by side. Regardless of their origins and their backgrounds, a shared passion united the marchers in 1913 and again in 2017.

Finally, the world of the New York gangsters was brought vividly to life by Herbert Asbury's *The Gangs of New York*. That's where I first learned of the role of the women gangsters, especially a woman named Battle Annie. Two other characters are based on real people: Captain Tunney, who wrote his own book and whom you will meet again in future Delafield & Malloy books, and "Owney the Killer," who became famous during Prohibition.

While the textual and film sources (and many others) were incredibly useful, my main inspiration came from the stories my mother used to tell me of my paternal grandparents, whom I never got to meet. They had a chauffeur-driven Rolls Royce (my grandfather never did learn how to drive), an apartment on Central Park and a mansion on Long Island, where the gardener and his wife had their own house. My grandmother's idea of gardening was to point out which roses the gardener should clip for her. I asked my mother once if they would have been part of Edith Wharton's set (whose books I re-read religiously), and she shook her head emphatically. My grandparents would have been considered "new money," and since my grandfather was an Irish immigrant who started out as an office boy, they would have been eschewed by New York society. I don't suppose it mattered to them. According to my mother, they "lived at the top of their income" but when my grandmother was diagnosed with a debilitating illness, whatever money they had left after the depression went to keep her alive. Their fortune was gone by the time they died. I never got to meet them.

I also keep a picture of my maternal great-grandmother on the bookshelf by my desk. In it she wears a black hat topped with some sort of elaborate lace and flower adornment and sits in front of a typewriter. According to family documents, "After her divorce in 1900, Mary Page Field worked as a local newspaper reporter and was Probation Officer for the Town of West Haven."

Of course, no author is an island. I could not have written this book without the help of my front line readers, Tamara Titus and Vicki Moreland. Thanks also to readers of various drafts, including Pam Ball, Kathleen Laufenberg, Donna Decker, Patti Wood, and Kevin Murphy. Thanks to Katrina Harkness for her insights. And most of all, thanks to my husband, Joe, for his ceaseless moral and technical support.

I hope you enjoyed your time with Louisa and Ellen. If you like, you can check out Chapter One from the next book, *The Butterfly Cage*. And you can connect with me through my web page (www.trishmacenulty.com) to subscribe to my blog or newsletter to find out about future books. And, of course, you can follow me at either or both of the following:

Facebook: Trish MacEnulty, Writer
BookBub: https://www.bookbub.com/profile/trish-macenulty

The Butterfly Cage

Chapter 1
Louisa

Louisa Delafield ripped the page from her typewriter and handed it to a copy boy.

"This has to make the next edition," she told him, donning her hat and grabbing her purse from the lower drawer in her desk.

"Where are you off to now?" Ellen, her assistant, asked.

"Penelope Gaines is having a small reception for the former president while he's in town. She insisted I come early, which means I must dash home and change into something presentable," Louisa said. "Hold the fort, please."

She hurried out of the building and found a cab.

The summer of 1913 had been idyllic if somewhat hectic. Panama hats bedecked with ribbons and bows were all the rage, knee-length bathing costumes gave women new-found freedom to enjoy the surf, and socialites dashed from horse races to tennis matches to costume parties as if their lives depended on being seen in every possible venue from Newport to Saratoga. Louisa had documented it all for her readers in *The Ledger* as well as in her nationally syndicated column.

Now a slight autumnal melancholy tinged the early September evenings, and the white shoes were put away for next year. September and October would provide a lull as one by one, the yachts returned to their berths, families streamed back to their Fifth Avenue houses and Central Park apartments, and the women who ruled the upper class began plotting the next season's events.

The unexpected death of New York City's mayor had temporarily thrown the schedule into disarray, but it had given her something important to write about during the social doldrums.

The taxi dropped her off in front of the Dakota on the Upper Westside. This area had become more fashionable as of late, and she wasn't surprised that Penelope Gaines had chosen to live here. As wealthy as she was, she was not a member of Caroline Astor's "old money" crowd. Not to mention, Penelope was divorced. However, she had made her own name in society by regularly hosting a number of charitable soirées and tea dances. In the process, she had also gained a reputation of being the 'life of the party.'

Louisa took a private elevator to the third floor. A butler opened the door and showed her into the reception area of the luxurious apartment. While she waited, she glanced around and took mental notes. All the apartments in the Dakota had been custom designed. She glanced up at the high ceiling and then down at the parquet floor, inlaid with mahogany and cherry wood. It was as nice as any town home.

"Louisa, I'm so glad you could come a few minutes early. I have some news for your column," Penelope said, holding a highball glass in one hand. Tall and blond, she wore a flattering rose chiffon dress with a fashionable raglan waist and a high-neck collar. She had been the daughter of a successful banker when she married Charles "Spend a Million" Gaines, a boisterous barbed-wire mogul, who never fit in with the staid society of New York. The marriage had not worked out, and they'd been separated ten years ago. Recently they made it official with a divorce.

"I hope it's happy news and not another funeral," Louisa said, "although I will say that was a spectacular event."

"No, no, this is happy news," Penelope said, leading Louisa into the drawing room. In front of a huge fireplace stood Dominic Gallo. Louisa was not terribly surprised to see him there as he had been seen out and about with Penelope since the spring. A dashing man with black hair, dark eyes and a dazzling smile, he smiled now as Penelope took her place at his side.

"The news I have is that Dominic and I recently got married." Penelope gazed up at him with adoring eyes.

"Married?" Louisa asked. She had not expected this. "Why didn't you tell me beforehand so I could have announced it in my column?"

"It was rather spur-of-the-moment. I wanted to get married before Caroline's coming out this season so that Dominic could be at my side for the balls. Of course, now with the mayor's death, we'll also be busy with other plans."

"Such as?"

"Dominic's political career," Penelope said, slipping her hand into the crook of her husband's elbow.

So that's what this reception was about. Penelope was grooming her new husband for political office, and they were hoping to get William Taft's blessing.

The doorbell rang, and Penelope gulped down her drink before hurrying off to greet her guests.

"Miss Delafield," Dominic said, turning his full attention to her. "I read your columns religiously. Thank you for promoting the women's right to vote, a cause near and dear to my heart."

This was even more surprising than the news of their nuptials. First, that he was reading her column and secondly that he cared about women's suffrage. Then again, if he were hoping for a political career, he was certainly the sort who could win the women's vote if they had one. He was not only handsome, he was so charismatic it was almost uncomfortable being alone with him.

"Thank you," she said. "I didn't know you were interested in politics, Mr. Gallo."

"When I came to New York ten years ago, I fell in love with this city. I was born in Italy, but moved to San Francisco as a boy. With a small inheritance, I bought some land. Land was cheap in California then. But I always wanted to come back to the city that I had seen as a young boy. And so I sold the land, came here, and bought an import/export business. New York welcomed me with open arms. Look at me, Miss Delafield, a poor boy from Italy, and now I am married to a beautiful woman, and I am surrounded by luxury. I want to give back to this city which has given me so much."

He smiled, and she melted a little. No wonder Penelope was so smitten.

She noticed a severe-looking woman in black, sitting in a chair in the corner of the room, reading a book.

Louisa wasn't alone with him, after all. But who, she wondered, was this woman? A relative? She certainly was not a member of society or she would never have simply ignored Louisa, but she was no servant either.

At that moment Penelope entered with Katherine Murphy and her husband, John, and behind them, Katherine's sister, Hester French. John Murphy was the president of his father-in-law's company, which made springs for railroad cars. This had created enormous wealth for their family. In New York society, the Murphys were considered "new money," which would make them natural allies for Penelope and her new husband. If John Murphy was looking for political influence, what better place to start?

"Forgive me. I hope we can talk more soon," Dominic said, smiling at her once again as if she were the only person in the room.

Katherine Murphy immediately bustled over to Louisa. She was always eager for a mention in Louisa's column.

"Miss Delafield, I haven't seen you since the races in Saratoga. Tell me, what should we look forward to this Season?" she asked.

"Debutante balls, debutante teas, and debutante afternoon dance parties," Louisa said. "The season overfloweth with young women coming out. And perhaps mayoral candidates coming out as well." She glanced toward Dominic Gallo.

"Isn't he divine?" Katherine whispered with a giggle, nodding in Gallo's direction.

"What are you giggling about, sister?" Hester French asked.

More guests had arrived, among them the burly former president, William Taft.

"Oh, look, it's the former president!" Katherine exclaimed, ignoring her sister's question, and off she went.

Hester French put a hand on Louisa's arm.

"Miss Delafield, may I ask how Miss Malloy is doing?" Hester said, blinking her large, slightly bulging eyes.

"Ellen?" Louisa said in surprise.

"She and I met at the Washington women's march in the spring. I've been traveling all summer with my sister and brother-in-law, but I hope to see her again." Hester added, "to enlist her help with the suffrage committee."

"I'm sure she'll be delighted to help," Louisa said. "Ellen is quite in favor of anything that disrupts the hierarchy. I sometimes believe she's a closet radical."

"She is a dear," Hester said and took a glass of champagne from a passing waiter. Louisa thought it odd that Hester, a wealthy heiress, would show an interest in an Irish immigrant and former lady's maid, but Hester had a reformist zeal. Unlike her stout little teapot of a sister, Katherine, she seemed to have no interest whatsoever in fashion and society. Her dress was a plain pale green gown, the only flourish being a bit of eyelet embroidery around the collar.

"I shall tell her you asked after her," Louisa said.

Hester French wandered off, and a few minutes later Louisa overheard her talking volubly to Dominic Gallo about an upcoming meeting of the suffragists.

It had been a long day, but Louisa needed to get a quote from the former president before she left. She pulled out her reporter's notebook, looked up and saw an ethereal looking creature in the doorway holding a cocker spaniel in her arms. It was Penelope's daughter, Caroline, the debutante — or at least she would be a debutante when the season started. The young woman slipped through the guests and stepped out onto the balcony. Louisa decided to follow. It was always good to have mention of a debutante in her column. New Yorkers seemed endlessly fascinated with them. Louisa had not had a season. By the time she was eighteen, there was no fortune left to attract a rich husband. Instead she attended Barnard on a scholarship, a fate she had never regretted.

She went through the French doors onto the balcony where the cool night air sparkled with city lights.

"Oh, hello," Caroline said, looking up. She was sitting on the floor beside the dog. "You're Miss Delafield, aren't you?"

"I am," Louisa said. "And you're Caroline Gaines."

"I am, and this is Beauregard Vrai Amour, the Second," the girl said. "He's a champion show dog."

"He's quite handsome," Louisa said. Louisa reached over to pet Beauregard's golden head, but he bared his teeth, and she thought better of it.

"I read that Mayor Gaynor's dogs keep waiting for him to come home," Caroline said, wistfully. "It's so sad."

"I don't suppose it's easy for dogs to understand death," Louisa said, though she didn't really know. She'd never had a dog. She had a pony when she was young and now she had a cat, or she should say a cat had her. No one actually "owned" a cat. "Your mother told me she recently married. Was it a lovely wedding?"

"Well, it was small," Caroline said. "They're going on a late honeymoon to Panama sometime next month. They want to see the moment when the water goes gushing through the canal, and I'm off to Wyoming to see my father, who's on a hunting expedition. He doesn't know she's gotten married. Can you imagine? I'm going to be the one to tell him."

Louisa wondered if that's why Penelope hadn't announced the marriage beforehand.

"Well, she's told me now, so I'll have to let the world know," Louisa said.

"Go ahead. They won't get any newspapers out in the wilderness of Wyoming," she said. "The worst part is I can't travel alone. So they're sending my 'aunt' Rosa with me."

"I didn't know that Penelope had a sister."

"She's Dominic's sister. A former nun," Caroline said.

"Is she that woman sitting off in the corner by herself. Dressed all in black?" Louisa asked.

Caroline crinkled her nose.

"Yes. She's still a nun at heart. She didn't quit for some romantic reason like falling in love with the gardener or something. She said she had to do God's work out in the world. She lurks around train stations to make sure young, unaccompanied women aren't 'cut out' of the herd by evil doers and forced into a life of sin."

"That sounds rather admirable," Louisa said. She glanced at Caroline, who rolled her eyes, and then added, "But she's probably not much fun as a traveling companion."

"She's a horrid choice," Caroline said.

A peal of laughter sounded from inside.

Louisa leaned on the balcony railing and looked out over Central Park. People walked along the paths, enjoying the balmy night.

"My publisher, Mr. Calloway, has also gone to Wyoming for a hunting expedition with the Prince of Monaco," she said.

"That's why my father went. He heard about the big hunt with the prince, but when he got there, the prince and Buffalo Bill refused to let him join. So Pops made his own expedition. There won't be any wild animals left in Wyoming with all those expeditions." Caroline scratched her dog behind the ears, and the creature drooled.

"I'd love an interview with the Prince of Monaco," Louisa said. "My readers clamor for anything having to do with royalty. You'd think they'd never heard of democracy."

Caroline stood up and leaned close to Louisa.

"Why don't you come out with me?" Her eyes gleamed in the light from the windows.

"What? I couldn't do that," Louisa said. "I have stories to cover here in New York."

"The season doesn't begin until November. You'll be back in plenty of time for all that. Oh, come on, Miss Delafield. Have you even been out west? Can you imagine going to Yellowstone National Park?"

"You must go if you can," a voice said.

Louisa turned and saw none other than William Taft himself standing in the doorway and lighting a cigar.

"Mr. President," she said.

Taft strolled onto the balcony as he blew a plume of smoke into the night air. "While I was in office, I had the opportunity to visit — and name — the Shoshone National Caverns, a treasure of beautiful crystals and sparkling stalactites. Quite unlike anything you can imagine."

Louisa mulled over the idea. There really was nothing of importance for her to cover for the next month. Why not? Why not surprise Forrest? In New York it was near to impossible for them to be alone and with all her activities in Saratoga and Newport over the summer, she had only had that one delirious night with him, a night she would never forget.

"I shall have to ask my editor, Mr. Thorn," Louisa said.

Caroline grabbed her hands and gushed, "He'll have to let you go. What a coup for your paper to have an interview with a prince!"

Louisa chuckled.

"I can't promise anything, but I shall ask. In the meantime, may I get a quote from you, sir?" Louisa said, turning to Taft. "What are your thoughts on women's suffrage?"

The portly man puffed his chest out and answered, "On the whole, it is fair to say that the immediate enfranchisement of women will increase the proportion of the hysterical element of the electorate."

Of course, at that moment who should come out on the balcony but Hester French whose eyes fairly blazed when she overheard his response.

"Hysterical? Do you mean to say that men, with their drunkenness and their violence, are calmer and more rational than women?"

Louisa took this as her cue to leave. She returned to the reception and glanced around. Everyone seemed to be infected with a sense of hilarity. That was an aftereffect of the funeral, she supposed. Everyone was giddy to be alive — except for Dominic Gallo's sister, who sat in her corner and knitted, unfazed by the laughter and conversation bubbling around her. No wonder Caroline dreaded the idea of having such a joyless woman for a traveling companion.

As she waited for the elevator, she had a sudden sense of dread. The elevator doors opened, but for some reason she was reluctant to go inside it. She had no idea what was wrong. She'd been fine coming up. She looked to her right and saw the door to the stairwell. Without knowing why, she turned away from the elevator and took the stairs to the lobby. A few minutes later she was in the cab and forgot about the whole incident.

To order this book, please visit my series page: https://www.amazon.com/dp/B0BBDGKRKK?

About the Author

The Whispering Women is Trish MacEnulty's debut as a historical fiction novelist. She has previously published four novels, a short story collection, and a memoir. A former Professor of English at Johnson & Wales University in Charlotte, NC, she currently lives in Tallahassee, Florida with her husband, two dogs, and one cat and teaches for the School of Journalism at Florida A&M University.

Made in United States
North Haven, CT
26 January 2024